STEVE VESCE

One ORDINARY MAN

*A novel based on the
true story of Harry Hopkins*

Early acclaim for *One Ordinary Man*

"Beginning with page one of the novel, One Ordinary Man, I recognized the importance of this book... It is not only historically accurate, but it also reveals the author's knowledge of the major players on the world stage, especially Harry Hopkins. I could hear the echoes of my grandfather's voice in the words Steve Vesce put in his mouth and I recognized the familiar tone of the conversations he creates. His descriptions of my grandfather's interactions with world figures as well as family members all ring true... my grandfather came to life for me...a fascinating read from cover to cover."

Dr. June Hopkins
Harry Hopkins's Granddaughter
Professor of History, Emerita
Author: Harry Hopkins and The Grand Alliance of the Second World War; Harry Hopkins: Sudden Hero, Brash Reformer; Jewish First Wife, Divorced: The Correspondence of Ethel Gross and Harry Hopkins (co-edited with Allison Giffen)

———————

"Vesce...manages to pique reader interest through his passionate dedication to historical detail.... he knows how to spin a good historical yarn. Vesce's larger-than-life portrait of Hopkins reminds that there really is some truth to the whole "Greatest Generation..."

Kirkus Reviews

———————

"Fleet, revealing novel of FDR's indispensable deputy fighting the Depression and the Nazis. This brisk, lively novel imagines the world-changing life of Harry L. Hopkins.... crafting fictionalized incidents that honor the historical record. Vesce favors a reportorial approach...with... plenty of canny dialogue... many crisply told moments that breathe life into the historical facts. Vesce's fleet scenecraft captures sharp exchanges... the material... abounds with achievements and surprises."

Booklife Reviews

"Steve Vesce's 'One Ordinary Man' is a wonderful gift to us... a fascinating page-turner of a read... This story serves to remind us of a time past when brilliance, tireless dedication and self-sacrifice could make the world a better and safer place... Read this book for inspiration and hope that there are still such men and women out there to lead us to a better future.

David Heiman
Retired Management and Practice Leader Partner
Jones Day, a global law firm

"There is nothing ordinary about the Man and nothing ordinary about the Book. As a lifelong history buff, One Ordinary Man elevated my love of history to a new level. It's like a time machine. I actually felt like I was there with Harry. Steve's writing is bold and brilliant."

Bob Trimper
Retired President, Rank Xerox, Middle East Africa
Retired Chairman Comstec, UK

Steve Vesce's first novel is a cinematic piece of historical fiction about Harry Hopkins.... It's a smooth read, which is calling for a smart producer to turn into a film. Enjoy this story about the FDR era, and you'll inevitably contrast it with what's going on today.

Michael Hirsh
Author/Journalist

"This captivating historical novel brings Harry Hopkins, one of the country's greatest unsung heroes, to life.... It is rare to read a book that is, in equal measure, so factual yet so enjoyable."

Judge Thomas A Wallitsch (ret.)

This book is a work of fiction based on the true story of Harry Hopkins.

There are fictionalized scenes, characters, dialogue, situations, relationships, and events that are the product of the author's imagination and which the author believes are consistent with the historical truth of Hopkins' fascinating life, the themes of his remarkable story, and the times in which he lived. Any fictional character in this book who resembles an actual person, living or dead, is purely coincidental.

Copyright © 2025 Steve Vesce

Published by Verlibri Media LLC, Atlanta, Georgia
First Edition: November 2025
ISBN: 979-8-9996453-0-2 (ebk)
ISBN: 979-8-9996453-1-9 (bk)
ISBN: 979-8-9996453-2-6 (aud)

DEDICATION

This book is dedicated to my father, Joe, who, with millions of other Americans, believed in the vision of FDR's Four Freedoms and fought World War II to defeat fascism and help American democracy become the guiding light for the free world.

AUTHOR'S NOTE

This is a biographical and historical novel about Harry L. Hopkins that is based on historically accurate information, and years of research including books, newspaper articles, correspondence, and public records.

It is an inspiring story of one ordinary man who journeyed from obscurity to a place behind the wizard's curtain to pull the levers that helped America overcome the Great Depression, defeat fascism, and win World War II.

For continuity and entertainment purposes, however, I have included imagined story elements—scenes, characters, dialogue, situations, relationships, and events—which I believe are consistent with the historical truth of Hopkins's fascinating life, the themes of his remarkable story, and the times in which he lived.

There are scenes, characters, dialogue, situations, relationships, and events in this book that are fictional, and any fictional character in this book who resembles an actual person, living or dead, is purely coincidental.

July 9, 2025
Steve Vesce

TABLE OF CONTENTS

PROLOGUE 14

CHAPTER ONE 18

CHAPTER TWO 39

CHAPTER THREE 60

CHAPTER FOUR 73

CHAPTER FIVE 84

CHAPTER SIX 94

CHAPTER SEVEN 109

CHAPTER EIGHT 134

CHAPTER NINE 145

CHAPTER TEN 160

CHAPTER ELEVEN 178

CHAPTER TWELVE 198

CHAPTER THIRTEEN 214

CHAPTER FOURTEEN 226

CHAPTER FIFTEEN 240

CHAPTER SIXTEEN 254

CHAPTER SEVENTEEN 265

CHAPTER EIGHTEEN 273

CHAPTER NINETEEN 291

CHAPTER TWENTY 300

CHAPTER TWENTY-ONE 320

CHAPTER TWENTY-TWO 350

CHAPTER TWENTY-THREE 378

CHAPTER TWENTY-FOUR... 402

CHAPTER TWENTY-FIVE 425

CHAPTER TWENTY-SIX.. 444

CHAPTER TWENTY-SEVEN 467

CHAPTER TWENTY-EIGHT 482

CHAPTER TWENTY-NINE.. 503

CHAPTER THIRTY.. 516

CHAPTER THIRTY-ONE 530

CHAPTER THIRTY-TWO... 560

CHAPTER THIRTY-THREE.. 585

CHAPTER THIRTY-FOUR 597

EPILOGUE.. 617

ABOUT THE AUTHOR 620

ACKNOWLEDGMENTS

Researching this novel, was a rewarding journey of discovery. Though I had read about FDR's presidency and Harry Hopkins many times over the years, I gained a deeper appreciation of this remarkable American hero while preparing a lecture about him several years ago. This historical and biographical novel was born out of the research for that lecture.

After months of research, it became clear to me that Hopkins's story was the story of the hero's journey. He was one ordinary man with extraordinary talent and grit, who journeyed from obscurity to a place behind the wizard's curtain to pull the levers that helped America overcome the Great Depression, defeat fascism, and win World War II.

I am grateful and fortunate for the time and opportunity to share Harry Hopkins's remarkable story with a new generation.

My wife, Carol, deserves the lion's share of credit for always supporting my endeavors and encouraging me to pursue this particular dream to tell Hopkins's story well.

I also want to thank my entire family, and my many friends and colleagues who gave me their unconditional support and guidance, and took the time to read the many drafts of this, my first novel. Special thanks to Kat Lansbury, Charles Lansbury, Bill Vesce, Zoey Ripple, David Heiman, Mo Winograd, Jill Force, Bob Trimper, Liz Mageira, Mike Hirsch, Janice White, Howard Simon, Beth Wilson, and Jack Romanos for your time, input, candid comments, suggestions, and continued encouragement.

I am also grateful for the many authors, historians, and news organizations who chronicled Harry Hopkins's life and times, providing the historical facts and opinions about the man, and insights into his accomplishment's, colleagues, friends, and adversaries.

Robert Sherwood, the Pulitzer Prize and Academy Award-winning author and Harry Hopkins's friend and colleague, deserves special recognition for his seminal work entitled *Roosevelt and Hopkins: An Intimate History*. Sherwood's Pulitzer Prize-winning biography, which was published in 1948 just two years after Hopkins died, and was written using Sherwood's personal knowledge of Hopkins as well as Hopkins's personal papers. In my view, Sherwood's book remains the definitive work about Harry Hopkins and his relationship with Franklin Delano Roosevelt.

Among the other works were several standouts such as David Roll's book, *The Hopkins Touch, The Citizens of London* by Lynne Olson, Doris Kearns Goodwin's *No Ordinary Time,* Jonathan Alter's *The Defining Moment,* Henry H. Adams's *Harry Hopkins: A Biography,* Michael Fullilove's *Rendezvous with Destiny,* June Hopkins's *Harry Hopkins and the Grand Alliance of the Second World War,* Matthew Wills' *Wartime Missions of Harry L. Hopkins,* Kristin Downey's *The Woman Behind the New Deal,* Harvey J. Kaye's *The Four Freedoms,* and William Shirer's *The Rise and Fall of the Third Reich.*

All of these authors and others have taught us all about the remarkable story of America and the world during one of the most challenging twelve-year periods in history.

I never got to meet my grandfather, but even as a child, I realized that Harry Hopkins was an important and famous man. As I grew older, I grew curious about him and I wanted to understand how and why he became such an extraordinary public figure. So, I became a historian.

Over the past three decades I did all the things historians are supposed to do. I immersed myself in the political and social history of twentieth century America. I took university courses and earned a Ph.D. in history; I visited archives, analyzed the documents, and read the many books written about him and his era; I listened to his speeches and read his letters; and I wrote about my grandfather's contributions during the Great Depression and the Second World War. As my research progressed, pride in my grandfather's achievements grew.

With the above as background, I approached reading the novel, One Ordinary Man, by Steve Vesce, with some reservations. Though he does not present himself as a trained historian, he does have an excellent grasp of the events that set the stage for the players who drove the action. Consequently, the book reads like a drama.

I heard my grandfather's voice in the words that Steve Vesce put in his mouth and recognized the familiar tone of the conversations he created. His descriptions of my grandfather's interactions with world figures as well as family members all rang true. Consequently, a three-dimensional figure emerged, and my grandfather came to life for me.

World leaders are humans, sometimes flawed, but a few manage to rise above petty differences when it comes to public service. Hopkins somehow was able to do this. Vesce recognizes that Hopkins often put service to his country, and to his president, above his responsibility to his family, but also shows that the enormous effort he put into his fight against poverty, fascism, and tyranny were meant to keep his family as well as his nation safe.

Hopkins' career should be an inspiration for those who seek public life in any form. Sitting at the right hand of President Franklin Roosevelt, he had enormous power but never sought fame, nor did he hope to benefit monetarily from his service. He was a skilled administrator and spent billions of dollars of other people's money providing jobs for Americans made destitute by the Great Depression, but not one dime stuck to his fingers.

Struck down by cancer in the middle of his career, he refused to slow down. The thousands of miles he traveled, in a time when travel was difficult and dangerous, often laid him low. It becomes clear that he sacrificed his health for the war effort. He died when he was just 55 years old, and was as much a victim of the conflict as any foot soldier. Harry Hopkins represented the best sort of man during an era when the best was essential.

This book is especially important today because it demonstrates how good leadership is crucial not only for one's country but for the entire world. The freedoms we have in the United States, the Four Freedoms articulated by President Franklin Roosevelt at the start of World War II, are under attack today—freedom of speech, freedom from fear, freedom of religion, and freedom from want. These are worth fighting for. At a time when our democratic system is at risk, we need men like Hopkins to stand against autocratic leaders at home and abroad.

Dr. June Hopkins

Professor of History, Emerita

Author

Harry Hopkins and The Grand Alliance of the Second World War

Harry Hopkins: Sudden Hero, Brash Reformer

Jewish First Wife, Divorced: The Correspondence of Ethel Gross and Harry Hopkins (co-edited with Allison Giffen)

Bellingham, Washington, 2025

PROLOGUE

April 1957
Kensington, London

Robert Hopkins walked along Kensington Road on an unusually bright and beautiful London morning with *destiny* on his mind. All morning long, as he prepared for his reunion with Winston Churchill, he had been preoccupied with how London and its famous citizen were woven into the fabric of his own life, and the life of his late father, Harry Hopkins—the man whose visits to London during the war years were part of the great work he did on behalf of the President of the United States and the cause of freedom.

Yes, Robert was thinking a lot about *destiny*.

It had been nearly fifteen years since he first set foot in London. Back then, he was a US Army soldier assigned to General Eisenhower's headquarters. Three years later, Germany was defeated, and he and his new British wife, Brenda, moved to Paris. It was easy for Robert to remember those difficult years when German bombers dotted London's sky and the spirit of the city seemed to swing like a pendulum between terror and exhilaration, often on the same day.

Though London's skies had been quiet since Germany's surrender twelve years earlier, Robert had the distinct feeling that a dark cloud remained over the entire city. It felt to him like Londoners were stuck in place, still living with the strain of the war years, and longing to break into the light of even one carefree day—a day without rationed food, or a long line at a butcher, or the stomach-churning concern of having enough money to live.

When Robert turned down Hyde Park Gate toward Churchill's home, past homes that stood proudly as reminders of England's glorious past, he knew it was fitting that the British Empire's last true believer lived on this street.

Robert last saw Churchill in February 1945, when General Eisenhower ordered him to the Yalta Conference on the Crimean Peninsula to photograph Prime Minister Winston Churchill, President Franklin Delano Roosevelt, Marshall Josef Stalin, and, of course, his father, Harry Hopkins. They were all in Yalta to plan the end of the war and beyond, and even after all these years, the images of their conference were still fresh in Robert's mind's eye. When he arrived at Number 28 Hyde Park Gate and approached the London bobby standing guard near the front door, he couldn't help but feel that his father, Harry, was walking with him.

There is no record or transcript of what Robert and Churchill discussed that day. The only thing we know for sure about their luncheon and conversation comes from a letter Robert wrote to his wife, Brenda, on Claridge's Hotel stationery. The letter was found in an otherwise ordinary box of their personal papers, not long after Brenda died.

In his letter, Robert described a very pleasant lunch with the eighty-two-year-old legend, filled with stories told about those challenging, often desperate, and occasionally euphoric war years. He wrote Brenda that Churchill had his cook prepare consommé and cold beef for lunch in honor of Churchill's first lunch with Robert's father, Harry, during his first visit to London in January 1941.

Churchill was still a master raconteur and shared story after story while eating his lunch, smoking his cigars, and drinking his favorite Pol Roger champagne with the vigor of a much younger man. Though Robert said it was a very entertaining afternoon with a wide-ranging discussion, he wrote Brenda of several comments the great man made, which "will remain etched in my heart for the rest of my life."

Apparently, at one point during their lunch, Robert asked Churchill what he remembered about his father, anticipating a humorous story of one of their many escapades, or a more serious, lesser-known tale of one of their wartime struggles. Instead, according to Robert, the great man sat for what seemed like a long time, wreathed in cigar smoke and sipping champagne as he peered out the dining room window toward Hyde Park.

"Everyone who came in contact with your father would confirm what I have said about his remarkable personality," Churchill said as he quietly puffed on his cigar and looked out upon a group of people standing in the park. Robert sat silently watching the old man filter through a torrent of his memories about Harry Hopkins through the haze of time and smoke and tears that were now welling in his eyes. When Churchill finally turned toward him, Robert could see the great man was losing his battle to contain the emotions that were filling his chest.

"Your father was an extraordinary man and a true leader of men," Churchill said directly to Robert. "His love of the causes of the weak and poor was only matched by his passion against tyranny, especially when tyranny was, for a time, triumphant. He had a soul that flamed out of a frail and failing body," the great man finished in a way that told Robert how much he missed his father.

Churchill then reached for his napkin and turned back to the window. The tears that had welled in his eyes moments before were now streaming down his cheeks. As he stared out at the park, he said quietly, "He was a crumbling lighthouse from which there shone the beams that led great fleets to harbor."

CHAPTER ONE

March 1933

Washington, DC

"You'll fit right in with this group, Harry."

"Union Station, Washington, DC, is next!"

The conductor's voice carried through the Pennsylvania Railroad train car, which had left New York City hours earlier and was now slowly approaching Union Station, carrying Harry Hopkins into the nation's capital.

Hopkins sat wedged between the seat and the train window with one leg over the other, a scuffed shoe dangling in front of him, and a bare leg showing between his trouser cuff and the top of his sock. The heavy wool suit he wore that day was the kind that wrinkled badly in the rain, and it had already lost its creases and shape.

With his face hidden behind a wide-open copy of *The New York Times*, a sleek stream of smoke from his Lucky Strike cigarette rose slowly above the paper and danced its way toward the train ceiling to join the cloud of cigarette and cigar smoke from the other passengers. As the train squealed, rumbled, and banged its way into Union Station, out of his window Hopkins noticed three hobos running through the rail yard to jump onto a freight train heading north. He watched the hobos scramble toward the open train door, clawing and crawling their way up and inside the moving train.

He was not surprised. Almost everyone in America during those dark days in 1933 sought to escape from the debilitating anxiety that consumed the country. For some, whether they were paying passengers or not, it was trains that held the promise of a new place, a new life, and perhaps, a better destiny. For others, with the country still under Prohibition, it was bootlegged beer, bathtub gin, or the homemade stuff they simply called "hootch." And for still others, it was prayers and worship that transported them and provided the hope and strength needed to meet and survive each new day. Unlike most Americans, Harry Hopkins boarded the train that morning, not trying to escape, but hoping he would be carried directly into the teeth of the storm.

Just three days earlier, on March 4, 1933, Franklin Delano Roosevelt, FDR as he was known, was inaugurated as President of the United States and promised to deliver a *New Deal* for Americans. Despite the fact that America was reeling from the economic tsunami called the Great Depression, the country's newly elected, wheelchair-bound President exuded remarkable—no, inhuman—confidence that all would turn out well for America and Americans. With steel braces on his legs and hands holding the podium with a vice-like grip, FDR stood alone on the East Portico in front of the Capitol and told Americans the only thing they had to fear was fear itself.

The new President's confidence, however, did not convince every American that all would be well. For the thirteen million people, 25% of the country's working population, who were unemployed, and for the millions more who were starving, just getting out of bed in the morning was like making a long shot wager that they would survive the day.

Hopkins entered Union Station's main hall in Washington, DC, carrying his briefcase, a cigarette, and a copy of *The New York Times* under his arm. He looked like most people in the Station— average build, average height, an overcoat, and a well-worn fedora on top of his head that covered his average brown hair parted on one side and combed over the top of his head. There was nothing in his appearance that would have told anyone who saw him that day that in a few years his would be a household name throughout America or, in just twelve short years, he would, for a time, be thought of as the most powerful man in the world. In fact, the only thing noteworthy about Harry Hopkins's appearance as he walked through the main hall that day was his loose-fitting, creaseless wool suit, which made him look thinner than he actually was and hid his determined stride.

Union Station was a chaotic blend of sound and activity with continuous announcements over the station's loudspeakers about lost items and departing or arriving trains. There were crowds of people arriving, others running to catch a train, and still more sleeping on station benches. Some in the hall were looking for handouts, removing items from lockers, or being greeted by friends and family, while a young newspaper hawker in the center of the building did his best to sell the latest information to a very concerned public.

"Hey, paper here! Roosevelt closes all the banks! Read all about it! Paper here!" the young newspaper hawker bellowed.

The newsboy was a master salesman. As a crowd of people surged toward him, begging him to take the coins in their outstretched hands, the newspaper hawker moved smoothly and quickly with the athleticism and dexterity of a trained athlete, handing out newspapers, making change, pocketing the money, and calling out for more, "Read it right here! Roosevelt declares a bank holiday! The Stock Market and all banks are closed! Find out when you can get your money! Paper here!"

It was early evening by the time Hopkins exited the main hall onto the plaza outside, and he was immediately pressed by blocks of people coming and going from the station. Beyond the station's entrance, there were dozens standing on the plaza looking for handouts, offering taxi rides, trying to carry luggage, selling apples, cooking potatoes, and roasting nuts, while several police officers in uniform actively patrolled the plaza.

"Can I give you a lift?" a thick, rough-looking man asked Hopkins.

Seeing the man approach Hopkins, a patrolling police officer closed quickly on them. "It's okay, mister," the police officer said to Hopkins over the man's shoulder. "He won't bother you."

The man did not move but kept his fists tucked into the pockets of his worn leather jacket and his eyes focused on Hopkins from under the brim of his wool flat cap.

"Move along," said the officer, tapping the butt end of his Billy club into the man's back just above his kidney.

Hopkins couldn't help but notice that the man's eyes were anything but menacing, and actually seemed to be asking Hopkins for help.

He decided.

"Here you are!" Hopkins blurted out, sounding relieved, as a smile crossed his face. "It's okay, Officer," Hopkins said to the policeman. "We're friends."

Hopkins couldn't tell who was more surprised by his response: the menacing man, the police officer, or himself.

"C'mon, Charlie," said Hopkins, motioning to the man. Dumbfounded, the man told Hopkins, "We're goin' this way," and directed him toward a line of cars on the other side of the park.

"Thank you, Officer," Hopkins said to the police officer, sounding a little too grateful, and turned to follow the menacing man.

As Hopkins and the man walked near the park, they were hit by a wretched smell that was a toxic blend of unknowable bits of food, soiled clothes, body odor, and human waste. The park was filled with dozens of makeshift dwellings, people and children barely dressed, dogs, cats, and rats roaming in the mud, and something they called "stew" cooking on small fires. As they walked past the park, Hopkins locked eyes with a ragged-looking man and woman who sat on wooden crates stirring a pot of something over an open fire.

"Hooverville?" Hopkins asked the man.

"Yeah, they're all over the city. Whaddaya gonna do? They're all starvin'," he replied matter-of-factly.

Hopkins knew what he saw was a sobering example of how men could fall. Less than a year after Herbert Hoover ascended to the presidency, the wheels started to fall off America's economic wagon, followed by the whole cart, and everything in it. His monumental failure to effectively counter the dung storm that became the Great Depression turned the once lauded hero into an object of scorn and worse. Newspapers that people used to provide warmth were called "Hoover blankets." When a man turned his pockets inside out, it was called a "Hoover flag." But "Hooverville" was the epithet that hurt the most.

"How much to go to the Women's University Club off DuPont Circle?" asked Hopkins as they walked to the car.

"Twenty-five cents, all right?" answered the man, hoping Hopkins would still agree to ride with him.

Hopkins nodded.

"Thanks for helping me out back there," said the man, sounding sincerely grateful.

"Tough times," Hopkins replied simply.

"You can say that again. Real tough. By the way, my name's Joe, not Charlie."

"Harry," replied Hopkins, and quickened his pace, anxious to get to the Women's University Club before his friend, Frances Perkins, the new Secretary of Labor, began her speech. He traveled to Washington that day with one goal in mind: get to the University Club, see Perkins, and convince her to champion his idea to put millions of Americans back to work.

Harry Hopkins and Frances Perkins were old friends and kindred spirits. It was Perkins, who two years earlier, convinced Hopkins to give up his directorship of the New York Heart Association to join Governor Franklin Roosevelt as Executive Director of New York's TERA, the Temporary Emergency Relief Administration. The goal then was to find jobs for New Yorkers who had succumbed to the soul-crushing cataclysm of the 1929 Stock Market Crash and the early days of the Great Depression.

As they approached a line of cars parked on the street, Hopkins picked out an old, dilapidated black Ford with rusted fenders parked at the curb. "That the one?" Hopkins asked, hoping Joe would say no.

"Yeah," said Joe. "She runs great."

When Hopkins opened the rear door of the car, he was greeted with the sickly, sour smell of a very old and worn-down car, and a large hole in the floorboard showing the street below.

"You can put your briefcase on the back seat, but ya betta sit up front with me," Joe suggested. "It gets breezy back there."

Hopkins walked to the passenger side of the car, and as he sat in the front seat, a broken seat spring pressed on his right leg, forcing him to sit on his left side. Hopkins tried to open his window to get some fresh air, but it didn't move.

"Cost more for the air conditioning?" Hopkins asked, nodding his head toward the hole in the floorboard, happy that at least some air would find its way into the car.

"Nah. It came with the car," replied Joe, ignoring Hopkins's wisecrack as he worked the gas pedal several times, trying to pump gas into the engine. Joe pressed the starter button, and though the car's engine strained to come alive, it collapsed under the weight of its age and disrepair.

"Always drive a cab, Joe?" Hopkins asked as Joe waited a few seconds before trying the engine again.

"Nah, I'm a steamfitter. But you know, construction went into the toilet. Got a wife and kids at home and gotta do something. How 'bout you?"

"Social worker," Hopkins explained.

"Oh yeah?" Joe said as he placed his finger on the starter button again and prayed a silent prayer that the engine would turn over. After a series of knocks, burps, and belches, to Joe's delight, the engine finally fired.

"Smooth as silk," Joe proudly announced as he madly pumped the gas pedal, trying to keep the engine alive. It took a few seconds, but the engine finally settled into a steady, and very loud, gargle.

When Joe put the car into gear, there was a terrifying grinding sound that inspired another silent prayer from him. After a couple of steel-on-steel screeches, several loud knocks, and a few shudders, he guided the old Ford out of the parking space and into the street. The car looked like it was dancing a Cha-Cha, moving to and fro down the block on its way to the Women's University Club.

Relieved to be making progress, and so far, uninjured, Joe took a moment to silently thank God for his good luck. Hopkins almost had the same thought at the same time, and removed a pack of Lucky Strikes from his pocket, lit one, and offered one to Joe.

"Thanks. Haven't had one in days," Joe said, happy for the chance to have a cigarette in his hand, and twenty-five cents in his pocket—if, that is, they made it to their destination.

"Here, take these," Hopkins said, handing Joe the unfinished pack of Lucky Strikes. "I've been smoking too much anyway."

"Thanks, Harry. Really appreciate it," Joe said, surprised by Hopkins's generosity. "Hey, what's a social worker?"

"I run New York's Temporary Emergency Relief Administration," Hopkins replied.

"Relief?"

"Yep."

"You mean like the dole?"

"Something like that. I help people find jobs."

"Are you gonna do that here?"

"I hope so, Joe."

"Me too, Harry."

#

Two months later, on a beautiful May morning, Hopkins approached the White House entrance for his meeting with President Roosevelt. Though the cherry blossoms were gone, the trees, lawn, and flowers on its grounds were in full bloom and color. Walking along the perimeter fence, Harry saw dozens of people standing in silence, looking toward the White House Portico and windows as if they were staring at a holy site. The angry protestors from the Hoover days had been replaced by desperate supplicants.

There were people placing notes and flowers inside the fence, and some reading Bibles. A Jewish man in a yarmulka stood shuckling as if he were in front of the Wailing Wall, and a woman and young girl, who reminded Hopkins of his own wife and daughter, appeared to be silently praying with their hands extended toward the White House Portico.

Remarkably, it was just a little more than sixty days since Hopkins first arrived in DC and made the trip from Union Station in Joe's Flivver to the Women's University Club to pitch Frances Perkins on his idea. When she saw Hopkins enter the auditorium that night, Frances let out with an oversized, "Oh my word! It is Harry Hopkins!" Many people thought Perkins sounded like Margaret Dumont, the woman who starred in the Marx Brothers' movies and who spoke in overdone, affected tones. And much like Dumont greeting Groucho, when Perkins greeted Hopkins, the people standing near the new Secretary of Labor that night thought she seemed to be a little too happy to see the man in the shapeless wool suit.

Now, DC being DC, Perkins's overly friendly greeting of Hopkins immediately had everyone around her wondering who this man was who made the usually dry and serious Secretary of Labor so happy. As they hugged, Hopkins picked up on the crowd's curiosity and whispered to Perkins, "They think we're an item." Knowing his assessment was likely accurate, Perkins quickly ushered Hopkins out of the auditorium and into a stairwell. When they disappeared, there were more whispers in the auditorium.

That night, in that dimly lit stairwell, Hopkins went right to the point, as always. He pitched Perkins on the idea of FERA—a Federal Emergency Relief Administration—that could disburse $500 million of federal funds to enable state governments to give jobs to the thirteen million-plus Americans who were out of work. Even though Perkins recognized that FERA was a fundamental, and some would later say, radical change for the federal government, like Hopkins, she and the President were deeply concerned that Americans and America would not survive the current economic catastrophe. She promised Hopkins she would take his proposal to Roosevelt, and today, as Hopkins walked to meet with FDR just two months later, his proposal was already the law of the land.

FDR had spent every single day since his inauguration waging war against an economic adversary whose assault on America was as grave, invasive, terrifying, and violent as that of any enemy ever faced by the country. On FDR's eighth day in office, Sunday, March 12, 1933, he delivered his first of many radio broadcasts, which America would later call his *Fireside Chats.* That Sunday night was the first time a US President spoke to the entire country at the same time over the radio, and FDR's goal was to educate and convince Americans that when America's banks reopened the next day, they would be safe to hold their money.

FDR's clear, optimistic, and steady voice entered people's living rooms that Sunday evening, and in under fifteen minutes, he gave Americans a primer on the banking system and won their confidence. When America's banks reopened the next day, Americans did re-deposit their money, and according to some, FDR saved American capitalism in his first eight days.

By the time Hopkins arrived for his meeting with FDR that May, the administration had delivered an astounding number of programs approved by Congress to repair or renew one or more segments of America's shattered economy, as well as Americans' trust in their country's institutions. Today, Hopkins's Federal Emergency Relief Administration—FERA—would be added to the growing list of FDR's achievements.

While the people standing outside the White House's perimeter fence implored their God and their President for help, FDR sat in his office reading a document as his secretary, Marguerite "Missy" LeHand, stood next to his desk waiting for his instructions. Also waiting were Edwin "Pa" Watson, the President's gregarious Senior Military Aide, Frank Walker the sharp, and always well-dressed political operator who was one of FDR's most trusted advisers and the leader of his National Emergency Council, and pacing the room was Louis "Louie" Howe, the former Albany, New York newspaperman who was devoted to FDR.

A political operative who chain-smoked Camel cigarettes, Howe was the protector of FDR's brand. His finely tuned political antennae, small stature, thinning hair, nicotine-stained fingers, acne-ridden, pockmarked face, and easily distributed nasty comments to anyone who doubted FDR earned him the nickname "the Medieval Gnome" from his friends and enemies alike.

Howe had been by FDR's side fifteen years earlier, convincing him not to divorce Eleanor, his wife, after Eleanor discovered FDR had a heated affair with her secretary, Lucy Mercer. He was with FDR three years after that, when the 39-year-old FDR contracted polio while vacationing with his wife, Eleanor, and their six children at their summer home in Campobello, off the coast of Maine. And Howe was still there years after that, when FDR wallowed in self-pity and depression at the loss of his physical prowess and his promising future. More than anyone, Howe knew that FDR intimately understood what desperation could do to a man.

When FDR, the tall, handsome, and once agile Assistant Secretary of the Navy believed his life was over and all hope of ever following in his cousin Theodore Roosevelt's footsteps to the White House was gone, it was Louie Howe, Eleanor, Missy LeHand, and Frank Walker who together lifted FDR up and pushed him forward into the political arena despite the terrifying and ego shattering loss of his mobility. Howe, Eleanor, and Frank Walker were the only people who called the President "Franklin," while Missy LeHand kept "Effdee" as her own, private name for the man she adored.

As Howe paced FDR's office, smoking and waiting for FDR's attention, the President finished reading the document, signed it, and handed it to Missy LeHand. "Missy, please make sure Harold Ickes gets a copy of that," FDR instructed LeHand, who nodded and left the office.

Roosevelt inserted a fresh cigarette into his enamel-tipped, five-inch cigarette holder, lit it, and sat back in his chair looking at Howe. "Okay, Louie. What's the news?"

Howe screeched to a halt and sat down on the arm of the sofa with his right leg vibrating. "Fear, and lots of it," Howe said quickly. "You remember what Walter Lippman told you—that you may have no alternative but to assume dictatorial powers? Well, newspapers everywhere are saying you should temporarily suspend the Constitution until we get out of this mess." Howe's right leg was now pumping up and down frantically.

"What?!" Frank Walker said in disbelief. "You're kidding."

"It's everywhere. I keep telling you, Frank," Howe admonished Walker. "You have to look in and under the stories. In and under. Just this morning, *The New York Times* happily reported, I repeat, happily, that Mussolini met with Hitler's man. Fascism and dictators are very appealing nowadays."

"Jesus," Walker muttered in disbelief.

"They are scared," said FDR quietly. "Louie, if I do what they suggest, I will be the last President the United States ever has."

Howe popped up off the arm of the sofa and started pacing again. "Franklin, you need to send your own message to these guys right away. Before this thing gets out of hand."

"Louie! Will you sit down for Christ's sake?" Walker demanded. The alarming subject and Howe's frantic energy were getting the best of him.

Howe found a chair in front of FDR's desk, sat, and waited for FDR's instructions.

"I want you to call Walter Lippman," instructed FDR, "and tell him I want him to stop disrespecting Congress in his articles and to stop talking about dictatorship."

"I'll take care of it," agreed Howe.

"What about the Hearst papers?" Walker asked.

"Not a chance," Howe responded quickly. "The word is Hearst is producing a movie called *Gabriel Over the White House*. It's supposed to get the country ready for a dictatorship."

"Gabriel? Like the angel Gabriel?" Walker's voice was incredulous.

Howe nodded with an "I know, it's crazy" look in his eyes.

"That sounds like quite a movie," FDR snickered. "I think I would like to see it."

"Who the hell else but Hearst would combine religion with dictatorship training," Walker scoffed.

"Let's start with Lippman," FDR ordered, "and then we will go from there."

The door to FDR's office opened, and Missy LeHand entered with Frances Perkins and Harry Hopkins in tow. Perkins was dressed in her usual dark suit, pearls, and tri-cornered hat, and Hopkins in a neatly pressed blue suit, shirt, and tie, and shined shoes.

"MisTAH Hopkins!" FDR exclaimed in a way that seemed to accent his accent.

Hopkins approached the President's desk with his hand extended. "Mr. President," he said, shaking hands with FDR across his desk.

"Good luck, Harry," Missy said as she turned to exit the office.

"Thanks, Missy," Hopkins replied casually.

"You two know each other?" Walker asked, surprised by their familiarity.

"Don't believe a word Missy says," Hopkins joked.

FDR laughed, and Missy smiled at Hopkins. "You'll fit right in with this group, Harry."

"Missy is a very good judge of character," FDR and LeHand exchanged knowing looks before she turned to leave.

"Harry, you know Louie," FDR continued. Howe and Hopkins acknowledged each other but said nothing, each never quite sure of the other.

"I don't think you know Pa Watson, Harry," Roosevelt said, introducing Watson. "Pa helps run things around here."

"Pa, say hello to Harry Hopkins. We worked together in New York, and Harry is going to run FERA for us, our new Federal Emergency Relief Administration."

"Great to meet you," Watson said, shaking hands with Hopkins.

"Please have a seat, Harry," FDR continued, smiling broadly. "I believe you set a new Capitol Hill record. A new federal program approved by Congress in just sixty days."

"Thank you, Mr. President, but it's all because of you and Mrs. Perkins," Hopkins replied.

"No, no," said FDR. "The credit entirely belongs to Mrs. Perkins and to you."

"Thank you, Mr. President," Perkins said, very pleased that FDR recognized her.

"How is your family doing?" FDR asked.

"Fine, sir. My wife, Barbara, and my daughter, Diana, arrived from New York, and we're settling in."

"We had to set up Harry's office in the old Walker Johnson Building on New York Avenue," Frank Walker jumped in, wanting to be sure FDR had all the facts.

"I'm told that old building smells like a locker room, a stable, and a hospital all put together. And I hear they have cockroaches the size of bullfrogs," FDR said, enjoying his own joke.

"Not to worry, Mr. President. I've worked in a lot of rough places in New York City," Hopkins said, smiling.

"I'm sure Frank and Frances have told you there are a lot of rough places in this town, too," replied FDR, his tone turning serious.

"Yes, sir, we did," Perkins assured the President.

"There are many people in this town who will try to slow you down, Harry," FDR counseled. "Don't pay them any attention. You just make sure we get our people working again."

"We will," Hopkins said confidently.

"Congress has given us five hundred million dollars to put our people back to work, and that's what we're going to do. Fast. Not the dole, Harry, but jobs—and lots of them," FDR emphasized.

"Yes, sir."

"And Harry," FDR was on a roll now. "I don't care if the people we help are Republicans, Democrats, Baptists, Jews, Socialists, Catholics, Moslems, or anything else. We need to get them all working again, and fast," he directed.

"I won't let you down, Mr. President."

"I know you won't."

Walker stood and extended his hand to Hopkins. Hopkins stood, and the two men shook hands. "If you need anything, you call me," instructed Walker.

"Thank you," replied Hopkins, and then turned toward the President. "Thank you, Mr. President."

"Welcome aboard, Harry, and Godspeed!"

#

Each day during those early years of the Depression was a challenge for most Americans, regardless of the weather. But whenever a day started with bright sunshine, it at least suggested the possibility of a better day ahead. And the next morning in Washington, DC, was just such a day.

The Washington Post sat on the mat outside Hopkins's apartment when Barbara, dressed in her bathrobe and slippers, opened the door to retrieve it. The bright and warm early morning sun poured out from inside the apartment, flooding over the newspaper and lighting the corridor.   Barbara picked up the newspaper from the mat and retreated back into her apartment.

Barbara Duncan had married Harry Hopkins three years earlier after their brief affair and his divorce from Ethel Gross, his first wife of sixteen years. Hopkins had three sons with Ethel, David, Robert, and Stephen, who all lived in New York City, and a daughter, Diana, with Barbara, who were both with him in Washington, DC.

A naturally beautiful woman, Barbara exuded warmth, intelligence, and optimism to everyone who came in contact with her. Though her dark-haired beauty initially attracted Hopkins, it was Barbara's internal glow, smarts, sensitivity, and innately free sensuality that ultimately claimed his heart.

Hopkins adored her.

The apartment was filled with the comforting aroma of brewed coffee and buttered toast, and Barbara read the newspaper's headlines as she walked to Diana's room and peeked in to see her two-year-old daughter sleeping soundly. She then continued to her own bedroom where she found Harry sitting on the edge of their bed in his T-shirt and shorts with his head in his hands. Hopkins looked like he was praying for more sleep when Barbara stepped in front of him with the open newspaper in her hands.

"You made the papers," Barbara announced, reading the article above his head.

Hopkins did not respond but reached around and pulled her to him so that he could press his sleepy face against her.

"Mmm, you smell good," Hopkins said, enjoying his new resting place.

"You made *The Washington Post* this morning. It says here, *Money Flies*."

"Let me guess. I'm going to bankrupt America," answered Hopkins, his voice muffled against her body.

"It says, *'The half billion dollars for direct relief of the States won't last a month if Harry L. Hopkins, the new relief administrator, maintains the pace he set yesterday in disbursing more than $5 million in his first day.'*"

Still holding her, Hopkins lifted his head to look up at her. "I'm not going to last six months here. I'll do what I please."

"You will, will you?" Barbara teased.

He stood up and kissed Barbara while he tugged at the sash on her robe. "Anything I please," he said as he kissed her neck and worked to get her sash untied. Breathing a little heavier now, Hopkins finally opened her robe and worked to lift her nightgown while Barbara tossed the newspaper on the bed and reached into his shorts.

"You are so aggressive," Hopkins whispered while he kissed her neck and slowly made his way toward her breasts.

"Me? You are," Barbara said breathlessly, punctuating each kiss and stroke with a new label for Hopkins. "You are a carousing… poker-playing… horse-handicapping… hard drinker… who can't wait for Prohibition to end..."

"You forgot social worker," added Hopkins as he finally raised Barbara's nightgown above her waist and pressed himself closer.

"Not as romantic," Barbara said, finally managing to slide Hopkins's boxers to the floor.

And then…

"Daddy!" Diana called from down the hall.

They both stood stock still, holding their breath.

"Daddy!" Diana called again.

After several moments, Barbara exhaled and, looking disappointed, lowered her nightgown and pulled up Hopkins's boxers. She stepped back from Hopkins and closed her robe as Hopkins tried to hold her arm and quietly convince her to stay put.

"Come back," he whispered.

"Diana doesn't think you can do anything you please," she whispered back. "You better get her, and I'll pour the coffee."

Still holding her hand, Hopkins tried to kiss her one last time as Barbara made for the door. "Stop that." Barbara smiled and exited the bedroom. She loved being loved by him.

"Good morning, Diana!" Hopkins called out as he put on his robe.

CHAPTER TWO

*"People don't eat in the long run, Congressman. They eat
every day."*

Harry Hopkins moved fast. In all things. All the time. Whether it was his sprint-like pace walking up a street or down a hall, or his unequivocal decisiveness, or his uncanny ability to quickly connect dots, Hopkins hit the ground running each morning, and fueled by too many cigarettes and cups of coffee each day, did not slow down until his head touched the pillow in the evening.

Working from an old, cramped office at the end of the tenth floor in the Walker Johnson Building, Hopkins soon engaged his network of social workers to deploy a small army in the crusade to put Americans back to work and food on their tables. Within months, Hopkins had FERA delivering funds to every state in the union, putting hundreds of thousands of Americans back to work.

It didn't take very long for Hopkins and his crew to become the front line in FDR's campaign to defeat the Great Depression.

During his first months at FERA, Hopkins spent much of his time on trains, traveling to state capitols and county seats to use his persuasive skills, be they official or "unofficial," to get men who should have known better to do better. If that meant twisting arms, Hopkins did it. If it meant playing political hardball, he did that, as well. Sometimes throwing a spitball or two.

One of the legendary Hopkins stories from those early days was often told by Aubrey Williams, one of Harry's key lieutenants. According to Williams, he and Hopkins visited a FERA office in the late summer of '33 in a small town outside of Macon in rural Georgia. The office was a storefront located on Main Street and Hopkins, Williams, and two FERA secretaries found themselves inside that office facing an angry crowd of several hundred burly men who peered at them through the storefront's windows, chanting "We need jobs! We need jobs!" over and over and over again.

Terrified, Williams and two secretaries sat behind the office's locked glass door and windows while Hopkins held the phone to his ear, waiting for Governor Jerry Jackson to come to the phone. They felt like fish in a fish bowl being watched by very hungry people.

According to Williams, Hopkins asked Williams to call the local sheriff. When Williams quickly pointed out that he didn't have to call the sheriff since the sheriff was standing right outside the office in the crowd, Hopkins kept the phone to his ear and calmly told Williams to open the door and ask the sheriff to come in. Whenever

Williams told this story, he freely admitted that he sat frozen in his chair and was unable to move.

"I can't open that door, Harry," pleaded Williams. "There are too many angry people out there."

"It'll be okay," assured Hopkins, but Williams knew Harry had no idea if it would.

Not wanting to appear cowardly, especially in front of the secretaries, Williams rose from behind his desk and slowly walked to the door. He cautiously unlocked the front door and opened it just enough to fit his lips through the crack between the door and the jam. Moving his lips like a guppy gasping for air, Williams asked a big farm hand in dung-encrusted boots and worn-out overalls standing near the front door to call the sheriff. When the sheriff arrived moments later, he looked at Williams standing inside the door with his lips protruding through the door crack and his nose in the air.

"Are you goin' to open this here door or are you just goin' to stand there like you smellin' cow shit?" asked the sheriff.

Williams stepped back to let the sheriff into the office, and fortunately, the crowd outside stayed put. Williams closed and locked the door behind the sheriff, and the crowd went silent, pressing forward toward the windows to watch the sheriff inside among their prey.

"Please ask Governor Jackson to call Harry Hopkins at the FERA office," Hopkins said loudly into the phone and then hung up. Williams always wondered if there was someone on the other end of the line or if Hopkins said the governor's name just so the sheriff could hear him.

The sheriff walked toward Hopkins. "Sheriff Clemmons," said the sheriff, but didn't offer his hand.

"Harry Hopkins. I run FERA," Hopkins replied.

"I know who you are," Clemmons said in a way that assured Hopkins he knew everything and everyone in his town.

"I will meet with Governor Jackson and get this straightened out," Hopkins assured Clemmons.

"That would be good," commented the sheriff, not believing a word Hopkins said.

"Would you do me a favor?" asked Hopkins calmly.

"If I can." The sheriff was a good Christian and wanted to be polite.

"Please go outside and tell everyone that you have taken care of this, and they will all have jobs next week."

"Can't do that," the sheriff said quickly. "How can you guarantee those people out there will have jobs next week?" asked Clemmons, making sure Hopkins knew he did not believe anything he said.

"You have my word," Hopkins said sincerely.

The sheriff thought it was time to set Hopkins straight. "The only word I believe, Mr. Hopkins, is the word of my lord and savior, Jesus Christ."

"Praise Jesus!" responded Hopkins instantly.

One of the secretaries made the sign of the cross, while the other raised her eyebrow.

"You a Christian, Mr. Hopkins?" asked Clemmons suspiciously.

"Yes, sir. Methodist. You?"

"Baptist. You know Psalm 118, Mr. Hopkins?" asked the sheriff, certain he would now prove Hopkins was a fraud.

"Better to take refuge in the Lord than trust in man," replied Hopkins as easily as if he were giving a sermon at a Sunday service.

The secretary who made the sign of the cross did it again, and the other, who was taking a sip of water, coughed it up as she tried to keep herself from laughing. "I'm sorry, wrong pipe," the coughing secretary explained as the sheriff and Hopkins looked over at her.

Aubrey Williams almost fell off his chair. He never did find out how Hopkins knew that particular Psalm.

"You are a Christian." Sheriff Clemmons was pleased. "I am going to trust you, Mr. Hopkins."

"Thank you, Sheriff. I will be sure to tell Governor Jackson what a great job you are doing here."

The meeting ended with Hopkins escorting the sheriff to the door, shaking hands, and agreeing to attend Baptist services with Sheriff Clemmons the next time he came to town. The sheriff exited the office, and after he spoke to the crowd for a few moments, they all left. Whenever Williams told this story, he always made it a point to say, "I'm not sure how, but that was that. It was almost like Harry hypnotized that guy."

But it was the next part of the story that Williams loved telling most, when the following week he and Hopkins went to visit Governor Jerry Jackson.

Jerry Jackson was a fifty-something-year-old politician who loved the trappings of his position and, in particular, enjoyed his slick hair, pencil mustache, gleaming white teeth, tailored suits, silk union suit, and custom-made shoes. Jackson would have been called a *dandy* by most, but he preferred to have people think of him as an English Lord. He even adopted the affected haughty tones heard during the grand days of the British Em-pie-ah.

If you didn't know better, you might have thought Jackson was a widely respected, polo-playing world traveler who attended Oxford. Unfortunately for Jackson, most everyone knew he grew up the son of a poor dirt farmer and was as corrupt as they come.

When Jackson's secretary, a feisty and capable old timer who had served many previous governors, opened the door to Jackson's office, the first impression Williams had was of stupendous splendor and wealth. The office was a mix of glowing fine mahogany, gleaming rich leather, an ornate gold-leafed hand-sculpted plaster ceiling, and floor-to-ceiling mahogany bookshelves filled with gold-trimmed leather-bound editions.

"Harry! To what do I owe the honor of this visit?" Jackson bellowed a little too friendly as he held out his hand for Hopkins.

Coat, hat, and briefcase in one hand, and cigarette in the other, Hopkins did not respond. Instead, he walked past Jackson and, ignoring Jackson's outstretched hand, deposited all of his belongings on top of Jackson's shiny mahogany desk. He then jammed and pounded his cigarette into Jackson's spanking clean ashtray, sending cigarette ashes flying from the ashtray to the top of Jackson's desk. Jackson could not stop himself from using the edge of his hand to gently brush Hopkins's ashes off his prized possession onto the rug below.

Seeming to be overwhelmed by the spectacle of Jackson's office, Hopkins didn't say a word, but walked to the bookcase to examine the dozens of leather-bound titles that filled the glistening mahogany shelves from floor to ceiling. "This is a very nice office, Jerry," Hopkins finally said, taking a book from the shelf.

"I tidied it up a year or so ago," answered Jackson proudly. "Can I hang up your coat, Harry?" Jackson asked, perturbed that Hopkins's belongings were lying on his desk.

"We won't be long," answered Hopkins as he flipped through the pages of the book in his hands. "Wow!" Hopkins exclaimed. "A first edition of the Lincoln-Douglas debates."

"Yes, it is," Jackson said, beaming.

"Must have cost a lot."

"A fair amount," replied Jackson, unsure where Hopkins was going.

Still examining the book, Hopkins said, "We've given your state 8.8 million dollars to create jobs for your people."

"Something like that," responded Jackson casually.

"Exactly that," Hopkins confirmed. "You asked us for $8,825,000, and that's what we sent to you."

"If you say so." Jackson retreated now to sit behind his desk, thinking it might be good to put a physical barrier between himself and Hopkins.

"Where's the money?" Hopkins asked as he returned the book to the shelf and turned to look directly at Jackson.

Aubrey Williams felt sweat begin to run in his armpits.

"Pardon me?" asked Jackson, sounding slightly offended.

"Where's the money we gave you to provide jobs for your people?"

"See here, Harry.   I am entitled to run my state as I see fit," Jackson said with feigned indignance as he tried to sort out what Hopkins really wanted.

"There are hundreds of people outside our offices every day who need jobs, and you won't release our money."

"Just poor dirt farmers and niggers," replied Jackson, instantly giving up his affected tones and noble pretentions as he sensed danger approaching. "Don't worry, Harry. I'll take care of it. You won't see them anymore."

"Jerry, Jerry, Jerry," Hopkins repeated as if he were speaking to his eight-year-old son Stephen. "Don't you know there are reporters and congressmen wondering where all the money is going?"

"So what?"

"So what?" Hopkins repeated thinking that perhaps Stephen was smarter than Jackson.   "The story will go something like this: Governor Jerry Jackson bought first edition books for his office, hired his relatives, and gave them cars and vacations while he refused to release FERA's funds to give jobs to the thousands of starving and desperate citizens of his state."

"No one will ever believe that," Jackson blustered, even though he knew everyone would believe it.

"Okay," Hopkins replied simply and retrieved his coat, hat, and briefcase from Jackson's desk. "We'll see what they believe after the reporters and congressmen start talking to your state auditor."

By now, Aubrey Williams's shirt under his armpits was soaking wet.

"C'mon, Harry. Why are you really here?" quizzed Jackson with a look of silent understanding.

Whenever Williams told this story, he always said that it didn't take a genius to know that Jackson was inviting Hopkins to dip into his till. He also said that this was the moment he thought Harry was going to jump over Jackson's desk and throttle the governor. Now, Williams didn't know it at that time, but in fact, that was Hopkins's impulse. Instead, Hopkins thought better of it, put on his coat, and looking directly at Jackson said simply, "You got the wrong guy."

"I'll release some of the money this week," Jackson said, and though it sounded like he was agreeing, he was really trying to quickly recover from his faux pas.

"All of it," demanded Hopkins. "This week, Aubrey here is going to hand out jobs to your citizens for a total payroll of eight million eight hundred and twenty-five thousand dollars."

"Up yours, Harry!" shot back a red-faced Jackson, giving up the last vestiges of his noble aspirations and going right back to his shit kicking days, riding a tractor on the back forty.

"Have it your way," said Hopkins easily, and turned toward the door with Williams following. Williams actually believed Hopkins was leaving too soon, but when Hopkins placed his hand on the doorknob, they heard Jackson calling out to them.

"I'll release the money today," said Jackson quickly, and then, realizing he may need to do damage control, he added, "Hey, Harry. How do I know this will stay between us?"

Hopkins stood at the door. "As long as your citizens get jobs and every penny we sent to you, I don't give a shit what you do, how many relatives you employ, or how much you steal from your own state. Just don't screw around with our money again."

Hopkins opened the door and again turned to look at Jackson. "By the way, your sheriff down there? Sheriff Clemmons? He does a good job."

#

By the fall of that first year, Hopkins became a victim of his own success. As FERA rapidly grew, so did Hopkins's workload, and so did his time away from Barbara and Diana. More than once during that first year, Hopkins thought back to the night he pitched FERA to Frances Perkins and remembered the saying, "Be careful what you ask for."

While Hopkins typically relied on his own eyes to ensure FERA was reaching everyone who needed its services, he felt like he was losing sight of FERA's effectiveness under the cumulative weight of his ever-increasing administrative burden and his need to engage in DC's political jockeying and hand-holding.

And then Eleanor Roosevelt phoned him.

Though married to FDR for nearly thirty years with six children, Eleanor had long before given up the physical and emotional intimacy of a loving marriage. The change occurred when Eleanor discovered in 1918 that Lucy Mercer, her beautiful secretary, was having a heated affair with FDR. Devastated by their betrayal, Eleanor proposed a divorce, but Louis Howe and the President's mother intervened. Howe discouraged them from divorcing to protect FDR's political career, and Sara Roosevelt forbade it to protect the family from scandal. Sara told her son she would disown him if he divorced.

Eleanor and Franklin remained married in fact, and certainly shared mutual respect for each other, but after his affair with Lucy Mercer and his bout with polio, Eleanor began to carve out her own independent path. With Louis Howe's help, Eleanor became a political force in her own right. And now, as First Lady, Eleanor Roosevelt was a big fan of Harry Hopkins.

Believing that she and Hopkins were both committed to helping the weak, overlooked, and downtrodden in America, Eleanor naturally gravitated toward him and his work. She championed equality for all Americans regardless of who they were, where they came from, the color of their skin, or who they worshipped and, like Hopkins and her husband, believed that it was jobs, work, and sustenance that provided dignity and self-worth to every American.

Eleanor was also a big fan of Lorena Hickok, who was widely considered to be the top female reporter in the country. For years, "Hick" worked for the Associated Press, but parted ways with them when she was invited to get a firsthand, inside look at FDR's new administration, the Roosevelts, and Eleanor. Hick was forty years old and described by one magazine writer as "a rotund lady with husky voice and baggy clothes." One would be hard pressed to find a less feminine-looking woman.

Over time, as Hick worked inside Roosevelt's camp, she and Eleanor became fast friends. After a road trip together up the East Coast of the country in the summer of '33, Hick and Eleanor grew to love each other, and eventually Hick took up residence in the White House. There were whispers of something more between the two women.

Eleanor's call could not have come at a better time for Hopkins. Just as he grappled with his inability to get out of Washington and into the field, Eleanor suggested he consider a role for Hick in FERA. Hopkins knew of Hick's proven skill as a journalist and talented ferret, capable of digging up important information, and believed she was just what he needed to stay in touch with FERA's impact on America. Most importantly, he trusted her eyes and knew he would be lucky to have someone with Hick's talent on his team.

"How do you think Hick would like the title of Chief Investigator?" Hopkins asked Eleanor.

"She will love it," answered Eleanor happily.

When Hick came to see Hopkins the next day, Eleanor had already sold her and even given her a car to use in her new role. "Eleanor can be very persuasive," Hick said as she sat next to Hopkins's paper-filled desk.

"Listen, Hick, it can be rough and tumble out there," warned Hopkins.

"I'll keep a pistol in the glove compartment," Hick answered casually. It was the same gun she took on her road trip with Eleanor the prior summer.

"It would be best if you didn't shoot anyone."

"That depends on who I shoot, doesn't it, Harry?" replied Hick, and Hopkins knew that was Hick's way of officially accepting her new job as FERA's Chief Investigator.

#

Knowing Hick's eyes were in the field, Hopkins now had time to deal with his own political backyard. While he expected the President's adversaries on the Hill and in the press to come after him, he didn't expect shots across his bow from people on his own team. He found himself regularly remembering FDR's comment when they met: "There are many people in this town who will try to slow you down, Harry."

Harold Ickes was FDR's straitlaced Secretary of the Interior and leader of the Public Works Administration, the *PWA*, responsible for deploying billions of dollars in a number of large projects like New York's Triborough Bridge, the Tennessee Valley Authority, and the Hoover Dam, among many others. Ickes started his career as a Republican and later heard the inspirational call of Theodore Roosevelt's Bull Moose Party. A sixty-year-old by-the-book administrator, Ickes was called "Honest Harold" by Conservative politicians and the press, and was known for being a hard case, especially when defending his own turf.

Though FDR really thought highly of Ickes and his handling of the PWA, he also believed *Honest Harold* was wired too tight and not particularly skilled when it came to political engineering or maneuvering. FDR found Ickes's fastidious vibe to be the exact opposite of Hopkins's, with none of Hopkins's charm. No one is quite sure how it all started, but as Hopkins's success and popularity grew with Americans, the press, and FDR, so too did Ickes's ire and competition with him.

Things between the two men moved from friendly competitors to outright adversaries soon after FDR ordered his friend, Treasury Secretary Henry Morgenthau, to move $400 million from Ickes's budget to fund Hopkins's new creation, the Civilian Works Administration, the *CWA*. By year's end, Hopkins's CWA was fast becoming the most popular weapon in President Roosevelt's arsenal against the Depression, and Harold Ickes decided it was time to slow down Hopkins's success parade—or at least rain on it a bit.

So *Honest Harold* lit a fuse.

Louie Howe, always concerned with FDR's political future, sounded the first alarm bells when he burst into Frank Walker's office, dropping a half dozen newspapers on his desk. Despite the two vacant chairs available to him, Howe stood in front of Walker's desk, vibrating and smoking the entire time.

"Frank. How many times do I have to tell you?" asked Howe. "You have to look in and under the stories. It's not Hopkins they're after, it's the boss."

"Who is?"

"I dunno. Maybe it's one of our senators or our Secretary of the Interior."

"Ickes? C'mon Louie. Why would Ickes want to slow down the boss?"

"I dunno. I am not a psychiatrist, Frank. Maybe he's jealous Hopkins is getting too much attention, he's a Republican, he has too much gas… whatever."

"Ickes has nothing to do with it."

"Are you taking nice pills or something? Grow up!"

Walker glared at Howe. "Those who don't know you, Louie, think you're a gruff, abrupt, and rude individual. And those who do know you think they're right." He picked up one of the newspapers and started reading.

"Yeah, well, I'm just an old newspaperman with a good nose, and I smell something," Howe retorted, confident in his assessment of the situation.

Walker looked up from the paper. "You're right about one thing. They definitely have Harry in their sights," he said, trying to connect the dots. "Do you really think Ickes is behind this?"

"Here's what I know, Frank," explained Louie. "The boss needs to put more people back to work if he's going to have any chance of getting elected to a second term, and it's Hopkins and Ickes who drive that bus."

Walker stared at Howe for what seemed to be a very long time, put down the newspaper, and quietly said, "I'll look into it."

This time, Walker knew Howe was right.

Ickes's burning fuse reached the point of detonation a few months later in early 1936 inside a Congressional hearing room. The room and gallery were packed with citizens, reporters, and photographers, and every seat on the dais was occupied by congressmen who exuded smug self-importance. Louis Howe and Frank Walker sat in the front row, directly behind the solitary man at the witness table— Harry Hopkins.

The Chairman of the committee conducting the hearing was a Southern Congressman known for his silky baritone voice, southern drawl, custom-tailored suits, flamboyant silk bow ties, and matching pocket handkerchiefs. This morning's gathering was the result of his committee's efforts to look into all things Hopkins. Their investigation was based on a number of inspired, well-placed stories about Hopkins that were anonymously concocted and gifted to receptive newspapers around the country. Some, like Louie Howe, believed Harold Ickes instigated much of the creative writing about Hopkins.

The Chairman banged his gavel to quiet the gallery, something he always relished doing. "Order, please!" said the Chairman in his silky voice. A hush quickly fell across the room and gallery.

"Now, Mr. Hopkins," the Chairman started, "you have given away more than half a billion dollars. That right?"

"Yes, that's correct," responded Hopkins easily.

"And how many people received those funds?"

"The States report putting more than a million people back to work so far."

"Work?" The Chairman laughed out loud. "You mean leaf rakers? Mowing lawns? What sorts of jobs are those?"

"Jobs that pay money and allow people to feed themselves," Hopkins answered simply.

"But Mr. Hopkins, how will these sorts of menial jobs affect our citizens in the long run?"

"People don't eat in the long run, Congressman. They eat every day."

Howe and Walker exchanged looks as the gallery came alive. Throughout the room, people were heard murmuring, "That's right," "That's the truth," and one older gentleman in the back of the gallery even let out an "Amen." Though they were not sitting on the dais that day, Harry Hopkins's supporters filled the room.

The Chairman lightly banged his gavel. "Order, please! Order."

When the gallery simmered down, the Chairman continued. "We have received reports that you gave funds to States that supported the President. Is that correct?"

Hopkins actually heard Louie Howe exhale the word "Asshole" behind him.

"Yes, that's true," replied Hopkins simply.

The Chairman proudly exchanged looks with several of his colleagues on the dais, while reporters furiously scribbled on their notepads.

"Mr. Hopkins. You admit giving funds to states that support the President and the Democratic Party?" asked the Chairman, his tone suggesting he was closing a prosecutorial vise on his witness.

"Yes, of course I gave funds to states that support our President," replied Hopkins easily. "I also sent money to other States, including your own state, Congressman. I think we put about fifty thousand people back to work in your state, and I'm pretty sure all of the folks in your state aren't fans of our President."

The gallery erupted with a few people laughing out loud, and the Chairman quickly rapped the gavel hard. Howe loved Hopkins's response, and he had a grin on his face from ear to ear, which on Howe's face made him look like he was in pain. Walker, who sat next to Howe, was trying hard not to smile.

"We will have order or I will be forced to clear the gallery," the Chairman announced and then turned back to Hopkins.

The room quieted.

"Mr. Hopkins, I think you'll agree there have been many mistakes made in the administration of your program."

"If we made mistakes, we have made them to help people who were broke. I haven't a thing to apologize for."

"Really? Well, we have reports that some people who receive cash from your program are... well… let's just say, less than honest."

"Congressman, it may be true that there are people in some states who are trying to take advantage of the system. Yeah, that may be true. But I have to tell you I am sick and tired of hearing that those people—who are out of work and need jobs—who are desperate, hungry, and unemployed—being called chiselers and cheats. The truth, Congressman, is that they are just like the rest of us. They don't drink any more than the rest of us, they don't lie any more, they're no lazier than the rest of us. They're pretty much a cross section of the American people."

The people in the gallery spontaneously rose up, cheering and applauding. Howe was delighted, and Walker proud. Reporters tried to capture Hopkins's comments while photographers' flashbulbs popped repeatedly. A scruffy-looking older man in the gallery shouted, "You tell 'em, Mr. Hopkins!"

Hopkins sat expressionless, looking directly at the Chairman, and didn't acknowledge anything going on behind him.

The Chairman snatched up his gavel and banged it hard again and again.

"Order! We will have order!" he shouted.

The gallery refused to quiet.

#

At about the same time, the Congressman was trying to maintain control over Hopkins's hearing, in Albert Lea, Minnesota, Lorena Hickok made a quick stop for a bowl of hot soup and a grilled cheese sandwich to hold her over in her quest to make Minneapolis by nightfall. When she burst from the warmth of the Early Inn Restaurant onto East Front Street, Hick was smacked in the face by a frigid, skin-cutting wind coming from Albert Lea Lake. The wind was so cold she felt her lungs heave and, for a moment, she thought she would not be able to catch her breath.

With her head down, hat pulled over her ears, and hands holding her coat tightly around her throat, Hick hustled to her parked car across the street. When she looked up, she saw three rough-looking, bearded men sitting on her car's fenders with their backs against the car's hood. She wished she hadn't left her pistol inside the car's glove compartment.

"Hello boys," she said without a hint of fear in her voice. "Time for me to go."

The three men looked startled to see her and slowly and reluctantly moved off the car's hood.

"Sorry, mister," apologized the red-bearded man.

"Ma'am," Hick corrected him.

"I'm sorry, ma'am," said Red Beard again. "It's so cold out here I can't even see anymore."

"Your car was the warmest thing out here," said the other man while the third man coughed a deep, growling cough. Hick had heard that kind of cough before and knew it was not good.

"We were about to lie down on top of your engine," Red Beard said, half joking.

Hick saw what looked like frostbite on the coughing man's nose. "Where are you guys staying?"

"Around the corner, ma'am. We got a little camp over there. Beautiful lake front property!" The two other men started to shuffle toward the lake.

"When was the last time you guys had something to eat?"

"Yesterday," answered Red Beard.

"You been down to the FERA office for jobs?" Hick asked.

Red beard scoffed at Hick's suggestion. "Jobs? There are no jobs here. It's too goddamn cold," he jeered and then quickly added, "Sorry for my bad language, ma'am."

Hick opened her purse and removed three one-dollar bills. She held them up. "You can have these if you go, right now, into the restaurant over there and buy a bowl of soup and a sandwich for each of you," Hick insisted.

Hearing her, the other two men stopped walking and looked back toward Hick and Red Beard.

"Thank you, ma'am," Red Beard said as he walked around the car toward Hick to pick up the bills. "That is very generous."

"No booze," Hick warned, handing him the bills. "And I need to see you guys go in that place across the street right now and buy some lunch."

Hick got into her car and watched the three men slowly cross the street to the restaurant. When she started the car, she found tears welling in her eyes. She didn't like feeling like a softy, and prided herself on being, in the jargon of the day, "a tough broad." She used her gloved hands to wipe her eyes dry.

As she pulled her car from the parking space, she was overwhelmed by the idea that the warmth of her car engine and three $1 bills were all that allowed three men in the little town of Albert Lea, Minnesota to survive that day. Three men, who like millions of others throughout the country, woke up each winter morning not knowing if they would see another day. More tears flowed.

CHAPTER THREE

"I do like Harry's style!"

Phil LoScalco, the heavyweight reporter from the *Brooklyn Eagle*, entered the Walker Johnson Building in a hurry and out of breath, worried he would miss the press conference. LoScalco was so big that when he walked through the lobby's glass doors in his oversized raincoat, he blotted out all of the daylight coming in from the street.

"I'm heah for da press conference," LoScalco said in his distinct Brooklyn accent as he quickly approached John Delaney, the Irish-born security guard who sat behind the lobby desk.

"Press conference?" Delaney asked, unsure for a moment.

"Judgin' by da smell, this is the Walker Johnson Building, right?" asked LoScalco as he adjusted the notebook, papers, and pencils he had tucked under his arm.

"Indeed, we are known for our distinct aroma," Delaney responded in his thick Irish brogue.

"Harry Hopkins?" LoScalco asked.

"Ah, yes," replied Delaney, realizing that was where everyone was going this morning. "My apologies. Tenth floor. Take the elevator over there," Delaney said, pointing toward the center of the lobby.

When LoScalco arrived in front of the elevator car in the lobby, he found it was already filled with reporters, with just enough room for one more average-sized person. And LoScalco was anything but average. As he stepped into the elevator, he turned and backed into the car, pressing against the crowd. There were several moans from the reporters being squeezed against the back wall.

Michael Gallagher, the elevator operator (and Delaney's cousin from Dublin), closed the inner cage against LoScalco's sizable stomach, shut the outer elevator door, and rotated the elevator handle to start their journey to the tenth floor.

Other than a clicking sound from the control apparatus, nothing happened.

"C'mon!" a voice from the back pleaded, while another complained, "I'm suffocating back here!"

Gallagher brought the elevator handle to the top and again rotated it.

The elevator still didn't move.

More verbal artillery was lobbed from the reporters on the back wall toward Gallagher.

"She's very sensitive," Gallagher said, defending his elevator's honor, and no sooner had someone in the back shouted, "Send her flowers!" than the elevator took off heading skyward.

"And we're off!" Gallagher happily announced like it was the start of a horse race.

The elevator arrived at the tenth floor with a jerk, and Gallagher swiftly opened the exterior door and slid the interior cage past LoScalco's sizable girth. LoScalco steadied himself as the elevator car bounced up and down, above and below the tenth floor, trying to find its equilibrium.

"Mind your step, gentlemen! Mind your step!" Gallagher announced loudly just as LoScalco tried to leave the bouncing elevator and tripped, spilling his notebook, papers, and pencils onto the corridor floor. Seeing LoScalco's difficulties, the remaining reporters quickly jumped to safety onto the tenth floor before the old elevator could give up the ghost and fall to the bottom of the shaft.

"Take ya life in ya hands in dis place," LoScalco complained as he retrieved his papers from the floor.

"Try the stairs next time. Might do you some good," Gallagher wisecracked, closing the elevator door with a smile.

After giving Gallagher an Italian salute, LoScalco followed the group of reporters toward Hopkins's office at the end of the corridor, where both people and daylight were spilling from the room. There were a few dozen reporters surrounding Harry's desk, and shouting questions while Hopkins sat cross-legged in his desk chair, wearing a brown pin-striped suit. The Washington Monument was visible through the window behind him.

Hopkins held up his hands, "Okay, boys. Let's do this one at a time. What's on your mind, Charlie?" Hopkins asked Charlie McAllister from *The New York Times*.

"Thank you, Mr. Hopkins. The Republican National Committee says your Civil Works Administration is guilty of, quote, 'gross waste and downright corruption,' end quote."

"Charlie, they can say what they want, but I'm very proud of what we've been able to do with FERA, the CWA, and are now doing with the new Works Progress Administration. So far, we've put more than four million people back to work, and helped to build thousands of schools, sewers, airports, and more."

A few flashbulbs popped, and before another reporter could ask a question, McAllister quickly added, "Mr. Hopkins, even Secretary Harold Ickes has said you're moving too fast to be able to control spending."

"Charlie, have you ever seen Harold Ickes move fast?" asked Hopkins with a smile, and the reporters laughed. "While Harold discusses, plans, and bids his projects, we put people—millions of them—back to work."

Hopkins looked over at Mickey Porter. "How's the New York Herald treating you, Mick?"

"Just fine, Mr. Hopkins," responded Porter, pleased to be identified by Hopkins. "Some people are saying you believe in socialism. That you think it's the way to fix the country."

"Mick, you know what I believe? I believe the days of letting people live in misery, of being rock-bottom destitute, of children being hungry, of moralizing about rugged individualism in the light of modern facts—I believe those days are over in America. They have gone, and we are going forward in full belief that our economic system does not have to force people to live in miserable squalor in dirty houses, half fed, half clothed, and lacking decent medical care."

The reporters feverishly scribbled in their notebooks.

Mike Brannigan from *The Washington Post* held up a copy of *Time* magazine with a picture of Hopkins on the cover. "What do you think about being on the cover of *Time*?"

Hopkins waved his hand dismissively. "Nah. The President should be on that cover. He's the one leading all of us out of this mess. I'm just lucky to play a small part."

"The article in here quotes one Senator, 'If Roosevelt ever becomes Jesus Christ, he should have Harry Hopkins as his prophet.' What do you think of that?" asked Brannigan.

"Was that a Republican or a Democratic Senator who said that?" Hopkins shot back with a smile, and flash bulbs popped.

"Tom LaBelle," LaBelle called out, jumping into the silence. "There are charges of corruption in your white-collar projects up in New York City. Are you going to call for a federal investigation?"

Hopkins responded quickly and evenly. "Why the hell should I? Those projects are damn good. They're excellent, goddamn it."

"I didn't mean to upset you," LaBelle said, throwing out bait and hoping Hopkins would bite. A few of the reporters in the room rolled their eyes at LaBelle's bush league move.

"I'm not mad, Tom," answered Hopkins casually, leaving the bait alone. "These people can make fun and shout at white-collar people if they want to, but I have no apologies to make. As a matter of fact, we have not done enough. I have a pile of letters from businessmen, if that is important, saying that our projects are damn good projects.

All these people think about is money to repair streets. We have one hundred and fifty projects up there that deal with pure science. Projects up there to make Jewish dictionaries—there are rabbis up there who are broke and on relief rolls. They can say let them use a pick and shovel to repair streets, but I believe every one of those research projects is a good project. We don't need any apologies."

LaBelle decided to throw out more bait, hoping to get Hopkins to bite down hard. "Isn't your former wife Jewish?"

Several reporters groaned, and Charlie McAllister growled, "What is it with you?" Everyone knew that wives and children were off-limits.

But Hopkins held up both of his hands. "It's okay, fellas. It's okay. Yes, my ex-wife is a Jew, and I'm a Methodist. So what? Do you think I'm paying off her rabbi? I wish you and your boss had a fraction of the intelligence my half-Jewish sons inherited from their full-Jewish mother. Then maybe, just maybe, you wouldn't ask such dumb questions."

"Get that dope outta heah!" LoScalco said loud enough to be sure LaBelle heard him.

LaBelle turned toward the door, thinking it was best to fight another day.

"Hey, LaBelle," Hopkins called out. "Wait a minute. You can tell your boss and your readers—and you can all quote me here—the job we've been doing and we're still doing is the kind of job where each day—if you forget to do something—like return a phone call or answer a telegram—it could mean someone doesn't eat that day. When this is all over and I am out of Government, I am going to be proudest of all of the people all over America—public officials, volunteers, paid workers—thousands of people of all political and religious faiths—who joined in this enterprise of taking care of people in need. It has been a great thing. I am tremendously proud of this country of ours, and I am tremendously proud I am a citizen of it."

The reporters in the room couldn't write fast enough to capture it all and actually had to compare notes later. LaBelle didn't record a word.

#

The year leading up to FDR's 1936 re-election campaign turned out to be a pivotal one for Roosevelt and Hopkins. After the incredible success of FERA and the CWA in putting people back to work, Hopkins not only created and ran the WPA, but he also joined forces with Frances Perkins to establish the new Social Security Administration. For the first time in US history, the government of the United States would provide a financial safety net for its citizens in their old age.

Despite their remarkable progress, the long knives were out, and forces were unleashed that threatened all of it. From the rise of reactionary groups and popular demagogues to the press keeping the stories of corruption and the feud between Hopkins and Ickes alive and in print, there were many in the country hoping to use Hopkins to sabotage FDR's bid for re-election.

When Frank Walker returned from a two-week field trip on behalf of FDR to see firsthand the effects of Hopkins's programs, he sat in an easy chair inside the White House residence with Pa Watson and Louie Howe waiting for FDR to complete the concoction he called a *martini*. After stirring the drink with great focus and deliberation, FDR poured the contents of his mix into four glasses and then raised his glass to the men. "Cheers," he said, and took a sip.

"What did you hear, Frank?" FDR asked Walker.

"Hopkins and his associates have done a magnificent job. That's what I heard," Walker said immediately. "It is truly amazing when you consider Harry has put more than four million people back to work. I saw some old friends the other day, and they said, 'Frank, this is the first money I've had in my pockets in a year and a half. Up to now, I've had nothing but tickets that I exchanged for groceries.'"

"I do like Harry's style," commented FDR as the effect of his martini settled in on him.

"Yeah, well," Howe jumped in, "before you guys get all misty-eyed about Hopkins, the papers are going after wonder boy every day."

"That's ridiculous," said Walker, fed up with all of Howe's intrigue.

"Ridiculous or not, Frank, you need to remember they are attacking Hopkins to get to Franklin. I don't like saying this," Howe said, looking directly at FDR, "but Hopkins may be a liability. The press will continue to go after Harry to air out any grievances they have with you."

"Well, my missus loves him, and those guys will be in for a good fight," FDR replied loudly, seeing Eleanor exit the elevator and enter the room.

"I'm too tired to fight, Franklin," Eleanor said as she made her way to an empty easy chair and collapsed into it. "Who do I love?"

"Harry."

"I adore Harry!" exclaimed Eleanor, leaving no doubt of her opinion.

"You see. The other guys do not stand a chance!" FDR cackled.

"All this talk about Harry's mismanagement and misuse of funds is embarrassing the President, Eleanor," Howe said, trying to bring her up to speed.

Eleanor removed her shoes and waved her hand dismissively at Howe. "Harry has done nothing wrong and certainly nothing to be embarrassed about. Unless you think putting millions of people back to work is something to be ashamed of."

Howe looked at the President, determined to make his point. "Well, Harry is an easy target, and to make matters worse, the thing going on between him and Secretary Ickes is trouble for us."

"You all have that election look in your eyes," Eleanor said directly to FDR. "Please tell me you are not turning your back on Harry."

"November, 1936 is just around the corner, Eleanor," Howe began, but before he could finish his thought, he was interrupted by a deep, dark cough.

"Louie, why don't you have some tea?" suggested Eleanor.

"Just a cold. I'm fine," Howe's voice sounded like it was rubbed with sandpaper.

"Louie may be right," Walker chimed in, picking up Louie's ball. "November will be here before we know it. It could only help us to put the problems between Ickes and Hopkins to bed. At the very least, it will give the other side less ammunition."

"Franklin will win in a landslide," predicted Eleanor and waved her hand at the men, dismissing their concerns.

"I like that idea, Eleanor," said Howe, catching his breath, "but we need peace in the family."

Roosevelt took another sip of his martini and turned to Watson. "Pa, I'm thinking of taking a few days off for some fishing. Let's invite Harry and Ickes to come along with us."

Pa Watson raised his glass to FDR. "I'll arrange it."

#

It seemed like forever and a different life when Hick last walked down F Street to her favorite Washington watering hole, the Old Ebbitt Grill. The Grill was a DC institution since the days when James Buchanan fiddled in the White House while the country smoldered.

Her road trip as FERA's Chief Investigator had been one hideous story after another of unimaginably cruel conditions randomly inflicting unthinkable suffering on Americans all over the country. No one place or person or group of people was immune from the Great Depression's devastating impact, and no one place or person or group of people knew what fate had in store for them each day as the economic cyclone ravaged the country.

As soon as Hick walked through the Old Ebbitt's doors, the sounds, sights, and smell of the place were instantly familiar, and a cascade of memories from years past clogged her brain. The same green velvet. Same stained glass. Same grotesque hunting trophies. And the same clusters of reporters, politicians, lobbyists, misfits, and other nefarious characters swapping long tales, juicy stories, outright lies, and an occasional truth.

Hick felt like she arrived home at a family reunion.

"Hey, Hick!" came a voice from the long bar. It was a reporter friend from the old days.

She smiled and waved back. "Any of you guys seen Harry?" she asked, walking past the Grill's bar.

"He's in the back," the bartender quickly replied.

Walking into the back of the restaurant, she found Hopkins sitting by himself in a booth just as a waiter dropped off a Scotch for him.

"Hey, Hick!" the waiter said, genuinely happy to see her. "Where the hell you been?"

"Dante's Inferno," she answered and made sure Hopkins heard her.

"What can I get you?" the waiter asked.

"Whatever he's having," Hick answered, pointing to Hopkins.

The waiter left the table.

"That bad?" Hopkins asked as she settled across from him in the booth.

"Worse. This was life-changing shit, Harry. Once you've seen it, there is no going back to life as usual." Hick looked around for the waiter with her drink.

"First, did you shoot anyone?" Hopkins smiled.

"Wise ass," replied Hick.

"Happy to hear that."

"Do you know, Harry, they've been starving over in West Virginia coal country since long before the Depression?" Hick asked Hopkins, not expecting him to answer. "Eight years at least. Some children there have never tasted milk. Disease is rampant. Many don't have shoes. They eat mostly green corn and string beans, and they're the lucky ones."

The waiter returned. Hick reached up and snatched the Scotch from the waiter's tray before he could put it in front of her. She took a big gulp and said to the waiter, "You better start lining these up, Ronnie." The waiter nodded and walked away. She turned back to Hopkins.

"Nobody seems to believe in the New Deal anymore. No-bo-dy," Hick emphasized. "One farmer told me that the President promised a New Deal, but all they're getting is a stacked deck. No food. No fuel. No medical care. It's as bad as you can imagine."

"Everywhere?" asked Harry.

"All over—from Iowa, to the Dakotas, to Texas, Florida, everywhere misery. Hell, even the animals look sick."

When Ronnie arrived at the table with another round, Hick put her empty glass on his tray and snatched the next one before he could reach for either.

"Take South Dakota," Hick continued, "that place is the Siberia of the United States. A lot of people up that way blame capitalism and are leaning toward Communism. I mean, really leaning into it. The meetings are packed. And it's not just in the Dakotas. The Commies are growing in Iowa as fast as corn used to."

"How about the South?"

"Christ, Harry, I heard one guy describe it as 'a spectacle of degeneration.' And it's the same for everyone—whites and colored. Hell, one asshole told me that 'Any nigger who gets more than a dollar a day is a spoiled nigger.'"

"We have to hold this together," Hopkins worried.

"It won't be easy. A Texas business guy told me that democracy is doomed and what we really need is fascism."

"Jesus," exhaled Hopkins.

"We could use his help," Hick replied, taking a long swig of her Scotch. "And just for the record, Harry," Hick continued as the Scotch further loosened her already relaxed inhibitions, "knowing what I know now, if I were twenty years younger and seventy-five pounds lighter, I'd be the Joan of Arc of the fascist movement in America."

Listening to Hick, Hopkins knew most Americans didn't appreciate just how far the country had fallen since the avalanche called the Great Depression had fallen on America. Though his programs were making some progress, that progress was not enough to push back the wave of suffering drowning the millions of exhausted Americans treading water every day just to survive. Hopkins worried that his programs might not be enough for FDR to win the next election, or worse, his programs might be the reason FDR lost.

Hopkins lit a cigarette, and as the waiter passed by their table, Hopkins called out to him and pointed to his glass, "Keep 'em coming, Ronnie."

CHAPTER FOUR

"Papa needs peace in his family."

Several days on a ship at sea was like a restorative elixir for FDR, and whenever he had the opportunity, that's where you could find him. Of course, gone were the days when he skippered a sailing vessel. Sailing nowadays for FDR meant being aboard a somewhat larger vessel, and his favorite of late was the USS Houston, a Northampton-class Navy cruiser.

FDR, along with Pa Watson, Frank Walker, Harold Ickes, and Harry Hopkins, left San Diego in late September, traveled south and then through the Panama Canal en route to Cocos Island near Costa Rica for fishing, relaxation, and, of course, the gossip FDR thoroughly enjoyed. As the sun set one evening, they were anchored in crystal-clear blue water, overlooking the stunning beaches, rocks, and lush cliffs of Cocos Island.

"Well, boys," FDR said, sitting on the deck facing a magnificent sunset with a martini in hand. "Isn't this a wonderful place?"

"It sure is," Ickes answered, taken with the beauty of the scene.

"But even here, in this beautiful place, I still find myself frustrated," FDR said, looking out over the water. "We're heading into an election year, and Papa needs peace in the family."

"Peace," repeated Ickes, wondering where the President was headed.

Walker picked it up from there. "You and Harry need to cease and desist in this feud going on between you. The newspaper boys are having a field day with you two."

"Feud? What feud?" asked Ickes with a look on his face reminiscent of a schoolboy caught putting a frog in the teacher's desk.

Hopkins chimed in, "There's no feud. Sure, Harold and I have disagreed a little, but that's it." And then, true to form, straight-faced Hopkins turned to Walker and said, "And it's only because it takes Harold a little time to realize that my way is always the best way to do things."

Ickes's jaw dropped. Walker almost choked on his drink. Pa smiled. And

FDR threw his head back, cackling at Hopkins's teasing.

An awkward silence followed, and seeing the look on Ickes's face, Hopkins knew the time for peace between them had arrived. "Harold, you know I'm kidding, right?" asked Hopkins, sounding sincere. He continued, "The truth is, I think you've done a

remarkable job with the PWA. And there is no way—not a chance—
I would have had the patience to do what you have done."

"Thanks, Harry," responded Ickes cautiously, still unsure of
Hopkins's sincerity.

"So, do we all agree to bury this thing here and now? A burial at
sea?" asked FDR, smiling and clearly expecting an affirmative
answer.

"Of course," responded Hopkins easily.

"Sure," agreed Ickes.

"Good," proclaimed FDR, and he turned to Watson. "Pa, let's tell
the captain to lower the ship's flag to half-mast in honor of this now
deceased and buried dispute."

Walker held up his near-empty glass. "Here's to winning in '36!"

#

On a quiet Saturday morning, the week after Easter, FDR sat at
his desk looking at the editorial page of the previous day's *Chicago
Tribune*. Missy LeHand had left the copy for him with an attached
note that read, "*Apparently, Col. McCormick has it in for Harry, too.
See page 14.*"

Under a headline that read, "The Tribune Platform for 1936: Turn
the Rascals Out," it said: *"Mr. Hopkins is a bullheaded man whose
high place in the New Deal was won by his ability to waste more
money in quicker time on more absurd undertakings than any other
mischievous wit in Washington could think of. The scandal of the*

political manipulation of funds under his control is growing, and to it may be added the scandal of the uncared-for destitute."

Roosevelt remembered Howe's often-told advice to look in and under stories, and he knew Louie was right. Colonel McCormick was using Harry to come after him. He reached for the intercom to ask Missy to have Hopkins come for lunch, when the door to his office opened and Eleanor entered with LeHand. They both carried handkerchiefs, and he could see they both had been crying.

"What is it?" he asked.

"It's Louie, Franklin," Eleanor answered. "I'm afraid he passed away."

The President was literally taken aback and slumped into the back of his chair. "When?" he asked.

"He died in his sleep early this morning," Eleanor informed him.

"At least that," said FDR quietly, surprised by the surge of emotion rising in him. As tears began to fill his eyes, and his throat seemed to constrict, he cleared his throat, put on his glasses, and opened the top drawer of his desk to remove a business card.

"Louie handed out these new business cards to everyone when we won in '32," FDR said as he looked at the card. "'Colonel Louis Rasputin Voltaire Talleyrand Simon Legree,'" read FDR. Though he smiled, a tear dripped on the bottom of his pince-nez glasses.

Still holding the card, FDR looked at LeHand over the top of his glasses. "We have a lot of 'yes' men, don't we, Missy, but Louie.... Louie was my 'no' man."

"I'm sorry, Effdee," said Missy, knowing how much Howe meant to him.

"We owe him so much, Franklin," Eleanor said. "If you agree, I would like to organize a state funeral for him in the East Room."

"Of course," replied FDR quietly, and when Eleanor and Missy left his office, he returned Colonel Louis Rasputin Voltaire Talleyrand Simon Legree's business card to his top desk drawer and closed that drawer shut.

#

Though as Louie predicted, Hopkins remained an easy target for some, by the 1936 election season, he was viewed by many as a powerful number two man in the government and the czar of a vast ministerial empire.

While FDR used cordial language filled with optimism and good cheer to move his audiences and followers, Harry dealt in simple, straightforward, and direct talk, sometimes sprinkled with insults. When asked, one man in the administration described Hopkins as having "a mind like a razor, a tongue like a skinning knife, a temper like a Tartar, and a sufficient vocabulary of parlor profanity—words kosher enough to get by the censor but acid enough to make a mule-skinner jealous."

Harry's way with words sometimes produced interesting, if not ironic, results. Like the time he insulted a Kansas Republican Governor who made a big show about balancing his state's budget. "Oh yeah?" Hopkins sneered when a reporter brought that to his attention. "And he's taking it out of the hides of his people!"

That Governor was Alfred M. Landon, and he managed to parlay Hopkins's insult into becoming the Republican candidate for President and Roosevelt's opponent that November.

The night before the 1936 election, the President retreated to the comfort of his Hyde Park, New York home, *Springwood*, his birthplace in 1882, and his cherished sanctuary ever since. The foliage on the trees across the property, though well past their peak color, was still bright and glistening in the sunlight. Roosevelt sat alone in front of a microphone in his small study off the main hall with its walls adorned with preserved birds and animals from his youth, as well as his etchings of Naval battles from the War of 1812.

A radio technician was just outside his study, wearing headphones and working a transmitter on a table. Franklin Roosevelt was on the air for another chat with his friends, the American people. Familiar, friendly, and comforting.

"I cast my first vote here in 1903," echoed the voice that by now was a regular visitor in America's homes. "Tomorrow, fifty-five million are eligible to vote. I hope all fifty-five million *do* vote."

As the President addressed the nation, the President's mother, Sara Roosevelt, sat with Eleanor and a small group of her son's inner circle, including Pa Watson and his wife, Frances, Missy LeHand, and Harry Hopkins with his wife, Barbara. All sat focused on FDR's voice from the nearby radio, and no one dared speak over the President. No one, that is, except his mother.

"What a wonderful speech, Pa. Who wrote it?" Sara Roosevelt asked.

"The President with Harry and Sam Rosenman," answered Watson.

The matriarch looked over at Hopkins. "You did a fine job, Harry."

Hopkins smiled and before he could thank the President's mother, they heard FDR say, "Theodore Roosevelt," from the radio's speaker. Just the sound of that name in her son's voice instantly turned Sara's mood sour.

The President continued over the radio, "The credit belongs to the man who is actually in the arena."

"Harry, why would you bring up cousin Teddy?" Sara asked Hopkins directly.

In the presence of Sara Roosevelt, Hopkins's usual confidence seemed to abandon him, and he began to stammer, "Well, Mrs. Roosevelt…, ah, ah, former President Theodore…"

Fortunately for Hopkins, Eleanor long ago gave up being intimidated by her mother-in-law and came to Hopkins's rescue. "Mother, many, many Republicans have fond memories of Uncle Teddy, and Franklin wants their votes too," Eleanor explained calmly.

Judging by the look on her face, Hopkins thought Sara Roosevelt was not convinced and didn't like it, though he couldn't tell if she didn't like Eleanor's explanation or just Eleanor herself.

The President's voice rang out from the radio's speaker, "…at least he fails while daring greatly, so that his place shall never be with those cold and timid souls who know neither defeat nor victory."

"This concludes President Roosevelt's Election Eve address to the nation," said the radio announcer. "We will now return to our regularly scheduled programming." Missy rose and shut off the radio.

"It was a good speech, Harry. Except for Teddy." Sara made sure Hopkins relived his guilt.

Never one to easily give in, especially to her mother-in-law, Eleanor defended Harry, "Uncle Teddy would've been proud of Franklin today."

"The Long Island Roosevelts proud of Franklin? Never," answered Sara, confidently instructing her foolish daughter-in-law just as FDR was wheeled into the room, smoking a cigarette.

"Franklin, I loved your speech," Sara said to her son.

"Thank you, Mother," replied FDR, genuinely pleased that she liked it.

"I actually thought it was perfect until you mentioned cousin Teddy."

"Mother, I included cousin Teddy because I wanted to be sure I had your attention right to the very end of the speech," joked FDR.

Sara did not see the humor. "You do not have to give credit to any of those people to keep my attention."

FDR looked at Missy and winked. "Missy, in the future, please make sure my mother sees a draft of all of my speeches for her comments."

"Yes, sir," answered Missy, smiling.

"Franklin, there is no need to show me your speeches. Just be sure you do not mention the Long Island Roosevelts." Sara Roosevelt was determined to be heard.

"Mother, if I am still President after tomorrow, I shall ask Congress for a law that will make it illegal for anyone in our government to ever publicly mention anyone associated with those Republican Long Island Roosevelts ever again," FDR replied.

"Now you understand," Sara replied, satisfied she had finally made her point.

#

Two days later, FDR returned to Washington in Marco Polo, his private rail car that had been built by the Pullman Company and modified for the President's use. The atmosphere inside the train was celebratory and, of course, refreshments abounded and alcohol flowed freely. The President reveled in the role of celebrant-in-chief, with a group that included staff, family, and even a few members of the press—friendly ones, at least most of them.

Toward the far end of the car, and as far away from the party as they could get in the small space, Harry and Barbara sat chatting with Frances Watson, when Pa Watson approached the group. "It's confirmed," Pa informed them. "The boss got 523 Electoral votes."

"How many for Landon?" asked Frances.

"Eight," Watson said, beaming, though his wife, Frances, was pretty sure Pa's glow had more to do with the fourth drink he was holding rather than the election. Frances had been counting; she always did.

"Well, that settles that," Barbara said, putting her arm through Harry's arm and squeezing him.

Hopkins squeezed back. "The people have spoken!"

Dorothy Thompson, the wife of award-winning author Sinclair Lewis and a well-known journalist in her own right, made her way over to them. Hopkins knew Thompson well and rose from his seat when he saw her. "Dorothy, have you come to celebrate with us?" teased Hopkins, knowing that she supported Alf Landon.

"Just hitching a ride back to New York City," parried Thompson, and sat with the group. "The President may not like what I write some of the time, but he's a classy guy and gave me a lift."

"He is a classy guy," Hopkins said with a smile and nod.

"I know we haven't always agreed, Harry, but a 523 to 8 box score has to make you very, very happy," Thompson said, knowing it was a breathtaking landslide by any measure.

"I was supposed to be a millstone around the President's neck. Am I rejoicing? Am I! I'm the happiest man in the world!" chirped Hopkins.

"Does this mean you will continue with the WPA and Social Security programs?" asked Thompson, neatly shifting into inquisitive reporter mode.

"That's up to the President," replied Hopkins easily, and then added, "But Dorothy, do you see any reason why we should stop now?"

"Harry, Dorothy is supposed to ask the questions," Barbara poked Hopkins.

Thompson smiled. "The truth is, Harry, I can't see any reason for you to stop, and apparently neither does our country," conceded Thompson.

"All aboard! Next stop, Washington, DC!" Pa Watson announced loudly, turning heads in the car. Pa's inhibitions had completely dissolved in his fourth cocktail.

"Oh, Pa," an exasperated Frances chastised her husband.

By the time the train made its way into Union Station a few hours later, the car had gone quiet, with most everyone, even the reporters, sitting silently with their own thoughts. It seemed like the closer they were to DC, the more the elation of the last twenty-four hours gave way to the sober realization that there was a lot more work yet to be done.

In that quiet moment, Harry reached for Barbara's hand. Since they met, fell in love, married, and left New York, Hopkins had this feeling in his bones that he was on a well-lit path toward a very bright future—a future he never could have imagined four years earlier when that other train carried him from New York City into Union Station.

Barbara was with him at the start of his incredible journey and for every step along the way. He swung his arm around her, and as he pulled her close to him, she turned and kissed him before nestling her head on his shoulder.

Hopkins couldn't remember ever feeling this much in love, nor could he ever remember feeling this good.

CHAPTER FIVE

"God... I love you, Harry Hopkins."

Just days after FDR's second inauguration on January 20, 1937, as a light snow fell in DC, Barbara stood in front of her bathroom mirror while Diana sang and played in the kitchen. Earlier that day, she saw Dr. David Shapiro, their family General Practitioner, and told him she had not been feeling like herself. It didn't take long for Shapiro to locate the source of her malady.

Barbara stood looking at her reflection in the mirror, with her left arm above her head. When her right hand touched the spot on her breast that Dr. Shapiro found during his examination hours earlier, she winced in pain. Barbara brought her arm down, raised it again, and tried again. More pain in her breast and dread in her heart as she heard Diana singing outside the door.

A week after her appointment with Dr. Shapiro, she and Harry followed the doctor's advice and boarded The Capitol Limited at Washington's Union Station, bound for Rochester, Minnesota, and the preeminent hospital in the country, The Mayo Clinic. Despite Hopkins's seeming confidence that all would be well, they were both enveloped by their worst fears as they traveled on their sixteen-hour train journey to the famed institution.

During their journey, Hopkins rambled on about his plans to take a real vacation during the coming summer and spend real time together as a family. He told her he would bring the boys to Washington for a visit and then all of them—he, Barbara, Diana, and his sons—David, who was twenty-one, Robert, who was fifteen, and Stephen, who was twelve—would go off and spend time together on Long Island and up in Saratoga, New York. Hopkins's summer plans helped both of them envision memorable days ahead together, and at least for a short while, forget the reason for their trip.

Unfortunately, it didn't take very long for their reality to return. Several days after their arrival at the Clinic, Barbara's tests came back positive and conclusive.

The prognosis was not good.

Weeks after winter gave way to spring, Barbara was feeling well and insisted that Harry arrange for his sons to visit. A longtime racing fan from his days handicapping too many horses at Aqueduct and Belmont race tracks in New York City, Hopkins planned for his boys to visit on the weekend of the Preakness at Pimlico. Always one of the three great races of the Triple Crown, this year's Preakness boasted one of the greatest horses of all time, War Admiral, as the favorite to win. Hopkins thought the race would be a perfect way to kick off his family's weekend festivities, and when

War Admiral won, their adventure at Pimlico quickly became a cherished family memory.

That summer, Harry managed to fulfill his promise to Barbara to put family first, despite the prevailing political winds that had shifted and now blew against FDR. While Roosevelt's political green thumb had turned brown over his "scheme," as his opponents described it, to pack the Supreme Court, Hopkins took Barbara, Diana, and the boys to Long Island and then off to Saratoga in August. They not only enjoyed swimming on Long Island's beaches and went to more horse races in Saratoga, but Hopkins made sure they did lots of fishing and boating with the kids, and many long walks along the lake for the two of them. It was a summer filled with more wonderful and cherished memories for all of them.

At the end of their Saratoga trip, Harry told his two oldest—David and Robert—about Barbara's condition, and he was overwhelmed by their reaction. Like their father, both David and Robert had fallen in love with Barbara and were distressed and disturbed to hear of her health issues. At one point, they even questioned Harry, asking if he was sure Mayo's diagnosis was accurate. Unfortunately, Hopkins had to relive Barbara's experiences over the past months, filling his sons in on her countless tests and hopeless results.

Hopkins was more than touched and very proud of them when both David and Robert asked Hopkins if there was anything they could do to help Barbara or him. Hopkins did not know how to answer them, but he took both of them in his arms, and the three hugged each other. He loved his boys dearly, and they loved him.

As the summer heat gave way to more temperate autumn days, the boys returned to school in New York, and Barbara and Harry returned with Diana to their apartment in DC. It was shortly after they returned, in October, when it became clear to both Barbara and Harry that things were changing rapidly.

A few days before Barbara was admitted into Garfield Memorial Hospital on Florida Avenue, she and Harry decided to shield Stephen and Diana from the news. They both believed less was best at their age.

#

Harry had his feet up on a chair, a blanket thrown across his legs, and his head and neck crunched up against the back of another chair as he slept in Barbara's hospital room. He woke suddenly and, for a moment, forgot where he was until he saw Barbara sleeping in her bed.

He quickly looked at his watch. It was three minutes past one o'clock in the morning. He unwound himself from the chair, straightened out his painfully crooked neck, and willed his aching body out of the chair and across the room to Barbara's bedside. Standing over her and watching her breathe, Hopkins was relieved and reached to touch her hand.

Barbara opened her eyes.

"I'm sorry I bothered you," said Hopkins as he looked at her serene face.

"It's okay. I'm thirsty." Barbara's voice was barely audible and sounded much deeper than normal as it scraped against her dry throat.

Hopkins walked to the other side of her bed to a stand with a water pitcher and a waterlogged cloth in a basin. As he dipped the cloth, he watched Barbara in her bed and noticed how the street light from outside the hospital cast a distorted shadow across Barbara's face and his hands as he worked the cloth in the water. The sound of the water dripping from the cloth into the basin sounded very loud in the quiet of the hospital room that night.

"Were you having a good dream?" asked Hopkins as he squeezed the excess water from the cloth.

"I think I was dreaming of you as the next President of the United States." Barbara smiled as Hopkins made his way back to her bedside with the wet cloth.

Hopkins placed the cloth on Barbara's lips, and she took as much of the water from it as she could.

"Let me get you some more."

"No, no. I'm fine. Where is Diana?"

"With Eleanor."

"Our daughter is in the White House?" smiled Barbara.

"Eleanor insisted."

"You be sure to thank Eleanor, Harry," said Barbara, her instructions and the drink of water making Barbara sound more like herself.

"Of course." Hopkins smiled, but before he could say, "I will," Barbara's face contorted in pain.

"Let me get the nurse." Hopkins turned to exit the room with the wet cloth in hand.

"No, Harry." Though weak, the emotion in Barbara's voice stopped him. "No more of that stuff."

"It will help," begged Hopkins.

"No," Barbara insisted. "No more."

Hopkins returned to her side and placed the water-drenched cloth on Barbara's lips again, and after she took whatever water was left in the cloth, he laid it across her forehead.

"That feels good."

"Let me get some more," Hopkins said, pleased his ministrations were helping.

Barbara's eyes never left Hopkins as he walked around the bed to the hospital stand to drench the cloth in the water basin.

"God... I love you, Harry Hopkins," said Barbara when he arrived at the basin with the cloth in hand.

Hopkins looked up and smiled. But before he could tell her how much he loved her, she was gripped by a ferocious pain that forced her to suck in air, raise her chest off the bed, and hold her breath. Hopkins dropped the cloth and walked around to her bedside.

It seemed like forever, but when Barbara finally exhaled, letting the air escape her lungs, she lay back on the bed and began breathing long, deep breaths as the pain loosened its grip on her. Hopkins was so relieved he almost wept.

"Breathe, sweetheart. Just breathe," he said quietly as he held and stroked her hand.

Barbara seemed to settle into a steady cadence of deep breaths for a few minutes while they quietly held each other's hands in the dark room.

"Can I get you anything?" asked Hopkins.

"You are all I need," Barbara replied, a slight smile creasing her face.

And then, again, she was seized with a sudden brutal pain that stiffened her entire body and forced her to close her eyes and inhale through her teeth.

Hopkins held her hand, waiting for the pain to let go of her. But as the moments went by, and the air she held finally did escape her lungs, Barbara seemed to relax into the bed and did not move.

Barbara was gone. No more breathing. No more pain.

Hopkins stood over her, holding her hand with tears running down his face.

"Goddamn it," whispered Hopkins.

#

When Frances Watson arrived at the hospital later that night to drive Harry home, the lights were on in Barbara's hospital room, and the room was empty except for Harry, who now sat in the same chair he had been sleeping in earlier. He was smoking a cigarette.

"Harry, I'm so sorry," said Frances, walking toward him.

Her immediate thought as she bent down to try to hug him was that he was in shock—incapable of thinking, or speaking, or perhaps, even moving. "Harry, C'mon. Let me take you home," she urged, not sure he would get up from the chair. Hopkins rose slowly, and when he arrived at the hospital room door, he turned to look back at Barbara's empty bed but said nothing.

Driving along Washington, DC's streets at this time of night, there were no cars, no trucks, and no people. It was a dark and quiet city. Hopkins had not said one word since Frances arrived, and, even now, he sat in the passenger seat of her Ford Roadster, silently staring out the windshield.   Just as Frances thought how worried she was leaving Hopkins alone, Hopkins quietly said, "Frances. Take me to Saint Matthew's."

"Harry, it's very late. Maybe it'd be better to go home and sleep a bit," she suggested.

"St. Matthew's. Please," he quietly insisted.

They entered through the rear door of the Cathedral, and, like the streets around it, the church was dark, empty, and quiet at this hour. Hopkins removed his hat and walked slowly down the center aisle toward the apse, never taking his eyes off the huge image of St. Matthew behind the altar, whose eyes seemed fixed on Hopkins. Frances followed quietly behind. When he arrived at the front of the church, he sat in the first row, and not wanting to intrude on his grief, Frances sat in the row directly behind him. They were the only two people in the church.

Harry's eyes remained fixed on St. Matthew, and St. Matthew remained looking down at him from his perch high above the altar. It was only a few moments, and Hopkins began to weep quietly at first, but then wave after wave of grief poured out of him, each more intense and louder than the one before. His cries echoed throughout the vast church.

Frances became quickly overwhelmed by the horrible grief that shattered her friend, and by her own feelings over Barbara's loss. With tears streaming down her face, Frances cried silently. She rose behind Hopkins to wrap her arms around him and hold him as he wept, her cheek nestled against the top of his head.   From high above the altar, St. Matthew continued to look down on both of them, giving each of them permission to grieve and to heal.

The night of Barbara's funeral, three days later, Harry put Diana to bed and tried his best to help her understand. And though he willed himself to be strong in front of her, he knew he was struggling, and worse, Diana knew it too. He all but fell apart when Diana looked at him from under her bed covers and said, "Don't worry, Daddy. Mommy is in heaven."

"Yes, she is, sweetheart," said Harry, and added, "I love you," kissing Diana goodnight.

When he left Diana's room, he sat at their kitchen table alone and cried, doing his best to cry silently.

Hopkins didn't know how long he'd been sitting there, but he knew it must have been quite a while because when he heard the doorbell ring, the tears on his cheeks and face were dry. When he opened his apartment door, he found Harold Ickes standing there with a shopping bag in his hand.

"Thought you could use some company tonight and some food for dinner," Ickes said, lifting up the shopping bag. "I brought a few sandwiches from Mac's."

"Any Scotch in that bag?" asked Hopkins.

"Two bottles."

"Damn, damn thoughtful of you, Harold. Come in."

Hopkins never forgot Ickes's kindness that night.

CHAPTER SIX

"Here's to you, Harry."

The White House was already showing the signs of the Christmas season with its halls, public spaces, and the residence decorated for the holidays. A blue spruce from Hyde Park stood in the residence living room, and Bing Crosby crooned seasonal songs from a console radio in the corner of the dining room. Hopkins and Missy LeHand joined FDR and Eleanor for dinner after politely declining several of FDR's martini concoctions during the President's cocktail hour.

They were all worried about an unusually quiet Hopkins, who picked at his food throughout dinner and seemed relieved when the waiter took his nearly full plate away. They were unsure whether he was struggling with Barbara's loss or just not feeling well, and when Eleanor pressed for some answers, Hopkins told her his ulcers were acting up. She immediately suggested that Dr. McIntire, FDR's personal physician, examine Hopkins as soon as possible.

Dr. Ross T. McIntire was a Naval officer who began his tenure with FDR shortly after FDR's inauguration in 1933. A board-certified otolaryngologist, McIntire checked FDR's sensitive sinuses each day like clockwork—at 8 a.m. and 5:30 p.m.

"Excellent idea!" FDR said to his wife. "Missy, call Dr. McIntire in the morning and arrange an appointment for Harry."

"It's okay, Missy," Hopkins jumped in. "I already booked a physical at Mayo."

"A better idea!" FDR said, sounding genuinely pleased that Hopkins was scheduled with the famed institution.

"I will watch Diana for you when you go to the Clinic," offered Eleanor.

"You have already done too much for us," said Hopkins, and meant it.

"I will not hear another word about it," replied Eleanor, determined to get her way. "Diana will stay with us here at the White House, and when you return from Minnesota, we will all celebrate Christmas together here."

Hopkins was touched by Eleanor's kindness and, deep down, relieved knowing Diana would be cared for. The President and First Lady could not have been more supportive.

"You are both too generous," said Hopkins, agreeing to Eleanor's proposal. "Thank you, Eleanor. Thank you, sir."

"No need to thank me, Harry," replied FDR, exhaling a stream of smoke. "You can see who the boss is around here."

#

A few days later, when Hopkins traveled by train back to the Mayo Clinic in Rochester, Minnesota, he couldn't help but relive his trip just months before with Barbara. It didn't take long for Hopkins's grief to resurface and the grayness to return. As his train banged its way to Minnesota, Hopkins worked hard to shed his dark memories and newfound fears.

Always the handicapper, he reminded himself that even though his father died of stomach cancer, it was a long shot that he would be diagnosed with the same disease that took Barbara. As it turned out, he should have made that bet, for when the doctors at the Mayo Clinic completed their tests, they determined it wasn't ulcers causing Hopkins's indigestion.

The day after they diagnosed his stomach cancer, and before his surgery, Hopkins was sitting in his hospital bed when he was seized by the same terrifying dread he had experienced with Barbara. How could he explain any of this to Diana? How could his cherished little girl possibly understand?

He immediately went to his briefcase and removed several pages of personal stationery to write to his daughter, who was staying with Eleanor in the White House. He penned "Dear Diana" on the page, and a deep and profound sadness swept over him. This letter might be the last communication he might ever have with his daughter.

The next day, December 20, 1937, the surgeons at the Mayo Clinic removed nearly three-quarters of his stomach.

#

Spring was already in the air when, in early March, FDR invited Hopkins to come to Warm Springs, Georgia, and rehabilitate at the place he called "The Little White House." FDR's Warm Springs compound was rustic, rural, and beautiful in its natural Georgia surroundings of abundant oak, pine, and magnolia trees, and fields of wildflowers. At this time of year, the clean, crisp air was a treat for any city dweller, and as its name suggested, the compound boasted a pool with water from a thermal spring that was believed to have healing powers.

Several years after FDR was stricken with polio, he had purchased the Warm Springs property and buildings from a friend using almost two-thirds of his inheritance. He believed the local spring waters strengthened his flaccid, polio-stricken legs and improved his mobility.

True to his nature, he opened Warm Springs to anyone who suffered from the debilitating effects of polio, offering a much-needed sanctuary to those whom the world called "cripples." The Warm Springs facility was always occupied by polio-stricken adults and children who, with the help of heavy jackets, braces, crutches, and wheelchairs, worked to overcome the effects of their soul-crushing and life-altering disease. While there was no evidence that anyone was ever cured of polio at Warm Springs, everyone who did spend time there found the next best thing—comfort.

On this morning, FDR was in the pool in his preferred bathing attire—a black one-piece suit—propped up on his elbows at the pool's edge with the ever-present cigarette holder between his teeth. Missy LeHand sat in a chair a few feet away on the pool deck, dressed in brown wool slacks and a white sweater with her hair tied back with a white bow. Hovering nearby were a couple of Secret Service agents and Irvin "Mac" McDuffie, the President's valet, who sat reading *The Warm Springs Mirror.*

There were patients in the pool with FDR who, thanks to his generosity, were assisted by caring and skilled therapists. No one in or around the pool seemed to think the President was anyone special, and FDR liked it that way.

"You should come in, Missy. The water's delightful!" said FDR.

"Effdee, how can you swim in that freezing water? Warm Springs!" Missy exclaimed, knowing full well the name of the facility did not accurately describe the temperature of its waters in the pool.

"It's invigorating! You should try it."

"Nooooo, thank you," Missy said, curling her legs up under her on the seat.

"Have you seen Harry this morning?" asked FDR.

"He was still asleep when I came out," Missy answered, and then added, "I hope he recovers quickly."

"The doctors at Mayo told Dr. McIntire it's better than two to one that Harry is in the clear and will fully recover," assured FDR. "Speak of the devil!" he exclaimed, seeing Hopkins rounding the tall hedges along the pool's perimeter, dressed casually in gray pants, black sweater, and an open-collared white shirt. Hopkins appeared to be at ease and relaxed, and walking like his old self, fluid and athletic. Very good signs considering the magnitude of his surgery.

"Harry the Hop!" FDR announced loudly with a broad smile. He was genuinely glad to see Hopkins up and around and looking well. "How are you feeling?"

"A little better, thanks." Hopkins sat in the chair next to LeHand, and taking a cigarette from his pocket, lit it. "Aren't you cold in there?" he asked FDR.

"Yes, he is," LeHand answered for the President.

"It's very refreshing. I wish you could jump in here," teased FDR, knowing full well neither Hopkins nor LeHand would ever swim in the cold water.

"I am very, very disappointed," Hopkins said sarcastically.

"A quick swim in this water would absolutely revive your appetite," FDR assured Hopkins.

"If that's what I need for a better appetite, I'll just put ice cubes down my pants," replied Hopkins quickly, and Mac and LeHand laughed out loud while the Secret Service agents did their best to hide their smiles.

"You must get in shape," said FDR, looking very concerned and serious. "There are some people who will not let you rest."

"Who's complaining now?" asked Hopkins, knowing by the look on FDR's face he was about to be teased.

"Well, for one, Congressman Martin Dies," replied FDR, trying to hide his grin behind the cigarette holder between his teeth.

"This ought to be good," said Hopkins.

"It is. It is. Tell him, Missy," FDR said, putting his cigarette holder on the pool's edge, and pushing himself into the middle of the pool to tread water while he listened to LeHand.

LeHand picked up some papers next to her and looked at Hopkins. "Congressman Martin Dies was named the Chairman of the Committee for the Investigation of Un-American Activities, and he announced today that he will ask Congress to investigate the WPA."

"What a surprise," responded Hopkins, sounding unfazed.

"Wait, wait," said FDR like a little boy with a secret. "There's more. Tell him, Missy. Tell him." FDR loved this.

Missy turned to one of the pages in her hand and continued. "Dies said he is determined to…" Missy said, reading the page in her hand, "…and I quote—'Remove subversives from the federal government like Hopkins, Ickes…'"

"Ickes!? Now there's a subversive for you," interrupted Hopkins, smiling.

LeHand continued reading, "'…and Frances Perkins…'"

"Of course. Frances is the real threat," Hopkins was trying hard not to laugh. It hurt.

"'…and other communists and fellow travelers,' end quote," LeHand finished reading, and FDR cackled in the middle of the pool.

Hopkins wrapped his arms around his stomach and closed his mouth tight to keep himself from laughing, but it didn't work. His laughter came out as quick, repetitive snorts through his nose that made him sound like a pig searching for food.

Treading water, FDR was determined to keep Hopkins laughing. "Frank Walker called and said that Dies received a congratulatory telegram from the Ku Klux Klan," announced FDR from the middle of the pool.

"Stop it!" Hopkins begged, holding tight to himself, but losing the battle. His snorting had Mac and the Secret Service agents laughing out loud.

"It's true. Read him the telegram, Missy." FDR would not let up.

LeHand picked up the telegram from her stack of papers and read. "'From the Ku Klux Klan to Congressman Martin Dies,' quote, 'Every true American, and that includes every Klansman, is behind you and your committee in its effort to turn the country back to the honest, freedom-loving, God-fearing Americans to whom it belongs,' end quote."

"It's comforting to know Dies stands in good stead with the Klan," Hopkins said, snorting loudly and trying to catch his breath. Everyone was laughing out loud, not at Dies or the Klan, but at Hopkins trying to keep himself from laughing.

"You know what," Hopkins said. "I'm getting very hungry."

"You see, Missy. I told you Warm Springs has healing powers," said FDR proudly. "Let's get some lunch."

FDR swam to the pool's edge and, using his arms, grabbed hold of the pool's coping, hoisted himself up, and smoothly twisted his body to sit on the edge with his powerless legs dangling into the pool. Mac rose and brought FDR's wheelchair to the pool's edge and helped him settle into the chair.

As Missy and Hopkins walked back to the cottage behind Mac, pushing the President, Missy slid her arm into Hopkins's arm, leaned into him, and said quietly, "It is good to have you back, Harry."

"It's good to be back," he said, squeezing her hand against him.

#

Hopkins recovered in the spring of 1938, and it didn't take long for him to pick up where he left off with the WPA. He continued pushing the edges of the envelope to find jobs for Americans, or create jobs with a little sleight of hand and help from his friends.

From the beginning, Hopkins had never been shy about knocking on Treasury Secretary Henry Morgenthau's door whenever he needed money for more jobs, often asking Morgenthau to transfer money from someone else's budget to the WPA. Hopkins's interagency money swapping requests had become so regular that Morgenthau decided he needed some cover and arranged a meeting with his old friend, the President.

FDR and Henry Morgenthau first met in 1913 when Morgenthau ran a farm called Fishkill Farms near FDR's home in Hyde Park. FDR, Eleanor, and Henry became fast friends, and in 1929, when FDR was Governor of New York, he appointed Henry as the Chair of the New York State Agricultural Advisory Committee.

Shortly after FDR was elected President, his Treasury Secretary at the time, William Woodin, became ill. FDR appointed Morgenthau to the same post, and Henry's posture as a strict monetarist had wide appeal for conservatives, the business community, and investors. Morgenthau successfully kept interest rates low and enabled America to finance the massive public spending required by FDR's New Deal programs.

"What brings you here, my friend?" FDR could tell his old friend had something serious on his mind.

"Hopkins," Morgenthau answered.

"What about him?" asked FDR.

"He keeps asking me to move money to the WPA."

"So?"

"I think I have my answer," said Morgenthau, relieved that he had done right by FDR's lights. "I wanted to be sure you were okay with us continuing to fund him."

"Keep giving him what he needs," said FDR definitively.

"I will," Morgenthau confirmed. "How should I handle Congress if they give us a hard time?"

"Ask them if they would like us to tell four and a half million of their constituents they will have to stop working," FDR wisecracked.

#

Invited for a nightcap in the residence, Hopkins thought the President and Frank Walker wanted to take his temperature after Congress's latest passive-aggressive move.

There was enormous pressure on Hopkins. The list of his enemies was growing in direct proportion to his popularity, and there were some in the press who found Hopkins an easy target in their attack on FDR and his administration. Reporters like Tom LaBelle regularly regurgitated their acidic accusations against Hopkins even when the stories were nothing more than rumors his enemies wished were true. For his part, FDR was glad to have Hopkins on his team and as the focus of his adversaries. He knew Hopkins was taking a lot of the heat that was directed at his administration.

There were creative stories written almost daily about Hopkins's corruption, the enormous amounts of money he spent, the failures of his agencies, and the ineffectiveness of his programs. Of all the contrived stories told about him, none had more staying power than the one filed by LaBelle claiming he overheard Hopkins telling his friend Bob Sherwood at Pimlico Race Track that the Democratic Party must "tax and tax and spend and spend and elect and elect." From the day LaBelle's article was published, "tax and spend liberals" became the rallying cry for every single person who was against FDR's policies.

For generations to come.

When the news broke, Hopkins said he never said any such thing.

It didn't take long before the creative stories being written about Hopkins at the behest of ambitious politicians and enterprising reporters motivated Congress to act. Using Hopkins's feeding frenzy, Congress sucker-punched FDR and voted to cut Harry's annual salary by $2,000, from $12,000 to $10,000.

"How about a martini, Harry?" FDR asked Hopkins as he entered the residence.

"No, thanks. But if you have a Scotch, I'll take it."

Though he had lost some weight, Hopkins looked energized and seemed as healthy as he had when he first joined the administration, five years earlier. Both FDR and Walker were pleased and amazed to see how well he had recovered from his surgery.

"Harry, who do you think should replace Justice Brandeis if he retires?" the President asked Hopkins as he poured his Scotch. Justice Louis Brandeis was a brilliant jurist who was appointed to the Supreme Court by Woodrow Wilson back in 1916. He was now in his eighties, and it was common knowledge he wanted to rest.

"Felix Frankfurter," Hopkins said easily.

Frank Walker agreed. "Frankfurter does make the most sense."

"Good choice," replied FDR. He had already decided on his friend Felix, but was happy to hear Walker and Hopkins concur. He handed Hopkins his Scotch.

"Harry, I want to apologize for the way Congress is treating you," Walker started. "We never imagined they would cut your salary."

"Don't give it a second thought, Frank. It's Congress," responded Hopkins, believing it was not worth their time to decipher Congressional motives.

"We think Congress keeps rolling logs in front of you because they're afraid you'd be a great candidate for President in '40," said Walker.

"Crazy," Hopkins replied, treasuring his first sip of Scotch.

"Well, then you can call me crazy, too," said FDR, sounding more serious than Hopkins would have expected.

Hopkins worried the President misunderstood him. "I meant Congress is crazy. I wasn't saying—"

FDR cut him off. "Someone capable of doing this job needs to replace me in 1940," said FDR, looking and sounding dead serious.

"You have made a real difference in the lives of so many Americans, Harry," added Walker, his tone also serious.

"Thanks, Frank, but we still have to put a lot more people back to work," replied Hopkins, unsure where the conversation was headed. He surveyed FDR and Walker.

"He's not listening," Walker said directly to FDR, and leaned forward in his chair toward Hopkins. "We," he said, nodding toward FDR, "think you should throw your hat in the ring for President in 1940."

Hopkins was hardly ever lost for words, but he suddenly felt like his senses were betraying him, and he was unable to hear or speak. All he could muster after several moments was an impotent, "You're serious?"

"We are," said Walker simply, while FDR sat watching his protégé digest the idea.

"I don't know what to say," Hopkins blurted out, really not knowing how he should proceed with the conversation.

FDR took the pressure off Hopkins by explaining. "Harry, I want to go back to Hyde Park at the end of this term. I've already studied all of the possible candidates our party can put forward in 1940, and none of them—not one, in my opinion—is capable of winning the race, doing this job, and finishing what we started."

"I am flattered you think I am capable," replied Hopkins, "but I may not be the best person. I am a widower with a young daughter. I have three sons from a woman I divorced who, by the way, may still be a card-carrying member of the Communist Party. Then there's the fact that I am not thought of favorably by conservatives or the business community…"

FDR held up his hand, and Hopkins stopped. "None of that will prevent you from winning in 1940," FDR said confidently.

"There are a lot of people who don't exactly have a high regard for me," Hopkins said to Walker, hoping he could prevail on FDR to reconsider.

"Actually, we do wish you were more likable," teased Walker.

"It is true your work has, at times, put you on the wrong side of our business leaders," said FDR, "but we just have to change their minds."

"Sir. I am honored you think of me in this way, but I can't see how I can get from here to that chair in your office over the next couple of years," Hopkins told FDR as the prospect of his running for President simultaneously thrilled and terrified him.

"One foot in front of the other. That's how," said FDR, and the irony of that statement coming from FDR did not escape Hopkins. FDR continued, "When the time is right, I will appoint you Secretary of Commerce to put you in direct contact with the country's business leaders."

As the implications of the discussion settled in, Hopkins was overwhelmed by FDR's confidence in him. "I want you to know that with or without a Cabinet post, I will serve you in any way you need," Hopkins assured FDR.

"I know Harry," FDR replied in a way that made Hopkins believe, for the first time, FDR had allowed him to see the real man. Hopkins knew in that moment that whatever else may happen, he had arrived at the center of FDR's inner circle.

"Let's keep all of this under our hats for the time being," Walker instructed.

FDR held up his glass with a smile. "Here's to you, Harry."

CHAPTER SEVEN

"Peace in our time."

Months later, in early September 1938, as the chill in the air began to morph the trees from green to shades of gold and rust and red in upstate New York, Hopkins and FDR traveled north on FDR's private train, Marco Polo, for a weekend at Springwood, in Hyde Park. Hopkins sat in an easy chair, drinking coffee and smoking, while FDR sat behind his desk a few feet away, working through a never-diminishing stack of papers. Both waited to hear Adolf Hitler's broadcast from the Nazi Party Rally in Nuremberg, Germany.

In January 1933, just two months before FDR was inaugurated, Hitler came to power when the declining eighty-seven-year-old President of Germany's Weimar Republic, Paul Von Hindenburg, appointed him as Chancellor. A month after his appointment, one of Hitler's key associates, Hermann Goering, secretly arranged to have the Reichstag, the seat of Germany's Weimar Republic, burned to the ground. As planned, Hitler immediately blamed the fire on the communists, who he said were attempting to take over the German government.

The very next day, Hitler convinced the feeble Von Hindenburg to sign a *Decree for the Protection of the People and the State*, ostensibly to protect the German government from the communists. In reality, the Decree restricted all personal liberties for everyone in Germany, including German citizens, and eliminated freedom of the press, speech, and assembly. It also gave the German government the right to search homes and spy on all German citizens.

With the stroke of a pen, it was game over.

Within twenty months after the Decree, Hitler substituted his personal dictatorship for democracy in the Weimar Republic, destroyed all political parties except for the Nazi Party, demolished State Governments and Parliaments, defederalized the German Reich, eliminated labor unions, abolished freedom of speech and the press once and for all, stifled the independence of the courts, drove Jews out of professional and public life, and had everyone in the German military and government swear an oath of allegiance to him directly.

By the time Hopkins and FDR sat on the train traveling to Springwood and waiting for Hitler's broadcast, Hitler had taken back the Rhineland from the French without firing a shot, annexed Austria, and now made it known he had his sights set on

Czechoslovakia in his quest for *lebensraum*—living space—for the German people.

"How was your summer?" asked FDR as their train chugged north and they waited for the broadcast.

"Relaxing," replied Harry. "I spent some time out on Long Island at Averell Harriman's place with Joe Davies, and a few of their friends."

"Davies is a good man," Roosevelt commented on his former Ambassador to the Soviet Union.

"I agree. I also met Bernard Baruch and Brendan Bracken this summer."

"Bernard told me you two met. He is a good friend," said FDR. "Did you know he advised Wilson in Paris at the Versailles Treaty negotiations back in 1919?"

Hopkins nodded. "Averell filled me in."

"You like Harriman, don't you?"

"I do," Hopkins nodded. "He's a very smart guy who doesn't mind working and getting his hands dirty."

"Honest?" asked FDR.

Harry smiled. "The kind of honesty and candor only the rich can afford."

"As long as he's not that rich man who thinks his own odor smells like perfume," said FDR, revealing his distaste for people who think their money and wealth make them better than others.

"Not Averell," assured Hopkins.

"Doesn't that Bracken fellow work with Winston Churchill in England?" asked FDR, as if he were trying to connect some dots.

Harry nodded.

"I don't like Churchill," commented FDR as he put his signature on a document he was reading. "I met him in London during the Great War. He acted like a stinker, lording it over all of us."

Harry loosened his tie and lit a new cigarette. As the pristine upstate New York countryside traveled past the train's windows, Hopkins felt a wave of relaxation sending him deeper into his easy chair. Somehow, with each passing minute, the serene and colorful landscape worked to soothe and wash away his tension. He took a long drag on his Lucky Strike and slowly exhaled. It had been a long while since he felt really good, and he was grateful for the moment.

Little did Hopkins know that in a few minutes, his life would be changed forever.

Missy LeHand entered the train car from her office in the next car and walked directly to the Philco Radio standing against the wall of the train. The Philco, which stood across from FDR's desk and next to Hopkins's chair, was a beautifully crafted piece of furniture, standing approximately four feet tall and made of solid maple. LeHand turned on the radio, and while the radio's tubes fired and warmed, she stood by waiting for the first hint of sound from its speakers.

"Effdee. I have the broadcast from the Nazi rally in Nuremberg for you," Missy said as the radio came to life with the sound of Gene Krupa's drums and Bennie Goodman's *Sing, Sing, Sing*. LeHand quickly turned the dial searching for the station she wanted and, after hearing several snippets of voices, chimes, and music, Adolf Hitler's strident voice filled the train car over the static from the speaker.

"Okay, Effdee?" asked LeHand as she turned up the volume.

"Good. Thank you, Missy." FDR placed the papers on his desk and sat back in his chair.

"Can you make out what he's saying?" Hopkins asked FDR.

"Every word," answered FDR, and he began translating Hitler's speech. "Dishonesty sets in the minute these democracies claim to represent government by the people and decry authoritarian states as dictatorships. How easily, however, are these supposed democracies stripped bare of their pretenses when one takes a close look at their stance in matters of foreign policy, which constantly change to suit the purpose of the moment. Throughout the Democratic countries, one laments the unimaginable cruelty with which first Germany, and now Italy as well, are striving to rid themselves of the Jewish element."

FDR grimaced.

"For decades," he continued, translating, "Germany nevertheless took in hundreds of thousands upon hundreds of thousands of Jews without batting an eyelid. Now that the burden has become overbearing and the nation is no longer willing to have its lifeblood sucked out of it by these parasites, it is now that there is great lament abroad."

FDR grimaced again and shook his head. He looked at Hopkins in a way Hopkins had never seen before—the usual confident look in his eyes, replaced by grave and utter concern.

"This is not good, Harry," FDR said out loud. "France and England may need us very soon. We had better get ready to defend ourselves."

"How can I help?" asked Hopkins.

"I want you to go to the West Coast and check on our aircraft production. We need to know how many aircraft we can produce in the event of a war," said FDR solemnly.

"I'll get the trip organized right away," Hopkins committed.

"No one can know the reason for your trip, Harry. Let's not put Congress on edge."

"Just another WPA trip for me," Hopkins said, assuring the President he had a good reason to travel to the Western states.

FDR turned his attention back to Hitler's speech, and as Hitler continued his harangue, Hopkins couldn't help but notice how the landscape and sky had changed. Dark clouds now hung over the horizon with gray and yellow light streaking through them to the farms and fields below.

#

By the time Hopkins visited the Douglas Aircraft Factory in Santa Monica, California, several weeks later, the British and French had signed an agreement with Hitler in Munich giving the Czechoslovakian Sudetenland to Nazi Germany. And they gave it to Hitler without even consulting the Czechoslovakian government.

Neville Chamberlain, the prissy, bird-like British Prime Minister and co-owner of a policy called *Appeasement*, returned to London from his meeting with Hitler and declared "Peace in Our Time" as he waved a piece of paper in front of reporters signed by the Nazi dictator. All in England, except for an out-of-favor MP named Winston Churchill, exhaled, believing war would not come to Europe.

Colonel Arthur Wilson from the War Department, accompanied Hopkins and Colonel Donald Connelly, the director of the WPA for Southern California, onto the main floor at the Douglas Factory, where they saw hundreds of people working at various stations. The noise on the floor was an almost deafening cacophony of hammers, drills, and grinders against metal and machinery.

Wilson shouted over the din, "These people here are working on our new bomber."

"How many have you built this year?" Hopkins shouted back.

"A little over a hundred, Mr. Hopkins," replied Wilson proudly.

As far as Wilson was concerned, Hopkins seemed impressed by his report, but in reality, Hopkins was shocked by Wilson's meager numbers. If the world went to hell in a handbasket, Hopkins knew it would take thousands of aircraft to defend the country.

After Hopkins and Connelly finished their tour of the facility, Wilson drove them to LaGrande Train Station in Los Angeles, and Hopkins thanked Wilson for organizing their visit.

"No, sir. Thank you!" Wilson emphasized, surprising Hopkins. "I'm glad at least someone in Washington is finally interested in what we're doing out here."

"Surprised to hear you say that," commented Hopkins.

Wilson looked at Hopkins like he was trying to decide what to say next.

"Respectfully, sir," Wilson plowed ahead, "you're the first people I've seen out here. We have to beg, borrow, and steal to get the people, equipment, and other things we need."

"That bad?" quizzed Hopkins.

"It seems anything related to the military is a challenge. It might surprise you to know, Mr. Hopkins, that Portugal has a bigger and better-equipped army than we have," added Wilson, deciding to go all in.

"Wasn't that factory we visited operating at full capacity?" Hopkins asked, hoping Wilson's answer would be "No."

Wilson scoffed. "Hardly. They have two other buildings on that property that are empty. Congress has us tied up in knots and red tape." Wilson paused for a moment to calm himself and then continued. "I'm sorry to bother you with this stuff. You guys at the WPA don't need to worry about the military's problems."

Hearing Wilson connect the WPA with the military, Colonel Connelly decided to make sure Wilson knew their boundaries. He was not going to take any chances that Wilson might tell some enterprising reporter the WPA had violated Congress's mandate.

"We're not worried about the military, Arthur," Connelly said. "Congress will not allow the WPA to have anything to do with the military."

Wilson got the message and decided to move off the topic. "Where to next for you guys?" he asked.

Connelly answered. "Frisco, Seattle, then Portland."

Wanting to leave Hopkins and Connelly on a positive note, Wilson decided a couple of sincere compliments couldn't hurt. "Well, for what it's worth, your WPA has made a significant impact on the lives of many people here in California. I see it every day. Those people you saw back at that factory are doing well because of a few War Department contracts. There are many, many others here in California who would not be doing well without your help."

"Thanks, Arthur. We appreciate that," Connelly said.

#

In early October, just days after Hopkins's inspection trip to the US West Coast, Winston Churchill, a back bencher and vocal critic of his party's policy of *Appeasement*, stood in front of his colleagues in the House of Commons and shredded the leadership of his own Conservative party over what became known at the "Munich Deal." As part of the deal, Great Britain, along with Italy and France, agreed to give Nazi Germany Czechoslovakia's Sudetenland, and they did so without even consulting the Czechoslovakian government.

In his forty-five-minute speech that would later be thought of as a memorable prosecution of his Conservative colleagues and his government, Churchill railed against his government's failure to confront the Nazis' aggression at Munich. Churchill warned his colleagues: *"We are in the presence of a disaster of the first magnitude. Do not let us blind ourselves to that. It must now be accepted that all the countries of Central and Eastern Europe will make the best terms they can with the triumphant Nazi Power."*

Though Churchill had many fewer friends than foes inside the House of Commons on that October afternoon, he mesmerized both and, more importantly, endeared himself to the British people when he concluded: *"Our loyal, brave people... should know the truth. They should know that there has been gross neglect and deficiency in our defenses; they should know that we have sustained a defeat without a war, the consequences of which will travel far with us along our road; they should know that we have passed an awful milestone in our history, when the whole equilibrium of Europe has been deranged, and that the terrible words have for the time being been pronounced against the Western democracies: Thou art weighed in the balance and found wanting. And do not suppose that this is the end. This is only the beginning of the reckoning."*

The following night, FDR sat in his office facing Hopkins and Joe Davies, who were both seated on the sofa. Joe Davies was the sixty-two-year-old, savvy, suave, and charismatic friend of FDR who had recently served as FDR's US Ambassador to the Soviet Union.

"How's your drink, Joe?" FDR asked.

"Hits the spot." Davies smiled.

"The Munich Deal has me concerned," said FDR, immediately launching into the reason for their meeting. "How long before Hitler helps himself to the rest of Czechoslovakia and Eastern Europe?"

"Not long at all," answered Davies quickly. He had already thought a great deal about that question after his sources in Moscow and Berlin intimated there was more on the horizon for the Nazis' ambitions.

"What will Stalin do?" FDR pressed.

"The Soviets will form an alliance with Germany as soon as they can on their own terms," said Davies without any hesitation.

"What about the British and French?"

Davies rocked his head side to side as he decided how to best answer FDR's question. "Those two have been diddling around with Stalin for almost a year," Davies finally answered. "The old bear will get tired of being cuffed around by the appeasing French and British."

"And you think Stalin will do a deal with Berlin even though he knows Hitler hates communists?" Though FDR framed it as a question, he really wanted Davies to confirm his own thinking.

"The one thing I learned while I was Ambassador to the Soviet Union is that Stalin is very, very practical and very, very ruthless. He will do a deal with anyone, including the Nazis, if it will protect his own power and secure his Western border," explained Davies. And then he added soberly, "With Hitler on the move, we should plan for the worst."

FDR looked at Hopkins. "Harry, tell Joe about your trip to the West Coast."

"I toured our West Coast aircraft manufacturers," Hopkins began immediately. "If everything went to hell in a handbasket right now, we would not be able to build the aircraft we need to defend ourselves, let alone help others."

"Not a surprise," responded Davies. "Congress has been shorting the military's budget for years now." Davies was very familiar with the US military's need for cash since the end of the Great War.

"Joe, this is very sensitive," FDR reminded Davies.

"Not a word outside this room," promised Davies.

FDR nodded at Hopkins, indicating he should continue.

"We are currently producing at less than 20 percent of our capacity," said Hopkins unemotionally.

"Damn," Davies said, surprised at just how deficient the military had become. He had no idea things had deteriorated that much, and neither did most Americans.

"I am meeting with George Marshall tomorrow—the Army's Deputy Chief of Staff—to see if we can jump-start production," Hopkins said.

"I thought the military was off-limits for the WPA," Davies said, trading looks with Hopkins and FDR.

"The Army and the Navy are sitting pretty," Hopkins responded, "to get a lot of money for our national defense in the next relief bill. We need to present a big program which will include the manufacture of modern airplanes and the employment of men, so they can go at top speed without regard for the current rules of relief labor and material."

"Risky business," cautioned Davies.

"A sign of the times," replied Hopkins.

#

Though it was the middle of October when General George Marshall entered the Walker Johnson Building, Washington, DC, was in the middle of record-breaking 85-degree days and blistering sunshine. The consecutive days of record temperatures had everyone in the city returning their coats, sweaters, and hats to their closets and bringing their summer clothes out for a second season.

Unfortunately for the people who worked in the old Walker Johnson Building, it was only hot, humid air that floated through its large old windows, and the heat from outside seemed to seep through its walls. John Delaney, the building's security guard, told his friends that on hot days like this one, the building's tenants "sweat like old Dublin whores goin' through the changes."

Hopkins was on the telephone in his Walker Johnson Building office, sitting at his desk in rolled-up shirtsleeves and a loosened tie. The large window behind his desk was wide open, with the Washington Monument visible across the city. When his secretary stuck her head in to announce "General George Marshall is here to see you," Hopkins stood up at his desk with the phone in his ear and waved at her to show the general in.

At fifty-eight, General George C. Marshall, who was the US Army's Deputy Chief of Staff under General Malin Craig, radiated integrity, dignity, confidence, and authority. During the Great War, Marshall worked together with legendary Generals Fox Conner and John "Black Jack" Pershing to lead the American Expeditionary Force and defeat Germany. He was, by far, one of the most capable and experienced military officers in the United States.

At Hopkins's request, Marshall wore a lightweight civilian suit for their meeting that morning, and he entered Hopkins's office just as Hopkins said happily into the phone, "Terrific work, John. Well done!" and hung up the phone. Though dressed in civilian clothes, there was no mistaking Marshall's military bearing. He shook hands with Hopkins and sat in a chair in front of Hopkins's desk.

"Sounded like you just won a battle," commented Marshall.

"A small victory. One of our WPA people in Arkansas just put about a thousand people back to work. We still have a lot more battles to win," admitted Hopkins.

"I understand," Marshall replied, thinking of his own challenges with the US Army. "Thank you for organizing this meeting today," Marshall said, happy to have the chance to speak with one of the President's trusted people about the Army. "I read your West Coast report and I agree with your assessment," Marshall offered, jumping right into the heart of the issue.

"It's good to know I'm seeing this correctly," replied Hopkins, pleased that Marshall confirmed his view.

"General Craig agrees, too. We know you focused on aircraft production while you were out there, but the truth is we are short of *everything*."

"Colonel Wilson said pretty much the same," Hopkins confirmed.

"Wilson is correct. Our army needs everything—from aircraft to ammunition," confessed Marshall.

"Are you saying the Army doesn't have enough bullets?"

"No, we have bullets," Marshall said, "but they are old bullets for antiquated guns."

"Can't we make new bullets?" Hopkins asked.

"If we had the money and machinery."

"And this is the case across the board? Vehicles, planes, weapons, artillery, the whole kit and caboodle?" Hopkins almost couldn't believe he was asking this question to the Army's Deputy Chief of Staff with the tinder box called Europe ready to ignite.

"Yes. Everything. Especially manpower," Marshall said clinically. "The plain truth is we need to make a modern army from scratch, and we need to build it fast."

Hopkins pushed his chair back from his desk and leaned forward with his elbows on his knees and his head and tie hanging toward the floor. Marshall, who was seated on the other side of the desk, was not quite sure what Hopkins was doing but decided to wait and see.

Before today's meeting, Hopkins had already thought there might be a way to blend the WPA's mission of putting Americans back to work with the Army's need to modernize. He was, of course, concerned that if Congress found out, there would be a knockdown, drag-out fight over such a strategy, especially if he was its architect. Hopkins knew it was a gray area, and if his adversaries in Congress knew he was involved, it was more likely a red one, as in full stop. After hearing General Marshall's assessment, however, and knowing America had to prepare to defend itself, the handicapper in Hopkins calculated the bet was worth the risk.

After several moments, Hopkins raised his head, pulled his chair forward to his desk, and said to Marshall, "The military needs to use the WPA."

"I thought Congress said you can't work with the military," Marshall said, unsure where Hopkins was headed.

"Yeah, well, you need ammunition, planes, tanks, guns, and equipment to defend our country, and I need jobs for our fellow citizens. Do we know the companies that can make the machines to produce the ammunition we need?"

"I'm sure we do," replied Marshall.

"How much money to get us started producing modern ammunition?"

"I don't know."

"Guess."

"Three or four million dollars to start. But that's just a guess," Marshall said, not wanting to commit.

Harry leaned over his desk and grabbed the telephone. "Please put me through to Treasury Secretary Morgenthau." He waited for a few moments and smiled at Marshall.

"Henry? It's Harry," Hopkins said into the phone. "Feeling much better, thank you for asking. Listen, the WPA needs to transfer four million dollars from its budget to the War Department immediately," he instructed and then listened.

After a brief moment, Hopkins assured Morgenthau, "No, Henry, the money is for *machines* to put our citizens back to work. That's what the WPA does."

Marshall watched as Hopkins listened to Morgenthau on the other end of the phone and then said, "No, this is all on me. But, Henry, we don't need to tell *The New York Times*, okay? How long to make the transfer?" asked Hopkins.

After several more moments, Hopkins looked satisfied and sat up straight. "Thank you, Henry," he said into the phone. "Appreciate it."

Hopkins hung up the phone and looked at Marshall. "The War Department will have access to four million dollars in a couple of days," he informed Marshall.

"Order the machines you need and pick a company to make the bullets."

"Thank you." Marshall was flabbergasted.

"Please let me know when those machines are operational. The WPA must continue to put Americans back to work quickly," advised Hopkins.

"I will," Marshall answered, not quite sure how this happened so fast or what was next.

Hopkins filled in the blanks. "General, I would like you to make a list of any other employment opportunities you can think of, and be sure to let me know." Hopkins smiled at Marshall.

"Employment opportunities," Marshall repeated, still unsure where Hopkins was headed or what he was referring to.

"That's right," responded Hopkins. "Manufacturing the machinery and things our military may need. The WPA has to put as many people back to work as quickly as we can."

"I will send you a list of other employment opportunities right away," Marshall said, grasping Hopkins's unsaid strategy and instruction.

Hopkins stood up and extended his hand with a big smile. Marshall rose from his chair smiling, and as they shook hands, Harry said, "I think we may have just won another battle, General."

#

Though they were sandwiched between an urgent need to prepare the country to defend itself and America's growing isolationist movement, the ever-increasing risk of all-out war in Europe had FDR, Hopkins, and Marshall prodding America and its deficient military forward via the backroads and backchannels of the US government.

Hopkins knew that Congress did not want foreign entanglements, but he also knew that to ensure America remained safe, America had to rebuild its military and invest in new weapons—weapons like the aircraft and submarines that Hitler and the Japanese were advancing which might easily overcome the defensive effectiveness of America's two moats—the Atlantic and Pacific Oceans.

In November, FDR called a secret meeting in the White House to discuss steps to help ensure America's total defense. Present at the meeting were FDR, Hopkins, the US Army Chief of Staff, General Malin Craig, General George Marshall, Pa Watson, General Henry "Hap" Arnold, Chief of the Army Air Corps, and Treasury Secretary Henry Morgenthau.

"Before we end today," Roosevelt said, sitting at the center of the conference table, "again I want to emphasize that our meeting here today is a secret." FDR surveyed the faces around the table, and they all nodded in agreement.

"Just to summarize," he continued, "we agree we need many more aircraft to protect our country. And though I see an Army Air Corps with 20,000 planes, and an aircraft industry capable of producing 24,000 planes per year, I think we also agree that Congress doesn't like me *that* much."

Some of the men around the table snickered at FDR's comment.

"Now, with these goals in mind, Generals Craig, Marshall, and Arnold agree to develop plans for the Army based on our projection that we will be able to produce 10,000 aircraft over the next two years. Harry Hopkins and General Marshall will ensure that we increase our production capacity, and Harry will be responsible for building new plants as needed," the President said confidently. "I think that about covers it, doesn't it?"

The men at the table staggered their affirmative replies and then, as the room fell silent, General Marshall spoke up. "Sir, I agree with your summary, but before we end today, it's critical for us to recognize we will not be able to defend our country with additional aircraft alone."

Roosevelt looked at Marshall, a little taken aback with his comment, and for a brief and tense moment, no one at the table flinched, blinked, or exhaled.

"What do you have in mind, General?" asked FDR.

General Craig decided to step in and help his deputy. "Mr. President, if I may, I think General Marshall is suggesting that when we produce our plans for you, we take a 360-degree view of all of our requirements for total defense."

"That's correct," Marshall confirmed. "To defend ourselves and fight a modern mobile war, we will need many more planes, ships, tanks, guns, artillery, ammunition—and many, many more men."

Roosevelt paused to puff on his cigarette. "Thank you for your comment, General," said FDR. "But as you well know, many in our country are not willing to invest in our military and still cling to the idea that our two oceans will protect us."

"Then we must educate them, sir," said Marshall evenly.

The room fell into a tense silence as FDR studied Marshall but said nothing. Most thought FDR was displeased. The truth was he was impressed with Marshall's candor and guidance. Like Marshall, deep down, FDR believed that now was not the time for half measures.

"Let's proceed with our aircraft plans," FDR said, and then turned to General Craig. "General, please also create plans to ensure we can defend our country, and please include *everything* the military needs to accomplish that goal. Thank you, gentlemen." FDR then pushed himself back from the table. The meeting was over.

Mac, FDR's Valet, entered the room and retrieved the President while all at the table stood at attention. As the men gathered their papers from the table, General Craig smiled at Marshall, "So,

General, have you thought about where you'd like to go for your *next* assignment?"

"That bad?" asked Marshall.

"You surprised him," replied Craig.

"I bet the President appreciated your views," Hopkins chimed in. "Get those plans done as quickly as you can. He has to know what it will take to defend the country."

"You guys are walking on the razor's edge," cautioned Morgenthau. "The isolationists in Congress will tear you apart."

"Not if you work your magic, Mr. Secretary," said Hopkins.

"I may be all out of tricks, Harry."

"That's impossible, Henry. You are the Houdini of government accounting," Hopkins needled.

"As long as I'm not the guy getting sawed in half!" Morgenthau sneered.

#

The Christmas Eve party was already well underway on the second floor of the residence, and everyone seemed to be having a wonderful time. The President sat toward the center of the room, with Eleanor at his side, and among the revelers were Pa and Frances Watson, Missy LeHand, Harold Ickes, Henry Morgenthau, Robert Sherwood, Dr. Ross McIntire, and Lorena "Hick" Hickok. Though Hick and Eleanor were spending less time together in recent years, they remained dear friends and didn't like spending Christmas away from each other.

Cocktails were in abundance, and waiters dressed in white moved through the room with trays adorned with hors d'oeuvres. Two photographers were busy taking pictures of Hick and Eleanor, each photograph confirmed by the pop of a new flash bulb.

Right then, the First Lady saw Diana and Hopkins enter the residence from the elevator. "Now, there's another person I want a picture with!" she said, and Diana ran to her. "Merry Christmas, Diana!"

"Merry Christmas, Mrs. Roosevelt!" said Diana, hugging the First Lady.

"I'm so excited you are spending Christmas with us this year," Eleanor said, hugging Hopkins.

"Merry Christmas, Eleanor," Hopkins returned her hug, and after retrieving a Scotch from a waiter, turned toward the President. "Merry Christmas, Mr. President!"

"And to you, Mr. Secretary," Roosevelt replied, holding up his martini.

Hopkins was stunned and walked over to FDR. "Mr. Secretary?" asked Hopkins.

FDR nodded. "Despite your awful Gallup Poll," FDR teased, "I appointed you Secretary of Commerce today."

"Thank you," Hopkins clinked glasses with FDR.

It was a memorable holiday party and a special Christmas for Harry.

When the party ended, only Hopkins, Eleanor, and Hick remained in the quiet residence while the White House staff straightened up and placed the family's presents and Hopkins's gifts under the Roosevelt family's Christmas tree.

"I'm done," Hick said, rising from her chair in her stocking feet and with her shoes in hand. "And to all a goodnight!" she announced and waddled to her room down the corridor.

"Would you like to peek in on Diana before you go to bed?" Eleanor asked Hopkins.

"I would love that."

The residence was very quiet and softly lit as they walked to Diana's room.

"You're sleeping in there tonight, Harry," said Eleanor quietly, pointing to an open door. "That's the Lincoln Suite."

"Eleanor, I can never thank you enough for all you've done," replied Hopkins.

"I just hope you don't feel like I am intruding."

"Intruding?" Harry was not sure what she meant. "I am so grateful for everything you and the President have done for us."

"Well, I must confess I have selfish reasons."

"You are never selfish," Hopkins said, and meant it.

"I hope you don't mind, Harry," Eleanor continued, sounding genuinely concerned, "but I have wanted to ask you about something for a while now."

"Eleanor, you can ask me anything."

"After Barbara died and you had your surgery, it made me think about who would look after Diana in the event something happened to you?" confessed Eleanor.

Hopkins stopped walking and turned toward her.

"I hope you don't mind talking about it," she said, afraid she may have made an error in judgment in bringing up the topic.

"No, no, Eleanor. It's fine. The truth is it has been on my mind, as well," admitted Harry.

"Do you have a Will, Harry?" she asked, feeling like she was walking on a frozen pond and the ice was crackling under her feet.

"Yes, I do. But there is nothing in my will about Diana," he said, embarrassed.

"In that case, would you please consider naming me as Diana's guardian should something happen to you?" *There, I finally said it*, she thought to herself.

"Eleanor, I don't have a lot of financial resources. In fact, hardly any," Hopkins responded. His easy confession made him realize just how close he and Eleanor had become.

"Do not concern yourself with any of that," Eleanor answered quickly. "You and Diana are very dear to me, and it would make me extraordinarily happy knowing I would be the one to take care of her," she said, tears welling in her eyes.

"I can't tell you what this means to me, Eleanor." Tears filled his eyes, as well, as he hugged her, touched by her friendship and her generosity.

"I hope it means your good health will continue," she answered.

"I will draft a new will first thing on Monday," promised Hopkins.

When Eleanor slowly opened the door to Diana's room, the light from the corridor spilled across Diana's bed, illuminating her as she slept soundly under the covers.

Her father and her guardian both quietly entered Diana's room together and looked at their charge as Diana slept, unaware that she had already received an incredible gift this Christmas.

CHAPTER EIGHT

"Like getting an advanced degree in world affairs."

As Joe Davies suggested, and Churchill predicted, Hitler was not content with the sliver of Czechoslovakia called the Sudetenland. It didn't take long before the Nazi dictator made a mockery of the so-called Munich Pact and humiliated those who had clung to a policy of Appeasement as their best hopes for peace. Less than six months after the Munich Deal, on the Ides of March in 1939, Hitler's troops marched into all of Czechoslovakia and took Bohemia and Moravia with no resistance whatsoever. By nightfall that day, the German Army made its triumphant entrance into Prague. Not a shot was fired.

The next day, after FDR and Hopkins had a dinner of rare roast beef and mashed potatoes, Roosevelt put a cigarette in his holder, lit it, and said, "I don't think we can wait to settle the issue of the new Army Chief of Staff."

"George Marshall understands better than anyone exactly what we need to defend our country," Hopkins replied.

"General Pershing and Fox Conner agree," the President said.

"Not surprised," Hopkins said, lighting his own cigarette. "Marshall is smart, honest, and there's not a lick of politics in him."

"Harry, do you think Marshall can convince Congress to give the military the money it needs?" asked FDR, sharing his biggest concern for his next Chief of Staff.

"If there's anyone other than you that Congress will listen to, it's George Marshall," Hopkins assured FDR.

#

Great Britain's King George VI and Queen Elizabeth toured Canada, and then became the first British monarchs in history to visit America when they crossed the US border at Niagara Falls, New York, on June 7. In a thinly veiled attempt to bolster support for the British cause in a war that now seemed inevitable, FDR invited the monarchs to a state dinner at the White House and to enjoy a hot dog-eating barbecue at his home in Hyde Park several days later.

On the night of the state dinner, FDR and Hopkins sat waiting with cocktails and cigarettes in the White House residence living room, dressed in white tie and tails—though Hopkins's suit was rented.

"I spoke with Bernard Baruch today," FDR told Hopkins, "and I asked him to spend some time with you to give you his take on the world situation."

"Like getting an advanced degree in world affairs. Thank you," replied Hopkins, excited to have the chance to spend time with the great financier and statesman.

"He suggested you visit with him this summer at his estate in South Carolina—Hobcaw Barony. A bit of work, a bit of school, and a bit of rest."

Eleanor entered the living room holding Diana's hand. Earlier in the day, Eleanor taught Diana how to curtsy, and Diana had been practicing ever since. *She looks like a princess*, Hopkins thought, as his little girl entered wearing a pretty new white dress with shiny white shoes and lacy ankle socks.

"The King and Queen are on their way," Eleanor told her husband and Hopkins. The President took one last sip of his martini, placed the glass on a table next to him, and stubbed out his cigarette. Harry followed suit.

King George and Queen Elizabeth entered the living room, and as they approached, FDR, Eleanor, and Harry greeted their guests warmly. Then Eleanor held Diana's hand and took several steps toward the monarchs. "Your Majesties," said Eleanor formally, "may I present Miss Diana Hopkins?"

Diana stood stock still, wide-eyed and speechless. Eleanor softly tapped Diana's shoulder, encouraging her to approach the royals and curtsy as they had practiced. Diana seemed unsure at first, but after Eleanor's gentle encouragement, she stepped forward.

"Your Majesties," Diana said and curtsied in front of the monarchs.

Eleanor could not have been prouder, FDR cackled, and Hopkins beamed.

"It's very nice to meet you, Diana," said the Queen. The King greeted her as well, but Diana could not take her eyes off Queen Elizabeth, who wore a stunning silver gown with a diamond necklace and a jeweled tiara.

"Are you the fairy queen?" Diana asked the Queen.

Queen Elizabeth smiled a warm and bright smile. "Diana," the Queen replied, "if you would like me to be, tonight I will be the fairy queen."

Everyone in the room was captivated watching Diana and the Queen, and it seemed that Queen Elizabeth was as much taken by Harry's young daughter as she was by her. A chorus of laughter filled the room as Diana curtsied again and then ran to Hopkins.

"Daddy, I met the fairy queen," Diana said, hugging Hopkins.

Every person there could not have hoped for a better start to the evening.

#

After a few weeks with Bernard Baruch at Hobcaw Barony and his master class on geopolitics and political economy, Hopkins was forced to make a return appearance at the Mayo Clinic during the last week of August. Ironically, both he and FDR now shared the same physical condition. His chronic nutritional issues were impacting his muscles, leaving him unable to walk.

The doctors at Mayo informed Hopkins they had reviewed all of his tests, thoroughly discussed his case, and concluded that, unfortunately, there was nothing more they could do for his condition. They apologized, but said he was not absorbing nutrients, and that caused him to live in a state of near-starvation.

The phone rang in his hospital room, and when Hopkins answered, the President's cheerful voice said, "I thought I should send you a ribald telegram, but I decided to call instead."

"So great to hear your voice." Hopkins smiled, his first smile in days.

"I'm sure you've heard the news," FDR started. "Things are eroding quickly in Europe. With Hitler and Stalin signing that Non-Aggression Pact, it doesn't speak well for peace."

"Joe Davies said this would happen," Harry replied. "How is Marshall doing in the new job?"

"Just fine," answered FDR. "He'll be sworn in a few days from now."

"He'll do a great job."

"I wrote a letter to Hitler the other day, but I'm not optimistic it will have any real effect," FDR reported.

"I'm glad you let him know where we stand," Hopkins commented. "If the Brits and French allow another Munich, we're all at risk."

"Bernard taught you well," declared FDR. "Now, when they are finished with you up there, I want you to come to Springwood and Warm Springs to recuperate."

"I'll gladly take you up on that."

In the middle of the night, on September 1, 1939, the same day General George Marshall would be sworn in as the US Army's new Chief of Staff, there was a knock on FDR's bedroom door. The President stirred from his sleep and, trying to gather his senses, lifted himself up on his elbows to look about the dark room. His bedroom door opened, and a sliver of light cut into the room from the corridor. Mac, his valet, entered, followed by Pa Watson.

"Mr. President, I am sorry to wake you, but I have news," Watson said as he walked through the door and turned on a lamp.

"What is it?" FDR asked, already knowing the answer would not be good.

"Germany invaded Poland," reported Watson.

"It has come at last," said FDR sadly, and added quietly, "God help us all."

At the same time, a thousand miles to the northwest, Harry Hopkins was wide awake in his hospital bed staring at the ceiling, and over the protests of his nurses, listening to the radio he insisted on having in his hospital room. *"Today, the First of September 1939, at dawn,"* said the announcer, *"the German Army and Air Force crossed into Polish territory without a declaration of hostilities. Since then, the German air force, known there as the Luftwaffe, has been bombing cities and towns throughout that country."*

The following morning, Pa Watson received a call from the Mayo Clinic's Chief Administrator about Harry's prognosis, and Pa immediately informed FDR. He told the President it sounded like it was game over for Hopkins. Within minutes, the President summoned Dr. McIntire to his office and plainly told McIntire that he rejected even the possibility that Harry's life could not be saved.

"The doctors up at Mayo have given up Harry for dead," FDR told McIntire, more than a little perturbed. "I want you to arrange to bring him to the Naval Hospital here in Washington and organize the best team you can to help him," ordered Roosevelt.

"Yes, sir," McIntire replied, reverting to his military roots.

The President then turned to LeHand. "Missy, make sure Ross has everything he needs to get Harry back here fast. And, when you get back to your desk, get Harry on the line for me," he instructed.

In truth, Missy was terribly worried about Harry. She loved him. Perhaps not as much as she loved FDR, but she loved him nonetheless. With or without Dr. McIntire, she would see to it that Harry Hopkins arrived back in Washington quickly and safely, and got the attention he needed. She didn't wait for McIntire and immediately made the arrangements to transport Harry back to Washington.

When Hopkins arrived in DC, the Surgeon General of the Navy, Admiral Edward R. Stitt, was called in. Over the next several months, Hopkins functioned as a sickly guinea pig for countless experiments. Though it was a many-month-long, painful ordeal for him, it was an ordeal that eventually brought Hopkins back from the brink.

Throughout the winter months and into the early spring of 1940, Harry healed, first in the hospital and then at his home in

Georgetown, spending no time in his new role as Secretary of Commerce. His healing was slow going and advanced a little at a time. Though he remained weak, as the weather improved, he began to venture out, occasionally for short walks, drives, and White House dinners.

Harry repeatedly offered FDR his resignation, but FDR wouldn't hear of it. "You'll be back in your office at Commerce in a couple of weeks and going great guns!" FDR told Hopkins, seemingly still convinced that Hopkins would carry on and run as the Democratic candidate for President in 1940.

By May, however, it was sadly obvious to everyone, including FDR, that Hopkins was not only unable to function as Commerce Secretary, but was also unable to run for any office in 1940—let alone the office of President of the United States.

Harry joined the President for a late Friday evening dinner in the White House on May 10th, complete with the usual pre-dinner martinis and cocktails. Despite the fact that the news from Europe was not good, Hopkins felt well and especially glad to be back in the White House. While he nursed a weak Scotch and soda and Roosevelt sat sipping his second martini, Missy came in and began fiddling with the radio, filling the room with music, laughter, advertisements, and static as she tried to find the right station. After several moments, they heard, "This is the BBC," from the radio's speakers.

The announcer confirmed that German forces had invaded Holland, Belgium, and Luxembourg by land and air, and quoted the fanatical Adolf Hitler as saying, "The hour has come for the decisive battle for the German nation!"

Anyone with any sense knew Hitler's next stop was France.

"In Washington," the broadcaster said bringing his report home and personal, "at a news conference today, President Roosevelt was asked whether he thought Germany's invasion of the Low Countries would lead to US involvement in the war. He replied that it would not," the announcer said deliberately hitting the word "not" especially hard.

FDR was about to motion to Missy to turn down the radio when the broadcaster continued in his crisp British accent, "His Majesty King George has summoned Winston Churchill to Buckingham Palace following the collapse of Mr. Chamberlain's government and Germany's sweeping attack. Mr. Churchill pledges to form a coalition government to confront Nazi Germany."

"Having received His Majesty's commission," Churchill's distinct voice came through the speaker, "I have formed an administration of men and women of every party and almost every point of view. We have differed in the past, but now one bond unites us all: To wage war until victory is won, and never to surrender ourselves to servitude and shame, whatever the cost and the agony may be."

The President motioned for Missy to turn off the radio.

"France will surely be next," said FDR, sounding resigned to the crisis developing in Europe.

"And then England," Hopkins added.

"I suppose Churchill is the best man they have over there," commented Roosevelt, "though I hear he likes to drink."

Eleanor entered FDR's office looking tired and worried after completing a scheduled trip to New York, where she gave a number of speeches to women's groups. She had looked forward to spending a couple of days in her former home, but when the news broke about Hitler's invasion of Belgium, she could not find her way back to DC fast enough.

"Oh, Harry, it's wonderful to see you," Eleanor said as she entered and went directly to him.

Hopkins started to rise, but she held up her hand. "You stay put," she insisted and bent down to hug him in his seat. "You are a light on a very dark day, Harry."

For Eleanor, Hopkins's presence somehow represented sanity in a world going insane as it moved inexorably toward war. Little did she know that, despite his New Deal bona fides, Hopkins was a prime mover in getting America's military ready and prepared.

Are you feeling well?" Eleanor asked Hopkins.

"He needs to get his rest," answered FDR.

"Well, then you will stay here tonight," Eleanor said simply.

"No, no," Hopkins protested with a raised palm. "That's not necessary. Much appreciated…"

Eleanor cut him off instantly. "You'll stay here and that's that, Harry. We'll put you in Lincoln's rooms," Eleanor ordered. "Who's watching Diana?"

"The boys are here from New York. They are with her."

"When things settle, Diana will come here as well," Eleanor insisted, leaving no room for rebuttal.

Though he had stayed in the White House's Lincoln Suite down the hall from FDR's bedroom before, Hopkins truly never expected to call those rooms his home that night—and for the next three-and-a-half years.

CHAPTER NINE

Seven-year-old-Diana Hopkins loved living in the White House, and so did her father. Even when Harry was up to his neck with work, as he always was, he found living and working there to be helpful to his now nearly full recovery. Hopkins especially liked the fact that there were so many supportive people in Diana's life on a daily basis. They both quickly settled into the kind of easy domestic routine shared by families around the country—except they happened to live with the President and First Lady.

With a file under his arm, Harry entered the President's bedroom dressed in his bathrobe, pajamas, and slippers for their usual morning meeting, and found FDR sitting up in bed, with a blue cape with the letters "FDR" monogrammed in red stitching draped across his shoulders, and a breakfast tray in front of him—scrambled eggs, toast, orange juice, and coffee. As usual, Hopkins went directly to the table with a carafe of coffee next to his usual chair, poured himself a coffee, and lit a cigarette.

"Things are not good in London," Roosevelt said, holding out a cable for Hopkins, and then said, "Churchill."

Hopkins walked to the President and took the cable from him, reading Churchill's message aloud. "'I trust you realize, Mr. President, that the voice and force of the United States may count for nothing if they are withheld too long.'"

"Clever," said Hopkins, appreciating Churchill's tactic to reel in FDR and the United States.

"I hope it's not *desperate*," replied FDR. "We need to get ourselves in proper shape, Harry."

"I'm working with General Marshall to make sure we have what we need and our stocks are full."

"You're looking so much better," Roosevelt said as the Westminster clock chimed eight o'clock in his bedroom. "I see an improvement every day."

"Rest is overrated," Harry said with a wry smile.

The truth was he was feeling much better. It was a mystery, but the regimen of vitamins and nutrients prescribed by the doctors at the Naval Hospital, coupled with his work in the White House, had accomplished what months of rest in Minnesota and Georgetown could not. Though the concoctions McIntire administered were important, Hopkins knew it was his work with FDR that had a way of invigorating and restoring him to his old form.

It was a kind of occupational therapy.

With his White House bedroom doubling as his office, Lincoln's Suite was always cluttered with papers, old coffee cups, dirty plates, overflowing ashtrays, and stacks of file folders. They installed three telephones in the room, one on a desk in a corner, one on a small round conference table in the living area, and the other on a nightstand next to his seldom-made bed. Visitors—and there was always a steady stream of them vying for Hopkins's attention—not only wondered how the man worked like that, but also how he lived there.

Later that day, when Pa Watson walked into Hopkins's room, he found him sitting on the phone in his boxers, with his pants down around his ankles, while he injected himself in the thigh with one of Dr. McIntire's magic elixirs. After he finished injecting himself, Hopkins put the syringe in a tray on the table, stood up with the phone clenched between his ear and shoulder, pulled up his pants, and tucked in his shirt.

"That's right," Hopkins said into the phone, "Total national defense. Not partial defense or defense a little at a time, but total national defense."

After several more moments listening, Pa could see Hopkins was becoming agitated. "I don't get what's so hard to understand. This is not that difficult. We need to store at least six months of fuel," he said, his voice rising in volume.

Pa Watson was enjoying the show. He knew Hopkins. And he knew by Hopkins's tone that whoever was on the other end of that phone, making excuses, was headed for a lot of heat. Sure enough, after a few moments more listening, Pa saw Hopkins's face turn dark, and Pa smiled. *Here it comes.*

"Jesus! Enough!" Hopkins shouted into the phone.

Hopkins looked at Watson and shook his head.

"Yeah, well, I belong to the school that does not talk about things," Hopkins told the person on the phone, "You do them! Get this done fast and get back to me," Hopkins hung up the phone hard.

"These goddamn New Dealers. All they do is talk, talk, talk," complained Hopkins, and Watson laughed out loud at the irony of Harry Hopkins railing against one of his New Deal colleagues.

"One of these days, Harry, someone is going to take a potshot at you." Watson smiled.

"Pa, there's a long line of highly motivated people who are working very hard to secure my demise."

#

Though it was clear that Hopkins's health would prevent him from making a presidential run in 1940, FDR didn't broach the subject with him until just several weeks before the Democratic convention when they were traveling on FDR's train to Hyde Park. To the soft strains of Ray Eberle crooning Glenn Miller's latest release, *Fools Rush In*, on the radio, the President finally brought it up in an almost off-handed way.

"I really wish you could have made a run for it this year, Harry," FDR said casually.

"I'm sorry I let you down," Harry replied, disappointed his health forced him to back away from campaigning for the highest office. "Who knows, after you win again in 1940, maybe I'll be able to make a run in '44?"

"No President has ever had three terms," commented FDR. "The only way I'll stay in the White House is if the party—" FDR didn't finish his thought because Glen Miller's song on the radio was interrupted with, "*We interrupt this broadcast,* the announcer said, *"to bring you a special bulletin. We have just learned that France has surrendered to Germany. It has been reported that under the terms of their surrender, France will allow Germany to occupy the majority of the country, including Paris. Please stay tuned to this station for more updates. We now return to our regularly scheduled broadcast in progress."*

"That didn't take long," FDR said as the music resumed.

"You have to stay on. It is only a matter of time before that reaches us," Hopkins said, nodding toward the radio. Who else can lead us through this?"

FDR pushed back. "Harry, I won't run for the office again, and I will only stay on if the party wants me to."

"If that's what it will take," replied Hopkins undaunted, "then I'll go to the convention in Chicago and make sure they ask you."

#

True to his word, a few weeks later Harry set up shop in a suite at the Blackstone Hotel in Chicago, a place that was synonymous with behind-the-scenes political machinations. In the days before the convention was scheduled to begin on July 15, Hopkins worked the phones, twisted arms, called in favors, and otherwise worked his unique and sometimes manipulative magic on behalf of his boss.

Hopkins was not only working against whatever lingering feelings he had about his own political future, but also against history itself. No President had ever even seriously considered a third term. A popular slogan of the day said: "Washington wouldn't; Grant couldn't; Roosevelt shouldn't."

By the middle of the convention, Hopkins had enough confidence in FDR's chances to be the Democratic Party's candidate for the third time that he phoned and informed FDR the nomination was his for the taking if he would travel to Chicago and deliver a speech. FDR flatly refused. The Democratic Party would have to nominate him, and he would not ask for the nomination. Period.

With the Democratic Convention grinding to a conclusion, Hopkins asked FDR if he would mind if Eleanor gave a speech. FDR told Hopkins he had no objections, but it was up to Eleanor.

Hopkins closed the deal, and on July 18, Eleanor flew to Chicago and stood in front of the delegates. *"This is no ordinary time,"* Eleanor said to the thousands of adoring people standing and cheering in the convention's warm arena. *"No time for weighing anything, except what we can best do for the country as a whole. And that rests, that responsibility, on each and every one of us as individuals. No man who is a candidate, or who is President, can carry this situation alone. This is only carried by a united people*

who love their country and who will live for it to the fullest of their
ability with the highest ideals..."

Thanks to Hopkins's political engineering and Eleanor's speech, the Democrats nominated FDR for an unprecedented third term on their first ballot, with 943 of the 1,093 delegates demanding he stay on for the third time in 1940. Three months later, on November 5, 1940, America agreed and again elected Franklin D. Roosevelt as President of the United States with 55% of the popular vote and 449 electoral votes.

The following morning, Harry joined FDR and Eleanor for their traditional scrambled-egg victory breakfast at Springwood. When they finished breakfast, as was customary, a crowd of local Hyde Park well-wishers formed outside the front door, and the President was wheeled out to meet the crowd while reporters and Secret Service agents looked on. As FDR's Hyde Park neighbors cheered and applauded, Hopkins walked to the end of the porch out of the spotlight and stood alone.

There were cries of "Speech! Speech!" as Roosevelt waved to his friends and held up his hand to quiet them. "You are wonderful friends and neighbors," he said. "I appreciate you visiting me this morning to celebrate our victory with us," and then, after pausing for effect, he added, "for the third time!"

The crowd cheered.

A reporter noticed Hopkins standing off to the side and shouted, "What are your thoughts, Mr. Hopkins?"

Hopkins looked at the reporter, smiled, and shouted, "We made it!" and then broke into a tap dance on the porch to the cheers and laughter of everyone watching.

#

After the election, in early December, FDR recruited a posse of the usual suspects, including Hopkins and Pa Watson, for a trip to the Caribbean aboard the USS Tuscaloosa. Though the "official" reason for the two-week cruise was to inspect newly acquired military bases in the Caribbean, it was no state secret that the real purpose of the excursion was fishing, fellowship, poker, and Cuban cigars, which had been acquired during a brief stop at Guantanamo Bay.

The group was relaxing on the deck of the Tuscaloosa after lunch when the Tuscaloosa's executive officer delivered the pouch to FDR. Among the assorted papers requiring the President's attention and signature was correspondence from Winston Churchill.

Today's fifteen-page letter from Churchill was different, and even before he read it, FDR knew the sheer size of the letter was foreboding. Neither Hopkins nor FDR realized, however, that the letter FDR held in his hands would not only change the course of history but, once again, the trajectory of Hopkins's life.

Never known for an economy of words, Churchill used more than 4,000 of them in his eloquent way to paint a panoramic portrait of Great Britain's situation from Singapore to Gibraltar to Suez and the North Sea. As usual, he asked for more ships to carry food, supplies, and equipment to his weakening country. Unusual, however, was his secret revelation that Great Britain was going broke.

When he finished the last of fifteen pages, FDR removed his pince-nez glasses and handed the letter to Hopkins to read.

"Churchill?" asked Harry.

The President nodded his head. "He says they're almost out of cash."

"Morgenthau worried this would happen," Hopkins commented. "Baruch, too."

Hopkins stood up and read the letter as he paced the deck. After several minutes, he returned with the letter in hand and found FDR staring out across the water, deep in thought. FDR turned from the water, took the letter from Hopkins, and looked him squarely in the eyes. Harry knew that look. He had seen it so many times before whenever FDR thought he had solved a pressing problem.

"We will *lend* them everything!" FDR said out loud.

"Lend," Harry repeated, unsure what FDR meant.

"If they agree to pay us after the war, we'll lend them whatever they need—planes, tanks, guns, food, oil—all of it," said FDR, convinced he had found the solution.

"What about Congress and cash and carry?" Hopkins asked, referring to Congress's current law that all supplies and ammunition provided to foreign countries had to be purchased in cash and shipped by the purchaser.

"I don't know how this can be done," admitted FDR, "but I'm certain we must provide the British with the resources they need to win."

Pa Watson stepped onto the deck from the ship's radio room and approached FDR and Hopkins with a telegram in hand. "This cable just came in," Pa said, handing a document to FDR. "Lord Lothian, the British Ambassador to the US, has died."

"Damn," FDR whispered in reply. "No ambassadors when we could use them most."

FDR had recalled US Ambassador to England, Joe Kennedy, just before the election, and managed to briefly charm his wealthy benefactor into making a speech to America's Catholics to support his re-election. The truth was that as ambassador, Kennedy had been a thorn in Roosevelt's side, and his indiscreet public statements about Britain's poor chances against the Nazis an embarrassment. After he won the election, FDR promptly accepted Kennedy's resignation, and it was common knowledge that the President fired him.

"A lot could be worked out between Churchill and me if we could just sit down together. I'm sure of that," FDR said to Hopkins.

"Why not send me over there?" suggested Hopkins.

"We need you here," FDR answered emphatically. "The State of the Union is coming up, then the inauguration, and now this new program," he said, holding up Churchill's letter.

It didn't take long for FDR to engage his creativity and architect the idea that would help sustain the British. When they returned home, refreshed from their fishing trip, the White House was already decorated for the holidays. FDR asked Steve Early, his press secretary, to organize a press conference in his office so he could use his tried-and-true technique of sending up a trial balloon and airing out his new idea with the press.

"What I am trying to do is eliminate the dollar sign," FDR told the reporters in his office, some of whom raised their eyebrows as he plowed ahead. "I know that is something brand new in the thoughts of practically everybody in this room, but I think—get rid of the silly, foolish old dollar sign." A few of the reporters in the room looked at him like they were puppy dogs with their heads tilted to one side, listening to a strange noise.

"Let me give you an illustration," offered FDR. "Suppose my neighbor's home catches fire, and I have a length of garden hose four or five hundred feet away. If he can take my garden hose and connect it up with his hydrant, I may help him to put out his fire. Now, what do I do? I don't say to him before that operation, "Neighbor, my garden hose cost me $15; you have to pay me $15 for it…"

After the press conference, a fierce debate ensued during the following months, but it soon became clear that FDR had successfully sold his novel idea to the country with the help of two simple words: "Garden hose."

#

It was late at night, three days after Christmas, when Hopkins, Sam Rosenman, and Robert Sherwood sat together with FDR in the Oval Office to put the final touches on FDR's Fireside Chat scheduled for the following evening.

Sam Rosenman had been writing the President's speeches for years and, in fact, coined the phrase "New Deal" for FDR's first run for office. Robert "Bob" Sherwood was the six-foot-eight-inch-tall, forty-four-year-old, Pulitzer Prize-winning American playwright and author, who was an original member of The Algonquin Roundtable, and a close friend of Hopkins. Sherwood, Rosenman, and Hopkins were birds of a feather—all fervent believers in American democracy and determined anti-fascists.

By the time they met that evening with the President, Poland, France, Italy, Sicily, Sardinia, Belgium, Luxembourg, Austria, Denmark, Norway, Romania, Hungary, Czechoslovakia, and Holland were all conquered by the Nazis, and only England remained as the last, free-standing democracy in Europe. As if the disappearance of entire countries from Europe's map wasn't concerning enough, had the men in FDR's office that night known about Hitler's recent order to invade the Soviet Union, they would have been doubly concerned that England would soon join the list of disappearing nations and the United States would follow soon after. They were all keenly aware that, while the entire world burned, America fiddled, believing it was still protected by its two moats.

FDR sat behind his desk reading the draft of his next Fireside Chat, which the three had drafted, and he looked up. "I like it—especially the way you handled the doubting Thomas's. "*'Let not the defeatists tell us that it is too late. It will never be earlier. Tomorrow will be later than today,'*" he read. "That's excellent, Bob," the President said to Sherwood.

"Thank you, Mr. President," Sherwood said. "We wanted to be sure we addressed the isolationists."

"And this—*'We must be the great Arsenal of Democracy.'* It's perfect!" crowed the President.

"That was Harry," Sam Rosenman said.

FDR read the document and again tested it as he read, *"I have the profound conviction that the American people are now determined to put forth a mightier effort than they have ever yet made to increase our production of all the implements of defense, to meet the threat to our Democratic faith."*

"Indeed, that must be our conviction and our action right now," FDR confirmed. "Thanks, boys. I love it."

Rosenman and Sherwood collected their papers and stood up.

"I will send you my thoughts on the State of the Union in a couple of days, and I'll need that draft soon after," FDR reminded Rosenman.

"We will have it ready for you," Rosenman assured FDR.

A few days later, on January 2, Rosenman and Sherwood visited with Hopkins in his paper-strewn White House bedroom office to review their draft of FDR's State of the Union address. Rosenman paced around Hopkins's room with the draft in his hand, navigating through the file folders on the floor, while Hopkins sat with one leg hanging over an easy chair, reading the document.

Hopkins looked up from the document. "The boss wrote this?" asked Hopkins, sounding like he suspected that it didn't come from FDR.

"He did. He wrote those lines himself," said Sherwood. "No good?"

"Too good. There's no turning back from this," Hopkins answered, picking up the document and reading it out loud.

"*In the future days, which we seek to make secure, we look forward to a world founded upon four essential human freedoms. The first is freedom of speech and expression—everywhere in the world... The second is freedom of every person to worship God in his own way—everywhere in the world... The third is freedom from want—The fourth is freedom from fear...*" Hopkins stopped and looked at Sherwood and Rosenman. "This is a breathtaking vision for our world," Hopkins told the men.

"It's not a vision," Sherwood pointed out. "Here he says, '*This is no vision of a distant millennium and it is a definite basis for a kind of world attainable in our own time and generation.*'"

"He's defining America—who we are, what we stand for, and who we want to be," said Hopkins, captivated by the implications of FDR's Four Freedoms.

Steve Early knocked on Hopkins's door and, without waiting, burst into the room.

"Congratulations, Harry!" announced Early with a big grin.

"For what?"

"Your trip."

"What trip?" Hopkins asked sharply.

"Your trip to England," answered Early. "The President just told the press you are going over to London for a few weeks so you can talk with Churchill like an Iowa farmer."

"Of course, Churchill is very interested in this year's corn crop," Hopkins joked, and the group laughed with him.

"I'm not kidding, Harry," Early said seriously. "You're going."

"Bon Voyage, Harry!" Sherwood said, toasting Hopkins with his coffee cup.

CHAPTER TEN

"Welcome to London."

It was a gray and blustery late afternoon on January 9, 1941, when the men in Anti-Aircraft Battery One on the dock at Poole Harbor, England, heard aircraft engines in the distance over the English Channel. Surrounded by sandbags, the British officer in charge raised his binoculars toward the sound while his gun operator worked the anti-aircraft gun's wheel to swivel his seat and the turret of the ominous-looking gun in that direction.

"KLM one four from Lisbon with Spitfire escorts," announced the British officer in AA Battery One, as he peered through his binoculars toward the three black dots in the gray sky. "That's them all right."

The radio operator turned on his radio set and flipped the transmit switch. "Sussex Fighter Command, this is Poole Harbor AA Battery One," the Radio Operator said into the microphone perched on his chest, "We have eyes on KLM flight one four from Lisbon descending with two Spitfire escorts. Over." The Radio Operator flipped off the transmit switch and listened.

After a brief moment, "Yes, sir," the radio operator said crisply into his microphone. "Confirming. Escorts are to report to Sussex. Will notify immediately. Good day."

A smile spread across the British officer's face. "A good day indeed," he said out loud, still looking through his binoculars. "If they are sending them back to Sussex, that means no one is chasing them."

The radio operator adjusted the dial on the radio to the correct frequency, flipped the transmit switch, and then announced into his microphone, "Escort 0110. This is AA Battery One, Poole Harbor. Over."

After a moment of silence, the voice of the Spitfire Pilot came through a veil of static covering the radio's speaker, "Escort 0110. At your service, Battery One."

"Fighter Command requires you at Sussex if fuel allows. Over," the radio operator replied.

"Roger. On our way. Good day," the voice from the speaker signed off.

The British officer watched through his binoculars as the KLM flight continued descending toward Poole Harbor while its Spitfire escorts banked sharply toward Sussex, looking like two black pebbles sliding across the slate gray sky. The sky's dismal hue seemed appropriate considering the state of England. It was a dark and dangerous time.

Since Winston Churchill became Prime Minister seven months earlier, the Nazis had captured most of Western Europe. Though the British evacuation from Dunkirk in May was miraculous by anyone's standards, and spared the lives of hundreds of thousands of British and French soldiers, the equipment and weapons abandoned on the beach in France did little to secure Britain's future survival against the determined Nazi war machine. And after France's capitulation to the Nazis in August, England was left as Europe's lone survivor.

By now, in January 1941, the British not only stood against Herman Goering's Luftwaffe, which regularly bombed and burned Britain's cities, but they also had to contend with Karl Dönitz's U-boats, which effectively cut off all seaborne supply to their island nation. The relentless Nazi onslaught ensured that ever-increasing numbers of British citizens were killed or severely injured, and tons of the country's shipping, food, oil, weapons, and supplies found their way to the bottom of the Atlantic Ocean.

It was only the tireless valor, unselfish courage, and remarkable stamina of the Royal Air Force, the RAF, helped by the rough and unstable English Channel, that so far prevented Germany from invading Britain. As Churchill had rightly told Parliament five months earlier in August 1940 about the RAF, "Never in the field of human conflict was so much owed by so many to so few."

But as more and more RAF planes and pilots were lost defending their island home, nearly everyone in Britain was certain the German invasion would come when their country's tempestuous winter weather ended and their English Channel's turbulent seas calmed.

Young children were evacuated north to the interior parts of the country, while new recruits trained with cars and lorries pretending to be tanks, and pensioners and home watchers drilled with broomsticks as rifles.

Despite the fact that living in Britain was extraordinarily difficult, things were far worse in Nazi occupied Europe. Most people on the Continent had but three choices when it came to the Nazis: *cooperate, resist,* or *hide*. And when it came to resistance or hiding, people quickly learned about how skilled the German secret police—the Gestapo—were at getting people to turn on each other and turn *in* each other.

Everyone in occupied Europe lived in constant fear, and if they happened to be Jews, gypsies, eastern Europeans, homosexuals, mentally or physically challenged, professors, clergy, writers, intellectuals, prisoners of war, or political dissidents, typically their fear was not long-lived. When caught, these "vermin," as the Nazis called them, had their belongings and assets confiscated, and were either executed immediately or sent to one of the many Nazi Concentration camps to work and died shortly after.

The only truc way to ensure one's survival in Europe was to escape from the continent, and the short flights from Lisbon to Poole Harbor were not only a chance to live, but also a real chance at a new life and better destiny. England was the last waypoint for Europeans trying to live free, and London was quickly becoming their Alamo.

As the dozens of people waiting on the dock in Poole Harbor watched the KLM flight touch down in the harbor and taxi toward the dock, their excitement grew, and their voices rose in volume. With communications in Europe almost as difficult as travel, most of the people waiting had no way of knowing if the people they believed were on the plane, actually were. The waiting crowd pressed forward toward the plane as it approached the dock, excitedly waiting for its engines to shut down and its rear door to open.

One of the people waiting was Brendan Bracken, the polished, curly red-haired Irishman, who was Winston Churchill's Private Secretary. Bracken stood back from the crowd, with his foot on the bumper of his green Morris Eight as the plane shut down its engines and the crew secured its lines to the dock. It had been a couple of years since Bracken last saw Harry Hopkins at Averell Harriman's summer place on Long Island's gold coast, and he was anxious to see him again.

Bracken remembered how puzzled and terribly disappointed Churchill looked when he was told that President Roosevelt was sending Harry Hopkins to see him. Though the look on Churchill's face was almost comical as he removed his cigar and asked, "Who?" there was no comedy in his aspect as he quickly became angry at the idea of FDR sending a nobody to meet him at this terrible time. With things as desperate as they were in England, it took less than a moment for Churchill to launch into a full-blown, arm-waving, cigar-chewing, word-and-sputum-spitting rant about this unknown Hopkins fellow.

Churchill bellowed at Bracken as he rose from his seat with smoke escaping from his mouth, nose, and ears, wondering out loud if US Ambassador Joseph Kennedy was the man responsible for Hopkins's visit. "It had to be Kennedy," Churchill fumed. "Why else," he shouted, "would Roosevelt send someone who couldn't possibly help England during these desperate days, unless, of course, Kennedy convinced him England would never win nor deserved to win?"

Fortunately, Bracken knew Hopkins. So as Churchill flung himself into that dark and depressing place he called his "Black Dog," Bracken calmly told Churchill how much he liked and respected Hopkins, and how impressed he was by Hopkins, and about Hopkins's close relationship with President Roosevelt.

Despite Bracken's compelling endorsement of Hopkins, Churchill continued to sulk inside the swirling haze of his cigar smoke. That was when Bracken figuratively grabbed him by his lapels and insisted that he treat Hopkins as if he were the President himself.

"Whether you like him or not is unimportant," said Bracken firmly to his difficult boss, trying to shake him out of his self-pity. "We need America's help!" he added, almost shouting at a startled Churchill, and, truth be told, Bracken enjoyed it.

"And you, Mr. Prime Minister," Bracken continued, undaunted by his boss's petulance, "you need Hopkins to give FDR an accurate, unbiased assessment of our country's situation and our needs. It is up to you to make Mr. Hopkins feel very welcome here in England!" said Bracken firmly in closing.

Bracken's impassioned plea had the effect he hoped for, and Churchill seemed to pull back from the abyss. Churchill would later say that he sent Bracken to meet Harry Hopkins, President Franklin Roosevelt's personal envoy, and ordered a special train to transport him to London. The truth was, if not for Bracken, Churchill would have surely let Hopkins find his own way.

Bracken watched as the passengers disembarked from the rear door of the plane, and the dock became a frantic and emotional scene of people running toward each other, hugging, kissing, praying on their knees, looking frantically in the crowd for a loved one, and sobbing uncontrollably as they touched British soil for the first time. For those on the dock that day, these first moments with their loved ones who were able to escape Nazi Europe would remain among the most cherished memories of their lives.

But there was no Hopkins.

Bracken started walking toward the dock. "We must check that plane," Bracken said to his driver, a British Army officer, who moved quickly toward the aircraft. Bracken closed on the plane tied to the dock and climbed through its open rear door. He stood stock still in the center aisle and waited for his eyes to adjust to the darkness inside the aircraft.   In the darkness, Bracken heard the sound of water slapping against the plane's skis and fuselage, and a metallic clicking sound near the center of the plane. There was a dark shape in a seat against the window.

As Bracken made his way slowly down the aisle, he discovered the dark shape was Hopkins, who was slumped over with his chin in his chest, feebly trying to remove his seat belt. Judging by the way Hopkins looked, it wasn't obvious to Bracken that he was going to make it—either out of the plane, or at all.

"Harry?" Bracken called out, half expecting no reply.

"I can't open the damn thing," whispered Hopkins, barely lifting his head from his chest.

"They make these bloody things so damn complicated," a relieved Bracken responded. Bracken stepped into the row, reached in, and unclasped Hopkins's seat belt.

"Thanks, Brendan." Hopkins smiled weakly, pushing the belt off him. After a moment, he grabbed the back of the seat in front of him to try to stand, and his hand slipped. He fell back into his seat.

"Let me help," Bracken said, reaching in and putting his hand under Hopkins's arm to help him stand and move to the center aisle. "A damn long flight from America," Bracken said, helping Hopkins. "Three days?"

"Four," replied Hopkins, moving toward the open rear door using the backs of the airplane's seats to support and steady himself.

"The Prime Minister has arranged a special train to take you to London," Bracken informed Hopkins as he followed him to the open door.

"They have Scotch on that train?" asked Hopkins.

"Plenty." Bracken smiled.

"Feeling better already."

#

The special train waiting for Hopkins was Churchill's private train and just three cars long. It did not take long before the train's movement, the sound and cadence of its wheels against the track, and the Scotch in his hand had Hopkins feeling better. In fact, Bracken actually thought Hopkins's transformation from the plane to the train was miraculous. Bracken was not quite sure how Hopkins managed to go from barely able to speak and as pale as paper to looking fit and full of energy, but he was glad he did. As the train headed to Waterloo Station, they sat at a table against a window in the dining car. A white-coated waiter, who was actually a British Army sergeant, approached.

"Are you certain I cannot bring you something to eat, sir?" the waiter asked Hopkins.

"No, thank you. Just some more medicine," replied Hopkins, holding up his glass of Scotch.

"Right away, sir," the waiter replied. He turned to retrieve the bottle of Scotch on the bar and returned to pour another drink for Hopkins.

"We will pack a box for you with some food for later tonight," the waiter said.

"Thank you," replied Hopkins, "but that's not necessary."

"I have my orders, sir," the waiter responded with a smile and turned toward the galley.

"Cheers, Harry," Bracken said, raising his glass to Hopkins.

"Cheers," Hopkins responded, feeling like he was coming back to life.

Outside the train windows, they passed a small, empty British village with some of its buildings destroyed by German bombs.

"This has been going on since September?" Hopkins asked, pointing to the bombed buildings.

Bracken nodded. "Longer. Goering started out bombing our air bases but quickly turned his attention to our people. They are trying to wear us down."

Hopkins turned back to the window and saw a formation of twelve Spitfires—three groups of four—heading in the same direction as the train. Seeing Hopkins tracking the Spitfires, Bracken explained, "I suspect the Nazis are on their way. Happily, our Royal Air Force makes the Nazis pay dearly each time they cross the Channel."

After the Spitfires flew out of sight, the train passed several anti-aircraft batteries guarding the tracks and then rolled past a magnificent and majestic English countryside with a lone large estate standing in the distance. In the early evening light, it was a stunningly beautiful setting of green fields, hills, and trees surrounding the estate, untouched by the war.

"Is it any wonder you guys have the best damn poets in the world?" Hopkins said in awe of the landscape. "Look at this place."

Hopkins quickly turned to Bracken and looked him squarely in his eyes. "Are you going to let Hitler take these fields from you?"

"No," Bracken said, sounding very sure, though he really didn't know if his prediction was accurate.

As Bracken held Hopkins's gaze, he suddenly flinched when several bombs exploded nearby, followed quickly by several others in the distance. At the far end of the car, a British Army officer entered the dining car and spoke to the waiter. The waiter quickly turned toward the other staff in the car, motioning for them to pull down the train's window shades.

"I beg your pardon, sir," the waiter said, calmly approaching Bracken and Hopkins. "We will soon arrive at Clapham Junction, and we must black out the train."

"Of course," replied Bracken.

As Bracken reached to pull down his window shade, an incendiary bomb exploded several hundred feet from the train, and the fire from the explosion ignited the tracks. The bomb was too close for Bracken. He and Hopkins felt the concussion and saw the blaze erupt just as he lowered the shade.

"Sir. We should be ready for a rapid evacuation, if necessary," the waiter's tone was calm and suggested to Hopkins that he had seen this many times before.

"Thank you," said Bracken, sounding like he, on the other hand, was not accustomed to being bombed. "Clapham Junction and Waterloo Station are favorite targets for the Nazis," Bracken explained to Harry.

As the train slowed, making its approach into Clapham Junction, there were several explosions in succession that shoved a wall of air against the side of the train, moving dishes, glasses, and ashtrays inside the dining car. Hopkins's Scotch looked like it was on a ship in a heavy sea and spilled on the table.

Moments later, they heard the thunderous repetitive blasts of the large anti-aircraft guns guarding Clapham Junction. The sound of the big guns competed with the explosions of the Luftwaffe's bombs, to create a frightening medley of explosions, thuds, rattles, and whistles, with the sounds of gravel and falling debris hitting the roof and sides of the train.

At Waterloo Station, there were more than a dozen British reporters standing on the platform waiting for the American President's emissary. With each explosion and anti-aircraft round, the reporters flinched in unison. It looked like a macabre dance routine that would have been comical were it not for their dangerous circumstances. Though they didn't know it, every single reporter, to a man, had the exact same thought at the exact same time: "I am not paid nearly enough to be out here waiting for some American no one knows."

As Hopkins's train stopped and clouds of steam escaped from its bowels onto the platform, the bombs thankfully seemed to move further away from the station, and the pulsating booms from the anti-aircraft guns seemed to slow. When Hopkins and Bracken appeared at the train door, the reporters waiting on the platform almost let out an audible sigh of relief. In fact, on seeing Hopkins, one of the reporters from the *Daily Mail* shouted, "Thank bloody Christ!"

Hopkins had hardly touched the platform when the reporters began shouting questions at him, most of which were difficult to hear. When one reporter with a high tenor voice shouted, "Mr. Hopkins, how was your trip?" a bomb exploded very close to the station, causing all of the reporters to instinctively duck and squat.

"The trip was good and I feel fine," Hopkins shouted back and, at Bracken's urging, continued to move through the crowd toward the terminal. As Hopkins and Bracken navigated the platform through the reporters, a distinguished-looking, middle-aged man emerged from the crowd with his hand extended.

"Hello, Bracken," said Herschel Johnson, shaking hands with Brendan.

"Herschel," said Bracken with a nod.

"Mr. Hopkins," Johnson extended his hand. "Herschel Johnson, the charge from the US Embassy. Would you come with me, sir? We will see to your luggage."

Hopkins turned to Bracken. "I appreciate all of this, Brendan," Hopkins said, shaking Bracken's hand.

"We are happy you are here, Harry. I will see you tomorrow," Bracken replied, sounding anxious to keep moving out of harm's way amid the backdrop of distant explosions.

By the time Hopkins sat with Herschel Johnson in the rear of the US Embassy car on their way to Claridge's Hotel, the early evening had turned to night, and London's streets were dark. Inside their car, the radio played Edward R. Murrow's broadcast from a London rooftop as German bombs fell and fires erupted. Like millions of other Americans, Hopkins was a regular listener of Murrow's broadcasts, which began with him declaring, "This is London calling," and finished with the sounds and descriptions of real-time London bombings.

Long-faced and dark-haired, Edward R. Murrow had a similar look and gravitas to that of famed screen actor Humphrey Bogart. Murrow was CBS Radio's top European Correspondent, and along with William Shirer in Germany, was America's eyes, ears, and voice in London and Nazi Germany. Winston Churchill may have mobilized the English language and sent it into battle, but it was America's thirty-two-year-old Murrow who regularly brought

Britain's conflict into the homes of Americans. His descriptions of London under siege not only gripped America but transformed its understanding of Britain's duress and grit.

"I am Edward R. Murrow and this is London calling, Murrow said, launching his broadcast over the car's radio. *"I'm standing on a rooftop looking out over the city. For reasons of national as well as personal security, I am unable to tell you the exact location from which I am speaking. Off to my left, far away in the distance, I can see just that faint, red, angry snap of anti-aircraft bursts against the dark sky. A few minutes ago, the guns in the immediate vicinity were working. I can look across just at the building not far away and see something that looks like a splash of white paint down the side. And I know from daylight observation that about a quarter of that building has disappeared, hit by a bomb the other night..."*

"Where is he broadcasting from?" Hopkins asked Johnson.

"Don't know. Probably near the BBC. About a half mile away from here."

"Can you organize a meeting with Murrow for me tomorrow evening at 9 p.m. in my hotel room?" Hopkins asked.

"Sure. I'll do it as soon as we get back," Johnson replied easily.

Outside the car, Hopkins could hear the drone of many aircraft flying above London, and the constant thud of anti-aircraft fire searching for the German planes that were unloading their bombs onto London's dark streets.

Despite Murrow's bravery standing on a rooftop, and his skill in capturing the imagination of his listeners with his vibrant descriptions of the devastation descending on London from above, he was never able to completely describe the sheer human terror of Londoners in the city's dark streets below. Murrow and others were always left to sort out London's human tragedy the morning after.

Most Londoners spent their nights in the Underground Station to shelter themselves and hopefully live another day. Others, like the group of young men drinking pints at the corner pub or the young couple making love in the dark alley between two buildings, lived their lives with the certainty that they would live forever.

The young couple was about a half mile away from Hopkins's car against a wall in a narrow, dark alley. She, with her coat open, skirt up, back to the wall, and legs around his waist, and he inside her, with his face buried in her neck, relishing the feeling of the two of them striving toward mutual relief in a world gone mad. Though there were dozens of people running down the street and screaming over the horrific sound of the planes, bombs, and guns, the couple was unseen and heard none of it. They only heard the sound of their own heavy breathing as they worked themselves toward a climax, thinking how they couldn't wait to do it again.

The woman held tight to her partner with her eyes closed, loving the feeling of him breathing on her bare neck and driving his hips into her. She held tight to her lover, and when she heard the loud drone of engines above, she opened her eyes and saw the silhouettes of eight Heinkel He-111 bombers flying directly overhead in the dark night sky. At first, she wasn't sure. But as they made love between those two buildings and she saw the bombs from the Heinkel's belly descending directly above her, she was certain. She closed her eyes just as one of the Heinkel bombs landed, tearing apart her, her lover, and the two buildings.

No more lovers. No more heavy breathing. No more buildings.

The constant sound of streams of anti-aircraft fire lashing the night sky joined with the deafening sound of German bombers and their deadly bombs. Within seconds, another German bomb struck the corner pub, killing the young men with their pints, while a third bomb struck the building directly across the street from where the lovers stood. The explosion from that bomb sent a wave of bricks, glass, and debris flying across the street just as fifteen Londoners were running past, trying to reach the Underground Station at the end of the street. They were all killed instantly. Unknown until the following morning, on this night, three German bombs killed twenty-five people on that street in London and wounded forty others.

There was no reason. It was all random. Just bad, bad luck.

As Hopkins drove through the dark city, he couldn't help but feel like he was listening to some sort of macabre symphony of wailing sirens, exploding bombs, people screaming, buildings burning, planes flying, anti-aircraft guns thumping, and debris falling.

"Will this go on all night?" Hopkins asked Johnson.

"Most nights there are a couple of waves," replied Johnson. "Usually, an early show with incendiaries to light up the city for their friends and then a late show with the real big ones. They started early tonight," he added matter-of-factly. "Since you're staying at Claridge's, we will have dinner tonight at Claridge's. They have a bomb shelter in their basement."

"I hope it's not inconvenient for you," Hopkins replied.

"Not at all. I live at Claridge's too. I also invited General Raymond Lee, our Military Attaché, to join us. He will help you figure out if the British really need everything they ask us for."

"Actually, I'm more interested in understanding if they will ask for enough,"

replied Hopkins, turning to look out the window into the dark street. A bomb whistled and exploded several streets away, lighting up a dark London neighborhood in a ghastly orange glow. Hopkins looked through the windshield as the light from the explosion dissipated and a deep blackness returned to the streets outside the car.

"How the hell can you see?" Hopkins asked the driver.

"You get used to it," the security officer said, never taking his eyes off the road. "You have to go slow and watch out for people walking out here."

Hopkins turned to look out his window and, backlit by a fire that was burning blocks away, he saw dozens of silhouetted, frightened people quickly walking down the dark street in front of crumbling buildings. It was an unnerving and eerie scene.

"Where are they going?" Hopkins pointed to the silhouettes.

"The Underground tube entrance at the end of the road," answered Johnson, looking out Hopkins's window at the silhouettes. It's their bomb shelter."

After a moment, Hopkins turned to Johnson. "You really have to admire these people," he said. "Stay at home, and a Nazi bomb might get you. Go to a bomb shelter, and one of your near-sighted neighbors might cripple you with his car."

"Welcome to London," said Johnson.

CHAPTER ELEVEN

"You are, it seems, Lord Root of the Matter."

The following morning, Hopkins was up early and feeling surprisingly good after his long trip and adventurous night. When he entered the well-appointed living room of his suite, he was pleased to see a small table set up with a crisp linen tablecloth, napkins, polished silverware, a pot of coffee, and a basket of toast, scones, and biscuits. He was not sure how it all got there, but he was glad it did.

Hopkins pulled a briefing document from his briefcase that was prepared for him by Secretary of State Cordell Hull. He sat at the table, poured himself a cup of coffee, and lit a cigarette. The first cigarette of the day, especially if it was accompanied by good coffee, always tasted the best.

The US State Department had arranged for Hopkins to stay at Claridge's and, unknown to him, had also arranged for a valet to take care of him during his stay.   As he sat reading his briefing document, an immaculately dressed middle-aged British gentleman in a custom-tailored black suit and black tie, entered Hopkins's suite carrying Hopkins's pressed suit, shirt, tie, and shined shoes. "Good morning, sir," the valet said as he walked past Hopkins into the bedroom with his clothes in hand.

"Good morning," Hopkins responded, not quite sure who the man was, but thinking that by his look, he may have dropped in from Buckingham Palace.

The valet emerged from the bedroom with Hopkins's hat in his hand, and Hopkins noticed his hat looked to be in better shape than it had in a long time. "My name is Lyons, sir," the valet reported, his accent perfect upper-class British English.

"Did you arrange for this, Lyons?" asked Hopkins, pointing to his breakfast table.

"Yes, sir. I hope it is satisfactory," Lyons replied cheerfully. "If there is anything else you would like, I would be pleased to see to it."

"Thank you, Lyons. This is fine," Hopkins assured him, and trying to determine what else Lyons may have done, asked, "Did you press my suit and shine my shoes?"

"Yes, sir."

"Any chance you would like to live in America, Lyons?" Hopkins teased.

"I would like to visit New York City someday," Lyons politely answered.

"It's a great city."

"May I pour you some more coffee, sir?"

"I can do it."

"It is my pleasure, sir."

As Lyons picked up the pot and poured more coffee, Hopkins put out his cigarette and opened his briefcase.

"Do you like eggs, Lyons?" Hopkins asked, removing a box from his briefcase.

"Eggs, sir?"

"They gave me this box on the train last night," Hopkins said, handing the box to Lyons. "There are a couple of hard-boiled eggs in there, with some crackers, and celery. It would be a shame if it went to waste."

"I should not accept it, sir," Lyons demurred, holding the box in his hand.

"Please, enjoy it," insisted Hopkins, and sat back at the table to light another cigarette.

"With your permission, sir, the eggs would be a treat for my two sons," said Lyons, genuinely touched by Hopkins's generosity.

"Sure."

"Sir, I want to mention that when I unpacked your suitcase, I put your medicine bag in your night table."

"Thank you, Lyons."

"Sir, if I may, I also noticed you forgot your long underwear. January in London can be very cold."

"Long underwear, huh?"

"Yes, sir. If you agree, we should purchase several sets of long underwear for you," Lyons suggested.

"Thank you," Hopkins replied, grateful he might be able to stay warm.

"Not at all, sir. I will have the underwear here for you this afternoon," replied Lyons, sounding like he had accomplished his mission. Hopkins returned to his briefing document, thinking Lyons was done.

"One final thought, Mr. Hopkins," Lyons started again.

"I need a new hat," Hopkins said, seeing Lyons holding his hat.

Lyons smiled. "I took the liberty of steaming and shaping it this morning, and did wonder if you would like me to purchase a new hat for you."

"Lyons, I'm pretty sentimental about that old hat," Hopkins said, deciding to draw a line on his clothing needs.

Like the good valet he was, Lyons understood their conversation about clothes was over. "I completely understand, Mr. Hopkins."

"I really want you to consider moving to America," said Hopkins, and this time he wasn't kidding.

"You are too kind, sir," Lyons replied, satisfied he had gotten off to a good start with his new charge.

"Lyons, are you on duty this evening?"

"Yes, sir. I have been assigned to you for your entire stay, and I am available whenever you may need me."

"Do you know Edward R. Murrow?"

"Yes, sir. Everyone in London knows Mr. Murrow. We listen to his radio broadcasts regularly."

"He will be visiting me tonight at 9 p.m. for drinks. If I am late, please make him comfortable."

"By all means, sir."

#

After Hopkins finished his morning meetings at the Foreign Office with Anthony Eden and Lord Halifax, Hopkins had come to the conclusion that Lyons was right. He would definitely need long underwear.

With London's gray day, frosty wind, and damp, old buildings, Hopkins was cold from head to toe, through and through, down to his bones. By the time he drove to 10 Downing Street for his luncheon with Churchill, he found himself longing for a glass of Scotch to restart his internal boiler.

Hopkins's driver, last night's US Embassy security officer, drove slowly as he approached Number 10, knowing his car was being closely watched by the armed soldiers standing next to stacks of sandbags against the buildings and the soldiers with machine guns above the car in the second-floor windows across the street. Hopkins exited the car and saw huge timbers braced up against the walls of the Treasury building next to Number 10. On seeing Hopkins, the soldiers on duty snapped to attention, and Brendan Bracken opened the door of the famous building.

"Did you sleep well?" Bracken asked, shaking hands with Hopkins.

"Very," replied Hopkins, still too cold to start up a conversation.

"Come in and warm up," Bracken suggested. "The Prime Minister is finishing a meeting."

A butler entered the entrance hall to take Hopkins's coat, and though Hopkins thought about keeping it on, he decided that good form required him to hand it over. With Bracken leading the way, Hopkins was surprised to see how tired and worn the inside of the famed address looked, with its black and white floor and main staircase in need of repair. Then again, he realized, the British government had bigger fish to fry than keeping up appearances.

After a brief tour of the building, Bracken escorted Hopkins to the Basement dining room, whose walls and ceiling were supported by heavy wooden beams and trusses. In addition to a dining table set for two people and a roaring fire in the fireplace, Hopkins spotted a cloth-covered table in the corner of the room with whiskey, Scotch, sherry, and several bottles of champagne in a bucket.

"How about a sherry, Harry?" asked Bracken as he approached the table.

"A Scotch would be good. Thanks," Hopkins responded, looking at the formidable beams supporting the ceiling. "Has the building been bombed?"

"Just once. A few months ago. Actually, it was Treasury next door that took the brunt of the blast, but our upstairs kitchen and dining area were destroyed," reported Bracken as he poured Hopkins his Scotch.

"Anyone hurt?"

"Unfortunately, we lost three people," Bracken said, returning to Hopkins with a glass of Scotch in hand. Though Bracken sounded unemotional about the bombing, Hopkins sensed he had tucked that memory away for another day.

"Sorry to hear that," Hopkins offered, and Bracken simply nodded.

"I must go now, but I will see you after your meeting with the PM. He should be in soon. Glad to see you are feeling better." Bracken smiled and left the room.

Alone in the room, Hopkins walked to another cloth-covered table that held several frames with photographs and surveyed the pictures in each. As he picked up a frame that held the photo of a beautiful woman and a child, the door to the dining room opened, and Hopkins turned to see a very old, plain-looking woman enter the room carrying two cups of soup on a tray. "Good afternoon, sir," the older woman said to Hopkins and placed the cups on the plates already on the table.

"Good afternoon," Hopkins answered politely and turned back to look at the photo.

As the server approached the door to leave, the door flung open, and in walked Winston Churchill wearing a black jacket, a vest, and striped trousers with a gold chain across his midsection. He seemed in a hurry, walking directly toward Hopkins with his hand extended. He was much shorter than Hopkins expected.

"Good afternoon, Mr. Hopkins. Welcome," Churchill said, smiling.

Hopkins returned the photograph to the table and shook hands with Churchill. "It's good to meet you, Prime Minister."

"I see you have already met my daughter-in-law Pamela and my grandson Winston," Churchill said, pointing to the photograph.

"She is very pretty," Hopkins complimented.

"My son Randolph is a very lucky man. He is currently overseas. A lieutenant in my old regiment, the Fourth Hussars," Churchill replied, and Hopkins sensed there was more to the story of Churchill and his son.

"I am pleased to see we have given you a drink," commented Churchill as he noticed the Scotch in Hopkins's hand.

"Your staff is taking good care of me," Hopkins assured him.

"Please come and sit before our soup gets cold. I don't like cold consommé."

As Churchill and Hopkins sat at the table, the older woman returned.

"Margaret, please pour me a glass of champagne," instructed Churchill, and then turned to Hopkins. "I have a weakness for Pol Roger," Churchill confessed to him, and dove into consuming the cup of consommé on his plate without waiting for Hopkins. Hopkins followed his host.

"I hope your trip went well," said Churchill between spoonsful of soup. Hopkins had the impression Churchill was very hungry.

"It did," Hopkins replied. "Thank you for sending the train for me."

"Considering our nightly Nazi visits, I was more than a little concerned about your safe arrival in London."

The older woman placed a glass of Pol Roger in front of Churchill.

Churchill picked up the glass and held it toward Hopkins. "Cheers," he said.

"Cheers," replied Hopkins, lifting his glass.

"Please convey my regards to the President and tell him the Former Naval Person looks forward to meeting him as well."

"I will. The President regrets not being able to leave Washington at the moment," replied Hopkins, knowing that Churchill had begun a dance of sorts and was now moving him to the center of the dance floor.

"I understand how that can be," answered Churchill, wanting Hopkins to know he was not unreasonable. "Unfortunately, our long-distance communications are difficult and often result in more questions than answers. A face-to-face meeting to discuss all of the issues thoroughly would help tremendously."

"The President agrees," Hopkins said simply, painting his first strokes of FDR's image as sympathetic to England's cause.

As the older woman removed their consommé cups and placed a plate of cold beef in front of them, Hopkins layered in more color to his picture. "He sent me here to tell you that at all costs and by all means he will carry you through."

Churchill looked across the table at Hopkins, thrilled to hear Hopkins's message of support. "It is of great comfort to me to know President Roosevelt supports our cause," Churchill said sincerely, though he remained suspicious after his experiences with Ambassador Kennedy.

"He does, and I am here to find out exactly what you need to win," said Hopkins, assuring Churchill of the purpose of his visit.

Churchill was more than a little surprised by Hopkins's directness and unequivocal support. He didn't expect it and certainly didn't expect to hear it so clearly and so soon. He sat observing Hopkins and balancing his own personal caution against his country's desperate need for help. He quickly determined he would follow Hopkins's lead and get to the point.

"I have instructed our ministers to provide you with every detail of information and opinion we have so you can know the exact state of England's urgent need and exact material assistance Britain requires to win the war," Churchill said, repeating the very instructions he had given his ministers just days ago.

"Good," Hopkins said simply, comfortable knowing that they had completed their first dance together.

Churchill sat across from Hopkins, slathering large amounts of jelly on his cold beef while Hopkins, who was not hungry, watched him.

"Harry," Churchill said, calling Hopkins by his first name and confirming Hopkins's positive assessment of their emerging relationship. "You must eat cold beef with a large amount of jelly."

"Thank you, but this is fine. I don't eat large amounts of anything anymore," Hopkins said, trying to give himself some room if Churchill interpreted his behavior as impolite.

Churchill pushed the plate of jelly across the table in front of Hopkins. "Have more jelly with your cold beef." Churchill was selling now. "You will like it."

Hopkins thought that if the foundation of their whole relationship was based on his eating enough jelly with his beef, he would immediately reach across the table for more.

"Just to be polite," Hopkins said, reaching for the jelly.

"What can you tell me of America's view of England and our current situation?" Churchill asked, trying to determine whether Kennedy had poisoned America's well as far as Great Britain was concerned.

Hopkins sensed this question signaled a new dance and an inflection point in their relationship. He decided to tell Churchill the unvarnished truth.

"There is a feeling in some quarters that you don't like America, Americans, or the President," Hopkins said, intentionally sounding casual.

Again, surprised by Hopkins's candor, Churchill put down his fork and wiped his lips with his napkin. "I must say that is very disturbing to hear," Churchill said, clearly annoyed. It made Hopkins wonder if he had made a tactical error.

"I am convinced Ambassador Kennedy," continued Churchill, "promoted that idea, but it is certainly not true. The President must recognize that opinion was put forward by someone with a number of poorly formed observations and judgments."

"Our ambassador has strong opinions," Hopkins replied, pleased that Churchill was blaming Kennedy and knowing there was no love lost between Kennedy and FDR.

"His opinions are unsubstantiated, like his opinion that we will not survive against the Nazis," Churchill said, abandoning his lunch as the heat rose in his gullet with the red in his cheeks. "Such caustic opinions have inserted doubts into the relationship between our two countries, and hampered our ability to fight back against the Nazis. Not to mention that his distorted views continue to help our adversaries."

"So, England will hold up against the Nazis," Hopkins stated off-handedly, seeming to ignore Churchill's emotion.

Hopkins's comment caught Churchill off guard, and he felt his Kennedy-induced distemper subside. Churchill sat looking at Hopkins, thinking how he liked the tenor of this man sitting across from him at his table. Despite the fact that he looked cold and a bit pale, Churchill assessed that he was genuine, honest, and there was no fluff about him at all. He seemed to cut to the chase and speak directly to the point at hand. It did not escape Churchill that his assessment of Hopkins spoke volumes about FDR's judgment in sending him to London.

"The truth is I do not know if we will hold up against them," answered Churchill calmly. "We have held up so far, and I believe we will hold up again. And I am very confident we will continue to hold our own in the air in the face of the Luftwaffe. Our Royal Air Force performs incredibly well."

"And if the Nazis invade?" Hopkins asked the question that was on everyone's mind, including Churchill's.

"Even if they did gain a foothold on our island—even with one hundred thousand men—we will drive them out. And if Hitler decides to use poison gas, we will reply in kind." And then he quickly added to be sure Hopkins did not misunderstand, "Though you and the President must know we will never be the first to use such weapons."

Churchill put down his fork and knife and lit his cigar. Hopkins lit his cigarette, and as he blew out the match, Churchill noticed him shudder in the cold and damp room.

"Another Scotch?" Churchill asked.

"This is fine. Thank you," Hopkins replied with his cigarette between his lips, his hands folded together in his lap, and his shoulders scrunched forward in an effort to keep warm.

"Let's go up to the Cabinet Room. There is a better fire there."

"You must tell me everything you need," Hopkins said as he rose from the table.

"Our most urgent need, in light of the attacks on our shipping, is for the United States to reassert the principle of freedom of the seas. We need escorts in the North Atlantic, more destroyers, more fighter aircraft," Churchill said as the men walked. "I believe our strategy for winning should be based on our sea power, supported by air power. We will be sure to provide you with detailed reports and lists before you return to Washington."

The door to the dining room opened, and Brendan Bracken entered. "Sir, apologies for interrupting, but Sir John Dill needs to see you," Bracken said to Churchill.

Churchill turned to Hopkins. "Forgive me. I must attend this meeting. Sir John Dill is the Chief of the Imperial General Staff. Please plan to stay with us this weekend. I usually spend weekends at Chequers, but our security people say they are expecting a full moon. And since the Nazis know you are visiting us, we will spend this weekend at Ditchley instead. It's a beautiful estate just north of Oxford. Brendan will see that you get there."

Churchill extended his hand, and Hopkins shook it.

"I am glad you are here," Churchill said, and he was.

"So am I."

#

When Hopkins arrived back at his suite at Claridge's shortly after nine o'clock, his pockets carried dozens of papers and his brain an equal number of mental notes that he had made during his many meetings that day. Despite the very long day of introductions, meetings, and a deluge of information, he was feeling surprisingly good.

As he entered his suite, Lyons came to the door to retrieve his hat, coat, and briefcase. "Mr. Murrow is inside, sir. Can I get you something to drink?"

"Scotch."

"Sir, I am happy to report that I was able to secure three pairs of long underwear for you today," Lyons said quietly as he took Hopkins's coat.

"Not a minute too soon. I'm freezing my ass off," replied Hopkins.

"British long underwear has a long and successful history of curing that condition, sir," reported Lyons with a straight face. "I have a fire in the living room fireplace for you."

"Thank you, Lyons," Hopkins said, flattening down his hair as he walked into the living room to find Edward R. Murrow seated on the sofa and smoking a Camel cigarette with a Scotch in his hand.

"Ed, it's great to meet you." Hopkins shook hands with Murrow and settled into an easy chair across from Murrow. Lyons entered the room and placed Hopkins's Scotch on the table next to him.

"Should you need anything, sir, please ring for me," Lyons said and quickly left the room.

Hopkins raised his glass to Murrow. "Cheers, Ed," he said and took a sip.

"Cheers," replied Murrow, holding up his glass. "Damned courteous of you to allow me to interview you," Murrow said, smiling.

"The other way around," responded Hopkins, putting his glass on the table.

"Sorry?" Murrow's smile disappeared. He really wasn't sure what Hopkins meant.

"I'm interviewing you," Hopkins said easily.

"Interviewing me?" Murrow had no idea where this might be going.

"Yes. I want your views on Britain's capabilities, their spirit, and specifically Churchill," Hopkins said definitively.

"Is that why you're here?" Murrow was now intrigued and thought there might be a worthwhile story in tonight's meeting after all.

True to form, Hopkins responded candidly. "I'm here to figure out, first, if the British can make it. Second, assuming they can, what they will need to win."

"I heard you didn't beat around the bush," replied Murrow, realizing that Hopkins had just brought him into his circle of trust.

"Life's too short." Hopkins smiled.

"You want to know if they can make it?" Murrow decided to follow Hopkins's lead and cut to the chase.

Hopkins nodded, sipped his drink, but said nothing as he waited for Murrow to answer his own question. Murrow jumped into the water.

"Just look around," offered Murrow, a bit more impassioned than Hopkins expected. "They are tough. And I believe they finally have the right leader in Churchill."

"Win, place, or show?" Hopkins asked Murrow for his bet.

"I would put it on them to win."

"What do they need?"

Murrow leaned back into the sofa and lit another cigarette. He realized that Hopkins was now inviting him to play a new role—a role that would take him from being a radio reporter to someone who could possibly influence America's policies toward a foreign country. He took another sip of his Scotch.

"Unfortunately," Murrow began, "after Dunkirk and France's capitulation, they need everything."

"Everything," Hopkins repeated the word, urging Murrow to continue.

"Pretty much. They lost huge amounts of guns, ammunition, and equipment at Dunkirk. Lord Beaverbrook is doing a good job reviving their aircraft production, but the Nazis have been methodically cutting off the island—literally starving them on all fronts—food, supplies, everything."

There was a moment of silence, and after taking a long drag on his cigarette, Murrow decided to go all in by directly declaring his deeply held personal belief in a way he never would publicly. "The British desperately need America's help."

Hopkins had heard what he hoped he would hear and decided to pull Murrow in further.

"Off the record?" Hopkins asked Murrow and waited for his response.

"Sure."

"When Congress passes the new Lend-Lease Bill, we will be able to provide them with everything they need," Hopkins said, telling Murrow in so many words that he agreed with him.

"That bill is the President at his best," Murrow declared and by doing so told Hopkins exactly where he stood on America's isolationism.

"We think it will. But Ed, it's more than just the Lend-Lease Bill," cautioned Hopkins.

"How so?"

"There needs to be a working understanding between Britain and America, and I need to be the catalyst that will allow two prima donnas to see eye to eye."

"How can I help?" Murrow smiled, now understanding why he was the one being interviewed.

"I need to better understand Churchill and the men he sees after midnight."

"Let's get started," replied Murrow and raised his glass to Hopkins. "Cheers."

#

It was a clear, crisp, late Saturday night—early Sunday morning under a charcoal-colored sky filled with a bright moon, many stars, and German bombers flying above the blacked-out Ditchley Estate. While Churchill normally used Chequers as his weekend retreat, it was moonlit nights such as tonight that prompted his security staff to ask Ditchley's owner, Ronald Tree, a conservative MP, if the Prime Minister could use his estate.

The blacked-out building and the soldiers patrolling its perimeter were just silhouettes and shadows—hardly visible, even in the moonlight. Despite the darkness, the drone of the aircraft flying back to France and Germany had all of the soldiers guarding Ditchley craning their necks to make sure the giant, black, steel birds flying overhead did not release any of their lethal eggs.

Though it was nearly two in the morning, inside Ditchley's library, Churchill, Hopkins, and Bracken were still awake, drinking, smoking, and continuing their long day's talks. Hopkins was drinking Scotch and smoking Lucky Strikes, while Churchill and Bracken had brandy with cigars.

"I trust you packed the right clothes for this time of year?" Churchill asked Hopkins.

"My valet takes very good care of me. I have the best long underwear Fleet Street has to offer." Hopkins smiled.

"Clever man, your valet," Churchill said and then added casually, "the King told me he and the Queen enjoyed meeting with you. Is it true you believe our people are courageous?"

"I do," Hopkins said simply. "I am impressed by their courage and determination to meet the challenges facing the country."

Churchill took a long puff of his cigar and a sip of brandy, pleased to hear Hopkins's view of their efforts. "It is important for you to know we seek no treasure," said Churchill, "we seek no territorial gains, we seek only the right of men to be free. As a humble laborer returns from his work when the day is done and sees the smoke curling upward from his cottage home in the serene evening sky, we wish him to know that no banging of the secret police upon his door will disturb his leisure or interrupt his rest. We see government with the consent of the people and man's freedom to say what you will. What do you think the President would say to all of that?"

Hopkins stubbed out his cigarette, took a drink of his Scotch, and looked directly at Churchill, who thought Hopkins was going to launch into a commentary on the social responsibilities of a democracy.

Instead, Hopkins simply said, "I can tell you neither the President nor I gives a damn for any of that. You see, we're only interested in seeing that goddamn son of a bitch Hitler gets licked."

Churchill was taken aback, and after a few moments smiled at Hopkins. "You are, it seems, Lord Root of the Matter."

 "To Lord Root of the Matter," Bracken declared, holding his glass toward Hopkins.

"Hear, hear," Churchill affirmed, and he raised his glass to Hopkins. Bracken was right about Harry Hopkins after all.

On Monday morning, Churchill, the Former Naval Person, sent a cable to FDR, "I am most grateful to you for sending so remarkable an envoy who enjoys so high a measure of your intimacy and confidence."

CHAPTER TWELVE

"I shouldn't stay there too long, Harry."

Churchill gave Hopkins complete access to the inner workings of the British military and government, and Harry spent his days in London in a nearly constant series of meetings, conferences, and luncheons with military, production, foreign service leaders, and even the King and Queen. The result was a 360-degree view of Great Britain's faults, failures, requirements, and capabilities.

From insights provided by Foreign Minister Anthony Eden, to airplane production estimates freely offered by the often cantankerous Lord Beaverbrook, to General John Dill's less than optimistic outlook for the British Army, Hopkins was given an unimpaired view of England's challenges. It was a testament to Churchill's confidence in Harry that what began as his two-week visit became a six-week crash course on Great Britain and the war in Europe.

Perhaps the pinnacle of Hopkins's visit, and best evidence of Churchill's opinion of Hopkins, was Churchill's invitation to attend a meeting of his War Cabinet in the highly secret War Rooms under London's Whitehall. It was the first time a foreigner had ever been included inside that privileged circle.

The War Rooms were originally a group of basement offices under the New Public Offices, but they were now only accessible via a secret passage. They were the hub of Britain's wartime information and activity and the place where Britain's leading government ministers, military strategists, and Prime Minister Winston Churchill would meet, plan, and manage the continuous flow of emergencies that poured into the country.

When an intelligence officer entered the secure War Cabinet Room with a stack of folders in hand, Hopkins was seated at a U-shaped set of tables with Churchill; the Chief of the Royal Air Force, General Charles Portal; Churchill's military adviser, Pug Ismay; the Chief of the Imperial General Staff, General Sir John Dill; Chief of Home Defense, General Alan Brooke; the First Sea Lord of the Imperial Navy, Admiral Dudley Pound; and a second cousin of King George and a member of the Imperial Staff, Lord "Dickie" Mountbatten.

The intelligence officer handed a folder to Churchill.

"As of…?" asked Churchill as he opened the folder.

"Seven this morning, sir," replied the intelligence officer, passing the remaining folders to each person at the table.

"It appears they are proceeding with their invasion plans," Churchill said out loud as he read the folder. "May?" he asked.

"At the latest," said John Dill, the Chief of General Staff, emphasizing the word "latest." "If they do not invade by May, I do not believe they will invade this year," Dill announced confidently. "Hitler is slow to recognize just how difficult it will be for them. He is trying to maintain pressure on us while he decides."

"That would account for the on-again, off-again reports we get from Intelligence," Pug Ismay said directly to Churchill.

"Herr Hitler will not give up his invasion dreams easily," Churchill mused, still reviewing the reports. "Shouldn't we reinforce Dover?" he suddenly asked Dill.

"And if all of this activity is just a feint to keep us focused on the Pas-de-Calais?" asked Dill, clearly believing it was.

"Sir," General Alan Brooke, the Chief of Home Defense, spoke up. "They have brought in a very large rail gun in the Pas-de-Calais, and Dover has already reported several hits. That would seem to suggest their fleet of invasion barges in the French port is likely legitimate," he counseled Dill.

"Will their guns alone allow them to control the Straits of Dover, Admiral?" Churchill asked First Sea Lord Dudley Pound.

"I don't see how," Pound replied. "They must defeat our Navy to land in Dover. However, with their U-boats in France and the Atlantic, should they succeed in securing Dover and maintain their hold on the Pas-de-Calais, they can control the Straits with their guns and planes, and cut off our Navy from the Channel."

"Giving them access to our entire coast at will," Churchill added, sounding as if he were solving a riddle. Churchill then turned to Dill and asked, "Shouldn't we deploy more troops to Dover?"

"At this point, I think we should wait to see what his next move will be," Dill said, again sounding confident and certain.

"His next move?" Churchill was clearly irritated and waved the folder at Dill. "My dear general, they are loading barges with equipment, guns, and supplies twenty miles from our shore," he said, tossing the folder on the table.

Churchill then turned to General Brooke. "What do we have in reserve?"

"We can move a regiment immediately to Dover," responded Brooke quickly.

"Do it," Churchill ordered Brooke.

"Yes, sir," replied Brooke.

Observing the tense exchange, Hopkins sensed that Brooke had already had this argument in private with Dill and had been ordered to sit on his hands. He could tell that Brooke felt vindicated and Dill was, in his cool and unemotional British way, steaming hot. Hopkins surmised that General Alan Brooke wanted Dill's job, and Dill knew it. As it turned out, he was right. Within the year, Dill would be sent to the United States, and Brooke would take his job as Chief of the Imperial Staff.

"Just to be certain we all understand," said Dill directly to Churchill. "If we reinforce Dover, we will weaken the middle of our country."

"General. The Germans are not seafaring people," replied Churchill, sounding like a headmaster speaking to a middle school boy. "Should they invade, it is highly probable they will invade across the shortest distance between France and our island—and that is Dover from the Pas-de-Calais. We must prevent the Germans from ever gaining a foothold there at all costs," Churchill finished, angry with himself that he felt compelled to embarrass Dill in front of Hopkins. "Thank you, gentlemen," Churchill ended the meeting.

Everyone around the table rose, collected their materials, shook hands with Hopkins, and left the room, leaving Hopkins and Churchill in their places at the table. Churchill smoked his cigar and brooded.

"I wish you had witnessed a better meeting," said Churchill quietly to Hopkins.

"I'm honored you allowed me to attend," Hopkins said, sincerely pleased he was offered a firsthand look at the inner workings and personalities of Britain's War Cabinet.

"As you can see, General Dill and I have significant differences of opinion."

"With all the country is facing, it would be unusual if there weren't differences of opinion among your key advisers," reasoned Hopkins, trying to take some of the pressure off Churchill.

"Sometimes, Harry, it is difficult for me to see how we can possibly defeat our enemies in the face of our own differences," Churchill said out loud, and it made Hopkins realize just how far their relationship had grown in a short time. They were becoming colleagues.

"You will pull through this," Hopkins assured him.

"That is the interesting thing of it, Harry. I know we will. I know it."

#

Hopkins was again honored and more than pleased when Churchill invited him to join Clementine and Pug Ismay on his trip to inspect the British Fleet at Scapa Flow in the Orkney Islands off Scotland. Their itinerary was to travel by train and ship to tour the British Fleet at anchor and see Lord Halifax off to America. Churchill had appointed Halifax to replace Lord Lothian as Britain's new US ambassador.

Hopkins really didn't give the trip itself a second thought until he noticed Lyons had packed every bit of clothing he brought, and all three sets of his long underwear. When Hopkins asked Lyons why so many clothes, Lyons replied, "Because people who visit Northern Scotland in January have been known to plead with the devil himself for a brief stay in hell to warm up."

Hopkins boarded Churchill's private train, the same train car he and Brendan Bracken had taken from Poole Harbor to London when he first arrived. As they headed north through the British countryside to Scotland, Clementine and Pug Ismay were seated leisurely drinking tea and eating scones, while Churchill sat sipping a glass of whiskey and reading some documents.

Clementine, Churchill's silver-haired wife, was taller than her husband, and both regal in her stature and beautiful in her looks. A formidable person in her own right, her calm and even demeanor served her well as a counterbalance to Churchill's emotional impulsiveness.   Churchill loved her deeply and relied on her ever-rational intelligence and comforting support.

Clementine took to Hopkins almost immediately after they first met. In the short time since his arrival, she and Hopkins had formed a close relationship, with Clementine shielding her new friend from her husband's overbearing instincts and workaholic schedule. Clementine regularly intervened to ensure Hopkins got his rest and stayed warm in their country's old, cold manor houses.   Secretly, Clementine loved Hopkins's sense of humor and the way he teased Winston with his perfectly timed jabs. Hopkins had the gift of making Winston and her both laugh without bruising her husband's sensitive ego.

As the train rolled its way north, Hopkins sat across from Clementine with a Scotch in his hand, his overcoat buttoned to his neck, and his aging fedora pulled down over his head. Clementine instantly felt sympathy for her friend.

"You poor man. You look so cold," Clementine said, signaling for the steward.

"The Scotch helps," replied Hopkins.

Churchill looked up from his papers. "Macallan," Churchill bragged. "The best there is."

"Please bring us a few blankets," Clementine said to a steward who was standing by.

"Right away, ma'am," replied the steward.

"Not necessary, Clemmie," said Hopkins, but though he lightly protested, he was happy to know more wool was on the way.

"This old train is so drafty I can feel my hair blowing in the wind," replied Clementine, looking at Churchill, who she knew was listening despite his seeming concentration on his papers.

"The trip to Scapa Flow is invigorating," Churchill said defiantly, never looking up.

"Winston believes if he says it is so, it will be so," Clementine pushed back.

"Harry is in for a great adventure," Churchill responded and would not give ground.

"I'm very excited," said Hopkins, sounding like he was being taken to a dungeon.

Ismay and Clementine laughed out loud as the steward delivered several blankets.   Clementine rose from her seat and placed one blanket across Hopkins's legs and the other across the back of his shoulders.

Churchill looked up from his papers and, observing his wife taking care of Hopkins, couldn't resist. "You must be very special, Harry. I don't ever remember Clemmie giving me such a warm and comforting treatment."

"You never required such warm treatment because you always have an excess of hot air about you," shot back Clementine, satisfied Hopkins was now snug and warm.

Ismay and Hopkins smiled at Clementine's jab, and Churchill pouted.

When they arrived in Thurso, Scotland, at nine o'clock that night, a car whisked them straight to the dock where a large tug boat was waiting to transport them further.   When they exited the car,

Scotland's blustery, ice-cold wind cut against their skin and howled and shrieked through the tug boat's rigging.   Though tied to the dock, the tug boat and its gang plank bounced violently up and down in the wind and rough seas.

Churchill was the first to leave the car and, without waiting for the others, he bounded up the gang plank onto the tug boat, refusing to be helped by the two sailors waiting for him.   Clementine, Hopkins, and Ismay followed him up the gangplank, assisted by the sailors.

"Isn't it invigorating?" Churchill asked gleefully.

"For Eskimos," Clementine replied, and made her way to the bridge with Hopkins in tow.

Inside the tug's bridge, Churchill pointed to a British Navy destroyer barely visible in the distance, anchored in the middle of the bay. "We are headed for that destroyer there, Harry," Churchill said as the tow boat captain released her lines and guided the bouncing tug away from the dock toward the destroyer.

The tug's captain had to perform a very difficult maneuver to bring the tug immediately next to the destroyer. It was tricky on a calm day, let alone on a night like this one with its heavy winds and pounding sea. As the tug boat closed on the destroyer, bouncing and slamming into the water, Clementine clung to a steel rail inside the bridge and did her best to stay on her feet. She wondered why she ever agreed to join her husband in this unforgiving place.

Suddenly, the tug's floodlights lit up the side of the destroyer, and the destroyer immediately responded with her own. As the two ships approached each other, the light from their lamps bounced against the raging sea, turning the night into an eerie scene of shifting light and shadows that sliced wildly up, down, and across the two vessels.

Churchill stood on the tug's bridge thoroughly enjoying the adventure of the maneuver as the captain slowly nestled the tug next to the destroyer, and sailors on the lower and upper decks cast their ropes across to sailors on the deck of the destroyer. The tug and the destroyer heaved up and down, to and fro, and side to side, moving closer to, and away from each other in a very dangerous dance.

"Time for us to go," announced Churchill to the group. "Thank you, Captain."

They exited the bridge onto the deck and into the ferocious wind that slammed and buffeted the heavy boat. They could see the two ships were very close to each other, close enough to clearly see the destroyer captain standing on the deck of the ship.

Churchill held out his hand for Clementine, and when she took it, each sailor standing near the tug's rail took one of her arms and steadied her as she approached the opening. The deck of the tug boat rose several feet above the deck of the destroyer, then quickly fell below the same distance, making the move across to the destroyer extremely dangerous. Clementine settled her arms into the grips of the two sailors and watched intently as the two decks rose and fell above and below each other in the howling wind and rough seas.

"Go ahead, my dear," Churchill said over the wind. "The sailors will catch you."

As the tug's deck passed below the deck of the destroyer, the sailor holding Clementine's left arm said, "As we rise, ma'am, just step across. We will hold you, and the two sailors on the destroyer will catch you."

Clementine nodded and smiled, and as the deck of the tug started to rise to meet the deck of the destroyer, Clementine extended her leg like she was stepping over a large puddle and landed the toe of her right foot on the destroyer's deck. She was smoothly taken across the chasm between the ships by the two sailors on the tug, assisted by the two standing on the destroyer. Safely aboard the destroyer, Clementine thanked the sailors for their help and turned to glare at Churchill, who remained standing on the tug.

"Are you all right, Mrs. Churchill?" asked the destroyer's captain.

"Perfect, thank you, Captain," Clementine answered as Churchill smoothly crossed from the tug boat onto the destroyer's deck.

The captain saluted. "Welcome aboard, sir."

"Exhilarating!" Churchill exclaimed with a broad smile across his face as he saluted the captain.

"So pleasant, Winston," Clementine drawled sarcastically with one hand holding her hat and the other clutching the ship's rail as the wind whipped across the deck and her face.

Clementine looked across and saw Hopkins walking like a drunken sailor on the tug's deck. The tug's sailors there took Hopkins's arms and waited with him, trying to time his leap across. But just as Hopkins stepped forward to cross over to the destroyer, the tug pulled away from the destroyer, and Hopkins's foot missed the deck.

Hopkins dropped toward the sea below, but one of the destroyer's quick-thinking sailors grabbed him by the arm of his coat, and another did the same. They held Hopkins by his arms against the destroyer with his legs dangling between the two ships, which were still bobbing and careening back and forth next to each other.

"Winston!" Clementine called out, and Churchill, who had been watching the scene unfold, said calmly, "I shouldn't stay there too long, Harry."

The two sailors leaned into the rail for leverage and together hoisted Hopkins onto the destroyer deck just as the tug pushed against the sea and closed against the side of the destroyer. Hopkins would have been crushed were it not for the quick-thinking sailors.

"Are you all right?" Clementine gasped.

"Fine," Hopkins said, trying to sound calm. "Thanks," he said to the two sailors, and they saluted him.

Ismay, the last in the group, crossed over to the destroyer, and when he set foot on the destroyer's deck, both captains immediately released their lines to separate.

"My God, Harry, I thought we lost you," exclaimed Ismay as he approached Hopkins.

Churchill looked at Hopkins. "Harry, it's very dangerous to linger between two ships at sea. You must be decisive when making the leap."

Immediately, Clementine came to Hopkins's defense. "He will remember that the next time someone asks him to jump from one ship to another, at night, in an ice-cold, forty-mile-an-hour wind."

Clementine then turned away from her husband and took Hopkins's arm, "Let's get you inside."

"Right this way," the destroyer's captain said, pointing his hand toward a door on the deck.

Churchill stood watching Clementine and Hopkins enter the ship. He then looked at Ismay in a way that told Ismay he didn't understand what he had done to offend his wife.

Pug shrugged his shoulders, feigning ignorance.

#

The following morning, the heavy wind was gone, and the sea was calm, but the cold remained. When Hopkins woke, he looked out his cabin porthole and was greeted by a glossy gray sea and sky that was backlit by a yellow light. If he weren't so damned cold, Hopkins would have appreciated it more.

Sent by Churchill to fetch Hopkins, Pug Ismay found him sitting in the Wardroom in his overcoat and hat, hunched over a cup of coffee and smoking a cigarette. "We are coming into Scapa Flow and the PM wants you to see the fleet at anchor," Ismay said.

"Too cold out there," Hopkins said. "I'll take a look when we transfer to the Nelson."

"The PM wants you to see it. Let's go to my cabin," Ismay suggested. "Some of my heavy sweaters and fur-lined flying boots should help."

Though the sea and wind had calmed during the night, an icy wind still ran across the destroyer's deck as the ship was underway.

When Hopkins and Ismay arrived on deck, Pug's thick wool turtleneck sweater was visible above the collar of Harry's overcoat, and his oversized fur-lined flying boots were flapping on Harry's feet. Hopkins kept his old fedora pulled down tightly around his head, the top of which he held tilted into the wind.

Churchill stood at the rail looking out at the British navy at anchor in the distance. "Look, Harry. There's Scapa Flow and our fleet!" Churchill shouted over the wind as Hopkins approached and stood next to him. "There is our shield! If that should go, we'd be in for it. The Nazis have tried a couple of times to reach us here, but we have made it so risky for them that they have decided they will not make too many attempts."

As the ice-cold wind struck his face, Hopkins looked out, trying to keep his eyes open and holding onto his hat with a gloved hand. He had to admit that the sight of dozens of battleships, destroyers, cruisers, and other vessels as far as the eye could see was an impressive and inspiring sight in the morning light.

Despite the extra clothing and inspiring sight, Hopkins was still very, very cold. Shivering, he looked around for a place to sit down out of the wind and, finding a metal surface next to Churchill, sat down with his back to the wind and his head below the rail. The captain came down from the bridge and stood in front of Hopkins, sitting on the equipment. "Excuse me, sir," he said to Hopkins.

Churchill and Ismay turned, and Hopkins looked up. "Sir, I would not sit there if I were you," the captain calmly informed Hopkins. "That is an armed depth charge."

Hopkins bounced off the depth charge and quickly walked to the other side of Churchill on the rail.

"Can you imagine me having to explain that to President Roosevelt?" smiled Churchill.

#

After the group transferred to the Battleship HMS Nelson, they attended a festive lunch complete with wine, champagne, Scotch, port, and sherry to wish Lord Halifax and his wife bon voyage and good luck in his new role as Ambassador to the United States.

Cold and tired, after lunch, Hopkins went below to his cabin to rest. He was there but a few minutes before Churchill and his personal physician knocked at his door.

"May we come in?" asked Churchill.

"Of course," replied Hopkins, stepping back from the door.

"This is Dr. Sir Charles Wilson, Lord Moran," Churchill said. "He is my personal physician, and Clemmie insists he examine you."

Hopkins smiled. "Please thank Clemmie for me, but that's not necessary. I am feeling a little cold, is all."

Wilson paid Hopkins no attention as he put his bag down on the table and removed his stethoscope, a thermometer, and a tongue depressor. "Please sit," Dr. Wilson instructed him.

Hopkins thought about resisting, but decided it was smarter for him to just allow the doctor to examine him.

"I am glad you had the chance to meet Lord and Lady Halifax before they left on the King George V," Churchill told Hopkins, making small talk as the doctor went about his business.

"The President will meet them as soon as King George arrives in Virginia," Hopkins assured Churchill.

Wilson listened to Hopkins's chest with his stethoscope, oblivious to his conversation with Churchill. After examining Hopkins's eyes and ears, he placed a thermometer in his mouth. It was clear that Dr. Wilson was following Clementine's strict instructions.

Wilson removed the thermometer. "Your pulse is very slow, and your body temperature is down. You need bed rest, Mr. Hopkins."

"That's not necessary," Hopkins said confidently.

"No, no," said Churchill quickly. "You are going to listen to Dr. Wilson, or Clemmie will hang me from the yard arm. I am scheduled to tour the fleet over the next couple of days. It would be a boring business for you anyway. Why not take advantage of that time and just rest here? In a couple of days, you and I will go to Glasgow."

"This is really not..." Hopkins started again but was immediately cut off by Churchill.

"Harry. There are two people I always listen to when they insist: Clemmie and Lord Moran," Churchill said, even though he knew it was not true.

CHAPTER THIRTEEN

"Whither thou goest."

Hopkins was feeling much better and more like himself when Churchill returned from his tour of the fleet several days later. Lord Moran's injection of vitamins and his couple of days of rest seemed to have revived him.

Churchill was scheduled to speak at a dinner in the Ballroom at The Central Station Hotel, and, together, he and Hopkins traveled by train to The Central Station in Glasgow. The hotel, built in 1883, next to Glasgow's main train station, was luxurious from top to bottom, covered in imported Italian marble and ornate handcrafted and gold-trimmed plastered ceilings throughout its public spaces. Though the weather remained cold, Glasgow was not nearly as frigid as Scapa Flow.

As Churchill inspired his listeners in the smoky room full of British and Scottish government officials and dignitaries, Hopkins sat on the dais along with six other men.

"We all know there are difficult days ahead for us," Churchill told the room at the conclusion of his speech, "but we are confident that our democracy, and our United Kingdom, will prevail against Herr Hitler and his odious Nazi regime."

The crowd instantly applauded and some rose to their feet shouting, "Hear, hear," and "God Save the King!"

Churchill basked in the applause.

"I would like to thank Scotland's Secretary of State, Tom Johnston, for organizing this evening's dinner," concluded Churchill, looking toward Johnston on the dais. "And Mr. Harry Hopkins, who has accompanied me on my tour of Scotland as a representative of the democracy of the great American Republic, and the personal representative of the President of the United States."

Again, the room applauded.

Hopkins acknowledged Churchill's mention with a smile and a nod and waved his hand to the men in the room.

"I would like him to say a few words." Churchill turned toward Hopkins, and the room again erupted into applause.

Hopkins was surprised. He had not prepared any remarks.

He slowly rose to his feet and moved toward Churchill at the podium, shaking hands with him when he arrived. Churchill surrendered the podium and returned to his seat on the dais. The men in the room settled while Hopkins collected his thoughts. The room fell silent. There was no talking, no coughing, no movement, no clinking of glass or silverware against plates—just hundreds of people waiting for the words of their American guest.

Hopkins turned from the audience to look at Churchill. "I suppose you wish to know what I am going to say to President Roosevelt upon my return," he said gravely to Churchill and then turned to face the room. "Well, I am going to quote you one verse from the Book of Books, in the truth of which Mr. Johnston's mother and my own Scottish mother were brought up."

Hopkins scanned the faces in the audience. "Whither thou goest, I will go; and where thou lodgest, I will lodge: thy people shall be my people, and thy God my God."

Hopkins then turned back to look at Churchill on the dais.

"Even to the end," Hopkins finished, and Churchill's eyes filled with tears.

There was only silence for several moments. And then suddenly, the men in the audience were on their feet, clapping and cheering as Churchill dabbed his eyes with his napkin. When Churchill stood, the men's applause and cheers grew even louder as if their hands and voices were somehow connected to the overwhelming feelings of pride and hope that swelled in their chests.

America's emissary had told them in the most eloquent way possible that they were not alone, and there was hope.

#

When Hopkins returned to London, he immediately dove into more meetings to digest as much as he could about Britain's fight with Hitler.   Scheduled to spend his final weekend at the Prime Minister's retreat at Chequers, Hopkins sat in his suite at Claridge's, with a Scotch in front of him and a cigarette in his hand, and wrote a long cable to FDR about his time in England, the people he met, and his opinion of England's ability to prevail in the war.

"The most important, single observation I have to make is that most of the Cabinet and all of the military leaders here believe that invasion is imminent.   The spirit of this people and their determination to resist invasion is beyond praise. No matter how fierce the attack may be, you can be sure that they will resist it, and effectively."

Hopkins closed his cable with, *"I am convinced this meeting between you and Churchill is essential—and soon—for the battering continues and Hitler does not wait for Congress. I cannot believe that it is true that Churchill dislikes either you or America. It just doesn't make sense. This island needs our help now, Mr. President, with everything we can give them."*

Already familiar with Churchill's morning habit of working in bed, Hopkins was determined to arrive before 9 a.m. at Chequers so that he could plow through his own work before Churchill showed himself around lunchtime.   Hopkins rose early on Saturday morning to snow-covered streets in London, and after eating half a scone and a few sips of coffee, he departed with his driver to Churchill's Buckinghamshire retreat.

At 9:30 that morning, a British military vehicle approached the sentries at Chequers' gate, and after clearing the sentries, a British officer entered Chequers' foyer with a briefcase in each hand.   John

"Jock" Colville, Churchill's polished twenty-six-year-old private secretary, descended the stairs to the foyer to greet the officer.

"You are a bit tardy today," Colville said to the British officer.

"Yes, sir," the British officer confirmed. "The US Embassy asked us to wait while they organized material for Mr. Hopkins. This briefcase is for Mr. Hopkins," the British officer said, handing one of the briefcases to Colville.

"Wait here a moment," instructed Colville, and turned with Hopkins's briefcase to walk down the corridor off the foyer. When Colville arrived at the door of the first-floor bathroom, he knocked.

"Come in," Hopkins called out from behind the closed door.

Colville entered the bathroom and found Hopkins in his overcoat and hat, reading documents while sitting on the lid of the closed toilet bowl next to a large heating pipe. That heating pipe was the largest one in the estate, and ran from the bathroom floor up through its ceiling. There were stacks of papers at Hopkins's feet.

"The embassy sent this material for you," Colville said, handing Hopkins the briefcase.

"Thanks, Jock," replied Hopkins, taking the briefcase and putting it down next to him.

"Are you comfortable?" asked Colville.

"Very." Hopkins smiled. "This loo is the warmest seat in the house."

"Be sure to tap on the pipe if you need anything," Colville teased, returning Hopkins's smile, and made his way back to the foyer to pick up the other briefcase from the waiting British officer and carry it upstairs to Churchill's bedroom on the next floor of the grand old country estate.

When Colville entered Churchill's room, he found him in bed, smoking a cigar, drinking a glass of white wine, and reading documents in a flaming pink kimono with a black dragon across its back.

"Ah, Colville." Churchill never liked waiting for paperwork or messages, and was glad to see the briefcase in Colville's hand.

"The US Embassy was delayed sending material for Mr. Hopkins," Colville explained, knowing how anxious Churchill could become waiting for his documents.

"Material?" Churchill asked. "What material?"

"I do not know, sir."

"Did he seem concerned?"

"No, sir."

"Well, how did he look?" inquired Churchill, seemingly worried about his guest.

"Cold, sir."

"Cold?"

"Yes. He was sitting on the loo in the main bathroom in his hat and coat," explained Colville.

"You walked in on him while he was sitting on the loo?"

"Yes, sir. He was sitting on top of the loo next to the main heating pipe."

"The heating pipe," Churchill repeated.

"Yes, sir, just like that one," said Colville, pointing to the large heating pipe in the corner of Churchill's bedroom. "Mr. Hopkins said the downstairs loo is the warmest seat in the house."

Churchill laughed out loud and jumped out of his bed with his letter opener in hand and his pink silk robe flowing behind him. Standing at the heating pipe in his room, he tapped the pipe with his letter opener, "dot-dash-dash-dot" and then, "dash-dash."

"Morse code, sir?" asked Colville.

Churchill nodded and smiled. "P, M," he explained.

Colville and Churchill waited, listening for Hopkins's response.

"Do you think he knows it's me sending him a message?" Churchill asked Colville when suddenly the pipe rang out with "dot-dot-dot," "dash-dash-dash," and "dot-dot-dot."

Churchill looked concerned and told Colville, "Perhaps you should go down and check on him."

"What did he say?" asked Colville.

"Help!"

"He knows it's you, sir." Colville smiled.

#

Fortunately for all of those who stayed at Chequers that night, the sky above the blacked-out estate was cloud-covered and starless, which reduced the probability that any bombs would land on or near the Prime Minister's retreat. The British sentries patrolling the grounds were especially grateful to know it would likely be a quiet night.

As was customary for Churchill on the weekend, he invited an eclectic group to join him for dinner, followed by hours of conversations and debates covering a wide range of subjects and issues. In addition to Hopkins, dinner guests that weekend included Clementine, Jock Colville, Lord Beaverbrook, Professor Frederick Lindemann, and Air Vice Marshall Charles Portal. Lindemann, Churchill's scientific adviser, was in his mid-fifties, and Lord Beaverbrook was the wealthy sixty-two-year-old businessman and publisher who was Britain's Minister of Aircraft Production. Like Churchill, Beaverbrook had taken to Hopkins.

When the dinner table was cleared, Churchill lit his cigar while his butler offered brandy to his guests. Clementine and Lindemann refused, and Hopkins asked for a Scotch instead. When he did, he caught the butler's eye and signaled him with a nod, which the butler returned.

"Air Marshall," Churchill spoke to Portal as he held a match to his cigar, coaxing it into a full burn. "When I consider that right now one Nazi bomb could take out our government, air force, aircraft production, and our scientific leadership, I am forever grateful for your RAF fighters."

Portal smiled. "Thank you, sir. I am very proud of our pilots."

"They are indeed the best of us," confirmed Churchill and raised his glass. "To the men of the RAF."

The entire table responded with "Hear, hear," and "To the RAF."

"Prime Minister," Portal said, "we would be remiss in not proposing a toast to Professor Lindemann for his work on our new radio beam detection system. The professor's aircraft detection system has given our brave RAF pilots a fighting chance."

Portal raised his glass to Lindemann and said, "To you, Professor," while all at the table raised their glasses and added their own "Cheers" and "Hear, hear."

"And we shan't forget the work of Lord Beaverbrook and his organization," Portal continued, "ensuring we have the numbers of quality aircraft we need to fight off the Nazi assault."

"Indeed," Churchill agreed wholeheartedly.

Portal raised his glass again, this time to Lord Beaverbrook, and the group followed his lead.

"Thank you, Charles, and thank you, Winston," Lord Beaverbrook appreciated his colleague's acknowledgment of his efforts.

When the butler returned to the dining room carrying a small radio, he looked at Hopkins, who rose from his chair and motioned for the butler to place the radio on top of the sideboard and plug it in.

"What have you there, Harry?" Clementine asked.

"My small way of saying thank you to you and to Winston for your generous hospitality during my visit these past weeks," answered Hopkins just as sound from the radio's speakers filled the dining room. Hopkins played with the radio's dial to tune in a station, and Clementine and Churchill rose from the table to stand next to him. After passing a number of stations, Harry captured a station playing Tommy Dorsey and Frank Sinatra's "*I'll Never Smile Again.*" He turned up the volume.

"How wonderful," exclaimed Clementine, delighted to hear Dorsey's music and Sinatra's silky voice fill the room.

Churchill opened his arms and presented himself to Clementine. "Dance, my dear?" he asked. Clementine took Churchill's hand and they began dancing around the dining room as Sinatra sang and Dorsey played.

Colville, Lindemann, and Portal all stood with Hopkins and, together, they applauded Churchill and Clementine. After a few more bars, they stopped dancing, and Churchill kissed Clementine's hand. She hugged him.

"Unlike the title of that song, I will always smile when I remember tonight and that wonderful dance, Mr. Churchill," pronounced Clementine, touched by both Hopkins's thoughtfulness and her husband's gallantry.

"I must say, you are a very handsome couple," Portal said approvingly.

"Very light on your feet, Winston," Lindemann added, sounding like he was considering a study on Churchill's agility.

"We learned all we know from Fred Astaire and Ginger Rogers," joked Churchill.

Clementine walked over to Hopkins and kissed him on his cheek. "Thank you, Harry. We will enjoy all of that wonderful music coming from America."

"Thank you for making me feel so comfortable."

As everyone returned to their chairs at the dining table, the music continued playing in the background, and Churchill couldn't help but think how wrong he was to be concerned about FDR's emissary. Hopkins was a godsend, and his presence was soothing for everyone he met in England.

As he took his seat, Churchill looked at Hopkins and simply raised his glass to him. There were no words said, and no accolades given. Just a steady and studied look between the men that informed them of their understanding and appreciation of each other. Hopkins smiled and raised his glass in return.

"Harry, will you give us your assessment of the prospect of America joining us in this fight?" Portal asked, surprising Hopkins.

"It's hard to assess," Hopkins said truthfully. "As you all know, the President is both guided and constrained by Congress, our laws, and public opinion.

"Where do Americans stand, Harry?" Churchill followed up, sincerely interested in the answer to Portal's question.

Hopkins thought for a moment about ducking the question, but true to himself, decided to give them his honest opinion. "At present," Hopkins said, "there are four divisions of public opinion in America: a small group of Nazis and communists sheltering behind Lindbergh, who declared for a negotiated peace and wanted a German victory; a group represented by Joe Kennedy, which says 'Help Britain, but make damn sure you don't get into any danger of war'; a majority group which supports the President's determination to send the maximum assistance at whatever risk; and about 10 or

15 percent of the country, including Knox, Stimson, and most of the armed forces, who are in favor of immediate war."

"Harry, I am to give a speech on the radio next week. What should I say to those Americans who may be sympathetic to our cause?" asked Churchill, genuinely seeking Hopkins's insight and guidance.

"Just say it simply," Hopkins advised Churchill. "Give us the tools and we will finish the job."

"Harry, you may be the only person to ever have helped write a speech for the President of the United States and the Prime Minister of Great Britain," Churchill said.

"I only work with the finest people." Hopkins smiled.

CHAPTER FOURTEEN

"It is a godsend Hopkins is in the White House."

The White House sent the bill to Congress on January 10, 1941, and cleverly called it HR 1776, *An Act to Promote the Defense of the United States*, an obvious attempt to frame the proposal in both historic and patriotic terms. The bill that started with FDR's two-word analogy, garden hose, entered the American lexicon as the two game-changing words: Lend-Lease.

As the legislation ground its way through America's legislative machinery, it wasn't clear whether Lend-Lease was the worst possible thing at the worst possible time, or the best thing for the world since sliced bread. According to some, it would save democracy from fascism, and according to others, it would be national suicide. It was really hard to describe the stakes.

Or the polarization.

"Quote me on that!" FDR thundered to the roomful of reporters. "That really is the rottenest thing that has been said in public life in my generation!" He had been asked for his response to what Senator Burton Wheeler—a *Democrat*—called the proposal before Congress part of the President's foreign policy efforts that would "plow under every fourth American boy." The gloves were off. The fight was on.

Knowing England's very existence was hanging in the balance should the Nazis invade before May, after Hopkins returned home, he worked as far away from the public eye as he could during the Lend-Lease debate. He and FDR had already determined he would run Lend-Lease, and Hopkins prepared to hit the ground running once the measure was adopted.

Despite the isolationists' best efforts, in early March, Congress passed Lend-Lease into law, and FDR, Hopkins, and the inner circle boarded the Presidential yacht, Potomac, for some fishing and poker off the coast of Florida. Accompanied by the USS Benson, they steamed to the Bahamas in rough seas and fickle weather.

As the Potomac bobbed up and down on its anchor, FDR sat holding his cards and looking like the Cheshire Cat, while Steve Early nervously played with his chips. Pa Watson, Harold Ickes, and Dr. McIntire all sat dead still at the table holding their cards with their eyes glazed as the color in their faces drifted toward varying shades of green. Of course, Hopkins didn't have enough stomach left to get all that churned up.

"Up to you. Harry," said Roosevelt impatiently.

"Anxious, aren't you?" Hopkins cracked.

"Time's a wasting," retorted FDR.

"I would like to catch a fish sometime today," Pa Watson chimed in, hoping he could move around before his stomach reached the point of no return.

Hopkins threw two chips into the pot and looked at Watson. "You're just jealous I caught the two biggest fish so far," Hopkins teased.

"Only someone with your strength could have wrestled those porgies into the boat," Watson answered, swallowing hard, trying to keep lunch in its place in his stomach.

"It's all in the wrists." Hopkins smiled.

Steve Early continued to play with his chips and stared at his cards. "Why do I have the feeling I'm being taken by you guys?"

"If you don't know who the sucker is, it's you," said McIntire, also trying to fight off the churning in his gut.

"I'll call." Early decided to throw two chips into the middle.

With his cigarette holder between his teeth, FDR broke into a wide grin. "Full house, gentlemen. Kings and Tens," he said, putting his cards on the table and scooping the chips in the center of the table toward him.

"We don't stand a chance today," lamented Watson as he and the others threw their cards in.

"I should've folded," whined Early as Hopkins collected the cards.

"Who dealt that mess?" asked Hopkins.

"I did," Early admitted.

"I won't object if Steve would like to deal again," FDR cracked.

"Not a chance," Hopkins said emphatically and put the deck in front of Watson. "Shuffle 'em good, Pa."

A Naval officer approached FDR with a large manila envelope in hand. "Good afternoon, sir. This came for you," he said, handing FDR the envelope.

"Thank you, Lieutenant." Roosevelt opened the package and removed the bulky document. He smiled as he read: "'The Act to Promote the Defense of the United States' with a seven-billion-dollar appropriation from Congress. Lend-Lease, gentlemen!" he declared to scattered congratulations. He then turned to the end of the document, took out his fountain pen, and signed it.

"Please take care of this, Pa," FDR instructed Watson.

"I'll send it back with the lieutenant," Watson replied, happy for the excuse to get up and leave the table.

The President put the cap back on his pen and turned to Hopkins. "This is for you, Harry," FDR said, handing him the pen. "Couldn't have gotten this done without you!"

Hopkins was moved.

Seeing Pa head off, Harold Ickes, who by this time was the greenest of the group, was glad to have an opportunity to break from the game. "I'm going to lie down for a bit. I'm a little queasy."

"Me, too," Early said, rising from his chair, though the truth was he was less queasy and more annoyed that he lost a bundle of money. "I need to settle my stomach and lick my wounds. Please let me know how much I owe you," Early said to the President.

"I will make a full and complete accounting of my winnings," said FDR cheerfully.   And everyone at the table knew he would. FDR had inherited his Dutch ancestors' fiscal conservatism.

Seeing Ickes and Early leave the table, McIntire couldn't resist the opportunity to flee, as well. "I think I'll grab a nap," McIntire said, glad he was not alone in abandoning the game. "I have seasick pills in my cabin if you guys need them," McIntire offered to the group.

Seeing his marks leave the table, FDR picked up the cards and began shuffling. "Doesn't that beat all. Now that I'm winning, you land lubbers are running for cover."

"Thank you for this," Hopkins said, holding up the pen. "It means a great deal to me."

"Harry, you and I have some unfinished business," said FDR, dealing himself a solitaire game, one of his favorite activities for relaxation. "How does this sound to you?" he continued. "I hereby designate you to advise and assist me in carrying out responsibilities placed upon me by the Act of March 11, 1941, entitled an Act to Promote the Defense of the United States, also known as the Lend-Lease Bill. In this capacity, you will receive compensation at the annual rate of ten thousand dollars. You're going to run this, Harry, and I feel better knowing you are back on the payroll," FDR said, looking squarely at Hopkins."

"It's good to be back." Hopkins smiled.

#

It was the hottest ticket in town on Wednesday, April 23, 1941, when Charles Lindbergh stood at the podium looking out over a sea of fluttering American flags and transfixed faces at New York's Manhattan Center, a former opera house located on West 34th Street.

Charles Augustus Lindbergh—a.k.a. "Lucky Lindy" or "The Lone Eagle"—was a tall and handsome forty-one-year-old with piercing blue eyes and wavy blonde hair. He was a pioneering aviator, an American hero, and one of the most famous men in the world. Long a proponent of America keeping its distance from the conflict raging in Europe, Lindbergh was fast becoming the voice and face of the America First Committee, an organization of America's determined isolationists and FDR's political opposition with more than 500,000 members.

"I know I will be severely criticized by the interventionists in America," Lindbergh said to those in attendance, "when I say we should not enter a war unless we have a reasonable chance of winning."

Over the clamor of supporters and protestors outside the building, Lindbergh concluded his speech to his adoring live audience and millions of radio listeners with a membership pitch to join the increasingly popular America First movement. "That is why the America First Committee has been formed," Lindbergh said, "to give voice to the people who have no newspaper or news reel or radio station at their command; to the people who must do the paying, and the fighting, and the dying, if this country enters the war."

The crowd inside the center burst into applause.

While it seemed that the famous Lindbergh was the perfect spokesperson for the isolationists, there was a little-known significant problem with the so-called American hero. Two and a half years earlier, Herman Goering, Hitler's second in command and head of the Nazis Luftwaffe, pinned the Nazi *Service Cross of the German Eagle* on Lindbergh's chest when he visited Berlin. Supposedly, the medal was given to Lindbergh for his contributions to aviation. In truth, it was also presented to him because he was an ardent proponent of Nazi Germany's military superiority, an antisemite, and a vocal advocate for American isolationism.

When Bob Sherwood called Lindbergh "a Nazi with a Nazi's Olympian contempt for all Democratic processes," Hopkins thought Sherwood was being too kind.

#

Hopkins wasted no time running Lend-Lease and putting FDR's garden-hose program to work. A month into it, he sat in an open bathrobe, T-shirt, and boxers at a table in his White House bedroom office with the phone in his ear and a syringe in his hand.

He was just about to start his regular morning meeting with his three analysts when Churchill called. The three analysts remained at the conference table with their lead analyst in the middle, while Hopkins spoke to Churchill and gave himself an injection in his thigh.

"Harry, this is critical!" growled the familiar voice through the phone.

"Yes, Winston, I know. We're working on it," assured Hopkins.

"We lost 40 percent of our convoy last week. How quickly can we get the next one underway?" Churchill sounded like he was close to the end of his rope.

"We're organizing new shipments as we speak. I need you to give Averell Harriman a list of just the items you need right away."

"I know. But my dear Harry, I am not at all embarrassed to tell you that it is quickly becoming more and more desperate over here," said Churchill.

"We won't let that happen, Winston," Hopkins told Churchill as he removed the syringe from his leg, placed it into a tray on the table, and dabbed a cloth on the site of his injection. "I promise."

"KBO, Harry."

"You, too," Hopkins answered, and hung up the phone.

Hopkins closed the flap of his robe over his leg and looked at the three men across the table. He had meetings like this one every single morning and afternoon as he wrestled with keeping America's supply chain well-oiled and its Lend-Lease material moving within and without the country.

"You guys ready?" asked Hopkins.

"Ready," answered the lead analyst.

"Shoot!" Hopkins said, and with that, the Lend-Lease factory's machinery began to turn.

"A strike has stopped production at the company making propellers for the new Navy fighter," reported the lead analyst as he read from the folder in front of him.

"Tell Secretary Perkins we need this resolved immediately," Hopkins instructed. "And ask her to update me this afternoon."

The lead analyst closed the folder and moved it to his colleague on his right, while the analyst on his left took notes.

The lead analyst picked up the next folder. "Yugoslavia is requesting two cargo ships for their use. They want…"

Hopkins cut him off. "Next," he barked, and without a comment, the lead analyst turned in his chair and dropped the folder behind him on the floor. Any folder that found its way to the floor behind the lead analyst was destined for oblivion.

On to the next folder.

"There is a group of congressmen," the lead analyst stated, "who want to see the President because they are concerned that communists will interfere with war production."

"What bullshit," responded Hopkins. "Next," he said, but before the lead analyst could drop the folder behind him, Hopkins stopped him. "Hang on a second. Give this to Secretary Hull. Tell Hull if he and the FBI believe there is a legitimate threat here, he should let us know immediately." The analyst sitting on the left feverishly made notes while the lead analyst moved the folder to the analyst on his right.

Next folder.

"Greece is asking for a dozen bombers," the lead analyst read from the folder.

Since Hopkins needed to decipher exactly what was going on with Greece and their allegiances, he decided to play for time. "Tell the Greeks their request is under consideration, and let's revisit this in a month or two. If they give you a hard time, tell their ambassador to call me," ordered Hopkins.

The Greek folder was moved to the analyst on the left for action in the future.

The lead analyst then spoke to Hopkins without consulting the next folder in front of him. "Almost every ship builder in our program needs the Navy's design specs and forecasted requirements," he informed Hopkins.

"Call Secretary Knox and tell him we need that information ASAP. Not tomorrow, not next week, but now," Hopkins said, annoyed at the lack of urgency of some over at the War Department. "Make Knox your first call after you deal with the propeller strike."

"Will do," replied the lead analyst, pleased that Hopkins instructed him to do exactly what he thought should've been done.

"And tell me right away if those guys over at the War Department start rolling logs in front of your feet," advised Hopkins.

"I will," the lead analyst assured Hopkins.

As the meeting wound down, the lead analyst said, "There are three other items this morning that we think are important. "A midwestern company says they have developed a new thermal process for producing aluminum; several manufacturers are asking about using steel alloys in their production; and several mining companies have inquired about the use of quartz crystals in certain military equipment."

"Give all of those to Vannevar Bush," Hopkins instructed, "and tell him I need a report on each within the week. Are they viable?

Valuable? And so forth. And please tell him to keep the reports brief. We don't need *War and Peace*."

There was a knock at the door, and Missy LeHand poked her head in. "Harry, Secretary Stimson and General Marshall are here for you."

"Give us the room, fellas," Harry said to the analysts. "See you this afternoon at four o'clock."

As the analysts collected their papers and exited, Stimson entered and cracked, "There go the bedroom boys!"

"Who?" Hopkins looked puzzled.

Stimson smiled. "That's what Morgenthau calls your analysts—Hopkins's bedroom boys."

"Tell Henry those guys are doing a damn good job getting supplies to England," Hopkins said, defending his team.

"That's what scares Admiral Land. He says your bedroom boys are doing such a great job that if we don't watch it, we'll find the White House itself en route to England, using the Washington Monument as an oar." Stimson laughed.

"Tell Land that if we don't get supplies to the British fast," replied Hopkins, "he may find himself goose-stepping his way to his office with his right hand in the air and a Weiss Wurst in his left."

Marshall smiled and Stimson laughed as they both took seats at Hopkins's conference table filled with folders, papers, ashtrays with old cigarette stubs, coffee cups, and a used syringe in a tray.

"Nice digs, Harry," Stimson needled. "Listen, I know it means you would have to put on a pair of pants, but why don't you move over to the Lend-Lease offices at Treasury?"

"Saving the taxpayers' money," Hopkins cracked.

"Now that's real news. I'll be sure to tell Morgenthau you are a changed man," Stimson joked.

"What can I do for you guys?" asked Hopkins, knowing full well that if Stimson and Marshall were visiting, they had something important on their minds.

"We just visited with the boss, and we thought it best to talk this over with you," Stimson said seriously.

Hopkins liked it when he was right.

"We are getting crazy requests and they are slowing us down," added Stimson.

"Just to be clear, some of the requests make no military sense," General Marshall weighed in, making sure Hopkins knew they were not wasting time.

Stimson continued. "For example, he asked us to look into getting money and arms to Chiang Kai-shek."

"He's listening to every crackpot who visits him," Hopkins knew Marshall and Stimson were right to be concerned.

"I don't think he wants to start a war with Japan," said Stimson.

"In fairness, we need to give the President a filter he can use to determine what makes good military and strategic sense," said Marshall. "He should know our position if Great Britain falls. Or if the Japanese continue with their expansion into China."

"Or if we're forced to fight Japan or Germany," Stimson added.

"You have the time for that kind of planning?" Hopkins asked Marshall.

"We can do it, but it would be best if we included Great Britain and Canada," suggested Marshall.

Hopkins nodded and said, "I'll call Churchill and King and ask them to send their guys over here to work with you." The "King" Hopkins referred to was Mackenzie King, the Prime Minister of Canada.

"In the meantime," Stimson said, "maybe you can encourage the President to discuss military matters only with us, Admiral Stark, or with Secretary Knox."

"Leave it with me," Harry said, and the two men rose from the table and collected their briefcases.

"Thanks, Harry," said Stimson, genuinely pleased to have Hopkins's help.

"Before you go," Hopkins stopped Marshall. "I spoke with Churchill this morning and asked him to request only the equipment and supplies they need immediately to replace the material they lost in the last convoy."

Marshall looked pleased. "That will help us get another convoy out faster."

"Yeah, well, I'm pretty sure Churchill will ask Harriman for everything plus the kitchen sink. I already told Harriman to double-check all of Britain's requests, and you should do the same on our side," cautioned Hopkins.

"Thanks for the heads up," Marshall said, pleased Great Britain was not being given carte blanche as everyone claimed.

"And Henry," Hopkins called out to Stimson. "Please tell Admiral Land that neither the Washington Monument nor the White House will ever cross the Atlantic on my watch."

"Happy to." Stimson smiled.

As Stimson and Marshall waited in the hall for the White House elevator, Stimson turned to Marshall. "I take back what I said about Harry using the offices at Treasury," Stimson told Marshall. "It is a godsend Hopkins is in the White House."

CHAPTER FIFTEEN

It was late June when Stimson, Marshall, Hopkins, and the President stood in FDR's office looking over a map of the Soviet Union. Three days earlier, Hitler, in a continued search for more *lebensraum*, "living space" for Germans, unleashed his war machine against the Soviet Union and Josef Stalin, the man with whom he had signed a "non-aggression" pact and carved up Poland less than two years earlier.

"The Germans crossed into the Soviet Union here, here, and here," General Marshall said, pointing to a large map given to the President by National Geographic after the Germans invaded Poland in September 1939. It was being put to good use.

"Initial reports," Marshall continued, "suggest a force of over 5,000 bombers and fighters, half a million motorized vehicles, and two million men deployed along an eighteen-hundred-mile front."

"Can the Russians hold out?" FDR asked Marshall. "How long does Stalin have?"

"It's not clear, sir," Marshall replied. "The Germans are moving fast. Very fast. They've already destroyed much of Russia's air force on the ground. And we have preliminary reports indicating that more than 300,000 Red Army soldiers have already been killed or captured," reported Marshall.

"We estimate three to six months before the Germans reach Moscow, Stimson predicted, "but it's still foggy at this point. And we don't know why Hitler decided to move east now, especially when he seemed to have England on the ropes."

"There are a few good reasons that I can think of," said Hopkins. "First, Hitler was afraid Stalin was going to invade Germany first. Second, he believes England will be starved into making a deal with him. And finally, he wants to free up Japan to come after us."

"My thoughts exactly!" exclaimed FDR.

#

No one was sure what happened. In the middle of a wonderful White House party on a perfect June night, Missy LeHand screamed and fell to the floor next to the piano. The attendees crowded around her, and though she was breathing, they found her unresponsive. It was clear that something terrible had happened to her.

Dr. McIntire examined Missy after they brought her to her rooms on the third floor of the White House and informed FDR that she'd had a stroke. He told the President that he needed to move her to the Naval Hospital the next morning, and he was not optimistic Missy would recover. FDR was distraught and, after McIntire left, he called his personal attorney and told him to revise his will to allocate 50% of his estate to paying for LeHand's medical bill for as long as she was alive. His attorney did as he was instructed.

Later that evening, Hopkins went up to see LeHand in her room. When he arrived, the nurse on duty told him that although Missy seemed conscious and aware, she had not moved at all. Hopkins sat down next to his friend's bed. Her eyes remained fixed on something on the ceiling. He took Missy's right hand in both of his and though her eyes and head did not move, he felt her index finger pressing against his. Hopkins smiled at her and at the possibility of at least some recovery. There was hope.

When he left Missy that evening, he had tears in his eyes, deeply saddened to see his friend in such a desperate condition. There was a part of Harry that always loved Missy—her smarts, her polish, and her innate understanding of the people and world around her. Harry knew she would never be able to work again for the man she adored, and he also knew the man she adored would find it almost unbearable to not have her at his side. And yet, despite the fact that Missy LeHand had been FDR's protector, adviser, champion, companion, inspiration, task master, and guiding light for so many years, FDR did not visit her or ever see her again.

#

A couple of weeks later, on a bright July morning, Joe Davies, the former Ambassador to the Soviet Union, arranged to see Hopkins and took a taxi from Hillwood Estate near Rock Creek Park to the White House. They met in Harry's bedroom office after Hopkins's morning meeting with the "bedroom boys," who all made a hasty exit after Davies was announced by Alonzo Fields, the White House butler. As Davies entered the room, Hopkins reminded his lead analyst, "Please don't forget to add Australia's material to the British shipment and let them send it to the Australians."

"I will let Mr. Harriman know," confirmed the lead analyst.

"And tell Secretary Stimson when you see him that we need the completion dates for the twenty-five-pound artillery shells," instructed Hopkins as the bedroom boys walked past Davies and left the room.

"Hi, Joe. Have a seat," Hopkins offered.

Though Davies moved toward the small conference table and put down his briefcase, he did not sit. "Let's go over here," Davies said, pointing to the large maps on Hopkins's wall, "I want to show you something."

"I'm hearing rumblings from Congress," Davies said, standing with Hopkins in front of a map of the Soviet Union. "I hear they want to stop us from helping the Russians." Davies's face showed deep concern.

"I've already received the calls," Hopkins replied, confirming there was an effort underway in certain parts of the government to stop the US from helping the Soviet Union in their fight against Hitler.

"Harry. We must—*must*—provide as much aid as possible to the Russians," Davies said passionately. Hopkins didn't expect so much emotion from the normally implacable Davies.

"These are the Ural Mountains," said Davies, turning to the map and pointing east of Moscow. "When I was ambassador, there were munitions factories on the eastern side—here in Chelyabinsk, here in Tyumen, and here, here, and here."

Hopkins stood next to Davies, taking in the distances on the map from the old Polish border across Russia to the Ural Mountains and the munitions factories. "How far is it from the Germans to those factories?" asked Hopkins.

"About fifteen hundred miles, give or take," Davies answered, and Hopkins immediately grasped the point of Davies's visit.

"So, it's not likely the Germans will cross the Ural Mountains any time in the next six months," said Hopkins, seeing the opportunity for the Russians to deliver a severe blow to the Germans.

"With winter coming, not a chance," declared Davies emphatically. "Listen, Harry, I know the Russians. If we can supply them with what they need, the extent of their resistance will amaze and surprise the world."

"What do you recommend, Joe?"

"We should not turn our backs on the Soviets now," answered Davies. "The President should send word to Stalin immediately that the US will go all out to beat Hitler—that our historic policy of friendliness to Russia still exists."

Davies turned from the map. "Harry, if we do this well, Hitler's invasion of Russia may be the first glimpse of dawn in a black night," he told Hopkins.

"Leave it with me."

#

At day's end, Hopkins was with FDR in his office, enjoying their ritual of cocktails, cigarettes, and the chance to trade ideas, invent solutions, and engage in a "can you top this" story competition with each other. It was a sign of the times that neither had time any longer for DC gossip.

"I think Davies is right," Hopkins said. "We must help Stalin stay in the fight against Hitler. It will help keep Britain in the game and hopefully keep us on the bench."

"As long as Japan stays put," FDR added cautiously. "Draft a note to Stalin for me."

"I will," replied Hopkins.

"How is Churchill holding up?" FDR inquired.

"Struggling. The convoys are getting slaughtered in the Atlantic," Hopkins said, stating what was common knowledge.

"We have to escort those ships," said FDR, his frustration clearly evident.

"Let's not give Congress any more reasons to want to impeach you," advised Hopkins.

"They will never run out of reasons," cracked FDR.

"The real concern with all of Britain's convoy losses," continued Hopkins, "is the British may not be able to hold off the Germans, or worse, they may be starved in place. If Russia collapses and Britain is worn down enough, Churchill could be pressured into making a separate peace with the Germans, or the House of Commons might decide to replace him," Hopkins speculated.

"If the British capitulate to the Germans, Japan will first move against them and then against us in the Pacific," FDR worried.

"That's how I see it, too," agreed Hopkins.

"And if Britain goes down and Hitler finishes off the Russians, it is only a matter of time before he moves against us in the Atlantic." This time, FDR sounded certain.

"Caught in a vise between the two of them," Hopkins said.

"Let me show you something," FDR said and put down his glass, stubbed out his cigarette, and picked up a National Geographic magazine from the table. FDR opened the magazine to a page with a folded map, ripped the map from the magazine, and opened it across his lap. Hopkins had the distinct impression this was not the first time FDR had looked at this map or considered the idea. Harry knew this was FDR's modus operandi—try out his ideas out loud and then hone in on the best version depending on the reaction of his audience.

"Supposing we did this in steps," proposed FDR, looking at the map in his lap, which showed the Atlantic Ocean from the US East Coast across to Europe and Africa. Hopkins rose and stood behind FDR to look at the map spread across his legs.

"First step, we extend our three-hundred-mile free zone out into the Atlantic," FDR said, pointing to the map. "Now the British continue to escort their own ships, but US ships will patrol all navigable waters lying west of longitude twenty-five degrees. From here to here," FDR showed Hopkins.

"Halfway between the Americas and the west coasts of Europe and Africa," Hopkins confirmed, sounding like FDR's proposal appealed to him.

"Right there," FDR pointed to the map.

"In addition to helping the convoys and Britain," Hopkins confirmed, "it will send all of the right messages to Stalin and Hitler."

"Draft this too, will you, Harry?" asked FDR, knowing he'd made the sale.

"I'll work on both drafts tonight," Hopkins promised.

FDR lit another cigarette and seemed to go to a private place in his head, his eyes focused across the room. Hopkins had seen this look before. FDR seemed to be clicking off the options in his mind one at a time as if he were moving tumblers into place to open a safe.

After several moments, FDR turned to Hopkins. "You and General Marshall need to go to London right away. We need to step up our British deliveries."

"I'll let Churchill and Harriman know we're on our way."

"The British supply situation has to be settled before my meeting with Churchill next month," FDR confirmed.

"Leave it with me."

#

Several weeks later, Harry arrived at 10 Downing Street and was escorted to Churchill's basement dining room, where Averell Harriman and Ambassador Gil Winant were already seated with Churchill.

John Gilbert "Gil" Winant was the former Republican Governor of New Hampshire, and, in his new role as ambassador to the United Kingdom, he was charged with undoing the damage done by his predecessor. The news of Winant's appointment was well-received, and as one British newspaper recorded, "There is no name that could have been more welcome." Of course, from Churchill's perspective, that could have been any name that wasn't Kennedy.

Hopkins was barely seated before the wait staff began serving. The old woman who had served him at his first luncheon had been replaced by two white-coated waiters who Hopkins thought were British soldiers. Hopkins noticed the photograph of Pamela and Winston's grandson was still on the table in the corner.

"Harry," Churchill said, getting down to business as the waiters delivered their lunch. "Please be sure to tell the President how much we appreciate your extended coverage in the Atlantic."

Harriman agreed. "It has already helped a great deal. Last week, almost 90 percent of the convoy arrived intact. That was not possible two months ago."

"Winston, what are your thoughts on the Russian invasion?" Hopkins asked, addressing his biggest concern and knowing full well that Churchill was a committed anti-communist.

"At the risk of sounding crude, I am grateful, Harry," Churchill responded. "Since Herr Hitler invaded Russia, it no longer feels like the Sword of Damocles is swinging above our necks," Churchill said, finishing his consommé with a flourish.

"Can the Russians hold on?"

"We hear they are experiencing catastrophic losses—of men and machinery, but we really have no way to know." Though Churchill seemingly answered Hopkins, he really side-stepped the question. He actually did know from active British agents inside the Soviet Union's White Russian community that things in the Soviet Union were very, very bleak indeed.

The waiters picked up Churchill's consommé dish and replaced it with Dover Sole.

Hopkins decided to use the same technique as FDR - test your idea and then adapt.

"Soviet Ambassador Maisky said it would be good for me to see things in Moscow for myself," Hopkins told Churchill, hoping to get his reaction.

Instead, the reaction came from Harriman. "You're not thinking of going there, are you, Harry?"

"A face-to-face with Stalin will tell us a lot," answered Hopkins without hesitating.

"That's a very difficult and dangerous trip. The entire German Army and air force are between here and Moscow," Winant cautioned.

"I have to admit, Harry," Churchill said after a gulp of Pol Roger, "it would be very valuable for us to have direct contact with Stalin."

"I agree," Hopkins said, pleased to hear he had Churchill's support.

"It's not even possible for you to go there and get back before the Prime Minister and President meet in Placentia Bay," Harriman commented, deeply concerned that Hopkins would make such a dangerous trek.

"You could leave this week, and we can arrange a military flight to Archangel from Scapa Flow," Churchill suggested, nixing Harriman's concern.

"Only if you let me hitch a ride with you to the meeting in Newfoundland when I return, Winston."

"Certainly," agreed Churchill.

That evening, Friday, July 25, Hopkins sent a lengthy cable to FDR, "For the President's Eyes Only—*I am wondering whether you think it important and useful for me to go to Moscow... If you think a Moscow trip is advisable, I will leave here no later than Wednesday.*"

The next evening, while Harry was with Churchill at Chequers for the weekend, he received a cable in reply from FDR, "*I highly approve Moscow trip,*" FDR wrote and concluded, "*I will send you a message for Stalin.*"

#

On Sunday night, inside a blacked-out Chequers, Hopkins sat, putting the finishing touches on a speech that he was minutes away from delivering over BBC radio. Clementine came up behind him and touched his shoulder. "Harry, I want to say goodbye to you now before you leave on your trip." She bent down and kissed him on his cheek.

Hopkins put down his pen, stood up, and hugged Clementine. "How can I ever repay your hospitality?" he asked, grateful and surprised by how much they had grown to care for each other.

"You can come back safely," she answered him as she kissed his other cheek.

As she hugged Hopkins, she saw her husband walk into the room carrying a box. "We have a gift for you," Clemmie said as Churchill handed Hopkins the box.

"A new hat!" Harry exclaimed, opening the box. "How did you know?"

"We have our eyes on you, Mr. Hopkins," teased Churchill. "This is one of my favorite hats from my own collection."

"You should not have done this. You are both much too generous," Hopkins said, grateful and proud to have one of Churchill's hats in his possession. He took the hat from the box and placed it on his head. The obviously big hat pressed on the tops of his ears.

"How does it look?" Hopkins laughed.

"Nothing your valet can't fix, Harry," Churchill replied casually. "There is a car outside to take you to the train immediately after your broadcast. Did Winant deliver your visa and papers for the trip?"

"Not yet," replied Hopkins.

A BBC technician interrupted. "Excuse me. We're ready for you, Mr. Hopkins. Right this way."

At fifteen minutes past nine o'clock, Harry Hopkins's voice and message of hope were broadcast over the radio. "*I did not come from America alone,*" he told those in the world who had access to the airwaves. "*I came in a bomber plane, and with me were twenty other bombers made in America.*"

After the broadcast, Churchill and Harriman escorted Harry to the front of Chequers and the waiting car.

"Where in the hell is Winant?" fumed Harriman as Hopkins put his new hat in the car.

"He'll be here," Hopkins answered calmly.

"You know the Russians don't like people running around their country without the right papers—like a passport and visa!" Harriman was angry with Winant for being late, and tense and worried about his friend, Harry, traveling across Russia above the raging German war machine.

In the distance, a car carrying Winant pulled up to the sentries at the front gate. "Finally," huffed Harriman.

Churchill shook Hopkins's hand. "Harry," Churchill said, "it is critical you impress upon Stalin just how important Russia's continued resistance is. Please tell him Britain has but one ambition—to crush that vile man, Hitler. And be sure to tell Stalin he can depend on us!"

"I will," Hopkins assured Churchill.

When Winant's car stopped, Gil jumped from the car and ran to Hopkins like a runner in a relay race with Harry's papers as the baton.

"C'mon, Gil. I have a plane to catch," teased Hopkins.

"Your passport is in there, and there's also a note from Ambassador Maisky saying you are permitted to cross any frontier in the USSR," Winant said, handing Hopkins the package.

"Did you hear about Japan?" Winant asked, and Hopkins shook his head. "We seized their US assets."

"That'll get Stalin's attention," replied Hopkins, tossing Winant's package into the rear seat and getting in the car.

"Let's go," Hopkins ordered the driver.

CHAPTER SIXTEEN

"You tell the President Joe pulls through!"

When Hopkins left the train in Scotland, he was driven to the harbor where an American PBY, a.k.a. the "Flying Boat," was waiting for him. The plane, piloted by twenty-eight-year-old British RAF Lieutenant David McKinley, had just landed and was hardly cooled down before Harry got on board and the plane took off again. In an effort to avoid the German Luftwaffe, the flight path took them over the northern tip of Finland and then down across the White Sea. The sun never set on the twenty-three-hour flight to the port in Archangel, Russia, on the banks of the Northern Dvina River.

Following a picture-perfect landing in the harbor, Lt. McKinley made his way to the back of the plane and saw a clump of blankets. He knew Hopkins was asleep somewhere in that clump and, after turning on the interior lights, called out, "Mr. Hopkins?"

He saw movement under the clump of blankets and a moment later heard, "Yeah."

"Time to go, sir. "

"Where the hell am I?" asked Hopkins.

"Archangel, sir."

His body aching and his eyes half closed, Hopkins was whisked to the Archangel airport and onto a Douglas American transport plane for the six-hour flight to Moscow airport. When they landed, Harry was greeted by Maxim Litvinov, the Soviet Union's Minister of Foreign Affairs, and US Ambassador to the Soviet Union, Laurence Steinhardt, and then taken directly to the American Embassy. Once inside and safe from the prying eyes and ears of the Soviets, Steinhardt asked Hopkins a couple of rhetorical questions, like "Why in the hell did you come here?" and "Have you lost your mind?"

As their car rolled through Red Square the next morning, Harry was struck by the brilliant colors and magnificent steeples of the State Museum, Saint Basil's Cathedral, and the other onion-topped roofs hovering over Moscow's Russian Orthodox Chapels. He'd seen pictures before, of course, but none that had done the place justice.

Once through security, Hopkins and Steinhardt navigated a labyrinth of hallways inside the Kremlin and were ushered into a large wood-paneled room filled with simple furniture and maps covering its walls. Harry Hopkins was face-to-face with Josef Stalin, who wore a light-gray tunic that had four pockets and smoked a pipe, which he placed in the ashtray on his desk.

Premier Josef Stalin, the rugged sixty-three-year-old dictator of the Soviet Union, did not utter a word as they entered but motioned for Hopkins and Steinhardt to sit in the chairs in front of his desk. He picked up a cigarette box from his desk and offered one to Hopkins. Hopkins took the cigarette, and the communist dictator lit it for him. After taking a puff, Harry reached into his pocket and offered his host one of his Lucky Strikes, which he lit for Stalin.

Stalin then circled to the front of his desk and sat down in a chair opposite Hopkins. Harry noted that Stalin's seat was slightly elevated above the others. Steinhardt interpreted for Harry, while Maxim Litvinov, who would soon become the Soviet Ambassador to the United States, handled the conversation for Stalin.

Stalin smiled at Hopkins. "American cigarettes are good!"

"Please tell Marshal Stalin," Hopkins informed Steinhardt, "that I will send him several cartons as soon as I return to the United States."

Steinhardt did.

"Spasibo," Stalin said, never taking his eyes off Hopkins. "We are pleased you have come all this way to visit us," Stalin said through Litvinov. "If there is anything you need, please ask."

As always, Hopkins did not waste time. "Our government is determined to provide the Soviet Union with all possible assistance. President Roosevelt believes Hitler and Hitlerism must be defeated."

Stalin smiled and nodded. "Already, the Soviet Union and America agree. Be confident we will stop the Germans," assured Stalin.

"Can you give me your assessment of the battle so far?" Hopkins asked.

"Initially, the Germans attacked with approximately three million men," Stalin replied easily. "We had 180 divisions when they attacked, but almost all were badly placed, so we were unable to repel the enemy," Stalin said all of this with no visible emotion.

"And your air force?" Hopkins queried.

"The German Luftwaffe attacked more than sixty of our airfields, and more than 1,800 aircraft were destroyed—most of them were still on the ground. After the first week, we lost 4,000 aircraft, and hundreds of thousands of our soldiers were killed or captured. We still do not know how many civilians the Germans have killed." It was clear to Hopkins that Stalin carried all the salient facts in his head.

"How can the United States help?" asked Hopkins.

"By joining us in the war against Hitler," replied Stalin with a crooked smile.

Hopkins interpreted Stalin's answer as sarcastic and thought to himself that it didn't take long for Stalin to flex his muscles in front of him. He held the Russian leader's gaze and decided to set the boundaries of his visit and their relationship.

"My mission here is entirely related to supplies," Hopkins told Stalin. "The matter of joining in the war will be decided largely by Hitler himself and his encroachment on our vital interests. President Roosevelt sent me here to find out what you need to defeat the Germans."

Though Stalin showed no emotion at Hopkins's response, with no hesitation, he replied, "We need airplanes, anti-aircraft guns, heavy machine guns, aviation fuel, a million or more rifles, artillery shells, aluminum for new planes, bullets, hand grenades. Give us such things and we can fight for three or four years."

"I am here to understand precisely what you need to fight Germany," Hopkins informed Stalin, emphasizing the word "precisely." "*How many* airplanes, guns, tanks, etcetera?"

Stalin smiled. "I have instructed my military leaders to provide you with a complete picture of our requirements."

"Thank you," Hopkins responded in kind. "That would be helpful."

Hopkins sensed that as fast as Stalin tested him, something had changed in their relationship just as fast. It occurred to him that he had passed some sort of test, and Stalin was now convinced that Hopkins's mission was sincere and legitimate.

Harry spent the following two days in Moscow gathering the information he needed to architect a full-blown Lend-Lease program for both the British *and* the Russians. Most importantly, his visit with the Soviet leader marked the beginning of a determined alliance between the US, Britain, and the Soviet Union to defeat Adolf Hitler.

After what seemed like the longest three days of Hopkins's life, on August 1, Stalin and Litvinov were at the Moscow airfield to say goodbye to Hopkins.

"I'm glad we met," Hopkins said, extending his hand to Stalin.

Stalin shook hands with Hopkins. "Thank you for making such a long and dangerous journey. You have great courage," said Stalin, and the look in the dictator's normally unemotional eyes told Harry he meant what he said.

"As do you, and the entire Soviet Union," replied Hopkins.

"Please give President Roosevelt my best wishes and tell him that I believe he has more influence with the common people of the world today than any other force," Stalin told Hopkins.

"I will pass along your kind words to the President," assured Hopkins, though he wondered if Stalin said it to be kind. "The information you've given me will help the United States and Great Britain to assist the Soviet Union in your great fight."

"Great Britain?" Stalin said mockingly. "Great Britain has its own problems."

"Prime Minister Churchill asked me to tell you that Britain's sole ambition today is to defeat Nazi Germany," informed Hopkins. "He said you can depend on Great Britain."

"From his lips to God's ears," replied Stalin.

The irony that Stalin, a man whose country forbade religion, mentioned God was not lost on Hopkins. "The US and Britain will do everything possible in the succeeding weeks to send material to Russia." Hopkins offered his hand.

"You tell the President Joe pulls through," Stalin said, shaking hands with Hopkins.

When Hopkins's plane arrived back in Archangel, Lt. McKinley was waiting on the tarmac ready to return him to Scapa Flow for his trip with Churchill on HMS Prince of Wales to the Argentia Conference in Placentia Bay. Hopkins exited the plane and walked with McKinley toward the terminal. Judging by Hopkins's appearance, it was obvious to McKinley that Hopkins was worn very thin from his journey.

"How was the flight from Moscow?" McKinley asked.

"Bumpy."

"I received a communication from Ambassador Steinhardt in Moscow," McKinley said. "He said you left your medicine satchel at the embassy."

"I know. Bad luck," commented Hopkins as they walked along the tarmac.

"Should I try to secure some of your medicines here?" McKinley asked.

"I'll be okay. Let's get back to Scapa Flow."

"The ambassador also said he received a cable from President Chiang Kai-shek requesting that you stop in China to see him on your way back home."

"China will have to wait," replied Hopkins.

"Would you like to rest before we start? It is a very long flight to Scapa Flow." McKinley was intent on persuading Hopkins to rest before they started out.

"Whatever the next twenty-four hours may bring, it cannot be as trying as the last three days," Hopkins told McKinley.

It was actually twenty-five hours later when they arrived in Scapa Flow. Another arduous journey in rapid succession that left Hopkins weaker still. When Lt. McKinley opened the PBY's door in Scapa Flow, a tender was waiting to transfer Hopkins to the battleship, HMS Prince of Wales. The plane bobbed in the water, and as Hopkins tried to make the jump into the waiting tender, he had to be saved from falling into the water. The two British sailors who caught Harry sat him down in the boat.

From Lt. McKinley's vantage point, as the tender slowly made its way across the harbor, Hopkins appeared to be a large round woolen heap in the middle of the boat. McKinley said out loud to his crew, "I don't think I've ever seen so much courage and determination in anyone, let alone a man so ill."

Though it was really just minutes, the tender ride to HMS Prince of Wales seemed to be hours long for Hopkins. He was warmly and officially greeted by Admiral Sir John Tovey, the Commander-in-Chief of the Home Fleet, but as he stepped onto the deck of the battleship, his legs buckled. Fortunately, a nearby sailor grabbed and steadied him. Admiral Tovey instantly ordered a sailor to put Hopkins in his cabin and have the doctor meet them there.

Inside Admiral Tovey's cabin, Hopkins told the ship's doctor that he had left all of his essential medicines behind in Moscow. He did his best to list them for the physician, who then organized several injections for him, including a regimen of vitamins that he hoped would help to revive his new patient.

Though they both appeared cheerful and optimistic, the doctor and Admiral Tovey were worried. In fact, judging by the look of him, they both privately wondered if Hopkins would live long enough to see Prime Minister Churchill, who was scheduled to arrive the next day.

Tovey told Hopkins, "The doctor says you need rest, Mr. Hopkins. You'll stay here in my cabin. The Prime Minister will come aboard tomorrow."

Hopkins did not resist and was glad to have a comfortable and warm bed. By the time Harry woke up the next day, he had slept nearly twenty-four hours, and HMS Prince of Wales was somewhere in the middle of the Atlantic Ocean.

Churchill was on board, having dinner in the ship's flag dining room with his entourage, including Lord Beaverbrook, Anthony Eden, the Secretary of State for War, Admiral Dudley Pound, General John Dill, Vice Air Marshall Portal, Pug Ismay, and Sir Alexander Cadogan.

The stewards had already removed their dinner plates from the table when Hopkins entered the dining room and heard Churchill's commanding voice.

"Admiral Tovey, might you have a decent port aboard?" asked Churchill.

"We do, sir, indeed." Tovey looked over at a white-coated and white-gloved waiter and ordered, "Port and glasses for us."

"There you are, Harry!" Churchill called out, seeing Hopkins enter the dining room. "How are you feeling?"

"Better, thank you," replied Hopkins.

"Can we get you something to eat?" asked Admiral Tovey.

"Just a coffee," Harry replied sluggishly. The others at the table all said their hellos, and a moment later, the steward delivered a cup of coffee to Hopkins, while two others poured port for the rest.

"You look a thousand times better than when you arrived." Admiral Tovey smiled. He was relieved.

"You had the admiral quite worried," commented Churchill.

"Admiral Tovey and his staff took great care of me." Hopkins raised his coffee cup to Tovey, who nodded.

"Do you feel up to telling us about your trip?" asked Churchill. He was desperate to know the state of affairs in the Soviet Union.

"The Russians are putting up one hell of a fight, and they will continue to fight if we can keep them supplied," replied Harry as the caffeine seemed to revive him.

"Our reports say the Russians have already lost a million men," Beaverbrook weighed in.

"I believe those reports are accurate," responded Hopkins, "but I believe Stalin will ruthlessly fight against the Germans regardless of the cost in human life."

Churchill puffed on his cigar, examining Hopkins. "He impressed you," Churchill stated.

"I think Stalin will make Hitler regret the day he decided to invade Russia," answered Hopkins.

"I will say this," Sir John Dill weighed in, "even if the Russians do not defeat the Germans, with Hitler invested in his Russian gambit, it will, at the very least, diminish his available resources for other adventures."

"Indeed," Pug Ismay commented. "Even mighty Germany has finite resources."

"Hitler's turn to the east certainly gives all of us more time to get our own ducks in a row," Hopkins said directly to Churchill.

"Did you meet his military advisers?" asked Churchill.

"I did. Military staff, production people, Litvinov, and others. Every single person I spoke with was very candid about the situation and the equipment and supplies they need. But it is important to know that no one in Russia decides or does anything without Stalin's approval," Hopkins told the table, and then turned to look directly at Churchill. "Stalin is the only person in the Soviet Union that you and the President need to be in touch with."

"Harry, what were your impressions of Stalin, the man?" Ismay asked.

"Austere. Rugged," responded Hopkins quickly, and as he looked at the men around the table, he realized they were hanging on his every word. "He wore no ornaments, either military or civilian. He has a clear and hard mind. Very clear about what he wants and what Russia needs. When we spoke, it was like talking to an intelligent machine. He didn't waste words, and there was little in the way of gestures or mannerisms. He is about five feet six inches tall, thick, and close to the ground. He must weigh close to two hundred pounds, and his hands are huge.

"Sounds like he would make a superb Rugby player," Admiral Tovey ventured, and the men around the table let out nervous laughs.

Churchill exchanged looks with Hopkins through the haze of his cigar smoke and said quietly, "I hope he joins our team."

CHAPTER SEVENTEEN

"We are not divided; all one body we, one in hope and doctrine, one in charity."

FDR loved cloak-and-dagger deception almost as much as he loved the sea, so he was particularly excited when he and several aides left the White House for a trip on the Potomac, his 165-foot Presidential yacht, to Cape Cod, where they planned to do some fishing. Or so everyone believed.

As HMS Prince of Wales carried Hopkins and Winston Churchill across the North Atlantic toward Newfoundland's Placentia Bay and the Argentia Conference with FDR, the President was secretly spirited off the Potomac and boarded the heavy cruiser, USS Augusta. While the Augusta proceeded at full speed to Newfoundland, the Potomac played the role of decoy, complete with a Secret Service man dressed as a Roosevelt look-alike, and with mannerisms to match. To the reporters covering the President, it looked like FDR was on a fishing trip in Cape Cod. Even Eleanor didn't know.

By the next morning, fog hovered over Placentia, and the USS Augusta, with all of her escorts, was anchored and waiting in the bay. Roosevelt was on the deck, accompanied by his son, Elliott Roosevelt. Elliott was an Army Air Force captain who, along with his brother James, regularly helped their father whenever FDR was determined to stand or walk in public. It was the former that day, as the President of the United States stood waiting for the arrival of the Prime Minister of Great Britain, who was somewhere out there in the fog.

Admiral Ernest King snarled at the ship's captain, "Where the hell are they?"

"With this kind of visibility, sir, they could be right there on the other side of the harbor and we'd never see them," the captain worried.

A moment later, "There they are!" the captain exclaimed, pointing toward ghostlike images taking shape in the mist. Soon, there were three massive ships visible as they moved slowly through the dense fog. As the last ship of the trio came into better view, making its way toward the Augusta, the waiting Americans noted swirls of camouflage on its side. It was HMS Prince of Wales.

"Excellent!" FDR exclaimed as the strains of The Star-Spangled Banner could be heard wafting across the harbor from the Prince of Wales. When the anthem was finished, the band on the deck of the USS Augusta returned the respect with God Save the King, after which the President remarked to King, "I don't believe I've ever heard 'My Country 'Tis of Thee' played better."

FDR looked across and saw Winston Churchill and Harry Hopkins standing together. In that moment, FDR was filled with pride and thought to himself, "Well done, Harry. Well done."

At almost the same time, Hopkins turned to Churchill, "I need to head over to the Augusta now."

"As you should," Churchill instantly agreed.

"We are preparing the tender for you," Admiral Tovey informed Hopkins.

When Harry boarded the Augusta, he was immediately taken to the President's cabin, where Roosevelt read some briefing documents for the conference.

"Harry the hop!" FDR exclaimed. "Welcome home! How are you feeling?"

"They took good care of me on the Prince of Wales. Did Harriman make it?"

"Yes, he arrived last night with Sumner Wells," replied FDR. Wells was FDR's second in command at the State Department under Cordell Hull. "How was Russia, Harry?" FDR dug right into his biggest concern.

Hopkins answered quickly. "Joe Davies was right. Stalin will make Hitler pay. It will be a hard fight, but with our help, they will hurt the Germans badly."

"I'm not so sure Winston agrees with you," Roosevelt said, airing his concern about Churchill's long-held negative views of the Soviets and communists.

"He's coming around. He knows if Britain is to have any chance against the Nazis, Stalin must keep fighting."

"I'm thinking about having a private one-on-one with Winston after dinner tonight," FDR said.

"Something more informal might be better to start," suggested Hopkins, knowing that, as he told Murrow, he had to carefully manage the two prima donnas if there was to be any hope of a successful first meeting and strong alliance. "If it's all right with you," Hopkins continued, "I'd like to brief the senior leaders on my Russia trip at our dinner here, after which I'd like to invite Churchill to give everyone his informal analysis of the war. It'd be a good way for everyone to better understand how he sees the world."

Roosevelt nodded, "I like it."

After dinner aboard Augusta that evening, and after Harry's briefing on Russia, as usual, Churchill waxed eloquent on the war and the situation in Europe and the Far East. To the delight of Hopkins and FDR, he closed his brilliant extemporaneous talk with, "Germany's invasion of Russia has offered Great Britain a significant opportunity to re-arm, re-supply, and re-train for the kind of mobile warfare required to best Hitler and Mussolini in the Middle East, the Mediterranean, and the European continent. And it has also freed up resources to allow us to address Japan, particularly should they choose to continue their aggression beyond Manchuria."

Everyone in the room applauded as Churchill sat down. And as he relit his cigar, FDR and Hopkins exchanged looks. They knew Churchill would support supplying Stalin.

President Roosevelt spoke up. "I'd like to make a couple of toasts," he said, "First to you, Prime Minister. Thank you for helping to organize this Argentia Conference. In addition to having the opportunity and pleasure to meet you and your fine staff, I know we all would have traveled here tonight just to hear your masterful assessment of the war. I know I speak for everyone when I say we are all much wiser as a result of your insightful talk." FDR raised his glass and everyone followed, responding with "Cheers" and "Hear, hear."

Roosevelt continued, "My second toast tonight is to Harry Hopkins. His timely and dangerous trip to the Soviet Union, along with his keen assessment of Russia's challenges and capabilities, has provided all of us with a greater understanding of what they need to defeat the Nazi war machine." Again, a chorus of "Cheers," and "hear, hear," filled the room as glasses were again raised.

Not to be outdone, Churchill said, "If I may, Mr. President, I would like to propose a toast to you, sir, on behalf of all the people of Great Britain. We thank you for your remarkable leadership in the great struggle against the blight of Hitlerism. We are all inspired by your courage, and we will be forever grateful for the many bold and important steps you have taken to help the freedom-loving people of Great Britain and throughout the world during this crisis."

"I must say, if this evening is indicative of the rest of our time together, our Argentia Conference here will be a smashing success!" commented Roosevelt cheerfully, and everyone at the table again responded.

Hopkins saw the opportunity and immediately decided to advance his idea for the conference with the two leaders. "You both may want to consider setting a goal to produce a joint declaration at the end of the conference."

"Excellent idea, Harry," responded FDR, and Churchill immediately picked up the ball.

"If I may, Mr. President. You must know that Great Britain aspires to live in a world committed to the four freedoms you so eloquently put forward in your State of the Union address last January. Freedom of worship, freedom from want, freedom of speech, and freedom from fear are values and principles the United Kingdom wholeheartedly shares with the United States. So, if you do not object, I propose we allow your four freedoms to serve as the foundation for our joint declaration."

"I've no objection whatsoever, Prime Minister," said FDR, pleased that his four freedoms would serve as the framework for the relationship between the two countries.

"I'll begin drafting the Argentia Conference Declaration for your review and any edits you may have," Hopkins said, and raised his glass. "Cheers!"

FDR and Churchill raised their glasses along with the rest of the attendees, and almost in unison, the entire group responded to Hopkins with a rousing "Cheers!"

"Harry," Churchill addressed Hopkins. "If I may, I would like to suggest the first edit to the conference communiqué. Let's change the title of the document from the Argentia Conference Declaration to simply the Atlantic Charter."

"I love it!" exclaimed FDR.

#

Over the next two days, the delegations spent their time in meetings discussing Britain's needs, planning convoy protection, and hammering out the language they would use in the Atlantic Charter to communicate their allegiance to the world.

At one point, the discussions stalled when Churchill said he could not agree to the Charter because the fourth clause committed both countries to free trade. The United Kingdom's requirement to trade with its commonwealth countries, called the Imperial Preference, required Churchill to consult with the leaders of those countries. When it looked like that issue would prevent them from publishing their joint declaration, Hopkins intervened and prevailed on both parties to agree to the fourth clause by including the phrase, "with due respect for their existing obligations." It worked, and the Atlantic Charter was finalized.

On Sunday, the last day of the conference, the bay sparkled in sunlight that was almost blinding compared to the prevalent gray mist since they had arrived. It was Roosevelt's turn to visit Churchill, and he was ferried to HMS Prince of Wales.

The deck was full of sailors, officials, and many others, but no one said a word, and not a photograph was taken of FDR making his way to his seat. There was nothing but silence as FDR gripped Elliott's arm with his left hand while bracing himself with the cane in his right hand. He shuffled his braced legs forward in a maneuver

FDR called his "two-step"—an act that required extraordinary upper-body strength and courageous determination. Many wiped tears from their eyes as they watched the President totter and sway, committed to arriving at his designated seat under his own power.

When FDR seated himself next to Churchill on the far side of the deck, the signal for the prayer service officiated by chaplains from both navies was given, and the two leaders joined in as everyone sang Oh God, Our Help in Ages Past, followed by the British navy hymn, Eternal Father, Strong to Save. Prayers were offered for the President, Prime Minister, the King and his ministers and admirals, as well as for all the generals and air marshals, the invaded countries, and the sick, wounded, and bereaved of the world. And then there was the final hymn.

Onward Christian Soldiers.

Hopkins watched FDR and Churchill as they sang the verse: "We are not divided; all one body we, one in hope and doctrine, one in charity," and he saw tears in Churchill's eyes. Those words were more than a declaration for Churchill. Indeed, they were his prayer.

The Atlantic Charter was published and delivered to the world on August 14, 1941. It was the joint vision of Great Britain and the United States for a world underpinned by FDR's Four Freedoms, where all nations, large or small, victorious or vanquished, would know freedom, peace, and prosperity through Democratic principles, free trade, and equal rights.

CHAPTER EIGHTEEN

"I love it when you talk dirty, Lulu."

The night Senator Robert Taft and his wife, Martha, held a dinner party at their beautiful Victorian home in Georgetown was one of those magical autumn nights in Washington, DC.   A warm evening breeze flowed into their dining room through floor-to-ceiling windows, carrying with it the sound of a light rain rhythmically tapping against tree leaves and shrubs in their front garden.

Dinner completed, the Tafts' guests, who included Senator Burton Wheeler and his wife, Lulu, the Southern Congressman who chaired Hopkins's congressional hearing, and the well-known communist baiter and hater, Congressman Hamilton Fish, sat under the glow of a fine crystal chandelier that dated back to the early nineteenth century. The table was set with fine Italian linen tablecloth and napkins, Italian candelabras, and 120-year-old silver, glass, and dinnerware that was given to Martha by her husband's grandmother.

Senator Taft was the fifty-two-year-old Republican Senator from Ohio and the proud leader of a conservative coalition of Republicans and Democrats in Congress who railed against all things FDR—from the President's New Deal all the way up to his present-day seeming inclination to engage America in Europe's woes.

Though Taft and his dinner guest from Montana, Democratic Senator Burton Wheeler, purported to be committed isolationists, no one was really sure if they actually were. Some believed both senators simply chose the isolationists' side of the argument because Lindbergh's America First Committee was a very large and painful thorn in FDR's side. Truth be told, as far as Taft and Wheeler were concerned, any thorn that managed to get under FDR's skin was good enough to garner their support.

Senator Wheeler's wife, Lulu, sat on the America First National Committee and served as its Treasurer for the Washington, DC chapter. Lulu was never bashful about letting people know she was a devoted isolationist, and she was also an inspired leader in the club that hated everything to do with Roosevelt. And though the Senator agreed with his wife's views on FDR, he preferred to focus his energies on ferreting out the communists, socialists, gremlins, and other unseen enemies he believed were infiltrating America's government and culture. Taken together, Lulu and Burton Wheeler were a DC power couple who, with their like-minded friends and political allies, prayed they could save God-fearing Americans from the terrible cataclysm that would befall the country should FDR continue on his chosen path to perdition. Amen.

With Duke Ellington's Take the A Train playing on the dining room radio, Miriam, the Tafts' African American housemaid and servant, entered the dining room through the kitchen's swinging door and began clearing the table in preparation for dessert. Martha Taft rose from her seat to help, and she and Miriam returned to the kitchen to clean the evening's dishes and prepare dessert.

Before the swinging doors settled in place, Lulu saw an opening to change their lighthearted dinner banter and chit-chat, and introduced the conversation she was longing to have.

"What do you all make of this Atlantic Charter?" Lulu asked in a way that told anyone listening of her disdain for the joint British-US statement.

Senator Wheeler knew what was coming and tried his best to steer his wife in another direction. "Lulu, we all have had enough politics for today," he begged.

"Burton, we are being pushed into a war," Lulu said, confirming her husband's intimate understanding of her. "And now we are going to help the Russians for mercy's sake. You mark my words, Burton. When we learn what went on at that secret Atlantic Charter Conference, Roosevelt will be considered a traitor."

In fairness, Lulu couldn't help herself. For some deeply personal reason, she felt compelled to share her theories and felt particularly alive when she could incite those around her into an orgy of grievances. So, while Martha Taft and Miriam prepared dessert in the kitchen, Lulu put out chum in the dining room, hoping to instigate an emotionally charged feeding frenzy against FDR and his associates.

When the Andrews Sisters' Boogie Woogie Bugle Boy replaced Duke Ellington on the radio, Congressman Hamilton Fish couldn't resist following Lulu's lead. "Did any of you notice there was no mention of freedom of religion in the Atlantic Charter?" Fish lobbed his seemingly innocent question into the middle of the table.

In the early days of FDR's presidency, New York Congressman Fish was Roosevelt's neighbor in upstate New York and a loyal FDR supporter. By 1941, and tonight's dinner, however, Fish had become a rabid anti-communist and an outspoken and acidic critic of FDR.

On hearing Fish's question, Lulu became flushed with excitement, knowing it was a good indication that the feeding frenzy had started.

"What of it?" the Southern Congressman asked Fish.

"Seems odd, don't you think?" Fish said, trying to lead him and the others to his idea of water. "Every one of FDR's Four Freedoms is in that document, except for Freedom of Religion. I'm just saying."

"I missed that," Senator Taft said, biting down on the hook.

"There is no doubt in my mind that FDR was forced to kowtow to Stalin and the communists," Fish said, reeling in Taft.

"Thank you, Ham!" Lulu said to Congressman Fish, ecstatic that there was someone else in the room capable of seeing the forest from the trees. She then turned to her husband. "You see, Burton, I told you."

"Hopkins's slimy fingers are all over that Atlantic Charter document," Taft said, using the opportunity to throw a dart at the man he thought responsible for most of the ills plaguing the country.

"What I want to know is how did that half-man go from giving out leaf raking jobs to running Lend-Lease? How did that happen?" The

Southern Congressman couldn't resist the temptation to join in the frenzy at the mention of Hopkins's name.

"Our very own Rasputin," Senator Taft chimed in.

"He's a traitor," Lulu said matter-of-factly. "It's that simple. He is working with the British and the Russians to get us into a war with Germany." Lulu always made sure she threw in more chum to keep the feeding frenzy going.

"I warned you all," Senator Wheeler reminded his guests casually. "I told you if that Lend-Lease Bill got passed, it would result in every fourth American boy being plowed under."

"And I warned you back in '34 when Roosevelt officially recognized the Soviet Union," Fish jumped in, heated and salivating. "I told you Roosevelt would be a dictator who would take us down the road to socialism. It won't be long and the communists will be living right next door to you."

"You were right then, Congressman, and you are right now," Lulu said, thrilled to have Fish on her side as she successfully ginned up the group. "Roosevelt reigns supreme over all of us," Lulu kept the chum flowing.

"And the communists are now among us," Fish added for good measure.

Lulu Wheeler thought for a moment that she might actually be in love with Congressman Fish! The frenzy of grievance matching and besting started by Lulu seemed to elevate the temperature in the room and, in short order, actually had most of the guests perspiring in the warm, humid night air. Senator Taft wiped his brow with his napkin, and so did Congressman Fish as Lulu rose from the table.

"Robert, do you mind if I shut off that awful noise?" Lulu asked Taft, referring to the jitterbug beat of the Andrews Sisters. The music was distracting her just as they seemed to be heading toward a memorable group climax.

"Please," agreed Taft.

When Lulu snapped off the radio, a silence enveloped the room that left everyone at the table stewing in their anger and frustration. Just then, Martha Taft and Miriam swung open the kitchen door, beaming with broad smiles and carrying Miriam's delicious hot apple pie into the dining room. They both stopped in their tracks; their smiles wiped clean by the tangible tension in the room and the snarling faces that greeted them.

Martha stood for a moment examining the angry, sweaty faces around the table and decided the apple pie she held in her hands was just what the doctor ordered to cheer up the group. She flashed her biggest smile.

"Anybody want dessert?"

#

It was a serene, sunny, and cloudless morning in Honolulu, with a gentle trade wind blowing across the lush green island and its cliffs. The trees and flowers were in full bloom, and the soft, warm Hawaiian breeze carried soothing floral scents everywhere. It was a perfect time of year in the Hawaiian Islands and particularly in Honolulu.

The Japanese Consulate and the Consul-General's residence in Honolulu were beautiful, white, Western-style buildings that sat behind a fence on Nuuanu Avenue. A manicured lawn bordered with Koa, Ohi'a Lehua, Hala, Sandalwood, and Banyan trees, and a dense, colorful flower garden surrounded both the residence and the Consulate, while a Japanese flag with its bright orange rising sun fluttered softly in the breeze atop a flag pole.

The Japanese Consul-General, Nagao Kita, was in his late forties and recently sent by Tokyo to Honolulu as Japan's new Consul-General, together with his thirty-year-old Vice Consul, Tadashi Morimura. Since their arrival earlier in the year, both men quickly became welcome additions to Honolulu's diplomatic society, not to mention esteemed guests at the many cocktail parties that were held regularly across the island by local officials, military officers, and Honolulu's affluent.

Though both men preferred to wear traditional Japanese kimonos and follow traditional Japanese protocol behind the walls of the Consulate, outside the Consulate, they wore custom-tailored Western clothing, maintained polished Western manners, and spoke almost accent-free English with at least some semblance of wit and humor—an unusual trait for Japanese diplomats.

As it turned out, it was more than just their clothes, wit, and humor that made these two unusual. Kita knew that his Vice Consul, Tadashi Morimura, was not actually a Foreign Service Officer. Instead, Vice Consul Tadashi Morimura was a spy, and his real name was Tadeo Yoshikawa.

When Yoshikawa arrived for his meeting this morning with Kita, he wore a blue kimono. He was shown into Kita's office, and, as protocol demanded, he stood inside the doorway waiting to be recognized by Kita, who sat working at his desk. When Kita looked up after several moments, Yoshikawa bowed to the Consul-General.

Dressed in an orange and black kimono, Kita rose and returned Yoshikawa's bow. Yoshikawa then moved to the front of Kita's desk and bowed again. So did Kita. Kita extended the open palm of his right hand with his fingers held together toward one of the empty chairs in front of his desk, and Yoshikawa sat down. Kita did the same and handed Yoshikawa a document from his desk.

"We received this cable this morning," Kita informed Yoshikawa. Yoshikawa read the cable as Kita continued. "You are to separate Pearl Harbor into five distinct zones and report on the number and type of warships held in each zone."

"How quickly?" Yoshikawa looked up from the document.

"As soon as possible."

"Is there anything else?" asked Yoshikawa.

"That is all for now."

"Yes, sir."

Yoshikawa rose from his chair and returned the document to Kita. Kita stood and took the document. Yoshikawa bowed, Kita returned his bow, and Yoshikawa turned and exited Kita's office.

Though their meeting was over as quickly as it started, it was more than enough time to firmly plant the seeds of war.

#

Except for the curious and solitary Building One, which stood alone in the back of the 14th Naval District, the Naval base at Pearl

Harbor was a bee hive of activity, with sailors working, ships being maintained, children going to school, men and women picking up items at the Post Exchange in the Quadrangle at Schofield Barracks, cars carrying officers, and tenders shuttling officers and VIPs across the harbor from ship to shore and back again.

Against the backdrop of all of this activity, the seemingly empty Building One housed the Combat Intelligence Unit responsible for capturing Japanese radio signals from their embassies and their Navy. The unit was code-named Station Hypo, and it was commanded by Joseph Rochefort, a brilliant officer who worked tirelessly with his small team to try to figure out what the Japanese were up to. Those who knew Rochefort believed he rarely slept, brushed his teeth, or changed his clothes.

Through Magic, Naval Intelligence's secret program tracking Japanese Embassy communications, Rochefort intercepted a Japanese cable sent from Tokyo to the Japanese Consul-General in Honolulu that he believed discussed information concerning the US Naval force at Pearl Harbor. Rochefort was fairly certain the cable was a Purple message, originating with Japan's latest encryption device and most recent codes. To be certain his instinct was right, he sent the cable to the War Department in DC and requested that Naval Intelligence analysts confirm his suspicions.

By the time Rochefort's Japanese cable reached the War Department in Washington, DC, more than two weeks had passed from the time he sent it. Two weeks after that, the decrypt analysts in the War Department finally confirmed there was a "high probability" the message was asking the Consul-General to inform Tokyo of the number of US Navy ships in Pearl Harbor, though they were sure to add the disclaimer that they could not be one hundred percent certain. They also commented that all the Japanese had to do to get that information was ask any local Honolulu driver. They didn't need to send encrypted messages to learn how many ships there were in Pearl.

All in all, it took almost five weeks for Rochefort to learn that his instinct was right, though he certainly didn't agree with Naval Intelligence in DC that any Honolulu cab driver would have done the trick for the Japanese. After tracking their communications for months, Rochefort knew the Japanese, like all good intelligence operations, followed a triangulation protocol that compared information from at least three unrelated and unaffiliated sources to ensure every piece of intelligence they acquired was accurate.

Washington's decrypt of the cable confirmed for Rochefort that there was something far more sinister going on in his own backyard. He knew that if Tokyo was secretly enlisting the help of their Consul-General to determine the number of ships in Pearl Harbor, that meant they had accessed that information from two other sources. It also meant the information was vital to their plans and efforts, whatever those plans and efforts may be.

Rochefort immediately alerted his team to be on the lookout for similar sequences broadcast from Japan and, more importantly, told his friends upstairs in Building One's Combat Intelligence Unit that it was highly likely the Japanese had an active spy network operating in Hawaii.

#

As the US Navy tried to keep its head above water in the Pacific, its twenty-three-year-old Wickes-class destroyer, the USS Greer, steamed its way in the North Atlantic on a remarkably calm and sunny September morning. The Greer was on a scheduled mail run and after making a delivery to Argentia, Newfoundland, it was now sailing about 200 miles south of Greenland on its way to its next stop in Iceland.

As the destroyer cut through the calm seas at standard speed, her captain sat in his chair on the bridge while the watch officer, helmsman, navigator, and two lookouts attended to running the ship. None of those on the bridge had ever seen combat, and their average age was twenty-two years old, and that included their captain, Lieutenant Commander Laurence Hugh Frost, who at forty-one, was called the "Old Man."

The executive officer or XO entered the bridge from the Combat Information Center—the CIC—carrying a document and walked directly to the Frost.

"Sir, we have been notified by a British aircraft that they spotted a German U-boat," the XO reported.

"Read it," ordered Frost, and he stood up to look out onto the open water.

"'To USS Greer from British Patrol Aircraft N19. U-boat crash dive ten miles due west of your position heading one four zero. Acknowledge.'"

"How long ago?" asked Frost.

"Ten minutes ago."

Frost was not happy. Ten minutes was far too long for this information to reach him on the bridge, and he made a mental note to have a conversation with the XO when this was over. "Sound battle stations," he ordered calmly.

"Aye, sir," replied the XO and looked at the watch officer. "Sound battle stations."

"Battle stations, aye, sir," responded the watch officer quickly, and turned the switch on the communications panel. The horns on the ship began to squawk and echoed loudly throughout the entire ship and the ocean around them.

The watch officer picked up the microphone. "All hands. General quarters. I repeat. All hands. General quarters. This is not a drill," the watch officer announced, and after several more seconds, he shut off the horn.

All of the men on the bridge withdrew their life vests and helmets from the lockers, and everyone, including the captain, put them on.

"I have the con," Frost said as he placed his helmet on his head and the two lookouts moved to either side of the bridge with their binoculars trained on the water.

"Captain has the con," the watch officer repeated loudly, telling everyone on the bridge Frost would now be giving orders and directing traffic.

"Make sure our flags are up and visible," Frost ordered the watch officer.

"Aye, sir. Checking the flags, sir," the watch officer repeated and left the bridge to check the Greer's mast.

"15 degrees to starboard," Frost ordered the helmsman.

"Aye, sir, 15 degrees starboard," the helmsman repeated.

"All ahead standard."

"Aye, sir. All ahead standard."

The watch officer entered the bridge. "Flags are up and visible, sir," he reported.

"Very good," Frost confirmed.

"Torpedo in the water! Bearing 75 degrees!" The shout from the port side lookout sounded hysterical. "U-boat!"

#

Three days after the USS Greer was fired upon by a German submarine, two formidable and indomitable icons were lost at FDR's home in Springwood. On that day, Sara Roosevelt, the President's mother, passed away with FDR at her side, and though it was a perfectly calm day, minutes later, the huge oak tree that had stood as a proud sentinel above Springwood's central meadow for hundreds of years split in half and tumbled to the ground. The normally confident and ebullient FDR was shaken to his core and grief-stricken.

His mother, Sara Roosevelt, not only gave him life, but as his devoted and doting mother, she provided him with unwavering belief and love that many believed was the source of FDR's remarkable confidence, courage, and self-reliance.

On hearing the news of Sara Roosevelt's passing, Hopkins called FDR from the White House and offered to join him in Hyde Park. "I appreciate that, Harry," FDR said, "but it isn't necessary. Eleanor and the children are here. I'd rather you worked on the draft for the

Fireside Chat. Every one of Cordell's drafts about the USS Greer incident makes us look weak and indecisive. The world must know we will take some action against Germany."

"Cordell" was Cordell Hull, the seventy-year-old US Secretary of State. Patrician in his bearing and his demeanor, Hull was born and raised in Tennessee, where his family could trace its roots back to the Revolutionary War. While it was true that FDR nominated Hull for the Nobel Peace Prize in 1945 and Hull played a role in the formation of the United Nations, it was also true that Hull was not one of FDR's favorites.

"Sam Rosenman and I will have a new draft for you later today," Hopkins assured FDR.

Four days later, on September 11, 1941, FDR sat in front of a microphone at his desk in the White House wearing a black arm band on his left coat sleeve. Hopkins and Steve Early sat in his office as his audience, while the rest of America listened over their radios.

When Hopkins drafted the speech, he remembered FDR's first Fireside Chat, which educated Americans on their banking system and convinced them to invest in their country's future. From Hopkins's perspective, FDR would have to educate Americans on the need to defend themselves against the authoritarian viruses that were growing rapidly around the world. There was really only one course of action for America, and it was not to stick its head in the sand.

"My fellow Americans," FDR began, looking at Hopkins and Early, and proceeded to recount how a week earlier, the USS Greer was fired upon by a German U-boat. Like his banking chat, he educated the American people and stated his case—the United States had the right to defend itself, and he, as President, had a duty to defend it.

While Hopkins and Early looked on, FDR spoke in his steady clear voice, "In spite of what Hitler's propaganda bureau has invented, and in spite of what any American obstructionist organization may prefer to believe," FDR said, "I tell you the blunt fact that the German submarine fired first upon this American destroyer without warning and with deliberate design to sink her."

Hopkins enjoyed aligning the American Firsters with Hitler's propaganda machine and smiled when FDR continued making his case. "When you see a rattlesnake poised to strike," FDR told the country, "you do not wait until he has struck before you crush him. These Nazi submarines and raiders are the rattlesnakes of the Atlantic. They are a menace to the free pathways of the high seas."

FDR's chat that night closed with the sort of strength and directness that he had wanted from Cordell Hull, but which Hopkins delivered. "So let this warning be clear. From now on, if German or Italian vessels of war enter the waters, the protection of which is necessary for American defense, they do so at their own peril."

The radio technician in FDR's office watched as the light on his transmitter panel turned off. "We're off the air, Mr. President," the radio technician announced.

FDR sat back in his chair and lit a cigarette. "What do you think?" he asked Hopkins.

Hopkins was pleased that FDR put a stake in the ground and in the Atlantic Ocean. "That was a perfect 'good evening' to the America

Firsters and 'good morning' to Herr Hitler and Signore Mussolini," replied Hopkins. "You just ruined their day for sure."

On the very same night, Charles Lindbergh, the America First Committee's leading man, stood at the podium looking out over a sea of fluttering flags and transfixed faces at an America First Rally at the Coliseum in Des Moines, Iowa.

The morning after FDR's Fireside Chat and Lindbergh's Iowa speech, Hopkins sat in his bathrobe and pajamas in his White House bedroom office reviewing a cable from Averell Harriman detailing Russia's most urgent requirements when Steve Early and Robert Sherwood burst into his room without knocking.

"Jesus! What gives?" a startled Hopkins exclaimed.

"Did you hear about Lindbergh?" Early asked, almost giggling.

"What?"

Sherwood, who never missed a chance to berate Lindbergh, couldn't resist. "His speech last night in Des Moines after the President's broadcast."

"And?"

"He doesn't know," Early said to Sherwood.

"Lindbergh is getting skewered by almost every paper in the country," Sherwood said gleefully.

"This morning's *The New York Times* front page," Early jumped in, "says 'Lindbergh Sees a Plot for War.' Get this. He told the crowd 'England cannot win' and 'the three most important groups which have been pressing this country toward war are the British, the Jewish, and the Roosevelt administration.'"

"Even Hearst said his assertion that the Jews are pressing the country into war is unwise, unpatriotic, and un-American," Sherwood could hardly contain himself.

"I should send Lindbergh a thank-you note," said Hopkins, sounding like he was serious.

"This is really going to upset the isolationists," said a giddy Early.

"The hell with those guys!" both Sherwood and Hopkins said at exactly the same time.

#

Inside Senator Burton Wheeler's office in the Capitol, a pretty red-headed staffer walked past a pacing Lulu Wheeler and placed a half dozen newspapers on the Senator's desk.

"Thank you, Kathy," Senator Wheeler said to the pretty staffer as she turned to exit his office. "Lulu. Sit down, please. You're going to wear out my rug." Wheeler told his wife and picked up one of the papers from his desk.

"This is a disaster, Burton," Lulu moaned, continuing to pace the room. "An unmitigated disaster. Everyone is against him. Did he have to say out loud that it is a Jewish plot? Even if it is true."

Reading the paper, Senator Wheeler exclaimed, "Lord in heaven," and shaking his head, gestured toward Lulu with the paper in hand. "Even Wendell Wilkie called it 'The most un-American talk in my time made by any person of national reputation.'"

"What is wrong with Lindbergh?" Lulu asked, looking up toward heaven. She seemed to be on the verge of actual tears, and Lulu never cried.

"He thinks he is so important he can say whatever he wants," Wheeler said clinically and picked up another newspaper from his desk.

"The Des Moines Register, for Pete's sake?" exclaimed Wheeler disbelievingly as he read the next article. "Even they say his speech was 'so intemperate, so unfair, so dangerous in its implications that it cannot but turn many spadefuls in the digging of the grave of his influence in this crisis.'"

"What are we going to do, Burton?" Lulu begged her husband for an answer.

"Not much," the Senator said, resigned to the fact that putting distance between him and Lindbergh was in order. "Listen, Lulu, Martin Dies called this morning and told me the Texas House of Representatives wants to pass a resolution saying that Lindbergh is not welcome to speak in their state."

"America First is dead, Burton. Dead!" Lulu repeated, unable to accept her fate.

"Yes," Wheeler agreed. "And its epitaph will read: Here lies America First. Murdered by one man who succumbed to the weight of his own bullshit."

As the implications of the disaster settled in on Lulu, it propelled her to pace faster and harder around her husband's office, accentuating each step she took with the word "fuck." "Fuck, fuck, fuck, fuck, fuck…"

Senator Wheeler stopped reading the newspaper and looked up to watch his wife pacing and cursing her way around his office.

"I love it when you talk dirty, Lulu."

CHAPTER NINETEEN

"A couple of days of rest will set me right."

"The Russians approved these lists?" Hopkins asked Harriman.

"Confirmed, reviewed, and confirmed again," assured Harriman.

It was very late at night in FDR's office when Hopkins and Joe Davies sat with FDR debriefing Averell Harriman on his Lend-Lease trip in Moscow with Lord Beaverbrook. Each man held a folder prepared by Harriman, which contained the Soviet Union's requests for supplies, guns, vehicles, tanks, ammunition, planes, and anything else they could possibly need to defeat Nazi Germany.

"Averell. I want to express to you and your associates the great satisfaction I have with the successful culmination of your mission in Moscow. I think that you all did a magnificent job," FDR said, and meant it.

Joe Davies concurred with the President, "This is well done, Ave."

"Thank you." Harriman was pleased.

"How was Stalin?" asked Hopkins.

"Our first meeting went great. It lasted about three hours. The next day, though, the bear's ass was on fire and he worked us over pretty good," Harriman admitted.

"How did Beaverbrook do?" Hopkins followed up.

"Fine, especially considering that at one point he handed Stalin a note from Churchill, and Stalin just shoved it into a drawer without even looking at it."

"Stalin has all of the diplomatic skills of Attila the Hun." Davies laughed.

"As subtle as a sledgehammer," agreed Hopkins.

"My sense of him is he is under enormous pressure," Harriman suggested.

"From without and within," agreed Davies. "If Uncle Joe doesn't lead the Soviets to victory against the Germans, there are more than a few of his comrades standing in the wings waiting to shoot him."

"Soviet democracy at work," commented Hopkins. "I would like you guys to stay in touch," Hopkins said to Harriman and Davies. "Joe, I think we can continue to use your insights with the Soviets."

"Happy to help," replied Davies easily.

The meeting ended, and FDR and Hopkins made their way up to the residence. At that hour, the White House corridors were very quiet. As Mac pushed FDR in his wheelchair toward his bedroom, Hopkins walked alongside the President.

"Joe Davies is our best man when it comes to Stalin and the Soviet Union," Hopkins said out loud, replaying the meeting in his head.

"He understands them far better than most," FDR agreed and then looked up toward Mac. "Give us a second, Mac."

"Good night, Mr. Hopkins," Mac said and entered FDR's bedroom.

"Night, Mac," Hopkins called out as Mac closed FDR's bedroom door behind him.

"Harry, I know you are not feeling well," FDR started, sounding very serious and concerned.

"Are you canning me?" Hopkins asked, smiling.

"Not yet." The President returned the smile.

"A couple of days of rest will set me right," assured Hopkins.

"The demands of running Lend-Lease will not change in a couple of days, Harry," counseled FDR. "Last week Churchill asked me for 375,000 75mm artillery shells, and when I asked the Army, they said we didn't have them."

"The gears are grinding a little," suggested Hopkins.

"I was later informed by Marshall that you personally found 250,000 shells stored in the basements of a couple of Army bases and then convinced five different manufacturers to produce 25,000 more shells apiece to fill the order. Isn't that true?" asked FDR.

"It wasn't that hard. Only two of the manufacturers were isolationists," Hopkins cracked, and FDR cackled.

FDR turned serious again. "You have more important things to do than chase down artillery shells, bullets, spare parts, kippers, canned beef, sausages, cheese, and whatever else the British and Russians might ask us for."

"If Lend-Lease is going to work, we have to increase our production."

"What's stopping us?" FDR asked.

"Our factories have to create more capacity and increase their output of military goods."

"Now that, Mr. Hopkins, is a project worth your time," confirmed FDR.

"Already on it."

"How about we hand the day-to-day of Lend-Lease stuff over to someone else," suggested FDR, though it was clearly an order.

"Who do you have in mind?" Hopkins asked immediately, telling FDR that he was open to the idea.

"Who would you recommend?"

"Ed Stettinus is the best man," answered Hopkins quickly and in doing so told FDR that he had already considered leaving Lend-Lease to someone else.

"Then give Ed the job, and let's go up to Hyde Park next weekend and rest for a few days," said FDR, happy to know he and Hopkins were in agreement.

"Will do," replied Hopkins, and he actually felt a little relieved.

"Good night, Harry," FDR said.

"Good night," Hopkins replied and started walking toward his bedroom. As Hopkins reached the door, he turned back to look at FDR and saw his boss had stopped at his door and was watching him.

In that moment, Hopkins was struck by how remarkable it was that a former social worker from Iowa, who was the son of a harness maker, and the handicapped, only son of a wealthy, original American family, shared almost the exact same views.

"Thank you," Hopkins said to FDR, looking back across the hall.

FDR simply nodded and smiled.

#

The following day, Ed Stettinus came to Hopkins's White House bedroom office for the Lend-Lease handoff. Stettinus was a forty-one-year-old executive who had worked for General Motors.

"Ed, thanks for stopping by. The President wants you to take over the administration of the Lend-Lease Program," Hopkins said, going right to the heart of the matter. "He thinks there is nothing more important now for the country than getting this Lend-Lease show moving at top speed. We stayed up late last night talking over the whole situation, and he feels you are the man to do it."

"I'm here in Washington to serve wherever the President feels I can be most useful, and if he wants me to run the Lend-Lease show, I'll take it on and do my best," Stettinus agreed.

"Great," replied Hopkins, and stood up to shake Stettinus's hand.

"Is there anything more to consider about this thing? Does the President want to talk it over with me first?" asked Stettinus, still in his chair, surprised at how brief the meeting was.

"Not unless you have something you particularly want to talk over with him," replied Hopkins. "So far as the President is concerned, you're elected, Ed."

When Stettinus left his room, Hopkins was not embarrassed to admit that for the first time in a long while, it felt like a huge weight had been lifted from his shoulders.

#

The following weekend, while at Springwood with FDR, Hopkins's body began to shut down, and his extremities became weak and failed. When he and FDR boarded the President's private train to return to the White House, he fell asleep on the sofa in FDR's private car and never woke up. Notified to meet them at Union Station, Dr. McIntire waited impatiently for FDR's Marco Polo to arrive on the President's private platform.

The train had not even come to a stop when McIntire saw a Secret Service agent standing on the train, motioning for McIntire to hurry on board. McIntire jumped onto the slowly moving train and entered the car, where he saw FDR seated at his desk and Hopkins unconscious on the sofa.

"He said he wasn't feeling well after we got on in Hyde Park, and he hasn't moved since," FDR told McIntire as soon as he entered the car.

Seeing Hopkins's gray pallor and almost translucent skin, McIntire immediately checked Hopkins's pulse on his neck and wrist. "His pulse is very weak," McIntire informed FDR, and then turned to the Secret Service agents standing in the car. "I am going to need a hand," he said, reaching under Hopkins's arms to try to lift him from the sofa. "Let's get him to the Naval Hospital."

Though it took several days for Hopkins to look and feel better, he was still confined to his hospital bed and plugged into intravenous bottles of nutrients and plasma when Eleanor Roosevelt walked into his room.

"Are you playing hooky again?" she asked, seeing Hopkins looking relatively good with decent color in his cheeks.

"I just wanted a chance to have you all to myself." Hopkins smiled, happy to see her.

Eleanor walked to Hopkins's bed and kissed him on his forehead. "I love spending time with you, but I wish it wasn't here," she said seriously.

"Me too. How is Diana?"

"She is a joy. You should be so proud of her," Eleanor said, opening her purse and retrieving a card. "She made this for you," Eleanor said, handing the card to Hopkins. "How are you feeling?"

"Tip top," Hopkins lied, and opened Diana's card.

"You can fool Franklin, but you can't fool me," warned Eleanor.

"Did you help her with this?" Hopkins asked, looking at the card Diana had made.

"She did it all by herself. She is so smart."

"Her birthday is coming up on November 15. I would love for her to have a party."

"We will. We will have it at the White House."

"I will be there."

"What brought this on?"

"Who knows," Hopkins answered, sounding like he was tired of thinking and talking about his condition. "We were in Hyde Park last weekend, and then my extremities just gave out. And here I am again—nurses and needles."

Eleanor smiled and touched his hand. "I thought you might like to know there are some who still appreciate you…"

"You're too nice, Eleanor," Hopkins replied, sincerely touched by her kindness.

"No, I wasn't referring to me," Eleanor corrected Hopkins. "Besides, I always appreciate you. Time Magazine, believe it or not, said you are missed."

"Are you sure?" Hopkins asked, surprised.

"They were very complimentary," Eleanor happily told Hopkins. "They said you cut through red tape to get things done, and when you checked into this hospital bed last week, many a defense project crawled in there with you."

"I should give Ed Stettinus a call. He is probably..."

"You will do no such thing!" she said quickly, worried that she might have encouraged him to go back to work too soon. "You can ride over to the White House for Diana's Birthday party if the doctors say it's okay, and then—and only then—can you install a phone here. Until then, it's only books, radio, and rest for you, Mr. Hopkins," she preached.

Hopkins loved Eleanor. Her incredibly generous spirit was beyond the reach of anyone Hopkins knew, and in fact, most mortals. Eleanor was America's alter ego, who cheerfully challenged every American to do better, be kinder, and more considerate of each other.

Unfortunately, he knew that in the near future, Eleanor's idea of a better and more tolerant America would have to take a back seat to what the country was required to do to defeat the dark forces that gripped the world, and some in America itself. While Hopkins was confident that Eleanor's internal strength would serve her well in the coming years, he also believed there would be little room for her remarkable kindness, sympathy, and empathy if America was to survive what lay ahead.

CHAPTER TWENTY

"We are all in the same boat now."

This time around, Dr. McIntire insisted that Hopkins convalesce inside the hospital, and his release was a gradual affair. Over many weeks, Hopkins drove himself to the White House in time for Diana's birthday party and several dinners with FDR, and then promptly drove himself back for more rest and recuperation. It was only after Thanksgiving dinner at the White House that McIntire allowed Hopkins to settle back into his old White House rooms down the hall from FDR.

Of course, FDR's adversaries in Congress and the press made big drama out of the fact that Hopkins was treated at a military hospital at taxpayers' expense. It was only after Secretary of War Henry Stimson told reporters that he approved Hopkins's stay that the curtain dropped on Congress's latest Harry Hopkins soap opera.

In the meantime, while Congress and the press ginned up the public's indignance over Hopkins's and FDR's supposed transgressions, the real drama unfolding in America never saw the light of day. By the time Harry returned to the White House in early December, the Navy's Magic program saw a significant increase in cable traffic between Tokyo and Japanese embassies both in the US and around the world. The increased traffic alarmed Secretary of State Cordell Hull, who asked to meet with FDR, Hopkins, and Secretary Stimson to discuss next steps.

When the meeting began, Hull reported to FDR that Japanese Ambassador Nomura's behavior over the past several weeks had changed from his customary pleasant and professional attitude to seemingly ill at ease and distracted. Hull was worried.

Grace Tully opened the door to the President's office. "Harry is here," she announced, and Hopkins entered the room. Tully was FDR's stalwart, forty-one-year-old private secretary who had worked with FDR and Missy LeHand since 1933. After Missy suffered her stroke, Grace replaced her as FDR's lead secretary. While both FDR and Tully knew she could never replace Missy in the President's eyes, they also knew she provided the President with a steady, professional hand when he needed it most.

"Harry the hop!" FDR greeted Hopkins. "You broke out, did you?"

"Released for good behavior." Hopkins smiled and sat on the sofa in front of FDR's desk.

"Good to see you looking well, Harry," Stimson offered.

"A tune-up, oil change, and grease job does wonders," Hopkins responded, and it pleased FDR to hear Hopkins sounding like he was back in form.

"Tokyo has been burning the midnight oil and sending lots of cables to their people," FDR brought Hopkins up to speed.

"It's not good," Cordell assured Hopkins. "Though it is also possible it is not bad."

There it was. Hull's constant equivocation annoyed the hell out of FDR. His jaw clamped down tight as he wished his Secretary of State spent less time seeing two sides of the coin and more time declaring, "It's heads!" Period.

"With the increase in traffic, there is something there for sure," Stimson said, reading FDR's ire and trying to rescue Hull.

"Last week, we gave them a ten-point memorandum that told them to stand down and get out of China. They left the table," Hull informed Hopkins.

"Diplomatic speak for 'Up yours!'" commented Hopkins.

"We have also intercepted cables saying that the solution they desire must be concluded by November 29 and that deadline could absolutely not be changed," added Stimson.

"And after that, they say, things would happen automatically," Hull informed the group.

"What will be their next move?" Hopkins asked.

"Probably Southeast Asia—Thailand," Stimson replied quickly. "Maybe Malaya, Singapore, or possibly the East Indies."

"If you believe Joe Grew, it will be Pearl Harbor," Hull said.

"That was an old rumor," Stimson said, clearly giving it no credibility.

"Can we go around Tojo and send a direct message to the emperor?" Hopkins asked FDR.

"It's a good thought, but we're not there yet," FDR replied, and then turned to Hull. "Cordell, let's try to get them back to the table."

"I'll work on Nomura and see if we can't get something in place by the weekend," Hull promised FDR.

"Please make sure I continue to receive their decrypted cable traffic," FDR ordered Hull, and then turned to Hopkins. "Harry, without being specific, get word to Churchill that we all must be prepared for real trouble soon."

Hopkins nodded and, despite the rising tension, he couldn't help but think how happy he was to be back in that room again.

#

While Hopkins and FDR were having dinner the next evening, the Army officer on duty in the Map Room requested that FDR and Hopkins come there as soon as practical. With the Japanese making moves and the Germans crushing the Russian Army in the Soviet Union, both FDR and Hopkins dropped their silverware and, without waiting for Mac, Hopkins pushed FDR to the elevator.

The Monroe Room in the White House was across the corridor from the elevator that FDR and Hopkins used each day and evening to come and go from the residence. With the help of National Geographic's cartographers, FDR set up a private Map Room that contained large maps across the walls to enable him to track the war in Europe and the Far East. Inside the room were Army and Navy officers fielding and sending communications for the President. Other than the President, the only other civilian allowed in the Map Room was Harry Hopkins.

"The Russians have counter-attacked the Germans, and we are calling it the Battle of Moscow," the Army officer standing in front of the map informed FDR and Hopkins. "Approximately fifty divisions are on the move here," he said, pointing to the map west of Moscow. "About one million men with tanks and aircraft."

"Where did those troops come from?" asked FDR.

"We believe from their reserves in the east and Siberia," the Army officer replied.

"A ray of sunshine in cold and gray Moscow," said Hopkins. "How close are the Germans?"

"We believe they have advance elements about twenty-five miles west of Moscow," stated the Army officer.

"They are knocking on Stalin's door," FDR said, deeply concerned by how far the Nazis had traveled in five months, and how fast they did it. It was imperative that the Russians stay in the fight.

Hopkins recalled his conversation with Joe Davies and turned his attention east of the Ural Mountains to the vast distance from Moscow across Siberia to Korea and Japan. "Would you leave your rear exposed by moving hundreds of thousands of men and tons of equipment west across the Ural Mountains if you believed you needed to defend yourself in the east?" Hopkins asked the Army officer.

"No, sir," the officer responded, certain in his answer.

Hopkins looked at FDR. "Somehow, the Russians know Japan is not planning to attack them."

"That seems right," FDR replied, never taking his eyes off the map.

#

Several days later, after dinner on Saturday evening, Hopkins and FDR were in the residence living room having their usual cocktails and discussing the latest DC turf wars and attacks on the administration. The residence always seemed the quietest at that time of night on a Saturday, and even if it was for only a few minutes, the two men enjoyed the chance to be away from the harsh lights of DC and the enormous weight bearing down on them and the world.

"This is Saturday night, and you should be out with one of your adoring fans," FDR teased Hopkins as he drank his martini and took a long drag on his cigarette. He felt his body relax into the chair as he exhaled the smoke into the room.

"I don't want to give the press any more ammunition than I have to." Hopkins smiled as he worked on his Scotch. "Any word from Emperor Hirohito?" asked Hopkins, trying to take the attention away from himself.

"Not yet," FDR replied and sounded concerned.

"It was the right thing to do to go around Tojo and write him," Hopkins said emphatically. "At least you are on record that you do not want things to spiral between the two countries."

"Not sure it will help."

Alonzo Fields entered the residence with Navy Lieutenant Lester Schultz carrying a briefcase. "Sir. Lieutenant Schultz is here to see you," Fields said, showing Schultz into the room.

"Good evening, sir," Schultz started and opened his briefcase as Fields left the room. "Sorry to disturb, but we thought you needed to see these," Schultz said, removing a folder of documents from his briefcase and handing them to FDR. "We picked these up, and Naval Intelligence in Honolulu intercepted similar traffic. Japanese embassies are being ordered to burn their telegraphic codes and secret documents, and destroy the machines used to encrypt and decrypt messages."

"They're planning to go to war," said Hopkins quietly.

"And trying to hide the evidence. The decision has been made," agreed FDR.

"When?" Hopkins asked Schultz.

"Judging by the volume of traffic, most any time," Schultz said solemnly and handed FDR another folder. "We also intercepted this thirteen-point memorandum from Tokyo to their embassy here in DC. They say they will send the embassy the 14th point, tomorrow."

FDR read the document and handed it to Hopkins, who stood and paced the room as he read it. After a few moments, Hopkins stopped and returned the memorandum to FDR.

"This means war," FDR uttered the words, wishing he was mistaken, but knowing he was right in his heart.

"It does," confirmed Hopkins. "What would be the most beneficial place for them'?" Hopkins asked Schultz.

"I don't know, sir," replied Schultz, preferring to avoid speculating. "We have not picked up any Naval traffic."

"If war is inevitable, does it make sense for us to strike first?" Hopkins asked FDR.

"No, we can't do that," FDR said quickly. "We are a democracy and a peaceful people."

FDR turned and ordered Schultz. "Lieutenant, please keep me informed of any new traffic you receive."

"Aye, aye, sir," Schultz saluted, closed his briefcase, and left the residence.

"We should contact Admiral Stark," suggested Hopkins.

"He's at the theater tonight," FDR thought about it for a moment, and then continued. "I'd rather not page him. People will wonder."

"I'd like to go down to the Map Room," Hopkins said, wanting to get a better look at the Pacific.

"Give me a hand," FDR requested.

Hopkins circled behind the President's wheelchair, and together they headed to the Map Room and the greatest confrontation America and the world would ever know.

#

The next morning, Sunday, December 7, 1941, was an unusually warm and sunny day for early December in Washington, DC, as Steve Early, his wife, Helen, and their children exited from the eleven o'clock mass at Saint Matthew's. As the church's organist played the recessional hymn, Steve Early and his family passed through the large wooden doors at the rear of the church to find cars dropping off and picking up church goers and several dozen others waiting to enter the church for the Noon Mass.

"I will be back before dinner," Early said apologetically to his wife. Though he pretended to be disappointed that he had to work, Early was actually secretly pleased he could use the White House as an excuse to skip helping his wife decorate the house for Christmas.

"It's Sunday. Steve," Helen said, "and Christmas is a few weeks away."

"And that means it will be quiet and a good day for me to catch up on stuff. I won't be long," he said, but knew in his heart he would probably be gone the entire day. He made a mental note to go to confession again for telling his wife that fib.

By the time Early arrived at the White House Press Office, FDR and Hopkins were sitting in FDR's office, eating turkey sandwiches and speculating on Japan's next moves. Both remained convinced that Japan would likely attack the British and take advantage of the fact that the British were desperately struggling against the Nazis.

As FDR discounted Hopkins's view that an attack on "Fortress" Singapore was a possibility, his intercom buzzed and Grace Tully announced, "Secretary Knox is on the phone for you, sir."

Frank Knox, FDR's sixty-seven-year-old Secretary of the Navy, was the former Republican candidate for Vice President under Alf Landon five years earlier, and a part-owner of the *Chicago Tribune*. Though by his own admission he was not a "New Dealer," he was a strong advocate for US preparedness and FDR's goal of total defense.

FDR put Knox on his speaker. "Frank?" FDR said.

"Mr. President," Knox's voice rang through the speaker. "We've received a radio communication that Honolulu is under an air attack, and it is not a drill."

"This has to be a mistake. Japan would not attack Hawaii," FDR replied, though he intuitively believed it might be true.

"The transmission came from Admiral Kimmel's office," Knox assured FDR.

"Frank, let's double-check this information and get back to me," ordered FDR.

"Yes, sir," Knox answered and hung up.

When FDR turned and looked at Hopkins, his face told the entire story.

"I really wanted to leave this office at the end of my term, having kept us out of the war," FDR told Hopkins, "and I did my damnedest to keep us out. If this report is true, Japan just made the decision for me."

"It doesn't make sense," Hopkins said, trying to decipher Japan's motives for attacking America.

"This is just the kind of thing Japan would do while we are negotiating peacefully with them." FDR pressed the buzzer on the intercom on his desk.

Grace Tully's voice came through the speaker, sounding tinny and thin. "Yes, sir?"

"Grace, get me Secretary Hull," ordered FDR.

Moments later, Grace Tully's voice came over the intercom. "Secretary Hull is on the line, sir."

"Mr. President?" Hull's voice came through FDR's desktop speaker.

"Have you met with Ambassador Nomura yet?" asked FDR, knowing Hull was scheduled to meet with the Japanese ambassador.

"No. He is late," Hull responded, and he was not happy.

"We have just received a report that Japan has attacked Honolulu."

"Is this confirmed?"

"We believe it's reliable."

"That bastard was supposed to be here right now negotiating with me," Hull said angrily.

"I think our negotiations with Japan have ended. Keep your appointment with Nomura and treat him as you ordinarily would. Don't let them know you know of their attack," instructed FDR.

"Yes, sir," Hull replied, and hung up.

No sooner had Hull hung up the line than the President's intercom buzzed again. "Mr. President, I have Admiral Stark on the line," Tully announced. Harold "Betty" Stark was the sixty-one-year-old

Chief of US Naval Operations who sat with General George Marshall on the Joint Chiefs of Staff.

FDR pressed a button on his console, and Stark's voice rang out from the intercom. "Mr. President?" Stark sounded unsure if FDR was on the line.

"Yes, Admiral," answered FDR.

"Our fleet at Pearl Harbor has been attacked and heavily damaged, with a significant number of casualties."

"Admiral, I want to know the extent of our damage and casualties right away," demanded FDR. "And we must prepare for more possible attacks in the Pacific."

"We will get our orders out to the Army and the Navy, sir."

"Keep me informed," FDR hung up the line.

"We should organize a meeting as soon as possible with the military leaders," suggested Hopkins.

FDR pressed the buzzer, and through the intercom, Grace Tully answered. "Mr. President?"

"Please reach Secretary Stimson, Hull, Knox, Admiral Stark, and General Marshall and ask them to be here for a meeting at 3 p.m.," FDR instructed Tully.

"Yes, sir," Tully said quickly, and hung up the intercom.

"We need to prepare a press release," Hopkins suggested. "I think Steve is working today."

"Get him here," ordered FDR.

#

It was about 2:45 p.m. when three unmarked cars pulled up the driveway of the White House in single file. All of the cars came to a stop, and their doors opened. General George Marshall and Henry Stimson exited the first car, Frank Knox and Admiral Stark the second car, and Cordell Hull the third. All of the passengers entered the White House, and minutes later, all of the men were seated around the Cabinet Room's conference table with FDR, Hopkins, and Steve Early.

"Sir, I apologize," Cordell Hull said, "but I couldn't resist giving Nomura a piece of my mind."

"No need to apologize," replied FDR, "It is a testament to your character and skill that you restrained yourself from throttling him."

"Any further news on casualties?" asked Stimson.

"We know we have lost the Arizona," FDR said. "There was a huge explosion, and she capsized in her berth. There are hundreds of men trapped below. The Oklahoma and Utah were also hit."

"That ties with our reports so far," Stark commented.

"Goddamnit." Stimson exhaled quietly, and he looked despondent.

"And we lost dozens of aircraft on the ground at Hickam Field with many men killed or wounded there," Marshall briefed FDR.

"They're going to pay," Stark said out loud.

"Yes, they will," FDR assured the men at the table. "I will ask Congress for a declaration of war tomorrow."

"What about Germany?" Stark asked.

"Hitler told Japan that if they entered into a war with us, he would join them. Let's see how Hitler responds," answered FDR quickly and then turned to Admiral Stark. "Are we covered in the Pacific?"

"Orders have gone out to all of our bases," Stark confirmed.

"General Marshall, earlier I ordered General MacArthur to execute all necessary troop movements in the Pacific from his base in the Philippines," FDR explained to Marshall. "I want to make sure our troops are deployed where Japan is likely to attack—even if it takes us away from our bases."

"Yes, sir," replied Marshall simply, and Admiral Stark followed with, "Aye, sir."

"Henry," FDR said to Stimson, "I want the Japanese Embassy and all of their Consulates protected and all Japanese citizens picked up and placed under surveillance."

"We should give that to the Department of Justice," suggested Hopkins.

"Agreed," FDR said quickly.

"I'll take care of it," offered Stimson.

"Henry, Frank," FDR continued. "Every munition factory, arsenal, and bridge needs to be under guard."

"The Army will guard the War Department and the White House," Marshall stated.

"Thank you, General, but just the War Department," commented FDR. "I do not want military guards around the White House."

"Yes, sir," confirmed Marshall.

"When you go to Congress tomorrow for the declaration of war, I think it would be helpful to review our country's history with the Japanese," Cordell Hull suggested.

FDR turned dark very quickly and glared at Hull. "Cordell, I plan to give Congress a simple and direct message of precisely what I want and why. We can always tell them more later."

Hopkins jumped in. "We should schedule a meeting with the entire Cabinet and with Congressional leaders for later tonight to bring them up to speed."

FDR turned to Early. "Steve, please put those meetings together, and schedule the Cabinet meeting first at 8:30 p.m."

"Yes, sir," Early agreed.

"I'll sort out a list of congressmen for you to invite, but Hamilton Fish is not invited to tonight's meeting under any circumstances," commanded FDR.

"Congressman Fish is the ranking member of the House Foreign Affairs Committee," Early reminded the President.

"I don't care. He will never see the inside of the White House while I am President," FDR said firmly.

#

It was a dark, moonless, overcast night above Chequers, as Winston Churchill sat in the dining room with Gil Winant and Averell Harriman after dinner, listening to Bing Crosby's "Along the Santa Fe Trail" on the radio that Hopkins gave to Churchill and Clementine.

As always, the topic of British convoys making it across the Atlantic was never far from Churchill's mind, and Churchill was commenting on how pleased he was to have American ships covering the convoys since the President expanded America's territorial waters. As Gil Winant was about to add his thoughts on how FDR's Fireside Chat did a lot to help, he was stopped by a radio announcer who declared, "We apologize for interrupting this broadcast, but we have a special report from Alvar Liddell at the BBC's News Service."

After several moments, Liddell's voice filled the dining room. "Japan's long-threatened aggression in the Far East began tonight with air attacks on the United States' Naval bases in the Pacific. Fresh reports are coming in every minute. The latest facts of the situation are these... Messages from Tokyo say that Japan has announced a formal declaration of war against both the United States and Britain. Japan's attack on American Naval Bases in the Pacific was announced by President Roosevelt in a statement from the White House tonight..."

Churchill jumped to his feet as Liddell's broadcast continued in the background, and went to the phone sitting on the sideboard in the dining room. "I will call the Foreign Office and instruct them to declare war on Japan," Churchill said, picking up the phone.

"I wouldn't do that," advised Winant. "I recommend you speak with the President first."

Churchill looked at Winant with his cigar clenched between his teeth and then picked up the phone. "Put me through to President

Roosevelt." As he waited for the connection, Liddell continued his broadcast, "The attacks on Oahu took place early in the morning…"

The phone rang in FDR's office, and Grace Tully, who was working there, answered it.

"Is he there?" asked Churchill even before Tully could announce herself.

"Good evening, Mr. Churchill," Tully said, instantly recognizing the Prime Minister's voice. She looked at FDR, who nodded his head.

"Invite Hiram Johnson to tonight's meeting," FDR instructed Hopkins.

"Put him on the speaker," FDR instructed Tully, wanting to keep his hands free. "Winston?" FDR said out loud.

"What's this about Japan?" asked Churchill.

"We are all in the same boat now," confirmed FDR.

"The radio report said there was damage to your fleet and casualties."

"It's true. I will go to Congress tomorrow to ask for a declaration of war."

"I will do the same in the House of Commons."

"Your support means a great deal to us, Winston."

"We should meet as soon as practical with our staff to review the whole war plan in the light of this new reality and new facts," Churchill suggested.

"I agree. Let's plan to meet here in Washington in several weeks. You should plan to stay here at the White House with us," offered FDR.

"That's very kind," Churchill said and then added, "We are with you, Franklin."

"Thank you, Winston," answered FDR, genuinely pleased to know that he had at least one solid ally in an endeavor that he was sure would be a monumental undertaking for his country.

By the time Churchill hung up the phone in Chequers, Liddell's broadcast was over and the music had returned to the radio. Winant and Harriman sat staring at Churchill.

"It's all true," Churchill said simply. "All true."

#

There was little sleep that Sunday night as both FDR and Hopkins worked during the night connecting the dots and squaring the circles of survivors' testimony, and half-reported news, rumors, and exaggerated reports. By morning's light, as they sat in FDR's office sculpting and trimming the address FDR was scheduled to give to Congress later that day, they were certain of the things that mattered most: Japan attacked America, Americans were killed and wounded, and American ships and planes were lost. Everything else was just details.

FDR had asked Hull to prepare his speech before Congress to declare war on Japan, but again was disappointed by Hull's flaccid approach that included too much history, too much back story, and not enough punch. From FDR's perspective, the task was simple: say it straight, say it simply, and ask Congress to declare war. He and Hopkins sat with copies of his speech in their hands hours before the address, making final changes.

"It's clear, to the point, and strong," said Hopkins after re-reading the speech. "It's good."

"Much better than Hull's," FDR said, happy with this latest version.

"My only suggestion," Hopkins said, "would be to add something about your confidence in our military and our people, and that God is on our side."

"What do you think?"

Hopkins scanned the speech again. "Next to last paragraph... just before you ask for the declaration, put in a sentence..."

Hopkins took out his own pen to write on his copy of the address as he spoke the sentence out loud. "With confidence in our armed forces and with the unbounding determination of our people, we will gain the inevitable triumph, so help us God."

"Yes, that's good," agreed FDR.

Hopkins stood and handed FDR his copy with his suggested sentence written on it.

FDR took the document and, while sitting at his desk, tried on the final draft. "Yesterday, December 7, 1941, a date that will live in infamy, the United States of America was suddenly and deliberately attacked by Naval and air forces of the Empire of Japan..."

As Hopkins listened to the President test his speech, he realized that after months upon months of resisting the need for total national defense, the President's domestic adversaries and resistance evaporated in just twenty-four hours. It wasn't just Lindbergh's arrogance and bigotry that finished off the America First movement; it was Japan, which, with one act in one day, silenced the voices of all of the diehard isolationists. America was going to war.

CHAPTER TWENTY-ONE

"As you can see, Mr. President, the Prime Minister of Great Britain has nothing to hide from the President of the United States."

Following a stormy eight-day trip on the battleship HMS Duke of York out of northern Scotland, Churchill and his entourage arrived in Norfolk, Virginia, on December 22, 1941. Though just fourteen days after the Japanese attack on Pearl Harbor, Christmas was in the air in Washington, DC, and the White House glowed with its traditional Christmas decorations.

The Prime Minister was flown to Washington on a Navy plane, and the President was there to greet him at Washington National Airport. Settled in the White House, Churchill quickly turned the second-floor White House Rose Suite into a small headquarters for the British government. Sort of like a second War Cabinet Room, only with better light. Hopkins's bedroom office was just across the hall, and that was no accident.

At 9 a.m. the following morning, a British officer, accompanied by Alonzo Fields, the White House butler, carried a small wooden box adorned with red Moroccan leather. The box—known as the "Dispatch Box"—bore the name J. H. Beck embossed in gold leaf and had a brass handle. It contained papers and messages of a sensitive and classified nature for the Prime Minister.

Fields knocked on the door, and from inside the room, Churchill bellowed, "Enter!" When Fields and the British officer entered, they found Churchill sitting up in bed smoking a cigar in his flaming red kimono. He was reading a document through his round horn-rimmed spectacles, and there was a stack of documents sitting on the bed on one side and a tray of empty dishes and glasses on the other.

"Ah, good," Churchill said upon seeing the British officer with his dispatch box.

"Good morning, sir," the British officer greeted his Prime Minister. "My apologies, but the embassy staff were delayed in Washington street traffic."

"Tell them to leave earlier," Churchill said. "I want all dispatches here by eight. Leave them here," Churchill pointed to an empty spot on the bed. "And send these," Churchill ordered, holding out a stack of documents for the British officer.

"I will take them to the embassy at once," the British officer said, taking the documents from Churchill.

"No, no. We can communicate from the Map Room here," Churchill instructed.

"Yes, sir," the British officer replied crisply and left the room with the dispatches.

"Good morning, Mr. Churchill," Fields said. "If you are done with your breakfast, I will take your tray, sir."

"Thank you. Now, Fields, you and I want to be friends, don't we?" Churchill asked.

"Yes, sir," Fields replied, standing next to the bed with Churchill's tray in hand, unsure where Churchill might be going.

"Every morning with breakfast, I would like a glass of good sherry—not in a sherry glass—but in a tumbler," Churchill instructed. "And I also like tea and American bacon with my eggs as well as some cold meat with English mustard if you have it."

"I will tell the staff, sir," Fields replied and turned to leave, but was stopped by Churchill.

"And Fields, before lunch, I would like a couple of glasses of Scotch and soda."

"Scotch," Fields confirmed.

"Served in a tumbler as well," demanded Churchill.

"Tumbler," Fields repeated. "Yes, sir."

"What time does the President have lunch?" Churchill asked.

"Mostly between twelve thirty and one."

"Good. Let's plan on having the Scotch here between eleven thirty and noon," Churchill replied, returning to the document in his hand, and after making notes on it, placed it face down on the bed.

"I will see to it, Mr. Churchill," Fields answered, and stood with Churchill's tray in his hand, not sure if he should stay or go. After several moments standing quietly watching Churchill absorbed in another document in his hand, Fields decided he was no longer needed and slowly left the room.

At the same time, across town in a conference room in the War Department's Navy and Munitions Buildings at Constitution Avenue near 18th Street NW, senior British and American military leaders kicked off the Arcadia Conference. The purpose of the meeting was simple in concept but difficult in execution—to agree on a war-winning strategy that would serve the interests of two countries.

Seated around the table were General George Marshall, General Hap Arnold, and Admiral "Betty" Stark on the American side and Lord Beaverbrook, Admiral Sir Dudley Pound, Field Marshal Sir John Dill, and Air Marshal Sir Charles Porter on the British side. The last time the men around the table saw each other was five months earlier in Placentia Bay when they met to discuss the Atlantic Charter.

George Marshall opened the meeting by distributing a single piece of paper around the table. Though the paper outlined in just several sentences America's preferred strategy for executing the war, its brevity and simplicity belied the days and hours of work, complex analysis, and planning at the US War Department performed in large part by a little-known US Army Lieutenant Colonel named Dwight D. Eisenhower.

"Gentlemen, Admiral Stark, General Arnold, and I would like to begin with a proposal for us to consider," George Marshall said, launching the meeting. "We propose that our joint military operations should be based on the following: Germany is the most important of the Axis powers, and despite Japan's aggression in the Pacific, Germany must be defeated first."

"What should we do with the rest of our time?" asked Sir John Dill.

"I don't understand," Admiral Stark said, concerned.

I'm confident we all agree with your proposal," Dill happily explained with a broad smile across his face. "This could possibly be the easiest and most pleasant conference I have ever attended."

There were smiles all around the table.

It was the good beginning to the Allies' relationship that George Marshall had hoped for.

#

FDR, Hopkins, and Churchill sat in the White House dining room after lunch, smoking while Fields cleared their plates.

"I hope you were comfortable last night, Winston," FDR said.

"Fields here is taking very good care of me," replied Churchill.

"Thank you, Mr. Churchill," said Fields as he handed their empty plates to a waiter standing by.

A US Army officer from the Map Room entered the dining room and handed a cable to FDR, who put on his pince-nez glasses and read the communication while Hopkins and Churchill looked on. FDR handed the cable to Hopkins, and judging by the look on his face, he was struggling with its contents.

"Bad news?" Churchill inquired.

"The Japanese have taken Wake Island," FDR said, and added, "We surrendered." He could not mask his disappointment.

"How many men?" Churchill asked in a way that told them he was accustomed to these types of gut punches.

"About five hundred Marines were taken prisoner," answered Hopkins.

"The Japanese are moving very fast," commented Churchill, puffing his cigar to life.

FDR nodded. "MacArthur declared Manila an open city and is withdrawing to the Bataan Peninsula," he informed Churchill. Hopkins knew that when it came to disappointing soldiers, almost always, MacArthur was first on FDR's mind.

"If it is any consolation," Churchill confessed, "I'm afraid all may be lost in Hong Kong in a matter of days and the Japanese are now advancing down the Malay Peninsula toward Singapore."

FDR was stunned by Churchill's admission. "You still have Burma and Singapore available for offensive operations," commented FDR, trying to determine just how severe the situation was.

"For the moment," Churchill replied evenly.

FDR and Hopkins exchanged looks. Both were taken back by Churchill's seemingly calm acceptance of the enemy's successes and the realities of this new war. It wasn't his intention, but Churchill's calm acceptance of America's bad news gave both FDR and Hopkins a better understanding of their new reality and what lay ahead for America.

It was going to be a long and very hard war.

#

That afternoon, as a bearded reporter was being frisked by a Secret Service officer in FDR's outer office, a wave of laughter erupted from the wall-to-wall reporters and photographers already inside. When the Secret Service officer completed his search and permitted the bearded reporter to enter FDR's office, the next reporter stepped up to be searched.

Inside, FDR cackled in front of the laughing reporters while Churchill sat next to his desk. "I am sorry to have taken so long for all of you to get in," FDR told the reporters, "but apparently—I was telling the Prime Minister—the object was to prevent a wolf from coming in here in sheep's clothing."

FDR then turned to Churchill. "Please stand up for one minute and let the reporters in the back see you."

Churchill stood up, and when the reporters applauded loudly, he climbed on top of his chair. Their applause grew louder, and some cheered.

"Okay, boys, go ahead and shoot," FDR announced, inviting the reporters to begin asking questions.

"What about Singapore, Mr. Prime Minister?" Mike Brannigan asked. "Isn't Singapore the key to the whole situation out there?"

"As a geographical and strategic point," Churchill answered, "it obviously is of very high importance. But the key to the whole situation is the resolute manner in which the British and American democracies are going to throw themselves into the conflict."

"Do you think the war is turning in your favor in the last month or so?" Mickey Porter asked.

"I can't describe the feelings of relief with which I find Russia victorious, and the United States and Great Britain standing side by side. It is incredible to anyone who has lived through the lonely months of 1940. Thank God."

Phil LoScalco jumped in. "Can you tell us when you think we may lick the Axis?"

"If we manage it well, it will only take half as long as if we manage it badly."

Everyone in the room, including FDR, laughed.

Brannigan took the opening given to him by the laughter. "Do you anticipate a German offensive on a new front in the near future?" he asked Churchill.

Churchill smiled. "I will be very glad to be informed. Gentlemen, if you have any information, it will be thankfully received."

The reporters laughed again.

Charlie McAllister shouted his question above the laughter. "Have you any doubt of the ultimate victory?"

"I have no doubt whatever," replied Churchill, sounding very, very certain.

#

Christmas Eve, 1941, was a cold and cloud-covered night as a large crowd stood behind temporary barricades, looking across the South Lawn of the White House, waiting for the lighting of the national Christmas tree. There was gloom in the air, and it reflected the feelings of not only those waiting for the President to light the tree, but the entire county. Anxiety, uncertainty, and fear were the bedfellows of most Americans since Japan's attack, made worse by America's not-too-distant memories of the challenges and struggles of the Great Depression.

Normally held in Lafayette Park, the tree lighting within the confines of the White House grounds told the country things were now different. While technicians ran cables to the unlit tree, the Secret Service and plain-clothed soldiers mingled with and covered the crowd to ensure the safety of FDR and Churchill. Mike Reilly, the lead Secret Service agent, even suggested that the President not light the national Christmas tree this year, but FDR would not have it. America would celebrate Christmas—no, must celebrate Christmas—and FDR would light the national tree. Besides, it was one of FDR's favorite Presidential tasks, second only to carving the Thanksgiving turkey.

When Hopkins exited his suite holding Diana's hand, Churchill entered the corridor from his room across the hall. "Miss Diana!" Churchill called out. "Are you very excited to see your Christmas tree?"

"I am." Diana giggled.

Churchill held out his hand. "You come with me and I will make sure you have a good view."

Diana left Hopkins and took Churchill's hand.

"Thank you, Mr. Churchill," Hopkins said, encouraging Diana to be polite.

"Thank you, Mr. Churchill," repeated Diana.

"You are very welcome," Churchill said, walking hand in hand with her to the South Portico with Hopkins following.

Out on the portico, Harry held onto Diana as she stood on a chair looking out over the lawn at the unlit tree while FDR stood with the help of his steel braces, holding tight to the podium and speaking to the nation and the crowd on the South Lawn.

"Our strongest weapon in this war," FDR said, "is that conviction of the dignity and brotherhood of man which Christmas Day signifies more than any other day or any other symbol. Against enemies who preach the principles of hate and practice them, we set our faith in human love and in God's care for us and all men everywhere." The crowd burst into applause while millions of Americans across the country listened on the radio.

At the end of his speech, FDR invited Churchill to share his own Christmas message, and the crowd welcomed their Ally. His was a message of resolve and determination which concluded with, "Let the children have their night of fun and laughter. Let the gifts of Father Christmas delight their play. Let us grown-ups share to the full in their unstinted pleasures before we turn again to the stern task and the formidable years that lie before us, resolved that, by our sacrifice and daring, these same children shall not be robbed of their inheritance or denied their right to live in a free and decent world.

And so, in God's mercy, a happy Christmas to you all." The crowd cheered and applauded.

"And now for the ninth time," FDR announced with a broad smile, "I light the living community Christmas tree of the nation's capital."

When FDR pressed the switch, chimes sounded, and the tree lit the night, accompanied by "oohs," "aaaahs," and applause from the people on the lawn. The US Marine Band immediately played Joy to the World, and when the crowd began to sing, for a moment, the fear, foreboding, and gloom seemed to disappear, replaced by hope.

Diana stood on her toes, holding onto Hopkins, straining to get a good look over the portico railing. Hopkins picked her up, and Diana's eyes sparkled in the bright lights of the beautifully decorated and radiant spruce tree below.

"Look at the tree, Daddy!" she exclaimed, clapping her hands.

#

The following morning, on Christmas Day, after rising early to exchange gifts and see what Santa Claus had delivered, Hopkins, Diana, FDR, Eleanor, James Roosevelt, and Churchill attended Christmas Day services and stood in the first pew at Foundry Methodist Church. Together, with the rest of the congregation, they all sang Oh Come All Ye Faithful, accompanied by a master organist.

In the pews immediately behind FDR and Churchill stood all of their military leaders, singing loudly. For all those who remembered that Sunday morning in Placentia Bay on the deck of HMS Price of Wales, it was a very moving and poignant moment. There was a common wish and prayer for everyone in those first two pews that Christmas morning. Each hoped for strength and success in turning back the fascist tide rising throughout the world.

"Merry Christmas to you all!" announced the reverend at the end of the hymn, and the entire church responded with a rousing, "Merry Christmas!"

"Merry Christmas, Diana!" Hopkins told his daughter as he hugged her close and kissed her.

"Merry Christmas, Daddy."

After Churchill exchanged Christmas greetings with FDR and Eleanor, he turned toward Hopkins and was moved to see him with Diana.

"Merry Christmas, Winston," Hopkins said, shaking Churchill's hand.

Churchill grasped Harry's hand in both of his and looked at him through misty eyes. "May God bless you, Harry."

"May He bless all of us, Winston."

#

It was only a matter of days before Churchill had changed everyone's routine in the White House into seventeen-hour days that included work, smoking, discussions, and planning, followed by eating, drinking, smoking, more discussions, more planning, more smoking, and more drinking. Before everyone knew it, Churchill had all of them retiring in the wee hours of the morning, having breakfast at eight, and considering an afternoon nap at 4 p.m.—that is, the same time Churchill took his. "You must sleep sometime between lunch and dinner, and no halfway measures," Churchill advised. "Take off your clothes and get into bed."

Neither FDR nor Hopkins, however, ever did.

Eleanor was particularly miffed with the way Churchill had taken over her White House. One evening, while FDR dressed for dinner, she stood in his bedroom airing out her opinions. "Franklin, I will not allow this to continue," Eleanor warned. "You are running yourself into the ground. He talks and smokes and drinks until two and three in the morning every single night."

"He is our guest and our time together is very important," replied FDR, focused on knotting his tie.

"You should have told me he would be here for so long."

"It was a secret," FDR responded, hoping the country's national security could save him.

"Well, it is no secret he has turned our house upside down," fumed Eleanor.

There was a knock on the door, and Hopkins entered with two documents in hand.

"And you!" Eleanor said, seeing Hopkins. "You are just as bad, if not worse."

Hopkins looked at FDR for some insight into what Eleanor meant, and FDR shrugged his shoulders, feigning ignorance.

"You are killing yourself," she continued with Hopkins, "drinking and smoking and working to all hours of the night."

"I actually think Harry looks a little better," said FDR sheepishly, coming to Hopkins's defense.

"You are both incorrigible," Eleanor had had it. "And I have to serve dinner again tonight for twenty people!" she complained.

"Mrs. Nesbitt will do a fine job," FDR tried.

"So now you like her cooking," Eleanor shot back.

"She's a great cook," Hopkins said, trying to help.

"I have had it with you two!" Eleanor stormed out of the room, closing FDR's door behind her with conviction.

FDR looked at Hopkins and again shrugged his shoulders.

"You really do look a little better lately," he told Hopkins

.

#

A master salesperson, Churchill loved working the room and those around him. It didn't take long before what Hopkins called "the Churchill effect" permeated the White House and affected all of the attendees of the Arcadia Conference. Stimson and Marshall quickly realized what "the Churchill effect" was and the effect it had on FDR, and they decided to visit Hopkins in his cluttered bedroom office to share their grievances. There was no amount of Christmas cheer that could chase away their view that the boss was ceding much too much to his eloquent and persuasive British counterpart.

"Harry, I'm telling you, you can't leave those two alone," Stimson said, sounding very concerned.

"Churchill can be very persuasive," agreed Hopkins.

"The President told Churchill yesterday," Stimson continued, "if the American troops we plan to send to MacArthur and the Philippines don't make it, he will give them to the British."

"Giving our boys to the British so they can use them to defend Singapore," responded Hopkins, grasping the potential danger in such a move.

"Exactly," Marshall confirmed.

"Harry, he cannot make those kinds of decisions without talking to me first. Or he can do this without me," said Stimson, sounding like he meant it.

"And me," declared Marshall.

"Our country needs you both," Hopkins replied calmly, knowing that neither man would have come to him if they really wanted to resign. Hopkins knew they were asking him for help.

"We just learned they asked you to run the Munitions Assignment Board separate from the Combined Chiefs," Marshall said directly to Hopkins.

"They did," answered Hopkins.

"The Combined Chiefs must control the distribution of military supplies to plan campaigns and prosecute the war," Stimson said evenly.

Hopkins sat back in his chair, disappointed in himself. "Damnit, I should've caught that one myself."

"You know I'm not trying to take your job..." Marshall started, but Hopkins waved his hand and cut him off.

"I couldn't agree more," Hopkins responded. "The Combined Chiefs must be in control of equipment and supplies. Period," confirmed Hopkins.

"Thanks, Harry," said Stimson, relieved he wouldn't have to tangle with FDR and Hopkins over the issue.

"One other point," Marshall said. "Unity of command is critical in winning this war. We learned that tough lesson in the first war. There has to be one man over all the forces in each theater."

"And I assume the British Chiefs are pushing back against the idea," Hopkins said, anticipating they would resist the idea.

"And so is Churchill," Stimson added.

"Leave it with me," assured Hopkins.

#

Before the Arcadia Conference ended, Hopkins was charged with organizing as many nations as possible into a group that would support both the US and Great Britain in their quest to defeat Japan and Germany. He spent most of his days on the phone with ambassadors, foreign ministers, and heads of state, trying to persuade, cajole, convince—and in some cases, strong-arm— dozens of countries to formally declare their allegiance to the Allied powers and against the Axis.

After Stimson and Marshall visited him, Hopkins looked for an opportunity to have a heart-to-heart with FDR, but the breakneck pace and schedule of conference meetings left little time for a private talk. Even late at night, when Hopkins, Churchill, and Lord

Beaverbrook sat in FDR's office with scotches and martinis, they spent all of their time recapping the day's discussions and events.

Hopkins looked at his watch and decided to approach FDR in the morning. "It's 2 a.m. Time for bed. I have Litvinov in the morning."

"What news from Stalin?" Churchill asked.

"He will sign off on the document with everything from the Atlantic Charter, including freedom of religion," Hopkins informed them.

"You, sir, are a master negotiator," Beaverbrook complimented and raised his glass to Hopkins.

"Have we settled on a title for the conference document?" asked FDR.

"Our working title is the Joint Declaration of Principles of the Associated Powers," replied Hopkins.

"We must have a better name," commented Churchill.

"Let me think on it," FDR suggested. "How many countries have agreed so far, Harry?"

"Twenty-six," confirmed Hopkins.

"Hear, hear," Churchill said, raising his glass to Hopkins.

"We are trying to organize the signing for New Year's Day," Hopkins informed them.

"Well done, Harry," FDR said, genuinely impressed with Hopkins's accomplishment.

"It was Winston's speech today in Congress that helped to bring around the last few holdouts," Hopkins said.

"It was a masterful performance, Winston," FDR complimented his Ally. "You may want to use your mother's American lineage to run for office here. I would, however, recommend you run as a Democrat."

Churchill laughed. "I have already changed parties twice in my life. It's only natural that if I crossed the Atlantic, I should also cross the aisle again.

"Your dear mother would be proud of your decision," FDR teased.

"By the way, Franklin," Churchill began, "the Combined Chiefs of Staff are discussing having one commander over each theater. I am not sure that is a viable command structure for us. It may be too much power for one man, and—"

"Let's tackle that one tomorrow," Hopkins quickly cut off Churchill, wanting the chance to tee up a meeting between the Prime Minister and Marshall.

"Let's," FDR agreed.

"Two prima donnas," Hopkins thought to himself, walking behind the others as they exited FDR's office.

Beaverbrook fell behind as well and leaned into Hopkins. "I was glad you cut short the Prime Minister on the command issue."

"The last thing we need," Hopkins quietly replied, "is for those two to take opposite sides on a military question."

"Harry, you need to work on Winston," suggested Beaverbrook. "He is being advised to take a stand against the unity of command. He is open-minded about it, but you will need to discuss it with him," counseled Beaverbrook.

"Leave it with me," replied Hopkins.

#

Churchill never sat still for very long and always found that moving about helped him to think better.   When Hopkins entered his room the following evening to fetch him for dinner, he found Churchill pacing with Hopkins's draft of the conference memorandum in hand.   Churchill stopped, looked up, and waved the document at Hopkins. "Harry, this is a very good draft of the declaration of principles for the Allies.   You have brilliantly incorporated the Atlantic Charter."

"Thank you," replied Hopkins. "It's almost there, but it needs a little more work."

"This is very well done, Harry," Churchill complimented, believing Hopkins was being too modest.

"Time for dinner," Hopkins said, holding the door for Churchill as they both entered the corridor on their way to the dining room.

"I want to set up a meeting for you with General Marshall," Hopkins informed Churchill.

"Why?"

"I think it's important for you to hear his unity of command proposal directly," Hopkins said matter-of-factly. "Can we do it tomorrow?"

"If you believe it's important," agreed Churchill. "Tomorrow after lunch, then."

"I will ask General Marshall to visit with you in your rooms," Hopkins confirmed.

"I have wanted to tell you that I think you are looking much better, Harry," Churchill said as they walked down the corridor. "You have gained weight, and it appears you are feeling well."

"I do feel good," replied Hopkins.

"And you are dressing better, too," Churchill complimented. "That is a very nice suit."

"You see, Winston"—Hopkins smiled—"you bring out the very best in me. I'm fatter, healthier, and better dressed since you arrived."

"If you spent more time with me, my friend, I would have you farting through silk," promised Churchill.

As they passed the President's bedroom, the door opened, and Mac pushed FDR into the corridor.

"Just in time for dinner," FDR exclaimed, seeing Churchill and Hopkins outside his door.

Churchill walked behind FDR's wheelchair. "May I?" he asked Mac, his hands pointing to the back of FDR's chair.

Mac stepped away, and Churchil! grasped the handles and pushed the President down the corridor to the elevator.

"I hope Mrs. Nesbitt made something edible for us tonight," FDR said.

#

When General Marshall arrived at Churchill's rooms for his 1:30 p.m. meeting, he found him seated at a small conference table reading and smoking a cigar. Churchill greeted Marshall cordially and invited him to join him at the table while he finished reading the document in his hand. Marshall sat and waited, and when Churchill put down the document on the table, he launched right into the purpose of his meeting.

"As you know, the first job of the Combined Chiefs of Staff is to come up with a strategy that everyone will follow to win the war, and the second job is to execute that strategy," Marshall began.

"What do you have in mind?" asked Churchill.

"One commander in each theater over all forces."

"Land, sea, and air?"

"Yes."

"What the devil does an Army officer know about handling a ship or a Naval officer know about tanks?" Churchill asked with one eyebrow raised.

"I am more interested in our commanders having the authority to get the job done, rather than their technical ability," replied Marshall directly.

"Theater Commanders will report to the Combined Chiefs?" asked Churchill.

"Yes," Marshall replied simply and then expanded. "One commander in each theater and all commanders under the Combined Chiefs. For example, we believe a good choice for our Allied commander in the Southwest Pacific Theater is your General Archibald Wavell," Marshall said, intentionally informing Churchill that unified command would not be an exclusively American show.

"Wavell is a good man," replied Churchill.

"In our view," Marshall continued, "Britain has a claim on Australia, New Zealand, the Philippines, Borneo, Malaya, and Burma. We see the Australian-British-Dutch-American Command, ABDA, under Wavell."

"And how will the Americans in that theater respond to being led by a British officer?"

"The same way a British soldier will respond to being led by an American officer. Every Allied soldier will obey the orders given to him by an Allied commander," replied Marshall.

"With due respect to you, General, it's difficult to imagine our respective officers behaving nicely with each other. As you know, they can be a very stubborn bunch," suggested Churchill.

"With due respect to you, Prime Minister, so can you and President Roosevelt," Marshall quickly responded, looking Churchill squarely in the eye. "And yet you work together daily with one goal in mind: defeat Germany and Japan. Your example every day clearly sets the tone for all of our officers and all of our efforts."

Churchill watched Marshall for what seemed like a long time, puffing on his cigar. Like Hopkins, Churchill liked the tone and tenor of the man sitting at the table with him and admired his candor. Most importantly, listening to Marshall, Churchill realized that if the Allies were to have any chance of succeeding in defeating the Germans, they had to fight as one unit. National differences were fine and appropriate when debating strategy, but execution required the one-eyed view of one person tasked with carrying out the Allied strategy and defeating the enemy on the ground. Churchill had seen the effect of having multiple officers from different countries operating in the same theater during the Great War, and it cost the lives of millions.

"You have pleaded your case with great conviction," Churchill said, responding to Marshall. "Give me the opportunity to discuss your proposal with the British Chiefs and the Dominions."

"Thank you, sir," Marshall replied and exited the room.

#

Just before dinner that evening, Hopkins put the final touches on his draft of the Declaration of Principles of the Associated Powers, the document that was to be signed in several days by twenty-six nations. He sat at the table in his suite, gave it one final pass, and, satisfied with it, headed to FDR's bedroom. When he entered, Mac was busy tying FDR's shoes as the President sat in his wheelchair.

"The final draft of the Declaration of Principles of the Associated Powers." Hopkins smiled, handing the document to FDR.

After reading the draft for a few moments, FDR suddenly looked up at Hopkins.

"How about Associated Nations?" he asked Hopkins.

"It's better," Hopkins quickly responded.

"Better yet..." FDR continued. "How about the United Nations?"

Hopkins smiled. "The Declaration by the United Nations. That's it!"

"Come on. Let's tell Winston," FDR exclaimed, sounding like a school boy giddy with the excitement of a new secret.

Hopkins pushed FDR quickly down the corridor to Churchill's room with the draft in hand, and when they arrived at Churchill's door, they were so excited they opened the door without knocking.

When Hopkins and FDR pushed into the room, Churchill, who had emerged from his bath seconds before, was standing in the room, stark naked like a plump, pink cherub with a cigar between his teeth. When they saw Churchill, Hopkins, and FDR, they stood stock still.

"I'm so sorry, Winston," FDR said immediately. "I wanted…" FDR continued, but Churchill, who stood facing Hopkins and FDR, made no effort to cover himself, waved his hand at them.

"As you can see, Mr. President," Churchill said, breaking the embarrassing silence, "the Prime Minister of Great Britain has nothing to hide from the President of the United States." Churchill smiled and then turned to retrieve a towel from the bathroom.

"I'm sorry for barging in on you," FDR called out. "I was so excited to tell you I have come up with a name to describe the Allies. The United Nations."

"Brilliant!" Churchill exclaimed and returned to the room wrapped in a towel.

"How does The Declaration by the United Nations sound?" asked FDR.

"I like it!" Churchill smiled and then asked, "Drinks before dinner?"

"In my office."

"I'll be ready shortly," Churchill informed them, and as he turned back toward the bathroom, bellowed, "You know, I believe I am the only man in the world who has received the head of a nation without any clothes on."

Hopkins and FDR laughed all the way to FDR's office.

#

Early in the morning on the day before his scheduled visit to Canada, Churchill lay in bed dressed in an open blue jumpsuit, with a blood pressure cuff on his arm, while his personal physician, Dr. Wilson, Lord Moran, examined him. Churchill chewed on his cigar while Wilson held a stethoscope to his chest.

"Winston," Wilson said, listening to Churchill's heart, "put down that damn cigar."

Churchill reluctantly did as he was told and placed the cigar in an ashtray on the night table next to his bed. Wilson removed a tongue depressor from his bag.

"Open," commanded Wilson, holding the depressor in front of Churchill's mouth.

"Stop this," Churchill said.

"Open, I say."

Churchill opened his mouth, and after checking his throat, Wilson removed the tongue depressor and threw it away.

"How long did it last?" asked the doctor.

"Several minutes."

"Do you have any pain now?"

"No."

"Winston, you must rest," insisted Wilson.

"I will rest on the voyage home to England," conceded Churchill.

Wilson returned his stethoscope to his bag and removed the blood pressure cuff from Churchill's arm.

"I believe you have had a mild heart attack," Wilson said. "The pain you described is not consistent with indigestion, and your blood pressure is elevated. I insist we take you to..."

Churchill would not hear any of it. "I am not going anywhere except to Canada tomorrow as planned, and then I will sail home. Do not utter one word about this to anyone," he ordered.

"Winston," Wilson pressed, "respectfully, you are putting the entire government at risk if you continue..."

Again, Churchill cut him off. "My dear doctor, my government is already at risk. The House of Commons is pushing for a no-confidence debate as we speak."

"Nonsense," Wilson replied, believing Churchill was making it up. "They are not that stupid."

"Apparently they are." Churchill closed the front of his jumpsuit.

"Don't they realize how that will make us look to the rest of the world? I cannot believe it."

"Believe it," confirmed Churchill, almost sounding resigned. "When we return to London, I will face a vote of no confidence."

"Idiots!" fumed Wilson. "Winston, you must enlighten them on the effort required for this undertaking."

"The House of Commons does not believe it needs to be enlightened."

Down the hall in FDR's bedroom, at almost exactly the same time, Hopkins and FDR were in the middle of their morning routine.

FDR sat in bed eating his breakfast of scrambled eggs and toast while Hopkins sat in his usual chair drinking coffee and smoking.

"Churchill's facing a vote of no confidence when he returns," Hopkins informed FDR.

"I would hate to start from square one with another Prime Minister at this point," FDR said, finishing his eggs.

"Harriman and Gil Winant think it will just be a slap on his wrist," assured Hopkins.

"Let's hope so," replied FDR, moving his tray off his lap to the bed. "All in all, I think this was a very good conference."

"We're off to a good start," Hopkins said, knowing there was a long way to go in the developing relationship between the two countries and leaders.

"Especially now that you convinced me to run all military decisions through Marshall and Stimson and let the Combined Chiefs dole out the equipment with you overseeing them," FDR needled.

"I didn't mean to—" Hopkins started, but FDR cut him off.

"I am just teasing you. It is for the best. Who do you see running the Production Board?" he asked.

"Don Nelson," Hopkins answered quickly.

"Please inform him and have Steve Early send out that announcement today."

"I will."

"Speaking of the Chiefs, have they decided yet where and when we will fight the Germans?" FDR asked.

"Not yet."

"Harry, I want us to get into this fight."

"Leave it with me."

#

By the time Churchill's Christmas visit to America came to an end on January 14, the Arcadia Conference, with Churchill living in the White House and the White House under the Churchill effect, was a resounding success. Both the President and Prime Minister could not have been more pleased with the tone and substance of their talks and the obvious goodwill between the two nations. Hope abounded in Washington, D.C. and in London.

FDR arranged for a private train to take Churchill and his entourage to Palm Beach, FL, for a brief rest before their flight to London via Bermuda. Though it was a bitterly cold day in DC, Hopkins buttoned up and walked with Churchill from their car to Union Station, carrying a shopping bag filled with treats for Churchill and Clementine at home. As the two walked past the park outside of Union Station, Hopkins noticed several children dressed against the cold, playing on swings and slides in the revitalized park.

"It's good to hear the sound of children playing," Churchill said, seeing Hopkins looking at the park.

"More than you know, Winston. When I first arrived here in March of '33, this park was filled with starving people living in ramshackle huts."

"The Depression?" asked Churchill.

Hopkins nodded. "A war on men's souls."

"And now it's Hitler and Tojo trying our souls," Churchill replied.

As they approached the plaza at Union Station, the police, who had been informed that Churchill would leave today, had cordoned off the area. Remarkably, despite the cold temperature, there were hundreds of people, reporters, and photographers standing behind police guarded ropes watching Hopkins, Churchill, and the British contingent cross the plaza to Union Station's main entrance. Many in the crowd, especially reporters, called out to Churchill, hoping he would stop and speak with them.

When they arrived at the entrance to Union Station, Hopkins handed Churchill the shopping bag. "There are some goodies in here for you and Clemmie," Hopkins informed Churchill, "And a note for her."

"You did not tell her any of my secrets, did you?" Churchill smiled.

"Only those she already knows."

Churchill shook Hopkins's hand. "You are a good friend, Harry," Churchill said and turned to enter Union Station through the door held open by his bodyguard.

"Winston," Hopkins called out, and Churchill turned.

"Hitler doesn't stand a chance," Hopkins said confidently.

With his cigar clenched between his teeth, Churchill, the bulldog, looked at Hopkins, smiled behind his cigar, and turned into Union Station.

Hopkins walked back across the plaza to the car that had brought them to the station, opened the rear door, and dropped himself into the warm back seat. He laid his head back on the seat, closed his eyes, and took a couple of deep breaths.

"Where to, Mr. Hopkins?" the driver asked.

Hopkins opened his eyes and connected with the driver through the rearview mirror.

"The Naval Hospital on 24th," Hopkins answered quietly.

CHAPTER TWENTY-TWO

"Will be seeing you soon, so please start the fire."

When Eleanor "Barry" Lowman entered the Naval Hospital to visit Hopkins, heads turned from the moment she entered the building all the way to Hopkins's hospital room. Both men and women had their breath taken away as they watched the strikingly beautiful thirty-six-year-old former editor of Harper's Bazaar magazine. She and Hopkins had been friends since Harry's days in New York City and had grown closer—when time allowed—after Barbara died.

When Barry entered Hopkins's hospital room, he was sitting up in bed, dressed casually, and reading a document with an intravenous attached to each arm. The radio was on and broadcasting the latest news, "In other news today," the radio announcer said, "Japan advanced in the Philippines and the Malaya

Peninsula, where they took hundreds of British soldiers prisoner north of Singapore...”

“Goddamn,” Hopkins swore, and when he reached to turn off the radio, he saw Lowman standing in the doorway.

“My God, he’s still kicking,” Lowman said, her presence and smile lighting up the sterile hospital room.

“Barry Lowman,” Hopkins replied, always smitten by her.

“You’re looking pretty good. The doctors here must be miracle workers,” she said, checking Hopkins’s intravenous bottles. “Tell me the truth. Are they feeding you Scotch?”

“Always the reporter,” teased Hopkins.

“How are you, Harry?” Lowman asked, leaning over and kissing him.

“Just some minor repairs. How’s Harper’s Bazaar?”

“My friends at the magazine tell me they’re very busy now that you guys got us involved in a war.”

“Not you, too,” said Hopkins, pretending to be offended.

“Harry, who else can jazz you like me?” she said, holding his hand.

“You are my one and only. Is that guy Laurence still in the picture?” Harry asked about the man Lowman had recently married.

“It’s nice to be in love again,” she said, half wishing she wasn’t.

“I’m happy for you, kiddo.”

“When are you going to bust out of this place?” asked Lowman. “I want you to meet someone.”

“Who?”

"Louise Macy. She was Harper's Paris editor, and she wants to work for her country. Everyone loves Louise," Lowman pitched. "She is good-looking, smart—without being chi chi—and she is as healthy and strong as ten horses. She is wonderful, Harry."

"We need all the talented people we can find," Hopkins answered.

"Is it possible to find her a job in England?"

"Not unless she wants to run an anti-aircraft gun. When I get out of here, I'll set up a time to meet her," Hopkins promised.

"I feel like I just asked Saint Peter himself for a favor."

"Stop that," ordered Hopkins, smiling. "Anything for you."

#

By the time Dr. McIntire cleared Hopkins to leave the hospital, it wasn't a minute too soon for Harry. The phrase "stir crazy" had taken on a whole new meaning for him, and just the thought of another hospital stay made him feel ill. He committed to himself that he would do everything he could to stay clear of beds, nurses, intravenous bottles, and harsh overhead lights as much as he possibly could in the future.

When Hopkins walked into FDR's office several days later, the President could not have been happier to see him up and around.

"You look great!" FDR exclaimed as Hopkins walked through the door.

"Much better," replied Hopkins. "Can't wait to get back in the saddle."

"Didn't you read the newspapers?" asked FDR with a straight face. "Marshall and Stark asked me to fire you, and I did."

"God, what a relief," replied Hopkins. The banter between them made Harry feel like it was good to be home.

Grace Tully's voice came through the speaker. "Mr. President. Mr. Filmore is here."

"Thank you, Grace," FDR replied. "Give me a couple of minutes and send him in."

"What does Filmore want?" Hopkins asked.

"Congress is planning to stop funding the Civilian Conservation Corps, and he wants me to keep the program going," FDR informed Hopkins.

"Those New Deal guys never give up," Hopkins said, sounding to FDR like he was very healthy and back to his old self. "Tell him, in case he hasn't noticed, we don't need people to clean up our parks. We need them to carry our guns. If he doesn't get the message, tell him to call me. Damned New Dealers," he fumed.

FDR threw his head back laughing. He loved seeing his friend back in fighting form.

#

By early April, though the weather in Washington, DC had turned warm and bright, the atmosphere inside the White House remained very chilly and gloomy.

The boss was not happy.

It was now four months after Pearl Harbor, and FDR wanted Americans to get into the fight. While Europe continued to fight for its survival under the boots of German soldiers, and Japan's military continued to acquire more territory in the Far East and Pacific, the American Army and Navy remained on the sidelines.

When FDR asked Hopkins, Marshall, and Admiral Stark to come to his office, Hopkins, who knew of FDR's frustration, expected him to lay into Marshall and Stark. Surprising Hopkins, and perhaps truer to himself, FDR pitched his position and views to his military leaders in a way that greatly enhanced their view of him as their Commander-in-Chief. He did not reprimand them but instead motivated them to deliver what he envisioned. He wanted America in the fight and asked them for the best way to accomplish that.

During the meeting, Hopkins, Marshall, and Stark persuaded the President that the best way to engage American troops was to insist on getting Britain's final agreement for an invasion of Europe, Operations Bolero and Roundup, and to coordinate Far East war strategy, supply, and tactics by forming the Pacific War Council. FDR ordered Marshall and Hopkins to go to London and named Hopkins as the Chair of the Pacific War Council. President Quezon of the Philippines told Hopkins, "I shall never forget, as long as I live, the part that you have taken in securing for my government the recognition which the President of the United States has accorded us in making the Philippines a member of the United Nations and giving me a seat in the Pacific War Council."

The meeting ended that day with FDR authorizing Jimmy Doolittle's raid on Tokyo using medium bombers launched from the deck of the USS Hornet, about 650 miles away from Tokyo. The Army-Navy mission planned to bomb Japanese industrial centers and inflict material and psychological damage upon America's new enemy. FDR made it known to the men around the table how much he valued the audacity of that plan and Dolittle's courage in executing it. They all heard the boss's message loud and clear. Get moving!

After the meeting, Stark returned to the Munitions Building, and Hopkins and Marshall took the elevator to the Map Room to send a communication to Churchill. The Army and Navy officers in the Map Room snapped to attention when they entered, and after Marshall held up his hand, they continued about their business of moving documents, tracking convoys and troops, and sending and receiving communications for FDR and Hopkins.   As was his custom, Hopkins walked directly to the convoy map on the wall and was quickly joined by a Naval officer holding a report in his hand. Marshall followed.

"We lost the India Arrow here in the North Atlantic. Convoy Eighty G twenty-one ninety is on its way to Liverpool," the officer informed Hopkins.

"Twenty B-17s we can't afford to lose," Hopkins said, examining the map.

"How did you know that?" The officer was amazed at Hopkins's ability to recall shipments.

"It's my job to know that," replied Hopkins as he calculated the distances from the coverage zone to the place where the India Arrow was sunk. "How many men?"

"Thirty-eight confirmed dead," the officer replied, the sadness in his voice unmistakable.

Hopkins turned to Marshall. "We have got to figure out a way to stop these bastards from sending our men and equipment to the bottom of the Atlantic."

"The escorts got one U-boat, sir," the officer reported.

"We need to do better than that," Hopkins said forcefully.

Hopkins walked over to the communications officer, who sat among multiple radios and communication devices in the far corner of the room.

"Send this to Prime Minister Churchill right away," Hopkins informed the communications officer, and put a paper on the officer's table. The message read:

"Will be seeing you soon, so please start the fire."

#

Harry arranged to go to New York to have dinner with his sons, David, Robert, and Stephen, before David shipped out with the Navy and Robert joined the US Army. Stephen, the youngest, was just days away from being old enough to sign up for his first choice, the Marines. Though he was enormously proud of his sons, Hopkins was more than concerned for what might lie ahead for them and all of America's young men.

The following day, before heading back to Washington, he scheduled lunch with Barry Lowman's friend, Louise Macy, the very attractive thirty-something-year-old, Harper Bazaar's Paris Fashion Editor, who was looking for a job to help America's war effort.

Spring came early to New York City in 1942. By the beginning of April, New Yorkers had shed their winter coats and were strolling along Fifth Avenue at lunchtime, enjoying the promise that beautiful weather was ahead. On 55th Street off Fifth Avenue in New York City, there was the usual traffic jam in front of the St. Regis Hotel with cars and yellow cabs stacked up bumper to bumper down the street. Scores of people walked in front of the hotel, with many of the richest, finest-dressed, and most attractive people in the city entering and leaving through its front door, assisted by the hotel's able doormen.

Inside the hotel's King Cole Room, Harry and Louise were having lunch when the maître d' escorted a polished, patrician-looking businessman and a very young, extraordinarily beautiful blonde woman past Hopkins's table. The maître d' couldn't resist looking at Hopkins and Macy as he passed their table, and heard Hopkins say loudly, "No. That can't be true!" and Macy answer just as loudly, "It is!"

The maître d' wished he knew what they were talking about.

"That can't be true," Hopkins said again, holding Macy's beautiful blue eyes in his own.

"It is," repeated Macy.

"A nun?" asked Hopkins in disbelief, and Macy nodded her head and smiled.

"Everyone in Paris loves fashion and lingerie. Even nuns." She laughed.

"Frisky lady." Hopkins smiled.

"She was. And not the least bit embarrassed by any of it," said Macy.

"What's that French expression?" Hopkins asked.

"Joie de vivre," she responded easily. "Joy of life. And Sister Mary Teresa had it in spades. Believe it or not, that was Paris just a few years ago," Macy added with a slight sadness in her voice.

"Not a lot of joy in France today," Hopkins said, picking up on her wistfulness for a vanished time.

"No more joy," agreed Macy. "No more fashion. No more art. No more books. And no more freedom. Just fear and foreboding."

"Fascism," Hopkins pronounced. "Keep everyone divided and afraid and control the information."

"A few of my Parisian friends are writing and distributing pamphlets in Paris," Macy confided.

"Very dangerous."

"I really admire them," Macy said with more passion than Hopkins expected.

"The Gestapo doesn't like free speech," cautioned Hopkins.

"Oh, don't worry, Harry. I don't have the courage to take on the Gestapo," Macy said, confirming the limits of her bravery. "But I would like to find a job to help the cause."

"Barry thought you were interested in going to England."

"I was. But then, she told me you asked if I could operate an anti-aircraft gun." Macy smiled.

"London is bombed regularly."

"Maybe I can learn to drive a tank," Macy speculated, and Hopkins laughed. "Fly a plane?" Macy continued. "How about Fashion Editor for the US Army's Stars and Stripes Magazine?"

"I don't think the Army is interested in the latest battlefield fashions," kidded Hopkins.

"You never know. New brightly colored uniforms with stylish boots might be great for morale. Could add a whole new dimension to our fighting men," Macy teased.

"Let me figure out if there is something for you to do when I get back to Washington," Hopkins suggested. "Give me a couple of days and I'll get back to you."

"Barry said you were the best."

"And she feels the same about you. Though I was a little taken aback," Hopkins added.

"I'm sorry if I imposed. I really appreciate—" Macy was going to tell Hopkins how much she appreciated his help, but he cut her off.

"No, no, not that," Hopkins said, knowing she was about to thank him. "I was taken aback because when Barry told me how beautiful and smart you are, she also said that you are as strong and healthy as ten horses."

"She didn't say that."

"She did. Made me think I should check your teeth." Hopkins smiled, and after a moment, he asked, "Would you smile for me?"

Macy looked at him across the table, and they both started laughing, punctuated by Macy throwing her napkin at Hopkins across the table.

They had a great time together.

#

Accompanied by Navy Doctor Commander Fulton and several others, Hopkins and Marshall had the Pan American Clipper all to themselves as they flew from Baltimore to Bermuda on the first leg of their trip across the Atlantic to London. Their mission was code-named Modicum, and they were both dressed in civilian clothes, traveling under aliases. Harry was "Mr. Hones," and Marshall was "Mr. Mell."

When they made their final approach into Hendon Field outside of London several days later on a typically overcast and rainy afternoon, General Marshall was transfixed by the devastation he observed firsthand from the air. Even for the lifelong warrior, the damage London had absorbed from Nazi bombs was shocking.

As their Pan American Clipper taxied toward Averell Harriman and Gil Winant waiting on the tarmac, the excitement grew within the group of reporters and photographers who stood waiting behind a cordon guarded by soldiers. The word was out in London and in Berlin that the Americans were coming to town. So much for secrecy.

When the door to the Clipper opened, Marshall and Hopkins emerged from the plane while luggage and mail bags were pulled from the plane's rear compartment and placed on the tarmac. When Winant and Harriman greeted Hopkins and Marshall, they could see that Hopkins did not look happy.

"Evidently," Hopkins said as he shook hands with Harriman and nodded toward the mailbags being off-loaded, "there are people who think these commercial planes should be used so Aunt Bessie can tell her friends how she is progressing with her lumbago. We need the fuel and space for more important things than chit-chat mail."

"I've been complaining about it for weeks," agreed Harriman.

"Keep raising hell here," Hopkins directed, "and I will get out some new instructions on our side."

"Glad to see you are feeling well, Harry," Harriman needled Hopkins.

"Never better. How are you, Gil?" Hopkins asked Winant.

"All good," Winant replied, and turned to walk to their waiting car.

As they made their way across the tarmac, the photographers behind the cordon took pictures, and the reporters shouted questions. "General," one reporter called out to Marshall, "can we expect more airplanes?" while another shouted, "How long will you be here, Mr. Hopkins?"

One of the more enterprising reporters in the crowd thought an antagonistic question asked in a snarky way might get a rise out of Marshall, but instead, he got Hopkins's attention. "Any plans to send any soldiers along with the guns you've been shipping us?" the reporter asked sarcastically.

Though Gil Winant touched Hopkins's arm and quietly said, "Let it go, Harry," Hopkins turned and approached the rope line of reporters. He stood in front of the group as the photographers took picture after picture. "This war," Hopkins told them, "is not going to be won by production alone. It is going to be won by tough fighting. You can be sure America's contribution will not be confined to the production of guns," Hopkins added, intentionally boring in on the sarcastic reporter.

Hopkins then turned and walked to the car.

#

The following day, Hopkins had lunch at 10 Downing Street with Churchill, Marshall, and Churchill's new Chief of the Imperial Staff, General Alan Brooke. As John Dill suspected months before, Brooke replaced him as Great Britain's senior military leader after Churchill promoted Dill to Field Marshall and sent him to Washington, DC as the Chief of the British Joint Staff Mission on the Combined Chiefs of Staff. Churchill got what he wanted. Dill was out of the way.

As always, it seemed the flight, work, and hectic schedule fueled Hopkins, and he never looked healthier. Marshall thought Hopkins's physical transformation was remarkable. What Marshall did not realize, however, was that part of Harry's recovery was due to General Alan Brooke, who had a profound medicinal effect on him. Brooke's prissy, imperious, and condescending manner always rubbed Hopkins the wrong way and turned up the heat in his belly. The more Hopkins interacted with Brooke, the angrier he became, and ironically, the better he felt.

"I was glad we had the chance to fly into Hendon Field and see London from the air. It is obvious you all have lived through a great deal here," Marshall said as the waiters cleared their table.

"We have," Brooke responded, sounding like he was speaking to a school boy.

"But the British people are committed to seeing this through," Churchill added, wanting to be sure Marshall knew they were in the fight for the long haul.

"Have you had the chance to review our proposal?" Marshall asked Brooke without any emotion attached to the question.

Before Brooke could answer, Churchill jumped in, "I believe your proposal will be well-received by the British Chiefs."

"The President views our proposal as vitally important to the US war effort," Hopkins said, clearly communicating FDR's wishes to Brooke and Churchill.

"It is the view of the American Chiefs that unless we immediately begin Operation Bolero—building up the men and material here in England—we will have no chance of executing a cross-Channel invasion next spring," Marshall added.

"Opening a second front in France next spring is a significant challenge," Brooke answered, again sounding like he was speaking to a dull school boy.

"Of course, the British Chiefs will need to review the plans for Operation Bolero and for Roundup and the invasion," Churchill assured Brooke, trying to move his Chief of the Imperial Staff off his high horse.

"It should be a lively discussion," Brooke said, making sure he informed Churchill and the others he had no intention of just "going along" with the Americans.

Marshall thought of responding to Brooke but decided to leave it in Hopkins's hands. Though he apologized for having to leave them for a meeting at the US Embassy, he was glad to end the conversation with Brooke and have a discussion with all of the British Chiefs the following day.

When Brooke and Hopkins stood to leave, Churchill decided he had better do a damage assessment. He stopped Hopkins with, "Harry, a word before you go."

Brooke stopped, clearly not pleased that Churchill did not include him in his after-lunch conversation with Hopkins, but he dutifully shook Harry's hand and left after Marshall.

When the door to the dining room closed, Churchill lit his cigar. "Harry, I think General Marshall has a good plan," he said, emphasizing "I" and in doing so told Hopkins there was a chasm between how he and Brooke envisioned the Allies' relationship.

For a moment, Hopkins thought about jumping into the differences between Churchill and his Military Chief, but instead decided to remain focused on the purpose of his visit. "Winston," Hopkins responded, "the President sent General Marshall and me here for Britain's agreement on the plans for Operation Bolero—the build-up of American troops and material here in England—and on Operation Roundup—the invasion of France and Europe. He wants you to know he is willing to take great risks to get in the fight to relieve the pressure on the Russian front and defeat Germany. US troops cannot sit idle indefinitely. We need to mobilize America's forces."

By this time, Churchill knew Hopkins well enough to know that by the formality and tone of his response, Hopkins just told Churchill the Americans were expecting the British to agree to invade France, and to invade it soon. For a brief moment, he considered lecturing Hopkins on the horrific trench warfare in Belgium and France that had wiped out a generation of young Britons just twenty-five years earlier. He wanted Harry to know that the challenge, quite simply, was that Britain today did not have the financial resources, military strength, or manpower it did before and during the Great War.

Instead, Churchill opted to tell Hopkins, "It will be a good meeting tomorrow. I am optimistic."

#

While General Marshall met with General Eisenhower, his newly assigned Chief of Staff for the US Army's European Theater of Operations, Hopkins spent his day with Lord Beaverbrook, Averell Harriman, and Gil Winant discussing Britain's supply situation and the strategy for keeping Germany's U-boats at bay. The British had lost more than a million tons of supplies and more than 12,000 men to U-boat attacks between January and March.

With Operation Roundup's tentative invasion date of April 1943, Operation Bolero would transport about a million American soldiers and airmen to England and more than 3,000 heavy, medium, and light bombers and fighter aircraft. If the British Chiefs of Staff agreed to Operations Bolero and Roundup the following day, it would be imperative for the British and Americans to win the Battle of the Atlantic very soon.

Though it was a very long first full day of work in London, Hopkins felt great. He knew—or at least, he believed—that Churchill would not have privately indicated his support to him without confidence that the British would accept Marshall's plan. The handicapper in him thought the odds were better than even that he and Marshall would leave London with the British Chiefs' approval of Operations Bolero and Roundup.

Later that night, after he sent Lyons home for the evening, Hopkins sat in his bathrobe and pajamas in his suite at Claridge's on the phone with FDR. "Yes," Hopkins said as he sat drinking a Scotch and smoking. "Churchill supports our proposal. If the British Chiefs bless it tomorrow, we can get started."

"By the way, what are you doing up so late?" FDR asked over a surprisingly good connection. "You better get some rest."

"I will. Just finishing up," Hopkins replied.

After FDR signed off, Hopkins hung up the phone and poured himself another Scotch. He retrieved Harriman's latest shipping report from his briefcase and sat back on the sofa. He couldn't help but smile, thinking how he seemed to adopt and abide by a typical Churchillian work day when in London. The "Churchill effect."

The doorbell to his suite sounded, and Hopkins opened the door to find General Marshall with Dr. Fulton. "What's happened?"

Hopkins demanded, concerned that Marshall was visiting him at a late hour.

"I just received a phone call from the President," Marshall said, "ordering me to put you to bed and keep you there under a twenty-four-hour Army and Marine guard if necessary. May we come in?"

"He didn't call you!" declared Hopkins in disbelief.

"He did," Marshall replied easily. "He also said I can ask His Majesty, the King, for additional assistance if I need to."

"My orders from Admiral Dr. McIntire," Dr. Fulton informed Hopkins, "are to stay as close to you as I can at any time of the day or night."

Hopkins turned and walked into the living room, allowing Marshall and Dr. Fulton to enter the suite.

"Doc, this is London and you should be out visiting your friends and doing whatever else might interest you," commented Hopkins, taking his place again on the sofa.

Fulton did not respond but opened his bag and removed his stethoscope.

"Breathe through your mouth," commanded Fulton as he listened to Hopkins's chest.

As the doctor examined him, Hopkins reached for Harriman's document and handed it to Marshall.

"From January to March 12, we lost 1.2 million tons of supplies to German U-boats in the Atlantic, with more than half the result of lost tankers," Hopkins informed Marshall.

"Stop talking," Fulton insisted, putting his stethoscope back in his bag and removing a tongue depressor.

"They are crippling us in the Atlantic," agreed Marshall.

"We should ship only the most vital and essential cargo until we have adequate defenses and escorts," instructed Hopkins.

"Say 'ah,'" demanded Fulton, holding the tongue depressor in front of his face.

Hopkins opened his mouth and sounded off as instructed while Fulton examined the back of Hopkins's throat. Fulton removed the tongue depressor and tossed it in a waste basket.

Hopkins reached for another document on the table and handed it to Marshall as well. "For General Stillwell," Hopkins said.

"China?" Marshall asked.

Hopkins nodded, and Fulton examined his ears.

"It's from T.V. Soong," Hopkins informed Marshall. "The shipments being flown by the Flying Tigers over the Hump are not enough. Soong strongly suggests we ship via the Arctic Ocean, Yensei River, and the Siberian Railroad."

"Dangerous," Marshall said simply.

"Outright desperate," replied Hopkins.

Fulton took several vials of pills from his bag, removed some of the pills, and held his hand open in front of Hopkins.

"Take these," commanded Fulton. "Two will keep you well and one will make it easier to sleep."

"Who said anything about sleep?" Hopkins pushed back.

"I did," Fulton said. "You need to rest."

Hopkins took the pills and rose from the sofa.

"Doc, don't you know anyone here in London?" Hopkins asked as he walked them to the door. "I can get Averell Harriman and Gil Winant to invite you to a few parties if it will help."

"Good night, Mr. Hopkins," Dr. Fulton answered.

As Dr. Fulton and Marshall walked down the corridor to return to their rooms, Fulton turned to Marshall. "That guy is a walking miracle."

#

It seemed Churchill worked at all hours of the day or night, regardless of where he was, and his relentless work schedule tested the patience and stamina of every one of his colleagues every single day. Very late the following night, Hopkins and Marshall were summoned by Churchill to the secret War Cabinet rooms.

The night was unusually quiet in the absence of German bombers overhead. During their entire car ride from Claridge's to Whitehall, there was little, if any, auto and pedestrian traffic inside London's dense, pitch-black darkness. Their car pulled to the curb on Horse Guards Road, and Marshall, Hopkins, and two British officers exited to make their way across the plaza to an unseen door that was tucked into a dark, shadow-filled crevice between two buildings. Though they didn't speak, their footsteps could be heard clearly in the dark night.

As they approached the door, one of the British officers heard rustling clothes, heavy breathing, and quiet moans in the darkness. The British officer stopped and held up his hand, while the other officer removed his revolver from his holster. Hopkins and Marshall stopped behind the British officers and strained to see what they were looking at.

"Come on. Off with you two," the British officer with the revolver said. "Take it over to the theater district."

The sounds stopped, and a young British soldier and a young woman emerged from the darkness into the moonlight—he, straightening his hat, and she, her skirt. As the lovers walked quickly past the four men with their heads down toward Horse Guards Road, the British officer holstered his revolver.

"Sorry about that, sir," the British officer said to Hopkins.

"Theater district, huh?" Hopkins asked.

"Yes, sir. They are absolutely barmy over there at this time of night," the British officer replied.

"Remind me to tell Dr. Fulton," Hopkins told Marshall, and Marshall laughed.

"Right this way, sir," the British officer directed and guided Hopkins and Marshall toward the space between the buildings where the couple had been moments before. The group approached a small steel door in one of the buildings. It was the street entrance to the secret War Cabinet rooms. The British officer knocked. A moment later, a sentry opened the door. He was standing in a vestibule bathed in red light.

When they took their seats around the table in the subterranean War Cabinet Room with Churchill; Brooke; General Charles Portal; Admiral Dudley Pound; Anthony Eden, the forty-five-year-old Foreign Secretary; and Clement Attlee, the sixty-year-old, balding leader of the Labor Party and Deputy Prime Minister, it struck Marshall that he and Hopkins were about to make history. Normally, that sort of thing never affected Marshall, but he knew this time was different. Whatever decision was reached at this meeting tonight would have a profound effect on America, Europe, and the world. Heady stuff that Marshall knew he must put out of his mind or, at the very least, keep in perspective.

"Our thanks to all of you here in the Defense Committee for taking the time to study our plans for the cross-Channel invasion," Marshall said, going right to the heart of the matter.

"Can we bring across the number of men we will need?" Churchill asked.

"Yes," answered Marshall confidently. "Men are not the issue. Landing craft, shipping, aircraft, and equipment might present some challenges."

"And we are confident we can overcome them," Hopkins added, wanting to be sure he removed any obstacles that may have been lurking unsaid in the minds of the members of the British Cabinet.

Brooke, of course, introduced a concern that neither Hopkins nor Marshall could have ever anticipated. "I think we all agree there must be an offensive in Europe, but I am concerned about Japanese control of the Indian Ocean." Brooke threw onto the table.

Hopkins immediately jumped on it. "I am sure we can work through whatever may come up in the Indian Ocean or elsewhere," he replied, his tone suggesting he thought Brooke's concern was frivolous.

Marshall decided to be very direct. "Americans must fight where the enemy can be fought on land, sea, and air. We want to engage the enemy now," he said directly to Brooke.

Clement Attlee, who was actually impressed by the Americans' plan and commitment, said, "There is little doubt a cross-Channel invasion will help our Russian allies—in fact, all of Europe."

"I agree," Anthony Eden said, affirming Attlee's statement. Remarkably, the conservative and proper English upper-class gentleman and Foreign Secretary threw in with his political adversary.

"The United States believes the cross-Channel invasion will be its major war effort," Hopkins added, making certain everyone at the table knew exactly where America stood.

Churchill stood up from the table, walking and puffing his cigar while the others watched him for several moments. Churchill, like Marshall and Hopkins, was more than aware they were making history on this night. He turned to the men. "The British Government and its people will make a full and unreserved contribution to the success of this great enterprise."

As everyone seated at the table answered with, "Hear, hear," Hopkins stood, walked to Churchill, and shook his hand. Marshall did the same with Brooke.

"I wish we had a drink to celebrate," Hopkins said to Churchill.

"That can be arranged." Churchill smiled.

"General Marshall and I will leave for home tomorrow," Hopkins informed Churchill. "There's a lot to do."

"You need to come back soon. Your visits, Harry, always seem to have a tonic effect."

"Thank you, Winston. I will remind the President that you said that the next time he calls me a pain in the ass."

It was a moment of intimacy between the two men. As they shook hands, Hopkins and Churchill smiled at each other, confident in their trust, comfortable in their friendship, and secure in the knowledge they had together moved themselves, their countries, and their world toward a new destiny.

#

Marshall and Hopkins sat in their civilian clothes in their room in the Port Patrick Hotel in Port Patrick, Scotland. Their hotel room sat on the Rhins of Galloway, a high bluff that overlooked the turbulent Irish Sea. Despite the fact that it was spring, the whipping wind ensured the need for a fire in the room to fend off the cold chill seeping through the hotel's old and porous windows.

As Hopkins stood in front of the fire waiting for his call to the President to be put through by the hotel's operators, he looked out at the rough and majestic sea battering the coast. He smiled to himself, thinking how he had come a very long way from his birthplace in Iowa and his days doing social work on the Lower East Side in New York City.

In the hotel lobby, General McClure, the Military Attaché from the US Embassy in London, stood at the reception desk dressed in a Navy blue, finely tailored business suit. McClure, who had accompanied Marshall and Hopkins to Port Patrick to see them safely off on their flight home, was checking on Hopkins's call to Washington, DC.

"I don't understand what is taking so long to place Mr. Hones's call," McClure said to the hotel receptionist.

"I don't know, sir," the receptionist replied. "The telephone operators may be having difficulty finding a long-distance line."

"It's urgent the call is put through," McClure insisted as two official-looking men in raincoats and hats entered the main entrance of the hotel and approached the reception desk. One of the men stood next to McClure, presenting his identification card to the hotel receptionist.

"Inspector Williamson, Scotland Yard. Do you have a Mr. Hones staying here?" he asked quickly while the other man surveyed the lobby.

"Scotland Yard?" McClure asked, turning to the inspector.

"That's right. Are you Mr. Hones?" the inspector asked McClure.

"I am General Robert McClure, the Military Attaché to the US Embassy in London. Can I see your identification?" McClure asked.

As Inspector Williamson showed McClure his ID, he told McClure, "Our office received a report that a Mr. Hones was trying to call the President of the United States from here."

"I see." McClure smiled and turned to the receptionist. "Please call the Prime Minister's Office at 10 Downing Street," McClure requested. "Ask to speak with Commander Thompson."

The receptionist looked frightened and turned to look at the two Scotland Yard detectives, who nodded their approval.

The receptionist picked up the phone and, after a moment, said, "Hello, Marion? Please, call the Prime Minister's Office at 10 Downing Street in London," and then quickly added, "No, Marion, I have not been drinking."

When McClure returned to Hopkins's room, he announced, "Your flight is cleared to leave tomorrow morning, and I'm told the weather will be perfect for your flight home. They are putting the call through shortly," McClure assured Hopkins.

"What was the holdup?" Marshall asked.

McClure smiled. "Who is this Mr. Hones fellow calling the President of the United States from Port Patrick, Scotland? They even got Scotland Yard on the case."

"You're kidding?" exclaimed Marshall, even though he suspected McClure wasn't.

"No, sir." McClure laughed.

The phone rang loudly in the room, and though the connection was poor and static-filled, when Hopkins answered it, FDR's voice was unmistakable.

"Harry? Where are you?" FDR asked.

"Port Patrick on the West Coast of Scotland," replied Hopkins.

"How's the weather?"

"Balmy," Hopkins lied.

"I'm sure not." FDR cackled. "How are you feeling?"

"Dr. Fulton took good care of me," Hopkins assured FDR. "We are scheduled to return tomorrow morning, but I didn't want to leave here without talking to you first."

"I'm glad you called," FDR replied. "Churchill cabled me and confirmed their full support of our proposal. You and General Marshall did a magnificent job. I'm planning to notify Stalin immediately."

"Welcome news for him," Hopkins said, knowing how much the Russians needed relief on their front.

"And very disheartening news for Hitler. This may be the wedge by which we shall accomplish his downfall," FDR declared, the excitement in his voice clear as a bell even through the static.

"What about France?"

"That worries me," FDR replied candidly. "I don't know if the Free French soldiers will take orders from Premier Laval and his German puppet regime."

"I wouldn't mind nailing that wood pussy Laval to your barn door!" Hopkins did not like any of the French leaders who had made a deal with the Nazis.

"I agree, but the odor would be too strong for the family of nations," FDR replied.

"Do you want me to stay here and discuss it with the Former Naval Person?" Hopkins asked.

"No, no," FDR responded quickly. "We need you and General Marshall at home. And I don't want to revive any conversation about us fighting in North Africa and Operation Torch."

"We will be back in a couple of days," Hopkins assured FDR.

Hopkins hung up the phone and turned to Marshall. "We go home tomorrow, and North Africa is off the table. Our focus is the cross-Channel invasion."

"Amen to that," Marshall said, smiling.

"You think they have some Scotch here in Scotland?" Hopkins asked McClure.

"I'm pretty sure we can find a couple of bottles," McClure said confidently.

CHAPTER TWENTY-THREE

"I feel damned depressed. We had a deal."

The contrast between London and New York City could not have been more startling. The former was a gray, dark, and desperate place of bombed and burned-out buildings that was holding on for its very existence, and the latter was the bustling, bright, and optimistic center of American finance and culture, which, ten years after the Great Depression, seemed to promise its inhabitants a dazzling future. Though some of its young men and women did go off to war, and some of its most prestigious buildings dimmed their lights at night, New York City remained as vibrant and energetic as it always was with its taxi cab traffic, well-dressed pedestrians clogging its sidewalks and streets, and packed subway cars filled with workers beginning and ending each day.

Hopkins loved New York City, and Louise was the perfect excuse for him to return, to see his sons, and further his courtship with a woman who was quickly capturing his heart.   Hopkins was falling in love fast, and Louise Macy was occupying more and more of his heart and soul.   She was everything Barry Lowman said and more. Not only was she the beautiful and intelligent person Barry claimed, but she was incredibly sensual—the kind of sensuality that surprised both of them as their commitment to each other deepened.

Since their first lunch together, and with each passing day, Hopkins found himself in an internal tug of war between his work commitments and his desire to spend more time with her. Fortunately for Hopkins, he was very good at compartmentalizing, else he would have never gotten anything done or gone happily mad as he fell more and more in love with her.

When Harry returned from London, he remained in New York, where he and Louise spent two wonderful days in the St. Regis Hotel. He'd missed her, and she had missed him. As they lay in bed, Louise gently traced her fingers over the surgical scar on Hopkins's stomach, with her head nestled between his neck and shoulder, and her leg draped over his. Being with Harry made her incredibly happy—"Paris happy" —she called it, and for his part, he gladly surrendered to her whenever they were together.   Barry Lowman was right. It was nice to be in love again.

"I missed you," Louise said onto Hopkins's chest.

"How would you like to live in the White House?" Hopkins asked.

"You're funny," Louise replied, giggling.

"No. Really. Would you marry me?"

"Harry," Louise pronounced his name like she was trying to soothe a man who had gone delirious. "You can't get married."

"Why not?" Hopkins asked, sounding a bit miffed.

"Because the President of the United States, Winston Churchill, Josef Stalin, and Chiang Kai-shek will never allow it," Louise answered, still circling her finger across his stomach.

"The heck with those guys," Hopkins responded, smiling. "How about it? Marry me and come live with me in the White House."

Louise raised herself on her elbow to look down at Hopkins. "Harry, seriously, we can't. You have too much to do. We should wait until this is all over," she said, but did not sound convincing.

"Here's what I know," Hopkins said confidently. "I love you, and all is right with this crazy world when I am with you."

Louise kissed him. "I love you, too. Very much," she said.

"So, what do you say?" Hopkins asked again.

Louise hovered above him for a long while and then answered him with a passionate kiss as her hand moved down from his stomach to stroke him.

"Are you negotiating with me?" Hopkins asked as he felt himself becoming aroused.

"Nope. This is 'Yes, I will marry you,'" Louise answered and kissed him again.

#

The White House was very quiet at this late hour, and as Mac pushed FDR's wheelchair into the living room in the residence, you could hear the wheels squeak and track across the wool carpet. Churchill was again inside the White House, occupying his rooms across from Hopkins for their second Washington Conference.

After meeting with FDR and Hopkins at Springwood, the President's home in Hyde Park, New York, Churchill traveled to Washington, DC with his military leadership for follow-up discussions on war strategy and plans with his Ally. Though there had been agreement on a second front and cross-Channel invasion, there remained much discussion among the military leaders of other initiatives put forward principally by Churchill, including winning the Battle of the Atlantic, and operations in North Africa, Greece, and the Balkans. While Marshall and the other US military leaders favored a direct and decisive battle with the main German Army on the Continent of Europe, it seemed the British consistently leaned toward an "Aren't I clever," indirect approach in their quest to defeat the Nazis. For his part, FDR just wanted Americans to get into the fight.

"Get me out of this thing, will you, Mac?" FDR asked his aide when he arrived in the residence in his wheelchair to join Churchill and Hopkins, who were already seated with cocktails in hand.

Mac parked and secured FDR's wheelchair in front of an easy chair and bent down with his head in front of FDR's chest. FDR wrapped his hand around Mac's neck and, in one fluid motion, Mac put his arms under FDR's legs and lifted the President from his wheelchair, placing him gently into the easy chair. It took no more than a few seconds for FDR to straighten his legs and find the chair's sweet spot.

"Thanks, Mac," FDR said. "Much better."

"How 'bout a night cap?" Hopkins asked FDR as Mac left the room.

"A small brandy would be good," FDR replied, and Hopkins went to the drink cart to pour.

"Your Navy's performance at Midway was nothing short of magnificent," Churchill told FDR.

"For the moment we stopped them," FDR said with a sigh, sounding very tired. "Let's see what they do next."

"Is the Yorktown finished?" Churchill asked about the US aircraft carrier hit during the battle. His question made Hopkins wonder what he really had on his mind.

"It is," Hopkins answered for FDR. "And so are four of theirs—Soryu, Akagi, Hiryu, and Kaga," Hopkins added.

Churchill puffed his cigar and took another sip of his brandy. "You have a great Naval leader in Admiral Nimitz."

Hopkins handed FDR his brandy, still unsure of what Churchill had on his mind and where he was headed.

"Nimitz is a fine and steady Naval officer," FDR commented. "But I am told it was Admiral Spruance who ran the battle from the Enterprise and directed the traffic at Midway."

Admiral Raymond A. Spruance was an unlikely hero. He was put in charge of Task Force 16, which included the carriers Enterprise and Hornet, by Admiral "Bull" Halsey, who lay in bed in Honolulu with a severe case of shingles. The appointment raised many eyebrows because Spruance had no carrier experience, though he covered Halsey's aircraft carrier Enterprise with his cruisers.

With the help of Joe Rochefort's intercepts and the Combat Intelligence Unit, Spruance ably guided the Americans to a crushing victory over the Japanese Navy. Though they didn't know it as they sat there that night, Spruance's victory north of Midway, that tiny, virtually unknown island in the middle of the Pacific, would later be recognized as the turning point in the US war against Japan.

"You are fortunate to have such impressive depth in your senior military ranks," Churchill commented, and it sounded to Hopkins like he was talking to himself.

Hopkins sat back in his chair, and as he studied Churchill, he realized Churchill had something on his mind about his own military leaders or the joint Allied military leadership. Hopkins was confident Churchill would eventually make sure everyone knew exactly what was bothering him.

"Harry, you look like you are feeling well," Churchill commented, wondering what Hopkins was thinking about.

"Never better," Hopkins answered.

"Have you told him?" FDR smiled at Hopkins.

"Told me what?" Churchill asked and sounded concerned.

"I am engaged to be married."

"Not so."

Hopkins nodded. "To Louise Macy, a former fashion editor for Harper's Bazaar in Paris."

"A good choice for you, Harry. You do need all the fashion help you can get," Churchill kidded, and then added, "Well done, Harry!"

"Thank you. I am very lucky," Hopkins said and meant it.

"When is the big day?" Churchill asked, hoping he could attend.

"Next month, here in the White House. The President has agreed to be my best man," Hopkins answered.

"I am disappointed I must return to England. I would have enjoyed sharing in your happiest day," Churchill said, and he meant it. "Do not lose the rings, Franklin," Churchill told FDR.

"They are safe with me." FDR cackled.

Churchill turned to look at Hopkins. "Harry, do you know that my greatest achievement was convincing my wife to marry me?"

"I've often wondered how you managed it," teased Hopkins.

"I owe it to my powers of persuasion." Churchill smiled and raised his glass.

"Congratulations, Harry."

As the three men raised their glasses to celebrate Hopkins's news, Alonzo Fields, the White House butler, entered the living room with General Marshall. When the three men saw Marshall entering the room at this time of the night, they knew, almost certainly, the news would not be good.

Marshall walked directly to FDR with a document in his hand.

"What brings you here at this hour?" FDR asked, expecting the worst.

Marshall did not respond but handed FDR the document. As FDR read it, his face turned ashen and his look somber. FDR looked at Churchill and held the document out for him. Churchill read the document and winced.

"Tobruk has surrendered with twenty-five thousand men taken prisoner," Churchill told Hopkins and handed the document to him. Hopkins now knew exactly why Churchill had commented on the depth of America's military leadership. He had been informed that the port of Tobruk was on the brink, and he knew his army had very little bench strength in its leadership. He needed fighting generals, and the British Army was very thin in that regard.

"What can we do to help?" FDR asked Churchill.

"Give us as many Sherman tanks as you can spare, and ship them to the Middle East as quickly as possible," Churchill immediately answered.

"We can send 300 Shermans and 100 Howitzers to Egypt in a few days," Marshall immediately offered and impressed Hopkins with his precise count of available resources.

"I would be grateful," Churchill said quietly as the magnitude of the disaster settled in on him.

"I'm sorry, Winston," Hopkins said, seeing Churchill crestfallen.

"First Singapore and now Tobruk. The entire Middle East theater may collapse. We cannot afford to lose the Suez and the oil," Churchill said out loud, again sounding like he was talking to himself.

"We won't let that happen," FDR assured him.

General Marshall addressed FDR. "With your permission, sir, I recommend we have General George Patton prepare his 2nd Armored Division for overseas deployment."

"Very good," FDR replied, pleased with Marshall's quick and aggressive action in the face of this devastating news. He then turned to Churchill. "I know this hurts Winston, but remember that England is no longer alone in this fight."

"Deeply, deeply appreciated," Churchill answered, though he appeared to be in shock.

#

After the fall of Tobruk in June of 1942, it became increasingly clear to Churchill and the British Chiefs that in order for Great Britain to survive the war with any world position at all, they must retain control of the Suez Canal and the Mediterranean. If the Nazis captured the Suez Canal and disrupted shipments in the Mediterranean and the Atlantic, England would not only be incapable of fighting, but would be starved into submission.

In addition to the loss of Singapore and Tobruk, and Churchill's realization of just how little depth there was in his military leadership, the British House of Commons was intent on holding a vote of censure against him. It seemed no matter how hard he tried, nor how much he was supported by America, he was not capable of defeating either the Nazis, the Japanese, or the naysayers in his own country. Churchill suffered under a seemingly constant cascade of catastrophic news and events that not only threatened his political future but his country's very existence.

It was against this backdrop that when Churchill returned to England in June, he set out to survive the censure vote, and with England's very existence at risk, he reevaluated his commitment to FDR and Hopkins to support the cross-Channel invasion in the spring of 1943. It was shortly after his return that he energetically began his campaign for the American military to consider attacking the "soft underbelly of Europe" by capturing North Africa, securing the Suez Canal, and then driving the German and Italian armies north through Italy and the Balkans, and into Germany.

Just weeks after Churchill returned to London and before Hopkins was to be married, FDR called a meeting in the White House with Hopkins, Marshall, and the new Chief of Naval Operations, Admiral Ernest King.

"Suddenly we are getting mixed signals from our friends," FDR said, "and I am increasingly concerned about their commitment to invade Europe next year."

"If the British are going to drag their feet, we should focus our resources in the Pacific," Admiral King said matter-of-factly.

"British forces in North Africa are about to be overrun, and they lost another 400,000 tons of shipping in the Battle of the Atlantic just last week," Marshall informed FDR.

"We should put our men and resources to work where we can to end this war fast," King said emphatically.

"I agree," FDR concurred.

"Time to fish or cut bait?" Hopkins asked Marshall.

"I believe it is," replied Marshall.

"Later this week, I will appoint General Dwight Eisenhower as Commander-in-Chief of the European Theater of Operations," FDR told the group.

"Eisenhower will do a good job," Marshall confirmed his support of the President's decision in front of the others.

FDR continued, "I will then tell our friends that you three—General Marshall, Admiral King, and Harry—will arrive in London next week to discuss the plan for the build-up and invasion and receive their firm agreement that US ground forces must be put into a position to fight German ground forces somewhere in 1942. Any comments?" asked FDR, surveying the faces of the men.

"We can't afford to wait," answered Hopkins.

#

When Hopkins, Marshall, and King arrived in London on a surprisingly warm and pleasant June day, they were greeted by Ambassador Gil Winant at the dock in Poole Harbor. The three men walked with Winant past two anti-aircraft batteries to a large black Daimler with a card on its windshield that read: PRIORITY.

"A different world here," Marshall said to King.

"Lucky for us," King replied.

"Churchill sent the car for you and is expecting you three at Chequers," Winant informed the group.

"We're going to London," Marshall declared, and he left no room for debate in the way he said it. "I have meetings with General Eisenhower, and Admiral King has to meet with First Lord Dudley Pound."

"He won't be happy, Harry," Winant said to Hopkins.

"Leave it with me," Hopkins said, knowing he was in for it.

Even though it was pitch-black by the time Hopkins's car approached the front gate at Chequers later that evening, he could make out the silhouettes of the estate in the distance and the two sentries standing in front of a barrier. The sentries unslung their rifles and took positions on the side of the road as Hopkins's car approached.

"We have a car approaching the gate," one of the sentries said into a walkie-talkie.

"We see him," a voice replied from the speaker.

Hopkins's car came to a stop at the barrier, and the British officer driving him rolled down his window. "I have Mr. Harry Hopkins here for the Prime Minister," the driver said.

"Open it," the sentry ordered, referring to Hopkins's rear window.

Hopkins heard the sentry and rolled down his window.

"Good to see you again, Mr. Hopkins," the sentry said.

"Good to be back." Harry smiled.

When Hopkins entered Chequers' foyer, a fuming Churchill approached quickly with a cigar clenched between his teeth. Harry had not even removed his coat.

"What is the meaning of this, Harry?" Churchill steamed.

"My apologies, but Marshall and King had meetings in London which could not be changed," Hopkins said easily.

"This is quite a problem," Churchill said angrily. "You do not have the right to go wherever you may please in my country, especially when I have asked your party to meet with me here at Chequers."

"Winston, I assure you, no one is trying to offend you," Harry said.

"Well, I find it very offensive," Churchill would not let go. "I set aside time today for us to meet here, and you all have determined you have more important things to do."

"This is really all my fault," Hopkins said sheepishly.

"Your fault?"

"I should have told you they had other meetings," confessed Hopkins.

Though Clementine Churchill was sitting in the dining room and could not actually hear their conversation, she knew from the sound of her husband's belligerent tone that Harry likely needed assistance. She decided to rescue Hopkins before her husband told their friend to find his own way back to London, or worse, back to the United States. She went to Harry's aid.

"Winston, are you going to let poor Harry take off his coat and get settled?" Clementine asked as she entered the foyer.

"Hello, Clemmie," Hopkins said through a beaming smile on his face as he hugged her.

"It is so good to see you again, Harry," she held him tightly.

"I hoped you would be here," Hopkins said, and Churchill grunted, interpreting Hopkins's comment as a slight against him.

"Oh, Winston!" Clementine exclaimed, defending Hopkins. "Winston is upset with everyone these days, Harry. Let's take your coat and get you settled. You will be happy to know it is much warmer here at this time of year."

As Hopkins removed his coat and handed it to the butler, Churchill sulked and absent-mindedly puffed on his cigar.

Hopkins walked over and stood in front of his friend. "Let me buy you a drink, Winston," he suggested as a peace offering.

"Please do, Harry," Clementine answered for her husband. "Perhaps you can cheer him," she added, and headed toward the dining room.

"I invited Professor Lindemann here this evening," Churchill said, explaining his disappointment through the haze of his cigar smoke, "in anticipation of a full-throated discussion with Marshall and King about our atomic research and the Tube Alloys project."

"I will be here through the entire weekend," Hopkins responded easily, "and look forward to speaking with the professor. By the way, we're now calling Tube Alloys the Manhattan Project."

"Let's get a drink," Churchill said, walking with Hopkins shoulder to shoulder toward the dining room.

"I was glad to hear you were able to silence the naysayers in Parliament," Hopkins said.

"I do not blame them for their doubts, Harry. Dunkirk, Rangoon, Singapore, Hong Kong, and now, Tobruk. The House of Commons has a right to be concerned. The idea of losing North Africa and the Suez Canal is terrifying to all of us."

Hopkins stopped walking and turned toward Churchill, who did the same. "Just know the timid and the faint of heart who run for cover with every setback will have no part in the winning of this war," Hopkins told Churchill.

"That is true, Harry," Churchill replied. "But we cannot win wars by retreating or surrendering."

#

In the middle of the following week, Marshall and King sat with Hopkins in his Claridge's suite, commiserating over the intransigence of their Allies. While Hopkins spent his time early in the week with Winant, Harriman, and Beaverbrook going over production and transport schedules to ensure the movement of men and critical equipment for Operation Bolero, Marshall and King met with Britain's military leadership and Churchill, trying to convince them to stick with their commitment to a cross-Channel invasion.

After multiple meetings over two days, it became painfully obvious to both Marshall and King that Churchill, Brooke, and the others had no intention of invading France and abiding by the commitment they had made just months earlier. While Hopkins sat examining his Scotch and smoking a cigarette, King paced the room, swigging long gulps of his drink, and Marshall sat in his chair, staring at nothing and uncharacteristically looking as if he had no idea what to do next.

"From the moment we first sat down, Brooke started backpedaling on the cross-Channel invasion," Marshall said.

"All I know is we just wasted two days listening to Churchill's lectures on his new strategy," King said to Marshall.

"What new strategy?" Hopkins asked.

"He wants to attack the soft underbelly of Europe," Marshall said.

"Whatever the fuck that is," King blurted out. "Let's just go home and kick the shit out of the Japanese and let these guys fend for themselves," King said, his voice rising in volume. King, who was ordinarily a caustic and seemingly unhappy guy when he was sober, became downright ornery and belligerent the more he drank.

"I wish I were there. We had a deal for Christ's sake," Hopkins complained to the air. "I just spent the weekend with him, and he still seemed supportive of the cross-Channel invasion."

"Not anymore," Marshall said simply. "Brooke probably got to him."

"I feel damned depressed. We had a deal," Hopkins repeated emphatically.

"Not anymore," Marshall repeated.

"Are you guys meeting again tomorrow?" asked Hopkins.

"I don't know why. More of the same bullshit," King said, finishing his drink and going for another.

"They have to put a stake in the ground," insisted Hopkins.

"We're wasting our time," said King, filling his glass with Scotch.

"I had a conversation with Brooke late today away from Churchill," Marshall revealed, "and I proposed we continue our build-up in England, land in North Africa in December, and delay the cross-Channel invasion."

"Did he bite?" quizzed Hopkins.

"Not really, but he seemed a little receptive," assessed Marshall.

"What's the earliest we can be ready to invade in North Africa if we had to?" Hopkins asked.

"Ballpark?" Marshall responded. "First week in November—plus or minus a week or two.

"When you speak with the British Chiefs tomorrow, see if they will agree to land in North Africa no later than October 30," Hopkins instructed, "and I'll cable the President."

#

King, Marshall, and Hopkins returned to Washington in early July with the knowledge that the cross-Channel invasion was on hold, and as dutiful Allies, they should now focus on the soft underbelly of Europe. Their Allies were getting cold feet. Not because they feared losing the war, but because they feared losing their empire and position as a world leader.

Hopkins, on the other hand, did not have cold feet. After he returned to the White House, on July 30, FDR handed him the rings, and Harry smiled at the President and turned to the Reverend Dr. Clinchy. Dr. Clinchy stood in front of Harry and Louise in FDR's private study, the Oval Office on the second floor of the White House. It was a small wedding that included the President, Eleanor, Hopkins's children, David, Robert, Stephen, and Diana, General George Marshall, Admiral King, Louise's brother, Navy Lieutenant Nicholas, Sam Rosenman, and Robert Sherwood.

After the ceremony, as Harry and Louise accepted congratulations from their friends, family, and guests, Eleanor announced lunch was served in the dining room. Though Mrs. Nesbitt prepared a buffet of turkey and ham with all of the trimmings for the reception, FDR asked Alonzo Fields if he would sneak him a plate of scrambled eggs.

"Congratulations," Marshall said, approaching Hopkins and Louise. "Where to on your honeymoon?"

"A farm in Connecticut, but that's a military secret." Hopkins smiled.

Marshall laughed. "Your secret is safe with me. I hope you both enjoy a much-deserved vacation."

"We are all so grateful to you, Louise," Eleanor chimed in. "Somehow, you were actually able to convince Harry to take some time off."

"I hope not too long." FDR cackled.

"I'll be back before you know it," Hopkins assured FDR.

"That's the spirit." FDR smiled.

"Oh, Franklin," exclaimed an exasperated Eleanor.

#

The farm they were given for their honeymoon belonged to a publisher friend of Louise, who offered it to her when she asked him if he knew of any secluded places where she and Harry could disappear for a few days. The publisher loved his Connecticut farm precisely because it was secluded and beautiful, especially during the summer months. He was happy to help Louise and especially happy to know he was also helping Harry Hopkins.

It took only a few days into their honeymoon—a lot less time than Hopkins had imagined—when he realized how relaxed he was and that almost all of the air had escaped from his pressurized balloon. Every day with Louise was easier and more comfortable than the one before, and his new daily life with her held none of the tension and anxiety that usually consumed him.

They sat on the front porch of the farm facing a setting sun and feeling the warm, gentle summer breeze rolling across the big, open field of wild flowers in front of them. Louise could not have been happier as she read Harper's Bazaar in a light summer dress with her legs curled up under her, leaning against Hopkins.

"This went by too fast. Do we have to go back tomorrow?" Louise asked Hopkins, who sat next to her barefoot, in casual pants and a short-sleeved shirt, reading one of his many reports.

"I know," replied Hopkins, and turned to kiss her.

"The light is magical tonight," Louise said, looking out at low-hanging golden sunlight dancing across the waving flowers in the field. "Reminds me of the vineyards in Bordeaux. Beautiful."

"Would you like to live on a farm?" Hopkins asked.

"I would like to live anywhere with you," replied Louise, and lifted her head to kiss him just as the phone on the table next to Hopkins rang.

"Don't answer it. Let it wait until tomorrow," Louise begged.

"It's probably nothing," suggested Hopkins, and picked up the phone. "Hello?" he said into the phone, and after a moment, "Hey, Bob!"

Hopkins turned to Louise. "It's Bob Sherwood."

"Hi Bob," Louise said out loud.

"Louise says 'Hi,'" Hopkins said into the phone.

When more than a little time had passed without Hopkins speaking, Louise straightened herself up and sat watching Hopkins's expressions.

"Sounds like we picked a good day to get married," Hopkins finally said to Sherwood. "How is the President handling it?"

Again, Louise watched Hopkins listening and, after several more moments, saw his expression turn dark.

"Arc you kidding?" he asked Sherwood angrily and listened again.

"Thanks for the heads up, Bob," Hopkins hung up.

"What?" Louise was concerned, seeing the strange look on Hopkins's face.

"Sherwood wanted me to know a couple of things in case some enterprising reporters showed up here," he told her.

"Here?" she repeated, worried and surprised.

Hopkins nodded. "The Combined Chiefs have changed their minds, and the President let them have it. He asked Winston to explain it to the Russians," he told her.

"That's it?" Louise asked, not convinced that it would make reporters want to find Hopkins's whereabouts.

"No," he replied, wishing he didn't have to include her, but knew it was the right thing to do. They were partners after all, and though Louise knew how the US press worked, she now lived on the other side of that fence inside the world he inhabited.

"Listen," he continued, "you need to know there are reports floating around that I took a government-owned yacht for our honeymoon."

"You did?" Louise asked, laughing.

"And Beaverbrook gave you a gift for our wedding," Hopkins continued. "An emerald necklace worth half a million dollars."

"Are you kidding?"

"My words exactly."

"How do you put up with this nonsense?"

"By staying focused on what's most important," Hopkins said and then kissed her. "I'm sorry," he said after several moments, disappointed that he had to share the outlandish accusations with her.

Hopkins usually paid no attention to the crazy conspiratorial claims people and the press made about him, but tonight, he found the more he thought of it, the angrier he became. Foremost on his mind was to protect Louise from the many purveyors of nonsense who had their sights on him. And Hopkins actually did not tell her everything Sherwood had shared with him. In addition to the yacht and necklace claims, Hopkins learned the press were maligning him and Louise for accepting a lavish wedding dinner hosted by Bernard Baruch while the rest of the nation was subject to rationing. They were framing him and Louise in the center of a national disgrace for a wedding dinner that was hosted and given to them by a friend.

Hopkins wanted a reckoning with those dark and destructive reporters who based their claims on nothing more than innuendo and their creative imagination, determined to make everyone in the country angry, suspicious, or afraid. Of course, he realized there was no practical way for him to win a lawsuit against the press, and he knew the best course of action was to just let it go.   Most importantly, he did not want Louise or Diana to have to experience any of this. Hopkins held Louise tightly—his apology to her for the dark and destructive musings of an ambitious and dishonest group of reporters.

#

When FDR and Hopkins learned Churchill had scheduled his visit with Stalin to inform him of the Allied change of plans, they asked if Averell Harriman could accompany him as an observer, and Churchill and Stalin agreed. Actually, Winston knew he was going into the lion's den, and he was glad to have at least some moral support from someone he was familiar with. On the day they met, Churchill and Stalin were joined by Averell Harriman, Soviet Foreign Secretary Molotov, a young Russian translator, and a British Army officer who translated for Churchill.

Stalin sat quietly, smoking and observing Churchill from across his desk while Churchill literally drew a picture, and eloquently rambled on about the status of England and Western Europe in the war. From the moment he entered Stalin's office—even before Churchill said "Hello"—Harriman had the impression Stalin would not believe anything Churchill said.

After his long dissertation, Churchill finally held up his drawing of a crocodile so Stalin could see it. Stalin didn't move or alter his expression.

"This," Churchill said, pointing to the picture he drew of a crocodile on the paper, "is Europe. And the top of this great beast is covered by the German Wehrmacht," Churchill explained. "And this," he continued, pointing to the crocodile's belly, "is North Africa. The soft underbelly of Europe from where we will enter Europe and defeat the Nazis. We are calling this Operation Torch," he finished, believing he had successfully communicated his clever strategy.

Stalin listened to his translator and waved his hand in the air. "You cannot win wars if you are afraid of the Germans and unwilling to take risks. You must open a second front."

"When we have defeated Rommel in North Africa," Churchill explained, "we will be able to send the Allied Air Force to Moscow."

"I would accept it gratefully," Stalin said without any emotion at all and added, "However, while Russian homes and factories are being bombed, and we fight more than 250 of Germany's best divisions, you promised Russia supplies which have never materialized, and said you would open a second front in France. And here you are drawing pictures and talking about soft bellies."

"Crossing the Channel is a very difficult operation," Churchill defended, "and securing the beachhead against the Wehrmacht once we landed..."

Stalin waved his hand again at Churchill, cutting him off. "You can easily land in Cherbourg to gain a foothold in France," Stalin said in Russian, looking like he was instructing a child on good military practice. "If the British infantry had fought the Germans like the Russians or the Royal Air Force in the Battle of Britain, they would not be so frightened of them."

"I pardon that remark," Churchill said, "only on account of the bravery of Russian troops."

This was not going well, either for Churchill or the Allied cause. To avoid eye contact, Averell Harriman examined the tops of his own shoes.

Despite his forgiveness of Stalin's comment, Churchill sat in the quiet of that room steaming, and as the heat rose in his belly, he delivered to Stalin an impassioned assessment of the events on the Western Front. "Great Britain," he started, "has stood alone in Europe against the German Wehrmacht for the last three years. When all of Europe and the French capitulated, we stood firm—defeating the German Luftwaffe, preventing an invasion of our island nation, sharing our equipment and supplies with you here in Russia, and providing the many freedom-loving people in Europe seeking to escape the Nazi regime with a sanctuary..."

Churchill stopped speaking when he realized the British officer who was his translator had stopped translating. The translator was captivated by his Prime Minister's passion.

"Why have you stopped translating?!" Churchill shouted at his translator. "Tell Premier Stalin every word I said!" he demanded angrily.

"I do not understand your words, but I like your spirit!" exclaimed a grinning Stalin. "And I look forward to Operation Torch and your victory in North Africa."

CHAPTER TWENTY-FOUR

"There is no doubt that great good will come out of our meeting here."

After months of discussions and delay, Marshall and Hopkins convinced FDR to approve the Combined Chiefs' plan for Operation Torch and the invasion of North Africa. The grand bargain made with their British Allies would finally deliver American soldiers into the fight against Germany in November 1942. Not exactly what Hopkins or Marshall expected, but FDR was happy American soldiers were finally getting off the bench and into the game.

Under the leadership of General Dwight Eisenhower, a joint task force of more than 100,000 US and British troops traveled through a dangerous Mediterranean Sea to make simultaneous landings in Casablanca, Oran, and Algiers along the North African coast. The American forces landing in Casablanca were commanded by General George Patton, who, during his meeting with FDR, promised the President that he would conquer Morocco or not come back alive. FDR loved Patton's fighting spirit.

On November 8, General Patton stood on the bridge of the heavy cruiser USS Augusta with Admiral Kent Hewitt, the commander of the Naval Task Force delivering America's boys to Casablanca's beaches. The Augusta's heavy guns pounded the Free French Navy and Free French forces occupying the city, shaking the entire ship with every blast.

After Germany's invasion of Belgium, Luxembourg, and France on May 10, 1940, the same day Churchill became Prime Minister of the United Kingdom, it took just a little more than six weeks for France to surrender. Marshall Philippe Petain, an aging hero of the Great War, signed an armistice with Germany on June 22, 1940, and established a "French State" which was an authoritarian government in Vichy. Though the Nazis allowed the French Vichy government to retain the French Navy and France's colonies in North Africa, the Vichy government was nothing more than a Nazi puppet regime. Petain and his Vichy government maintained an official policy of collaboration with the Nazis, including abiding by the Nazis' racial laws.

While everyone hoped the Free French in North Africa would stand down and not fight the Americans, their Naval guns and French troops returned fire all along the North African coast. It was clear that those in France's Vichy government were more afraid of their Nazi puppeteers than they were of the Americans and British. And to make matters worse, there was never any love lost between the French and British, even during the best of times.

As several French shells splashed next to the USS Augusta, the weapons officer confirmed with Admiral Hewitt and General Patton that Augusta had taken out France's battleship Jean Bart, which now sat dead in the Casablanca harbor. Hewitt was pleased and commanded his guns to continue pounding the coastal targets while the Allies' aircraft worked on the rest. He then ordered Augusta's captain to take the ship in closer to get Patton's men ashore.

"Kent," Patton said to Hewitt as he scanned the coast with his binoculars. "I take back every negative word I have ever said about you Navy boys."

"Let me get you and your men ashore before you give us a medal," Hewitt replied.

"This job is about as desperate a venture as has ever been undertaken by any force in the world's history," responded Patton. "Never in history has the Navy landed an army at the planned time and place. But if you can land us, within one week, I'll go ahead and win."

"The French are pretty tough, and they are putting up a really good fight," replied Hewitt.

Patton waved his hand, brushing aside Hewitt's concern. "The last great Frenchman was Napoleon, and he was a Corsican. If you can land us, I will be sitting in a Casablanca restaurant before the French finish their next bottle of wine."

#

FDR and Hopkins spent the weekend at Hyde Park tracking the developments of the North African landings, and sweating the staggering number of details from the War Department's updates. Despite their access to the most recent information available, their distance from the fight had both men wishing they were closer to the action. They decided to board Marco Polo and return to DC. At least they would be able to visualize the battle better in the White House Map Room.

They sat in their usual seats as the train passed through an upstate New York countryside that already began to show the signs of winter approaching, with browning fields and semi-barren trees trying to hold onto their leaves. The sun was low in a gray sky, and the air was already turning frigid. In addition to the frost permeating upstate New York, Washington, DC, was also becoming metaphorically chilly as the press and some members of Congress were calling for General Eisenhower's head after his decision to negotiate with the Vichy Government and their Nazi collaborator, Admiral Darlan.

As American troops landed on Moroccan beaches, Eisenhower looked for someone in authority whom the Free French forces would listen to and who could order them to stand down. Robert Murphy, a US covert operator stationed in the US Embassy in Morocco, suggested they speak with Admiral Francois Darlan, the head of the Vichy French Navy. When Eisenhower finally caught up with Darlan in Tangiers, he put the French admiral under house arrest.

While under arrest, Darlan, ever the self-preservationist, recognized the wind had shifted and was now blowing from DC and not Berlin. In his "negotiations" with Eisenhower, in return for his freedom and being named High Commissioner of France for North and West Africa, he agreed to order all French forces to cooperate with the Allied forces. When Eisenhower agreed, the French troops in North Africa stopped fighting the Americans and joined the Allies.

After Darlan cut his deal with Eisenhower to save his own skin, it took mere days after the Allied invasion of North Africa for the German Army to move into Vichy and occupy all of France—a quick end to the French State and the "free and independent government" of Vichy France.

Despite the fact that thousands of US lives were saved as a result of Darlan's order, many in the US Congress, British Parliament, and the press in both countries created an uproar over the fact that Eisenhower negotiated with a known Nazi collaborator like Darlan. While Eisenhower fought the Free French, Germans, and Italians in the battle for North Africa, FDR, Hopkins, and Marshall fought Congress, the press, the conspiracy theorists, and naysayers on the home front.

"Marshall and I think Eisenhower made the right decision to do a deal with Darlan," Hopkins told FDR, who sat at his desk and sipped his coffee as his train rumbled south toward DC.

"He has a duty to protect our soldiers," FDR agreed. "My understanding is the Free French would not take orders from De Gaulle."

"Or Henri Giraud," added Hopkins.

"And yet they did put down their weapons and joined us on orders from a collaborator like Darlan," FDR mused.

"Darlan is a finger licker who always checks wind direction," replied Hopkins.

"We have a few of those here, too." FDR cackled.

"We should plan next steps after we secure North Africa," Hopkins told FDR.

"What do you have in mind?" asked FDR, knowing Hopkins was ahead of him on this topic.

"A meeting between you, Churchill, and Stalin," Hopkins replied easily. "It will solve lots of issues, especially if we include Stalin in the discussions."

"Agree," acknowledged FDR. "I like that."

"I also think it's important for you to have the sort of free discussions with Stalin that you have had with Winston," suggested Hopkins.

"The question is where," commented FDR.

"Let's ask Churchill for his ideas," proposed Hopkins.

FDR nodded. "Cable Harriman and tell him to start working on it with Churchill," he instructed.

"Should we include Chiang Kai-shek?" asked Hopkins.

"Let's get a meeting organized first, and then decide. How was your meeting with Madame Chiang?" FDR queried.

"She was supposedly coming here for medical treatments but was healthy enough to drill me for an hour about our failing relations with China, how dissatisfied she was with our commitment in Burma, how much she disliked the entire British government, how they need more money and more supplies, and how much she and General Chiang really, really, really do not like General Stillwell."

"Yes, but... she's a very pretty woman." FDR cackled.

"And that's why I couldn't take my eyes off her while I listened to every complaint she had." Hopkins smiled.

"Chiang knows full well his wife will get Congress's attention," FDR commented. "Our congressmen will give her anything she wants."

"I hope Eleanor will forgive me, but I arranged for her to meet with Madame Chiang tomorrow," Hopkins informed FDR.

"Oh, I wouldn't worry about that," FDR replied. "Thirty minutes with my missus and Madame Chiang will be begging to go back to China."

#

Hopkins was wearing a tuxedo when he entered FDR's office just days before Christmas and found FDR sitting in his tux with a cocktail in hand. They were both scheduled to attend a Christmas party later that evening that would include a showing of a first-run movie. FDR always liked keeping up morale around the White House, especially during the holidays, and especially now in the thick of the war.

"It's confirmed," Hopkins said, going to the drink cart and pouring himself a Scotch. "We are meeting Churchill in Casablanca from January 14 to January 24. The codename for the conference is Symbol. Unfortunately, the battle in Stalingrad will keep Stalin in

Russia," Hopkins made sure FDR knew only the British would attend.

"There but for the grace of God," commented FDR at the mention of Stalingrad.

"Marshall says the reports from Stalingrad are unthinkable and unimaginable," Hopkins replied, taking a drink of his Scotch.

"We'll leave right after the State of the Union on the seventh," FDR said. "Where will we stay in Casablanca?"

"The Anfa Hotel. General Patton is responsible for conference security," replied Hopkins.

"Patton is one ornery SOB." FDR smiled. "I like him."

The door to FDR's office opened, and Eleanor entered dressed in a smart gray evening gown, accompanied by Mac, FDR's valet.

"Our guests are waiting for you two to start the movie," Eleanor announced.

As Mac walked behind FDR, Hopkins put out his cigarette and downed his drink.

"What's the movie tonight?" asked FDR.

"Casablanca, with Humphrey Bogart and Ingrid Bergman," replied Eleanor.

Hopkins and FDR exchanged looks with each other and smiled.

"I can't wait," exclaimed FDR.

#

By the end of the year, with the US Army's success in Morocco, FDR, Marshall, and Hopkins were able to make the Eisenhower-

Darlan deal old news in Congress and the press, and Churchill successfully defended Ike in Parliament.

General Patton controlled Morocco after clearing out the last vestiges of enemy resistance. Though the Germans, Italians, and Vichy French still maintained agents within Morocco's borders, Patton's military intelligence operatives were ruthless and relentless in eliminating spies, saboteurs, and criminals in their theater of occupation.

One criminal, however, got past Patton's intelligence people on the afternoon of December 24. A Frenchman named Fernand Bonnier de La Chapelle shot and killed Admiral Darlan while he stood in his hotel lobby. La Chapelle was apprehended immediately by the French Police, and in what appeared to be a miraculously quick application of French justice, he was executed the very next day for his crime.

Though supposedly a loyal monarchist and anti-Vichy, the word in Casablanca's coffee houses—depending on which one you visited—was that LaChapelle worked for the British, or the Free French, or the Americans, or the Germans, or all of the above. No one ever did find out if anyone other than La Chapelle was behind the assassination, but suffice it to say, there were many people everywhere who believed Admiral Darlan deserved his fate.

#

Weeks later, the wheels of FDR's jeep slowly turned and crunched against the Moroccan gravel road carrying him from

Medouina Airport to Casablanca's Anfa Hotel and the Symbol Conference with Churchill. In the rear of FDR's jeep sat General Eisenhower and General Patton, and following closely behind in another jeep were Hopkins, Marshall, and King. Though a bright and warm sunny day, the rut strewn road to the Anfa Hotel was anything but pleasant, and the jeeps bounced their way slowly forward. The road, which was cut through a barren desert, was unremarkable except for the hundreds of Patton's troops lining the road and standing at attention shoulder to shoulder to greet their Commander-in-Chief.

Behind the American soldiers lining the road were a dozen Arabs and their camels walking across the desert. They were watched closely by machine gun-carrying American soldiers who stood in a line fifty yards apart from each other with their backs to the President. Patton's orders to the US officer responsible for those soldiers were to shoot first and ask questions later.

"Stop here," ordered FDR, and the driver stopped the jeep in front of a US lieutenant who stood at attention with his eyes fixed. Patton did not like the unscheduled stop and did a 360-degree turn in his seat to survey the surrounding area.

"Lieutenant," FDR spoke to the young officer.

"Yes, sir," responded the lieutenant, saluting FDR.

The President returned his salute.

"At ease, son," FDR said with a smile. "I just want to tell you that everyone at home is very proud of what you have accomplished here in Morocco."

"Thank you, sir," replied the lieutenant, and FDR turned to look down the line of troops who all stood at attention.

"All of you have made our country very proud!" FDR said loudly to the men. "And you have all made me very proud!"

"We will not let you down, sir," the lieutenant said quietly, and then snapped to attention, saluting FDR again.

"Present arms!" the lieutenant shouted, and the men in the line all brought their weapons in front of them at the same time. George Patton sat in the back of the jeep, overcome with pride. He made a mental note to reach out to that lieutenant after this was over.

Hopkins, who was behind FDR in the car with Marshall and King, looked on, knowing FDR loved mingling with the troops. He was happy to see the boss in his best form.

"I hope you are as proud of these men as I am," FDR said to Eisenhower and Patton as the jeep continued down the gravel road. "Their victory here in Morocco was splendid."

"Yes, sir," Eisenhower replied. "We could not help but succeed with our soldiers and General Patton's leadership," Eisenhower said, putting in a plug for his friend and subordinate.

"Or without your timely negotiation with Admiral Darlan," FDR said easily, telling Eisenhower exactly where he stood on the Darlan affair.

"Thank you, sir. The job in front of us now is to engage with our real enemy, the Germans and the Italians," Eisenhower told FDR, revealing what kept him up at night.

"General Erwin Rommel and his Panzers will be next, Mr. President," Patton chimed in, his tone suggesting the soldiers on the side of the road were about to be tested.

FDR was beyond pleased with his American leaders and soldiers. "Fellas," FDR said to Ike and Patton as he waved to the soldiers with a big grin behind his cigarette holder. "If I accomplish nothing else while I am here, you and your men have already made this long trip worthwhile."

#

The Anfa Hotel in Casablanca was a beautiful building that, from a distance, looked like a white passenger ship sailing through a sea of palm, bougainvillea, and orange groves. Built on a hill, each room in the hotel and its Restaurant Panormique, promised wondrous views of the Mediterranean and the surrounding groves and desert all the way to the city. From Patton's perspective, the space around the hotel offered him the best possible location in Casablanca to ensure security for the conference.

The Symbol Conference was to be held at the hotel over ten days to allow FDR, Churchill, and their staffs to discuss their final plans to secure all of North Africa including the Suez Canal, dislodge the Japanese in the Far East, improve the safety of shipments across the Atlantic, and deliver to Stalin their promised second front against the Germans on the Continent of Europe.

FDR and Hopkins were keenly aware that the Russians, especially after the siege at Stalingrad, were doing the lion's share of the fighting and dying in the war against Hitler. Churchill and the British knew it as well, but they had a distinctly different view from their American allies on how to attack the Japanese, engage with the German Army, and "help" the Soviets. While everyone agreed they wanted to win the war on both fronts, as always, the devil lay in the details.

By the time Dr. McIntire's jeep drove up the hill at the rear of the hotel to the villas at the top, it was a beautiful afternoon with the sun glistening off white buildings and the Mediterranean Sea below. Were it not for the barbed wire barricade and the dozens of heavily armed soldiers guarding the perimeter and interior grounds, it would have been an idyllic setting. As McIntire's driver entered through the barricade, there was a lot of noise and activity across the compound with groups of soldiers unloading trucks, patrolling the grounds, and carrying crates, boxes, and weapons.

McIntire's jeep slowly threaded its way up the hill past dozens of soldiers, toward General Patton, who stood on top of a narrow lane in his shiny helmet and handsome ivory revolvers on his hips. Across the lane from Patton was Churchill's villa, and behind him stood the villa that housed FDR and Hopkins. Though Patton's intelligence staff had already determined that the hotel and its surrounding space were the best possible location to protect the Allied leaders, Patton worried about the details nonetheless.

"You've picked a perfect day and beautiful location for the conference, General." McIntire smiled at Patton, walking toward him.

"Well, Doc, I hope you'll hurry up and get the hell out of here," Patton replied, paying no attention to McIntire as he scanned the compound looking for gaps in their security.

"Tighten up the perimeter back there," Patton ordered a passing sergeant and pointed to a fence at the bottom of the hill. "I can drive a tank through that hole."

"Yes, sir. Right away," the sergeant replied, and broke into a trot down the hill.

"The Jerries occupied this place for two years," Patton told McIntire as he looked skyward, tracking a flight of US fighter planes above the compound, "and their bombers know how to hit it. They were around here about ten days ago, and it's a cinch they'll be back."

"What are those?" McIntire asked, seeing two thick and heavy-looking steel plates sitting flat on the lawn just outside the villas.

"There's a swimming pool under there that we covered with those plates and turned into a bomb shelter," Patton replied as a jeep approached carrying cargo. "They'll need that over there," Patton said to the driver and pointed. The jeep sped away in the direction of his finger.

"Which Villa belongs to the President?" asked McIntire, thinking it was best for him to get out of Patton's way.

"This one behind me," answered Patton. "That one across the way belongs to Churchill. Damn it!" Patton exclaimed, looking down the hill. "Hey!" Patton shouted in his shrill, high-pitched voice, walking away from McIntire. "Are you guys going to set up those positions!?"

When McIntire entered FDR's villa, he found the President and Hopkins seated in a luxurious living room with their sons Elliott Roosevelt and Robert Hopkins.   Robert was a US Army sergeant assigned by General Eisenhower to take photographs of the Symbol Conference, and Elliott was a lieutenant colonel in the US Army Air Force.

"There will be no press here at the conference until the last day," McIntire heard Hopkins tell his son, Robert.   "Take a lot of photographs and be sure you clear them with General Patton's intelligence officer," Hopkins instructed.

"I will," assured Robert.

"We have an hour before dinner, and I think it would be good for you and Churchill to have some private time," Hopkins suggested to FDR. "I'll invite him for drinks and get the party started."

"Good idea," replied FDR.

Hopkins rose and saw McIntire. "Hello, Doc," Hopkins greeted and left the villa.

"Ross!" FDR called out to McIntire. "Say hello to Elliott and Robert."

Elliott Roosevelt and Robert Hopkins rose, stood at attention, and saluted McIntire.

"Good to see you boys again." McIntire smiled. "At ease, please. I've known you boys too long, and besides, I am not that kind of admiral."

"How are you feeling?" McIntire asked FDR.

"Like a million bucks."

"You boys keep your eyes on your fathers," McIntire instructed Elliott and Robert, "and you let me know if either one of them is not taking care of himself."

"We will," Elliott said.

"And that father of yours..." McIntire looked at Robert.

"I know, sir," Robert replied quickly. "He can be a handful."

#

FDR hosted a dinner on the first night of the conference in his villa's dining room. Seated around his table were Hopkins, Harriman, Marshall, Ernest King, Hap Arnold, and Elliott on the American side and Churchill, Brooke, Dudley Pound, Portal, and Louis Mountbatten on the British side. There were many conversations underway around the table when Churchill tapped his knife on his glass for everyone's attention.

When the table quieted, Churchill raised his glass. "Mr. President. A toast to you for organizing this splendid dinner to inaugurate our Symbol Conference here in Casablanca," Churchill announced, and the entire table responded with "Hear, hear," and "Well done."

FDR raised his glass and responded, "Here's to architecting a clear strategy to defeat the Axis armies."

Both Hopkins and Marshall were well aware of Churchill's methods and tactics, so their antennae went up immediately when Churchill responded with, "Indeed, Mr. President. I believe the paramount task before us is, first, to conquer the African shores of the Mediterranean and set up the Naval and air installations there necessary to open an effective passage for military traffic..."

Marshall cut Churchill off before Hopkins had the chance.

"There will be a lot for us to discuss in the coming days," Marshall said, his tone so cold it left no doubt about where he stood on Churchill using social events to promote his latest theories and musings, not to mention continued British attempts to backpedal on their agreements.

Churchill didn't expect it, and for a moment there was an awkward silence around the table. Neither Churchill nor the British contingent were accustomed to their leader being cut off.

Brooke finally jumped into the silence, trying to allow Churchill to save face, "Yes, there will be a lot for us to discuss, and fortunately, we are all here in one place to thrash out the issues."

When Hopkins saw the look in Churchill's eyes as he puffed on his cigar, he knew Winston was trying to conjure up another way to introduce one of his new strategies to the group.

Though it appeared that Harry was answering Brooke's comment, he turned to Churchill, "I can't wait to start those discussions after a good night's sleep. Let's call it a night."

"I look forward to tomorrow," FDR responded immediately, pleased that Hopkins cut the discussion short and left no room for Churchill to continue.

#

A short while later, FDR's villa was dark and quiet after FDR and the boys went to bed, leaving Hopkins and Marshall by themselves in the living room.

"I hope I didn't cause you any grief tonight," Marshall said to Hopkins, knowing his statement was not received well by the Prime Minister.

Hopkins waved his hand at Marshall. "We can all wait until tomorrow morning to hear his latest sales pitch."

"If I have to listen to that soft underbelly story one more time..." Marshall's voice trailed off.

"I know, I know," Hopkins agreed.

"Harry, trying to defeat the German Army by fighting in North Africa is like strapping a windmill to our ass to try and swim across the Atlantic Ocean."

"He's terrified of losing the Middle East, the Suez Canal, and the Mediterranean," Hopkins responded. "They all are. It would be the end of the British Empire."

"That may be, but the fastest way for America to end this thing is to fight and defeat the German Army on the Continent of Europe," insisted Marshall.

"And we will," assured Hopkins.

#

As Hopkins knew he would, the next day Churchill aired out his latest strategy, proposing another invasion of Greece after securing North Africa and then a march through the Balkans into southern

Germany. This, despite the fact that Britain's first attempt in Greece several years earlier resulted in the British Army's retreat from both Greece and Crete. It took hours, and buckets full of frustration on both sides of the table, to move Churchill away from his latest gambit.

The Combined Chiefs, ironically led by Brooke and his own military leaders, finally succeeded in focusing the Prime Minister's attention on Sardinia and Sicily as possible targets after the Allies successfully secured the Suez Canal. While Marshall and the US Chiefs continued to press for the invasion of France, they were almost willing to entertain anything that might put the American Army facing the Germans on the European continent within the next twelve months.

After several days, the Combined Chiefs worked on the tasks at hand and did a deep dive into their current and potential strengths, weaknesses, opportunities, and threats. Though each side showed a lot of loyalty for their own team, as the conference progressed, alignment became evident, agreement apparent, and optimism pervasive among the military leaders of the two nations. No, they were not bosom buddies, but there was a mutual respect developing among the Chiefs and, more importantly, a deepening confidence in each other's capabilities.

One of the leaders most responsible for the respect and camaraderie between the Allies' military leadership was General Dwight "Ike" Eisenhower, the commander of Allied forces in North Africa. George Patton liked to tell a story about his friend Ike and his views on leadership. It occurred when Eisenhower learned an

American officer called a British officer, "a British son of a bitch." Patton offered to reprimand the officer, but Ike told Patton, "Let it go for now," and he then explained his view. "It's up to me to make it clear," Ike said, "that I don't mind if one officer refers to another as that son of a bitch. Everyone is entitled to their opinions. But if I hear of any American officer referring to a brother officer as that British son of a bitch, out he will go. They have to know that is what is expected of them." That was pure Ike. Take the responsibility, make it right, and then deal with it without any bias if it went wrong.

Eisenhower was called to FDR's villa one afternoon midway through the Symbol Conference to speak with FDR, Hopkins, Marshall, and Churchill about the status of the Free French forces in North Africa.

"Thanks for stopping by," Hopkins said, and thought Eisenhower looked particularly nervous.

"Have we learned anything more about Darlan's assassination?" Marshall asked, intentionally giving Eisenhower the opportunity to address the elephant he had been dragging around for months.

"Nothing new," Ike replied simply.

"It would seem the French here in North Africa believe in very speedy justice," Churchill commented.

"There is some talk La Chapelle was working on behalf of another organization, but it is just speculation," answered Ike briefly.

"Who will the French listen to here?" Hopkins asked, cutting to the chase.

"We hear it's a fellow by the name of Peyrouton," replied Eisenhower.

"What do we know about him?" asked Hopkins.

"We're working on getting our arms around him," Eisenhower assured the table.

"Thank you, Ike." FDR smiled. "Harry tells me you are concerned over the Darlan affair."

"I am not an expert in European politics, and I am prepared to be held accountable for the fallout from my negotiations with Darlan. Generals can make mistakes and be fired, but governments cannot," Ike said matter-of-factly.

"Well, General, I am pleased to tell you all of us agree that you should not be fired, and actually, we would like to award you a fourth star for your shoulder boards," FDR told Ike.

Eisenhower looked genuinely surprised and scanned the faces of the men around the table. "Thank you," he replied to FDR.

"You have our complete confidence," FDR said, smiling at Eisenhower. "Don't you worry about anything other than kicking the Germans and Italians out of North Africa and getting the Allied Army onto the continent of Europe as fast as you can.

"Yes, sir," replied Eisenhower. "I will."

"I'll go with you," Marshall said, rising from his chair and in doing so, telling Eisenhower the meeting was over. He and Eisenhower left the villa.

"I have great confidence in General Eisenhower," Churchill announced as he stood up and collected his papers. "And I regard him as one of the finest men I have ever met. He has managed to blend two nations and three distinct military services into one effective and harmonious command. Not an easy accomplishment. It is time for my nap. I shall see you both at my villa for drinks before dinner."

After Churchill left, FDR turned to Hopkins. "Ike looked jittery."

"That Darlan business smells," Hopkins replied. "With all the noise in the press and Congress, I'm pretty sure he thought his neck was in a noose.

"Where are we as of now?" FDR asked Hopkins for a recap of the conference.

"So far, the Chiefs have agreed to the following," Hopkins reported. "One, defeat the German submarine force in the Atlantic; two, increase the number of American troops in Great Britain; three, strengthen the air campaign against Nazi Germany; four, attempt to bring Turkey into the war against the Axis; —that was Churchill," Hopkins clarified and then finished, "five, prepare for the ultimate invasion of Western Europe, and last but not least, invade Sicily."

"I would like the Chiefs to agree on unconditional surrender," FDR said.

"I don't think you need them to agree," advised Hopkins.

"Shouldn't I discuss it with Marshall?" asked FDR.

"You can if you want to, but if you want unconditional surrender, then it's the military's job to achieve that," Hopkins told FDR.

#

The following morning, Hopkins stood outside FDR's villa on a sunny and warm morning with Patton and Eisenhower, saying goodbye to Eisenhower before he returned to his headquarters. Eisenhower's jeep was already loaded with his driver and luggage, and the two jeeps behind him sat waiting with several heavily armed soldiers in each.

"It was good to see you, Ike," Patton said, shaking his friend's hand. "Congratulations."

"Thanks, George," replied Eisenhower. "You and your men did a great job here."

"Thank you, sir." Patton saluted and then smiled. "Safe travels, Ike. My boys will look after you," he finished and looked down the path toward two sentries who were walking the grounds.

"Excuse me," Patton called out to the two sentries, and he started walking toward them. "You guys walk guard duty like my grandmother checking on her goddamn roses. C'mon! A little energy in that step!"

"I think George will be very happy when we leave Casablanca." Ike smiled at Hopkins. "I will see about this Peyrouton guy right away and get into his background," he promised.

"It will give all of us some peace of mind if we know there is someone the French Army will listen to," confirmed Hopkins.

Ike shook hands with Hopkins. "I cannot tell you how valuable it was for me to have a chance to talk to the President and yourself and the Combined Chiefs of Staff, particularly General Marshall. There is no doubt that great good will come out of our meeting here."

CHAPTER TWENTY-FIVE

"You can be Georges Clemenceau or you can be Joan of Arc,
but you cannot be both."

French General Henri Giraud sat at the Combined Chiefs conference table, looking like he was either slightly annoyed or somewhat amused by the discussion around the table. It seemed to him that his historical adversaries, the British, were up to their old tricks, and the Americans did not have the time or patience for any of it.

A French patriot to his core and a remarkably fit sixty-something-year-old, Giraud was captured by the Nazis during their invasion of France in May 1940. He was imprisoned at a mountain fortress called Konigstein Castle near Dresden and, two years later, escaped using a rope made of bed sheets, twine, and copper wire to repel his six-foot-two-inch frame down the cliff outside the fortress.

After his escape, he returned to France and, remarkably, his countryman, Vichy Prime Minister Pierre Laval, asked Giraud to turn himself in to the Germans. After Giraud refused, Heinrich Himmler, the head of the Nazi Gestapo, issued an order to assassinate Giraud. When Giraud couldn't be found, the Germans arrested seventeen members of his family as hostages to persuade Giraud not to help the Allies. Little did the Nazis know that, while Giraud held tight to France's historical suspicions of the British, he had already started to make plans with the Americans for the liberation of his country.

"There is little to gain by continuing this debate," an exasperated Marshall pronounced to the Combined Chiefs seated around the table. "I do not want to spend time going round and round about the cross-Channel invasion."

"We strongly believe," Brooke responded, "in attacking Germany via the—"

Admiral King cut Brooke off fast. "Yeah, we know. Soft underbelly. We know."

Determined to make his point, Brooke continued, "When we have cleared out North Africa—"

This time, Marshall did the cutting off. "General," Marshall said firmly, "America must keep up the pressure on the German Army. If invading France across the English Channel is off the table for this year, the next logical place to accomplish that is Sicily."

"Yes, I agree," Brooke replied. "And then onto the Italian mainland—"

Marshall cut Brooke off again. "General Giraud?" Marshall asked, turning to the French general.

"Naturally, I would prefer to liberate my country first," Giraud responded easily, "but we must fight the Germans wherever they may be."

"How soon can we mount operations in Sicily?" Portal asked.

"General Eisenhower believes we can be ready this summer," Marshall replied.

"General Montgomery agrees," Brooke said, wanting to secure a place for a British general in the decision-making process. "Shall we set a target date for July?" he asked.

"Any objections?" Marshall inquired, and on hearing no responses from the table, declared, "July it is. Name?"

"Operation Husky," Brooke answered immediately, confirming for Marshall and the Americans what they all already knew. This operation was discussed privately and drawn up by the British long before the conference.

"All agreed?" asked Marshall, and the group offered their affirmations.

"Done," pronounced Marshall.

#

The following evening, Hopkins and Harriman had dinner with Churchill and Beaverbrook in Churchill's villa while FDR dined with Elliott, Marshall, King, and Hap Arnold. Churchill was uncharacteristically quiet, and Hopkins saw there was something gnawing at him. The loose agenda for their dinner was a discussion on improving the flow of equipment and supplies to Great Britain and the Soviet Union. There were several times during the discussion when Hopkins thought Churchill would have commented, but instead remained silent. Hopkins decided to find out what was on Churchill's mind.

"I think the conference has been very productive so far," Hopkins said to Harriman and Beaverbrook.

When Churchill answered, "Because De Gaulle is not here," Hopkins said the word "Bingo" to himself.

"Isn't he coming?" Hopkins asked, inviting Churchill to expand.

"He refuses to attend in protest of our audacity," Churchill answered and then mimicking De Gaulle in a comical French accent, "How dare you invade North Africa without asking my permission?" Churchill then added, "There is no more frustrating man on our planet."

"It doesn't matter. General Giraud will meet with the President later," Hopkins told Churchill, trying to assure him the French were spoken for.

Churchill became instantly alarmed. "Harry, that is very dangerous. We must make sure Giraud does not know De Gaulle has refused to show up," Churchill pleaded with Hopkins. "Those two must work together to keep the French in check."

"I'll tell the President right now." Hopkins stood up, glad that he had decided to open up the subject.

As Hopkins headed toward the door, Churchill called out. "Harry, tell Franklin I am expecting a message from De Gaulle any minute. There is a chance he may decide to grace us with his presence."

Brigadier General Charles De Gaulle was an imperious, austere, ego-maniacal, stubborn, and humorless man who stood about six feet five inches tall and served as France's Undersecretary of War when the Germans invaded France in 1940.   When France capitulated and formed the Vichy government, De Gaulle fled to London, where he remained in exile and, with British help, urged French citizens and the French Resistance to take back their country. And though General Giraud remained in his country after he escaped prison, De Gaulle maintained that it was not Giraud who spoke for France and the French people, but he who was the country's rightful leader.   There was no love lost between Giraud and De Gaulle.

"Egos run amok," commented Harriman, after Hopkins left the villa to deliver the message to FDR.

Churchill lifted his nose in the air, imitating De Gaulle. "After all, Monsieur, I am De Gaulle, a graduate of the École Supérieure de Guerre."   Churchill downed his champagne and clamped down on his cigar. "We must have the French with us," Churchill fumed.

"Leave it with Harry and the President. They will convince De Gaulle to cooperate," Harriman said, trying to put Churchill at ease.

"I will happily hand them the reins of that stubborn French mule."

#

As the conference wound down to its conclusion, though compromises were made, it was also evident there was substantial agreement and more than a little competition among the Allies for the glory that would come with victory. The Combined Chiefs had developed a clear plan for the successful prosecution of the war over the next twelve months, and most importantly, at least from Hopkins's and Marshall's perspective, they agreed on the invasion of the European continent. All in all, the conference was a rousing success except for the French issue between Henri Giraud and Charles de Gaulle, which remained a loose thread blowing in the desert wind.

Just a few days before the conference was scheduled to end, De Gaulle finally accepted Churchill's invitation and deigned to grace those at the conference with his presence. On the morning of his arrival, Hopkins walked into FDR's villa to prepare for their meeting and found a half dozen Secret Service agents with machine guns stationing themselves behind doors, curtains, and the gallery above in the President's villa.

"What's going on?" Hopkins asked Lead Secret Service Agent Mike Reilly.

"De Gaulle is on his way," Reilly informed Hopkins.

"So?"

"There is no way he will get near the President without lots of guns pointing directly at his head," Reilly assured Hopkins.

"Where is General Giraud?" asked Hopkins.

"With Mr. Churchill in his villa."

By the time De Gaulle strode into FDR's living room several minutes later looking like Caesar entering the Roman Senate, all of the Secret Service agents except for Reilly were tucked away in their hiding positions with their guns trained on his forehead. Mike Reilly stationed himself in the room, not more than eight feet from the President.

"General De Gaulle," Hopkins greeted him politely, but did not offer De Gaulle his hand, and neither did the general. "It is good to see you again. We are pleased you could join us."

"How do you do," De Gaulle replied, and acknowledged FDR with a nod.

"Please be comfortable, General," FDR said, extending his hand toward the easy chair next to Hopkins.

"I have come a long way from London to be here," De Gaulle said. "A very tiring trip."

"Yes," replied FDR simply. "I hope you are not too tired."

"It is…" De Gaulle started, but seemed to be searching for the right word. "…exultant to be in my own country again."

"Can we get you something to drink?" asked FDR.

"A glass of wine would be good," De Gaulle replied. "C'est bon."

Hopkins looked at Reilly, who poured a glass of wine at the drink cart, and handed it to the general.

"I will get to the point," FDR said after De Gaulle sipped the wine. "We believe it is very important for you and for General Giraud to work together and show the French troops here in North Africa a unified face for the future of France."

"A unified face?" De Gaulle asked as if he were smelling a turd. "With Henri Giraud? That is not possible."

"I would think you would welcome Giraud in light of his accomplishments and his defiance of the Nazis," Hopkins commented.

"I do welcome Henri. But as my deputy, if he would like," De Gaulle said and put his wine glass down on the table in a way that told Hopkins and FDR he was not pleased with their wine or conversation.

"We believe the French people deserve to know they have two leaders of your stature who are united in the cause of liberating France from the Nazis," FDR said, trying his best to sound reasonable and rational.

"The French people know they have me," De Gaulle answered off-handedly.

"In France today," he continued as if he were lecturing FDR, "I am this generation's Georges Clemenceau."

Hopkins exchanged looks with FDR. They were both boiling.

"As I recall," Hopkins said, "Prime Minister Clemenceau united with General Ferdinand Foch during the Great War to save France from the Germans."

"That is true," De Gaulle replied and then added, "Perhaps I misspoke. It is better to say that I am more like Joan of Arc for today's France."

FDR stared at De Gaulle, and he couldn't resist the temptation to put the haughty general in his place. "You can be Georges Clemenceau," FDR said, "or you can be Joan of Arc, but you cannot be both."

Hopkins again exchanged looks with FDR and then turned to look at Mike Reilly, who thought the look on Hopkins's face said it all.

Shoot this guy.

#

The following morning, Hopkins visited Churchill in his villa to find him sitting at his dining table in a flaming pink kimono surrounded by empty dishes, chomping on his cigar, looking morose, and drinking a bottle of wine.

"Did he tell you he is Georges Clemenceau?" Churchill asked.

"He decided he is really Joan of Arc," replied Hopkins.

"Ah..." Churchill responded. "The Virgin Martyr of France. The man is unbearable."

"We have accomplished so much here. It would be an important exclamation point on the conference if Joan of Arc and Giraud would stand together at the press conference," Hopkins said, trying to inspire Churchill to action despite his distaste for De Gaulle.

"I wish you all the best," Churchill answered, pouring himself more wine. "I spent an enormous amount of time with him, exercising all of my considerable powers of persuasion, trying to convince him to stand side by side with Giraud. But, alas, no amount of emotion or logic could permeate that fortress of an ego. The entire time he was with me, he held his enormous proboscis in the air and peered down at me as though I had shat my pants."

"And now you are drinking a bottle of wine for breakfast," Hopkins chided Churchill.

"My dear Harry," Churchill offered. "I am sixty-eight years old, and I have taken more out of alcohol than it has taken out of me. I have no intention of giving up alcohol now or in the future," he concluded, and leaned back in his chair, drinking his morning tumbler of white wine. After he put down his glass, Churchill looked at Hopkins.

"It matters not how strait the gate," Churchill recited, "how charged with punishments the scroll, I am the master of my fate, I am the captain of my soul. Invictus by William Henley," Churchill added, and took another drink.

It occurred to Hopkins that while De Gaulle's irrational behavior and self-importance grated on Churchill, the general wasn't the only reason his friend was feeling blue and seemed to be descending into his "Black Dog." Churchill did not want the conference to end. Hopkins knew Churchill was happiest and felt most alive when he was in the company of people of substance who were in the midst of making momentous decisions.

Everything else for Winston was just boring routine.

#

All of the principals gathered on the last day at the final meeting of the Symbol Conference to hear the summary of Allied agreements. In addition to FDR, Hopkins, and Churchill, the Combined Chiefs sat at the conference table in the Anfa Hotel listening to Marshall's presentation. Everyone was given a copy of the summary.

"We unanimously agree," Marshall informed the table, "on all of the plans in the document in front of you. To summarize, going forward, in order of importance, the focus of our efforts will be: one, defeating the U-boats in the Battle of the Atlantic; two, provide assistance to Russia in relation to our other commitments; three, invade Sicily no later than July of this year; four, Operation Bolero—the build-up of men and material in England will continue; and five, advance in the Pacific Theater under Nimitz and MacArthur, and recapture Burma," Marshall concluded, finishing his briefing. He then invited Alan Brooke to weigh in. "General Brooke?"

"In the European Theater," Brooke picked up, "General Eisenhower will remain Supreme Commander and General Sir Harold Alexander will serve as his deputy. Admiral Sir Andrew B. Cunningham and Air Marshall Tedder will be in command of Naval and air forces, respectively," Brooke announced.

"I want to commend you all for your hard work and diligence in developing and organizing this historic plan," Churchill said. "You have constructed a clear map to victory."

"I am very proud to be associated with each of you," FDR added, "and very proud to be a part of this endeavor."

The table looked to Hopkins for his comments.

"I admit," he said, "I was a bit concerned about our progress here in Casablanca. But Sir John Dill gave me a preview of the plan last night, and I will tell you all what I told him." Hopkins held up the document. "This is a very good paper and a damn good plan. And I am feeling much better. If we achieve the goals in this document in 1943, the Nazis, Italians, and Japs don't stand a chance."

Smiles crossed all of the faces around the table, along with "Hear, hear," "Well done," and "Thank you," sounding off from various participants.

Later that afternoon, as Hopkins walked up the path to FDR's villa, he found Mike Reilly standing in front, watching a line of photographers and reporters being escorted by US soldiers behind a rope on the lawn next to the villas. Despite the fact that each reporter and photographer was thoroughly searched, a couple of dozen soldiers stood with rifles ready. Neither Patton nor the lead Secret Service agent was taking any chances.

"I think Churchill and Giraud are going to be coming out of Churchill's Villa shortly," Hopkins told Reilly. "Please come and get me when they do. I'll be with the President."

"You got it," Reilly replied, and Hopkins entered FDR's villa to find De Gaulle seated and listening to FDR.

Hopkins stopped and stood slightly behind De Gaulle's chair.

"General De Gaulle," FDR was in the middle of making a point, "it is imperative for you and General Giraud to put aside whatever differences you may have. You both must show the world you are on the same side and determined to free France, your home, from the chains of its oppressors. You and General—"

De Gaulle cut off the President. "I will," he said, "but only if Giraud agrees to serve as my deputy. I do not want there to be any confusion in the future."

"What future?" FDR exclaimed as the heat rose in his face. "France's future is bleak and not—" FDR started to go after De Gaulle, but saw Hopkins holding up his hands, silently encouraging him to go easy. "General," FDR started again after collecting himself and taking a deep breath, "your country is under the control of a monstrous regime that is determined to erase France, its past, and all of its culture from human history."

Just then, the door to the villa opened, and Reilly came in. Hopkins turned, and Reilly nodded.

When Hopkins exited FDR's villa, he found Churchill standing with Giraud as the general was telling him what everyone knew to be true. "Who can work with De Gaulle?" said Giraud to Churchill. "I apologize, Prime Minister, but it is not possible."

"The world must see there are French leaders who are willing to stand together and fight against the Nazi aggressors," Churchill implored.

"General," Hopkins interrupted. "The President would like to say goodbye if you have the time."

Churchill looked at Hopkins like he had lost his mind.

But when Harry put his hand on Giraud's elbow and extended his other hand toward FDR's villa, Giraud paused for a moment, and then followed Hopkins. Churchill and Reilly were right behind.

When Hopkins and Giraud entered FDR's living room, they saw a bored-looking FDR listening to De Gaulle's French history lesson. When the President saw Giraud walk in with Hopkins and Churchill, as if on cue, a big, broad smile swept across his face, and he let out a hearty "Hello, General! Welcome!"

De Gaulle turned to look over his shoulder and rose from his chair, but before he could say anything, Hopkins looked at FDR and said, "Sir, the reporters are waiting."

As if it were planned, Mike Reilly swooped in and began pushing FDR to the rear door of the villa. FDR grasped Hopkins's tactic and, as he was wheeled toward the rear door, announced, "Let's go and give them a joint statement. I will see you all out there."

Churchill understood and looked at De Gaulle. "Shall we go?" he invited, but still the aloof general did not move or answer.

"General," Hopkins then said to Giraud. "After you."

Though both Frenchmen stood quiet, it was Giraud who was the first to recognize that whoever presented himself to the reporters on that lawn would be viewed as aligned with the Allies and a future leader of France. And though it took De Gaulle a few moments longer, when he saw Giraud heading for the lawn, he arrived at the same conclusion.

Outside on the lawn, FDR and Churchill sat in chairs while the photographers seemingly could not get enough pictures, and the reporters shouted questions to De Gaulle, Giraud, Churchill, and FDR. Robert Hopkins took photos from a privileged position on the participant's side of the barrier and was able to deliver some of the most memorable pictures of the event.

As flash bulbs popped and FDR smiled his best campaign smile, he looked at Giraud and De Gaulle. "Why don't you boys shake hands?" FDR said to the two French Generals. Churchill could not believe his ears, and Hopkins, who stood off to the side, smiled.

There was a moment of tense silence as De Gaulle and Giraud looked at each other, each not sure what they should do. Even the reporters and photographers quieted down, watching the two men. And then, just like that, they shook hands. The reporters erupted, and the photographers struggled to take a picture and capture the moment. FDR cackled, and Churchill could not believe his eyes.

When De Gaulle and Giraud stopped shaking hands and looked up, several of the photographers complained: "Hey, I didn't get the picture of you. Can you do it again?"

De Gaulle and Giraud looked at each other once more and again shook hands amid another flurry of photographs.

Hopkins was grinning from ear to ear.

Afterward, De Gaulle and Giraud were escorted from the grounds, and FDR and Churchill remained in their seats to give their statements to the reporters.

"You will want to know about the presence of General Giraud and General Charles De Gaulle," FDR told the reporters. "They have been in our conference now for a couple of days, and we have emphasized one common purpose, and that is the liberation of France. They are at work on that."

FDR then continued. "The elimination of German, Japanese, and Italian war power means the unconditional surrender by Germany, Italy, and Japan. That means a reasonable assurance of future world peace. It does not mean the destruction of the population of Germany, Italy, or Japan, but it does mean the destruction of the philosophies in those countries which are based on conquest and the subjugation of other people."

FDR looked toward Churchill, who immediately picked up the ball. "I agree with everything that the President has said," confirmed Churchill. "I hope you gentlemen will find this talk to be of assistance to you in your work, and will be able to build up a good and encouraging story for our people all over the world. Give them the picture of unity, thoroughness, and integrity of the political chiefs. Give them that picture, and make them feel that there is some reason behind all that is being done. Even when there is some delay, there is design and purpose, and as the President has said, the unconquerable will to pursue this quality, until we have procured the unconditional surrender of the criminal forces who plunged the world into storm and ruin."

After all of the reporters and photographers were escorted from the compound, Hopkins walked with Harriman and his son, Robert.

"Were you able to get some good shots, Robert?" Harriman asked.

"I think I took a few keepers," replied Robert. "And, yes, I did turn over all of my film to General Patton's intelligence chief," he assured his father.

"Can't wait to see them," Harry responded. "Are you all packed?"

"Ready to go," Robert replied.

"After breakfast tomorrow, I have to issue the official communiqué of the conference and get cables off to Stalin and Chiang Kai-shek. Then we'll head out," Hopkins informed his son.

"Will you tell Stalin about the plans?" asked Harriman

"General Marshall will leave for Moscow tomorrow to brief Stalin."

"Brave man, Marshall," said Harriman, expecting the worst from their Russian Ally.

The following morning, after Hopkins finished the last of his conference duties, he stood with FDR and Robert in FDR's villa as the Secret Service agents put their luggage into their respective cars.

"I will ride with Robert to the airport," Hopkins informed FDR.

"See you there," FDR replied as he was pushed to his waiting car.

Outside, Churchill said his goodbyes to FDR, and when FDR's driver pulled out of the compound, he stood chomping on his cigar in his flaming pink kimono and monogrammed slippers, waving after him. Hopkins knew his assessment of Churchill was correct. He was certain that Winston did not want the conference to end.

"I hoped I would not miss you," Churchill said to Hopkins.

"I would never leave without saying goodbye," replied Hopkins.

"Goodbye, Robert," Churchill said. "It was a pleasure to meet you. You be sure to keep your head down out there."

"Thank you, Mr. Churchill. I will," replied Robert.

"Harry, would you mind if I accompany you and Robert to the airport so I can say goodbye to everyone there?" asked Churchill

"Perfect," Hopkins responded. "Should we wait for you to change?"

"Don't you like what I am wearing?" asked Churchill.

"You look stunning," Hopkins kidded. "Let's get you in the car quickly so we don't give the Germans an easy target."

#

When George Marshall arrived in Moscow to brief Stalin on the outcome of the Symbol Conference, the air was so cold, and the war in Russia so devastating, that few, if any, civilians were visible on Moscow's streets. The Kremlin looked like a fog-breathing fortress with frost-covered tanks and hundreds of heavily armed, wool-covered soldiers walking Red Square with their frozen breath filling the air around them and icicles hanging from their exposed hair, beards, and mustaches. There were dozens of anti-aircraft batteries populating the perimeter, and anyone who was foolish enough to be outside could hear multiple explosions and many planes flying in the distance. Marshall could not imagine a less habitable place on the planet.

Though it fell to Marshall to brief Stalin on the Allies' plans that were agreed to at the Symbol Conference, knowing how highly the Russians viewed Joe Davies, and anticipating Stalin's negative reaction to the delay of the cross-Channel invasion, Hopkins asked Davies to attend the meeting. Hopkins and FDR both thought Davies's presence might soften Stalin's response.

"I am very disappointed," Stalin said coldly. "Your President and Mr. Churchill promised a second front in France this year."

"The decision was reached by the Combined Chiefs after many days of discussions about the best strategy to defeat the German Army and support Russia," responded Marshall. "I know we all wished that you, your staff, and your officers could have participated in the conference, but it was understandable in light of what you must deal with here in Russia.

"The invasion of France will come, Premier Stalin, but not until next year," Marshall informed Stalin clearly. "After we conquer North Africa," Marshall continued, "we agreed that the most productive and efficient use of our resources is to attack from the underbelly of Europe through Sicily and Italy in 1943."

Marshall did his duty and informed Stalin of the decisions reached by the Combined Chiefs at the conference, and he did so with no visible evidence of his personal views. Though he did feel his own stomach rattle and saw Stalin wince slightly at the mention of the "underbelly of Europe."

"As I said, I am very disappointed," Stalin repeated, and the room fell silent.

Marshall did not respond.

Stalin liked and respected Marshall and sensed his integrity. But on hearing the news of his Allies' decision to delay the cross-Channel invasion, Stalin sat debating with himself whether he should let Marshall know he understood who was behind the delay.

Just as the tension in the room approached unbearable, Stalin looked at Marshall and said quietly, "But without America, Russia would have already lost the war."

Joe Davies knew that was Stalin's way of saying, "I know it's Churchill and the British."

Again, Marshall did not respond.

CHAPTER TWENTY-SIX

"I seem to be a mixture of a Baptist preacher and a race track

tout."

In the months after Casablanca, there was a sense among the Americans and British contingents that victory was assured. It certainly appeared that the more they pressed on the underbelly of Europe, the more they forced Hitler to send troops from the Russian front to support Mussolini, his weaker ally. It finally felt that after months of defeats and failures, hope was in the air again for all of the Allies, except Stalin.

Stalin had a different view.

The Soviet leader saw the delay in the second front as a direct assault on the Soviet Union by his so-called Allies. The delay, coupled with the horror of Stalingrad, convinced Stalin that Churchill, in particular, wanted the Soviet Union to break its back against the Nazis. Whether that was true or not really didn't matter. To Stalin's way of thinking, it was a smart strategy for the communist and fascist hating Churchill to allow two of his adversaries to kill each other and exhaust each other's people and resources. Of course, Stalin would have none of it, and he began a not-so-subtle campaign to upend the "special relationship" between the United States and Great Britain. There was no way the Soviet leader would allow Russia to trust an Ally and get caught with its pants down ever again.

By early March, Hopkins and FDR were once again back to their comfortable routine of early morning meetings in FDR's bedroom. Harry kissed Louise and left his bedroom office in his bathrobe, pajamas, and slippers for his first cup of coffee and cigarette of the day with FDR.

"We received cables from Stalin and Eisenhower," FDR said, holding out the documents for Hopkins when he entered.

Harry took the documents and, as he read, told FDR that he had already received word from Marshall and Churchill about Stalin.

"Stalin is not happy and, according to Churchill, the Soviets want the details of Operation Husky and a definite date," FDR reported. And Churchill seems to think Eisenhower is getting cold feet."

"That is a real problem," Hopkins commented. "After our setback at Kasserine Pass, Eisenhower thinks the invasion of Sicily is unlikely to succeed if we launch as planned in July. He believes we should wait," Hopkins said, handing the cables back to FDR.

"What did Churchill say about it?" asked FDR.

"He actually wants to move it up to June," replied Hopkins, sounding like he was not sure what to make of Churchill's suggestion. "He told me, 'If we yielded to the fears of the professionals, we would not have invaded North Africa.' The truth is, I think he's afraid to tell Stalin."

"What do we tell Uncle Joe?" FDR asked, his tone clearly suggesting he was very concerned about telling Stalin they had once again changed their plans.

"Eisenhower may be right to be cautious," Hopkins counseled. "There is still a lot of fighting to be done in Tunisia. I wouldn't commit to the exact plan or date for Husky until we're certain about the outcome in North Africa. If we commit and have to move the date again, I think we put a lot at risk regarding our relationship with the Soviets. By now, I'm pretty sure Stalin suspects we—the Allies—are hanging him out to dry."

"Let's get a cable out to Stalin," FDR suggested, "emphasizing the Conference plan is to invade Sicily in the summer as soon as the Axis in North Africa is defeated."

"Leave it with me."

#

By May of 1943, the British and American armies controlled North Africa. Eisenhower had captured the Axis forces in Tunisia, and the remaining German Army escaped to Sicily and Italy.

Two months later, on July 9, 1943, as planned at Casablanca, the Allies landed on the southern coast of Sicily with American General George Patton and British General Bernard Montgomery sharing the responsibilities of the mission. Patton's 7th Army was charged with the Western part of the country, and Montgomery's 8th Army with the eastern section.

As was their custom whenever time allowed, Hopkins and FDR sat in the residence one evening in late July, having a nightcap and smoking cigarettes.

"You heard?" FDR asked. "Stalin recalled Ambassador Litvinov from us and Ambassador Maisky from Britain."

Hopkins nodded. "When Churchill received the cable from Stalin accusing us of reneging on the deal to open a second front, Winston became so angry he sent Stalin a scathing note.

"Can't say I blame him," FDR said evenly.

"He should have spoken to me first," commented Hopkins.

"The Nazis will have fun with this if they learn about it."

"If Goebbels can come after me with an emerald necklace Beaverbrook supposedly gave to Louise that is now worth $5 million, he will certainly jump at the chance to disrupt the Allies' relationships," Hopkins said.

"You were right, Harry. I need to meet with Stalin face-to-face," FDR said after several moments, taking a deep drag on his cigarette and letting the smoke escape slowly from his mouth. "Harry, tell Churchill we want to organize a conference with the Soviets, and I would like to have private meetings with Stalin," instructed FDR.

"Wish me luck." Hopkins smiled.

"Stalin and I have to meet," FDR insisted, unsure what Hopkins meant.

"I'm all for it," replied Hopkins. "But private meetings between you and Uncle Joe will not sit well with Winston. You may want to arrange for Secret Service protection for me."

"He'll get over it." FDR laughed. "By the way, I have been meaning to tell you that was a really nice article about you in The New Yorker."

"Thanks, but I thought it made me look like an animated piece of shredded wheat. I seem to be a mixture of a Baptist preacher and a race track tout." Hopkins smiled.

"Sounds about right to me." FDR cackled.

"That reminds me," Hopkins said, putting down his glass and reaching into his coat pocket. "E.B. White, a writer with The New Yorker, received a letter from the War Board asking him for a statement on the meaning of democracy. I think you'll like this," Hopkins said, opening the magazine clipping and reading.

"'Surely the Board knows what democracy is,'" Hopkins read. "It is the line that forms on the right. It is the don't in don't shove. It is the hole in the stuffed shirt through which the sawdust slowly trickles; it is the dent in the high hat. Democracy is the recurrent suspicion that more than half of the people are right more than half of the time. It is the feeling of privacy in the voting booths, the feeling of communion in the libraries, the feeling of vitality everywhere. Democracy is a letter to the editor. Democracy is the score at the beginning of the ninth. It is an idea which hasn't been disproved yet, a song the words of which have not gone bad. It's the mustard on the hot dog and the cream in the rationed coffee. Democracy is a request from a War Board, in the middle of a morning in the middle of a war, wanting to know what democracy is," Hopkins finished with a big grin.

"I love it!" exclaimed FDR. "Them's my sentiments exactly!"

#

After victories against the Japanese in the Battles of the Coral Sea, Midway, and Guadalcanal, and against the Germans and Italians in Stalingrad, Torch, and Husky against the Germans and Italians, it was clear the tide of the war was turning in the Allies' favor. The British and Americans chased the German and Italian armies back into Italy, and in short order, Italy's Fascist leader and German ally, Benito Mussolini, was removed from power. With the American and British Armies pushing north in Italy, Soviet General Georgy Zhukov began to push the German Army in Russia back from whence they came.

In the Pacific, American forces were now adhering to the strategy put forward by Admiral Nimitz and General Douglas MacArthur to island-hop and bomb their way north across the Pacific Ocean to the shores of Japan. After amphibious invasions to recapture the Solomon Islands and New Guinea, preparations were underway to retake Burma from the Japanese and prepare for the subsequent invasion of the Gilbert and Marshall Islands.

All could not have been better for the Allies except that everyone, including Churchill, recognized that Great Britain was rapidly losing its position as a world leader. It was during this time that Churchill told Clementine that he could hardly bear it when he saw how much smaller the British Army was compared to the Americans. "In light of America's size, wealth, and industrial might," Churchill admitted privately, "it was quite logical they pressed for crossing the English Channel and invading France to confront the German Army head on."

Ironically, FDR and Hopkins privately said the exact opposite about Churchill's underbelly strategy. "In light of Britain's size and limited resources, it was quite logical they would put off a cross-Channel invasion and a direct confrontation with the main elements of the mighty German Army."

"Alas, with the Russian bear drunken with victory in the east," Churchill told Clementine, "and the US elephant lurching about in the West, Great Britain is like a little donkey between them, believing he is the only one who knows the right way home."

There was no avoiding it. Churchill's "Black Dog" was visiting him more often.

#

Despite Hopkins's schedule and the continuous barrage of complex issues that confronted him and the country, there were moments at the White House that he treasured, especially those he shared with Diana and Louise. With David and Robert both on active duty and Stephen recently joining the Marines, Hopkins realized how privileged and lucky he was to have at least some in his family with him.

During these challenging months, Louise and Diana's presence and steady support meant everything to him, especially when his health regularly swung from excellent to poor and back again. He found himself snatching every moment he could with his two favorite women whenever it was possible.

One really pleasant DC afternoon, even though it was just minutes before a scheduled meeting with FDR, Hopkins decided to sneak off and check on Diana and her Victory Garden in the rear grounds of the White House. Hopkins found Diana at work inside her garden while Louise, dressed in her Candy Striper hospital uniform, looked on from the garden's perimeter.

At eleven years old, Diana was now in that awkward stage of her development, and though there were some visible signs she was becoming a pretty young woman, she was not there yet. Dressed in overalls, and standing inside the garden tilling the soil, were it not for the bow in her hair, she could have been mistaken for any young, rough and tumble farm hand.

"I think my two girls have the best Victory Garden in the neighborhood," Hopkins said, approaching Louise at the garden's edge.

"Isn't it beautiful, Harry?" Louise commented admiring Diana's handiwork. "Diana did all of this."

Diana looked up and, on seeing her father, stopped her tilling and started pointing to all of the vegetables growing in the garden. "Peas, Daddy, and spinach, and beets…"

"And lettuce," Louise added.

"And Lettuce," repeated Diana.

"You're going to feed the entire house, Diana," Harry said proudly.

"Mrs. Roosevelt said we'll ask Mrs. Nesbitt to use my vegetables for dinner," Diana said, very excited that her produce would make it to the White House dining table.

"I can't wait," Hopkins said. "I wish I could help you."

"You're not a farmer, Daddy," Diana said matter-of-factly, and Louise laughed.

"Hey, I grew up in Iowa," Harry said, sounding offended. "I can farm. I should jump in there with you right now and show you how to work that soil and plant those crops."

"C'mon in," Diana dared.

"I would, but I have a meeting to go to," Hopkins answered.

"Sure, you do," Diana giggled as she returned to cultivating her garden.

"I do," insisted Hopkins. "Come on over here."

Diana put down her tiller and walked carefully through the garden to Hopkins.

"Give me a squeeze," Hopkins said, hugging her as Louise looked on. "I love you."

"Me too," Diana said, her face against his chest and her arms around him.

"And I'm very proud of you," Hopkins added, kissing her on top of her head, and Diana smiled up at him and broke away to return to her plants.

"Amazing, isn't it?" Hopkins said to Louise quietly. "Diana runs the White House's Victory Garden.

"She is amazing," Louise replied.

"I've got to go back to work," Hopkins said regretfully. He gave Louise a long, lingering kiss and headed back to the White House entrance with a little extra bounce in his stride. His five minutes with Diana and Louise were a little like taking one of Dr. McIntire's elixirs, except they made him feel far better than any of the doctor's concoctions.

#

The meeting he had to attend took place in FDR's bedroom with the President dressed casually and sitting in his wheelchair at his small conference table. Hopkins, Marshall, Stimson, King, Admiral Leahy, and General Brehon Somervell attended to discuss the situation in the China-Burma-India Theater. Brehon Somervell was the sixty-one-year-old general who Marshall put in charge of the Armed Forces Services, which oversaw supplies and logistics throughout the US Army.

Hopkins had been receiving numerous complaints from Chiang Kai-shek and T.V. Soong, Chiang's Finance Minister, about their lack of equipment and supplies. It seemed they always needed more of everything—equipment, supplies, and most of all, money.

"General Somervell," FDR began, "we are not making the kind of progress in the China-Burma-India Theater I had hoped for."

"It is the Wild West over there, sir," Somervell responded. "Our shipments are lost regularly in transit, and truthfully, sir, our guys don't know who to shoot first—the Japs or the Chinks."

"General Stillwell has made it clear he does not think highly of the Chinese," FDR said unemotionally.

Somervell thought he may have misread the tea leaves. "Sir, I wasn't suggesting—"

But Marshall defended Stillwell and Somervell. "General Stillwell doesn't dislike the Chinese, just some of their leaders. He will not stand by while Chiang steals and stockpiles our supplies."

"General Stillwell is right about one thing," Hopkins chimed in. "We really don't know what is going on in China even when we think we know."

"Can we get the OSS to take a look for us?" FDR asked Marshall.

"We can," Marshall assured FDR.

The US OSS, or Office of Strategic Services, was a trained group of covert operators who were used to infiltrate, sabotage, and spy on the enemy. The OSS maintained a camp embedded in the Burmese jungle near the Chinese border to harass the Japanese and maintain contact with Chiang's Chinese Nationalist forces.

"Let's find out what is really happening with our supplies," ordered FDR.

Somervell spoke up. "Do you want us to continue shipping to them?" he asked.

"Yes," replied FDR. "China and the Chinese Expeditionary Force must stay in this war, and the Chinese people must remain friends of the US."

"Yes, sir," Somervell replied.

FDR then turned to Hopkins. "Let's set up a meeting for us with Chiang Kai-shek. Somewhere between our two capitals."

"Leave it with me," Hopkins agreed.

#

It was a magnificent summer afternoon in August when FDR, Hopkins, Churchill, and their staff met at the Hotel Frontenac in Quebec for their conference, code-named Quadrant. Sitting high on a bluff overlooking the glistening St. Lawrence River, the hotel stood majestically over the old city, still on guard, watching for her enemies. One would swear you could still see the ghosts of British and French ships navigating the Saint Lawrence while they fought alongside the Algonquin and Mohawk Indians for ownership of the land. The place reminded everyone who attended the conference of Canada's long history of strength and courage under fire, and its importance as an ally that bridged England and the United States.

The conference discussions between the Combined Chiefs of Staff took place inside the hotel's conference room behind multiple layers of military guards. After their agreement to begin planning for Overlord, the new codename for the cross-Channel invasion the following spring, and an agreement to improve cooperation on the development of a nuclear bomb, Secretary of War Henry Stimson briefed FDR, Hopkins, and Churchill on the status of the Italian campaign.

"The Italian Army declared Rome an open city, and Mussolini and the Fascists are finished," Stimson reported.

"Congratulations, Franklin," Churchill said to FDR.

"To you, Winston. One member of the Axis down and two more to go."

"We may want to consider driving into northern Italy," proffered Churchill.

"Invading France is key now," Hopkins replied quickly.

"A drive north into the Balkans," Churchill continued, "and then into the south of Germany will cause the Germans to move several divisions—"

Hopkins did not wait long to cut him off. "The Chiefs are unanimous on Overlord and the cross-Channel invasion into France," Hopkins said emphatically, trying to put an end to Churchill's roaming.

"They are," reinforced Stimson.

Churchill was offended by Harry's short shrift, but decided to leave it alone and shift gears. "Who do you believe should be the Supreme Allied Commander?" he asked Stimson.

"George Marshall," replied Stimson quickly.

"Do you agree?" Churchill asked FDR.

"I do," responded FDR. "I want Marshall to be remembered as the General Pershing of this war, and he will not be, if we keep him in Washington."

"Harry?" Churchill looked at Hopkins.

"Marshall should command," replied Hopkins simply.

"I will inform Marshall of our decision so he can start preparing and tell him I will make Eisenhower acting Chief of Staff," FDR told the table.

Churchill did not respond, and as Hopkins collected his papers, he couldn't help but wonder what made Churchill raise the command issue.

#

When Harry returned to the White House a week later, he was worn out and struggling. Though it was a beautiful and bright summer day in Washington, he found himself buckling under the cumulative weight of his work and travels. He tried to convince himself he would be fine once he returned home to DC and saw Louise and Diana, but he seemed to become more tired with each passing minute.

"This trip took it out of you, didn't it?" Louise asked, searching her husband's eyes as they held each other close in Hopkins's White House bedroom office.

"My kisses not hot enough for you?" Hopkins deflected.

"How was it?" Louise asked, undeterred.

"The usual."

"There is nothing usual these days."

"The President will name Averell Harriman Ambassador to the Soviet Union," Hopkins said, offering Louise a tidbit of information, hoping to direct her attention away from him.

"I like Averell."

"Me too. You feel good," he said and kissed her again. "How are things here?"

"Eleanor thinks we should have our own home and take Diana away from here," Louise informed Hopkins.

"She told me the same," Hopkins replied. "I already told the President we rented the house in Georgetown and will probably leave here at the end of the year."

"How are you feeling?" Louise asked, not liking what she saw in his eyes.

"How is Diana?" he deflected again.

"Becoming a beautiful and smart young lady," Louise answered. "You're not feeling well, are you?" Louise pressed.

"Is she upstairs?" Hopkins asked.

"She is," Louise answered.

"Give me a few minutes. I want to go up and see her, and when I come back, maybe you can take me over to the Naval Hospital," Hopkins said as if it were a very normal request. He knew he had no other recourse but to check himself in.

"Oh, Harry," exclaimed Louise. Let me call Dr. McIntire."

"No, no. The doctors at the hospital will brew up a concoction for me, and I will be good as new in a few days," assured Hopkins. "Help me put together a bag and give me a ride over to the hospital. Maybe you and I can do this quietly."

#

A couple of days later, as Hopkins lay in bed in his hospital room reading a pile of documents and being fed Dr. McIntire's elixir of nutrients intravenously, Louise sat with him, reading a newspaper.

Sitting in the hospital bed, he found himself not only worn down by the work and travel, but also despondent over the time he spent struggling with his health and in hospitals. His regular hospital visits were no way for him to live or for Louise to deal with. Though he suspected he already knew McIntire's answer, he made a mental note to himself to ask McIntire what he could possibly do to stop visiting hospitals.

"Ça suffit!" Louise exclaimed as she sat forward in her seat in her Candy Striper uniform with the newspaper in hand. "Enough is enough!"

"What is?" asked Hopkins as Louise echoed exactly what he was thinking about his continuous hospital visits.

"Walter Trohan in the *Chicago Tribune*," Louise replied.

"Trohan?" Hopkins snickered. "Trohan thinks there is a secret cabal of Jews here in Washington controlling the government."

"And you are Rasputin," Louise said disbelievingly.

"Rasputin, huh?" Hopkins laughed. "Maybe I should grow a beard."

"I can't read this," Louise said, folding up the paper.

"Go ahead. I could use the entertainment." Hopkins smiled.

Louise unfolded the newspaper and turned to the article. She really did want to read it. "'On a May Day in 1933,'" she read, "'the lean, gangly figure with thinning brown hair and dandruff...'"

"I don't have dandruff," Hopkins said, sounding like he was offended.

"Sometimes," Louise said, and then continued reading, "'...thinning brown hair and dandruff made his way with his face twisted by a sardonic grin through an ill-assorted group of representatives, crackpots, senators, governors, jobseekers, political leaders, and toadies…'"

"I wonder who the crackpots and toadies are," Hopkins interjected.

"Doesn't say," answered Louise.

"Probably Henry Morgenthau and Felix Frankfurter," Hopkins cracked.

Louise continued reading. "He emptied his hands of other people's money. The strange and contradictory figure spent on and on to sway a nation and then the world."

Hopkins laughed.

"You should take this seriously, Harry."

"Please keep reading," instructed Hopkins. "I'm starting to feel much better."

"This is just crazy," Louise said, skimming the article before she continued reading. "'The President of the United States brought him into his official family and then into his private family and poured his innermost thoughts into the spender's prominent ears.'"

"I like my ears," said Hopkins

"Me, too," Louise answered and continued reading. "The wife of the President adopted his small child in all but name.'"

"I am starting to feel great!" Hopkins announced.

"How can you stand this?" asked Louise, disturbed by the article.

"Are you kidding, Louise?" Hopkins exclaimed happily and sounded very excited. "A few more articles like this, and I'll be sprinting down Pennsylvania Avenue."

"Some in the press want to know why American taxpayers have to pay for your penicillin," FDR told Hopkins during their ritual morning meeting in the President's bedroom. Hopkins sat in his usual chair, smoking and drinking coffee while FDR was in bed, smoking and reading papers with his finished breakfast plates on a tray off to the side. It only took a few days for the Naval Hospital doctors to reboot Harry's insides, and while he didn't sprint down Pennsylvania Avenue, he was feeling well enough to get back in the game.

"Sorry for the grief," replied Hopkins.

"Grief? I am grateful they watch you instead of me." FDR cackled and held out a cable he had just read for Hopkins. Hopkins rose and took it from him.

"What do you think?" FDR asked.

"I don't like it," Hopkins said evenly. "I hope you won't encourage Eisenhower to recognize Italy as a co-belligerent just because the King and Badoglio threw out Mussolini."

"They want to form a co-belligerent Army to fight alongside the Allies in Italy," explained FDR.

"I don't think there is enough evidence that Badoglio and the King can be trusted. I hate to see this business formalized until we have had a much better look at those two," Hopkins advised.

"Their own survival depends on their honorable capitulation to the Allies."

"I don't like the idea that these former enemies can change their minds when they know that they are going to get licked," cautioned Hopkins.

FDR stared at Harry while he took a long drag on his cigarette, and Hopkins knew the President was figuring out the next steps. "Let's tell Churchill we want Eisenhower to secure a formal armistice with the Italians before we recognize them," instructed FDR.

"Leave it with me."

#

Henry Stimson and Steve Early met with Hopkins in his bedroom office to discuss the latest batch of less-than-flattering newspaper stories about Hopkins. Harry was hot and particularly upset at the stories that included Louise in their so-called scandals or those that mentioned Diana. Spouses and children were supposed to be off-limits.

"Henry," Hopkins said sternly to Stimson. "Where does The Army and Navy Register get off printing this bullshit?"

"The conspiracy guys are saying you want Marshall appointed Supreme Allied Commander to get him out of Washington," Early explained.

"They're saying Marshall and Churchill disagree on strategy, and because of that, you want Marshall replaced as Chief of Staff with General Somervell," Stimson said, adding more color to the story.

"Somervell?" asked Hopkins, trying to figure out the connections.

"They know you worked with Somervell at the WPA," Stimson said.

"The Washington Times Herald says you want to create a Global WPA and that is the reason for the plot against Marshall," Early said, his tone suggesting that Hopkins should ignore the reports.

"They just make this stuff up. This is the emerald necklace story all over again," Hopkins said in disbelief.

"I wouldn't worry about it," Early suggested. "Hey, the Cheyenne Tribune says they can see Hopkins's Slimy Hand."

"Jesus," Hopkins whispered.

"No, not Jesus, but the Jews." Early smiled. "Your nefarious plot has expanded, it seems, to include your Jewish friends. Apparently, Justice Frankfurter, Henry Morgenthau, and Sam Rosenman are engineering a plot to turn America into a communist country."

"And your activities are nothing less than treasonous. You are turning my War Department into a global political organization," Stimson said, smiling. "And I want you to know, Harry, the War Department does not appreciate it."

"Goddamn. Anything else they want to throw in there?" Hopkins asked.

"There is more," Early assured Hopkins. "The Nazis broadcast this morning that General Marshall was dismissed two days ago and President Roosevelt has taken over his command."

"Positive proof our own imbeciles are helping the enemy," Hopkins said.

"I would be careful if I were you, Harry. The imbeciles are restless," Early cautioned.

There was a knock on Hopkins's door, and Grace Tully entered carrying a note for Hopkins.

"Sorry to interrupt, Mr. Hopkins," Tully said, handing him the note, "but I received this message from General Marshall, and when I told him you were in a meeting with Mr. Stimson and Mr. Early, he asked that I deliver it to you immediately."

"Thank you, Grace," Hopkins answered, and opened the note as Tully left the room.

He laughed out loud.

"Marshall wants to know if I am responsible for him getting fired," Hopkins said, and handed the note to Stimson.

"Steve, I'll get with the President about this nonsense, but I think we have to tell the press they are potentially hurting us—our military, our effectiveness, our allies..." Hopkins told Early and trailed off.

"I'll get on it," assured Early.

"Thank you for your time, Rasputin," Stimson snickered.

#

Later that evening, as Hopkins and FDR had their evening cocktails, Harry brought FDR up to speed on the trouble brewing over the decision to make Marshall Supreme Allied Commander.

"This Marshall business is getting out of hand. And to make matters worse, Churchill told me the agreement we reached in

Quebec regarding Marshall as the Supreme Allied Commander means that Marshall will only serve in an advisory role," Hopkins informed FDR.

"Advisory?" FDR asked, clearly annoyed at Churchill waffling again.

"We have to settle this issue with Churchill in Cairo next month before we sit down with Stalin at the conference in Tehran," advised Hopkins.

"Let's make sure we get it on our agenda when we are in Egypt," replied FDR. "I bet Winston has his hands full with Brooke and General Montgomery," FDR speculated.

"You may be right, but I feel very strongly that Marshall should have command of all the Allied forces crossing the Channel and attacking France and Germany," Hopkins said, concerned that Churchill would get his way.

"I agree," FDR said, confirming Hopkins's view on Marshall.

"Fortunately for us, Marshall is taking all of this in stride. He sent me this message today," Hopkins said, handing Marshall's message to FDR. "I think you'll get a kick out of it."

FDR opened Marshall's message and read it aloud. "'Harry. Heard a Nazi Broadcast that I was dismissed a couple of days ago. Are you responsible for pulling this fast one on me?'" FDR threw his head back laughing.

"Harry, send this back to Marshall," FDR said, picking up a pencil and speaking out loud as he wrote his reply on Marshall's note. "Dear George," said FDR as he wrote, "only true in part—I am now Chief of Staff, but you are President. FDR."

FDR cackled.

#

Later that evening, while Hopkins and Louise were lying in bed, Hopkins shared the latest conspiracy theories being told about him. Not exactly the usual pillow-talk most lovers enjoy, but Hopkins worried about how the stories floating around about him might affect her and Diana. Fortunately, having worked in the magazine business, Louise seemed to cope pretty well with the never-ending deluge of dung thrown at Hopkins, and recognized the stories were mostly a silly and, at times, a sad commentary on the stories' publishers, authors, and their audience.

"By the way, where did you put that $5 million emerald necklace?" teased Hopkins as he traced a line with his finger along her inner thigh.

"In my Swiss bank account with my gold bullion," Louise answered breathily, and turned toward him so that she could lie on top of his hand.

"Now I know why I married you. You're loaded!" Hopkins smiled and kissed her passionately.

"I'm going to miss you," Louise said, adjusting herself onto him under the covers. "When do you leave for Egypt and Tehran?"

"On the twelfth," Hopkins replied.

"Good. We have time," Louise said, kissing him and slowly moving her hips on top of him.

CHAPTER TWENTY-SEVEN

"If you think it'll help, tell him we're all Republicans!"

On Friday, November 12, Hopkins kissed Louise goodbye, and he, Roosevelt, and the rest of the Presidential entourage traveled from the calm waters of Chesapeake Bay in a small gunboat to a gray colossus rising out of the early morning fog.   It was the USS Iowa, the most powerful battleship afloat in the world. Nearly as long as the Empire State Building was tall, it was home to more than 2,700 men. Its 212,000-horsepower engines enabled it to knife through the water, and its powerful guns could dispense with anything in its way.

The Iowa was Hopkins's and FDR's ride—first to the Sextant Conference with Churchill and from there to the three-day "Eureka" conference between the "Big Three"—Roosevelt, Churchill, and Stalin—in Tehran, Iran. Hopkins thought Eureka was an especially fitting codename for the conference since all three Allied leaders would, for the first time, finally meet face-to-face.

Though FDR, Churchill, and Stalin were called the "Big Three," it was becoming clear to all that Britain was quickly becoming a junior partner in the powerful alliance, inferior to America in its industrial and military might, and subordinate to Russia in its significant contribution in blood and sacrifice.

Sensitive to Churchill's sensitivities, Hopkins informed him that FDR would have private meetings with Stalin in Tehran. Though Churchill seemed to acknowledge that FDR and Stalin should spend time with each other and have a good working relationship, he told Clemmie, he had the feeling the US elephant and the Russian bear were walking hand in hand down the road together, leaving the poor British donkey behind.

On their second full day at sea, on a beautiful, clear Sunday, the Iowa's Captain John L. McCrea had arranged to give the President a demonstration of the USS Iowa's ferocious firepower. When Hopkins and FDR came out onto the Iowa's top deck just outside the bridge, Hopkins was overcome by the breathtaking and wondrous sight of the many destroyers and cruisers sailing alongside the Iowa. The sight of America's warships cutting through the water and sailing together in perfect unison touched Hopkins deeply and filled him with awe and pride at how much his country's military had grown in the last five years. They had come a long way from those days of meager aircraft production in Santa Monica.

As Captain McCrea launched several large red balloons up to an altitude of 20,000 feet, Hopkins and FDR could hear the gears on the battleship's five-inch guns cranking and pushing their barrels skyward. It was a standard training exercise to practice hitting attacking aircraft, and the USS Iowa's gunnery officer and his gunnery mates took pride in quickly knocking the balloons out of the sky. Hopkins looked over at FDR, craning his neck to see the balloons, and he thought the President looked happier and more excited than he had seen him in a very long while.

"Commence firing," Captain McCrae ordered his executive officer.

"Aye, sir," the XO repeated, "Commence firing." The XO then gave the order to the gunnery officer.

Instantly, Iowa's five-inch guns began belching shells and fire at the balloons above, and with each blast, the ship shook and the spectators flinched. The sound of the guns was deafening, and fortunately for FDR and Hopkins, they had been given cotton balls for their ears. Preoccupied with watching the shells burst around the balloons, neither Hopkins nor FDR heard or saw an officer running from the bridge toward Captain McCrae. The officer was pointing to the water and yelling, "It's the real thing! It's the real thing!"

McCrae saw him before he heard him, and though he was unsure what the officer was referring to, the fear on the man's face made McCrae order his XO to stop firing at the balloons. As soon as the guns fell silent, FDR and Hopkins could hear the officer plain as day screaming, "It's the real thing!" and saw him pointing toward the water. In the distance, about 900 yards from the Iowa, was the unmistakable wake of a torpedo heading directly for the ship.

"Have the guns knock it out of the water," McCrae ordered his XO, and almost instantly the barrels of the five-inch guns began moving down from the sky toward the sea.

"Hard right rudder," ordered McCrae as the guns began sending shells toward the incoming torpedo. "Full speed ahead."

The massive battleship dug in and strained to turn sharply, as the shells from the five-inch guns splashed around the incoming torpedo. Hopkins thought about moving FDR off the deck, but when he looked at him, he was surprised to see FDR was thoroughly enjoying himself. Other than a reflexive twitch each time a gun fired, there wasn't a hint of worry on the President's face.

All eyes were on the wake screaming across the water and heading toward the Iowa as she turned away from the inbound torpedo and accelerated. FDR and Hopkins watched as the torpedo traveled past the ship's stern, and a five-inch shell finally detonated the torpedo in the ship's wake about 300 yards from the ship. The huge explosion sent a plume of water more than eighty feet in the air.

Though Captain McCrea's first thought was that there was a German U-boat nearby, he quickly learned otherwise.

It was friendly fire.

"Cease firing," McCrae ordered. "All ahead standard."

The guns fell silent, and the ship slowed.

A few minutes later, McCrea walked over to the President. "Sir," he said, "I'm very sorry. That was not part of our demonstration. Unfortunately, the William Porter, one of our escort ships, accidentally released a torpedo."

Roosevelt smiled and said, "Captain, please radio the skipper on that vessel and ask him not to shoot. If you think it'll help, tell him we're all Republicans!"

The Iowa arrived at Oran in Northwest Algeria on November 20. Eisenhower, along with Elliott Roosevelt, Franklin Roosevelt Jr., and Harry's son, Robert, all boarded The Sacred Cow, and flew to Tunis and then on to Egypt and the Mena Hotel in Giza.

Once a hunting lodge, the Mena Hotel sported long verandas and blue-tiled floors, and were it not for the British Army's overwhelming presence, it would have had the feel of a cozy country house. Cairo belonged to the British Army, and with FDR and Churchill in the hotel finalizing their positions for the upcoming Tehran Conference with Stalin, the British MPs made sure everyone was searched and their credentials viewed multiple times by multiple people before they were permitted even near the building. British soldiers covered every inch inside and outside the hotel.

The presence of the British military, however, could not take away the inspiring and stunning view of ancient pyramids in the near distance across from the front of the hotel. In the late afternoon sun, they seemed to rise from the desert floor and were a clear reminder of the thousands of years of human experiences and memories that were recorded in this place. They had witnessed it all. They were here then, they are here now, and despite the savagery of humanity's latest conflict, they would be here long after the war was finished.

Hopkins had arranged for China's Chiang Kai-shek to meet with FDR and Churchill at the hotel, and they sat inside the conference room together with Lord "Dickie" Mountbatten, the Supreme Allied

Commander South East Asia Command, and General Joe Stillwell, the US Commander in the China-Burma-India Theater.

"Burma is the key to the whole campaign in Asia," Chiang remarked, and after spending time with Chiang during the meeting, Hopkins thought Joe Stillwell might be right. There was nothing about the Chinese leader that told Hopkins he had any interest in the Allies or their initiatives other than their ability to provide him with more equipment, more supplies, and more money.

"The Joint Chiefs have unanimously endorsed our plan to recapture Burma. It's called Anakim," Mountbatten weighed in.

Chiang nodded. "This is critical," he said.

Churchill and Hopkins seemed to be thinking the same thing at the same time, but Churchill got there first. He exhaled some cigar smoke, and he told Chiang, "In the spirit of friendship, I should tell you there are concerns about supplies reaching your troops."

"Yes, yes," Chiang agreed easily. "We are having difficulty. If we are to be successful, General Stillwell must keep the Burma Road open. I have discussed this with General Mountbatten."

Mountbatten and Stillwell exchanged looks. Even though they were accustomed to Chiang's arrogance and tactics, his heavy-handed, one-sided approach to their relationship still grated on both men.

"Isn't the Chinese Expeditionary Force responsible for keeping the Japanese away from the Burma Road?" Churchill asked.

"Yes, they are. But as you know, I have put Chinese forces under General Stillwell," Chiang said, never taking his eyes off Churchill.

Hopkins looked at Stillwell, and for good reason, he was furious. That was the second time in as many minutes that Chiang embarrassed him in front of the others. Hopkins thought Vinegar Joe was going to leap over the table and pummel the Chinese leader.

"But to be fair to General Stillwell," Chiang added, directly to FDR, "even the best-trained soldiers need adequate supplies. And not even your General Chennault and the Flying Tigers can get supplies for his airplanes." Someone should have told Chiang that it was a bad idea to embarrass FDR, too.

FDR was doing everything he could to control himself when he removed his pince-nez glasses, rubbed the bridge of his nose, and looked directly at Chiang, "You have my assurance. The United States will deliver all of the equipment, material, and supplies you need to take back Burma and defeat the Japanese in China."

"I appreciate your confidence," Chiang said cheerfully to FDR, knowing he had, at least for the moment, successfully connived to get his way.

Upset by Chiang's blatant extortion, FDR decided to light himself a cigarette, while Churchill, red-faced, puffed madly on his cigar. So far, in a very short period of time, the Chinese leader had done extraordinarily well in securing a steady supply of goods for his coffers and alienating every one of his allies around the table.

Chiang stood up. "Please forgive me," he said, "but my wife and I are scheduled to meet King Farouk at Abdeen Palace this afternoon." And with that, he just walked out of the room.

The men around the table were flabbergasted. Translation: Farouk is more important to me than you guys around the table who are providing me with the resources to help save me and my country from a Japanese invasion. Stillwell had all he could do to remain sitting in his chair. He desperately wanted to follow Chiang out of the room and take him out back.

Churchill looked over at Mountbatten and, looking for a ray of light, said, "At least they are still in the fight."

"Chiang will stay in it as long as we continue to send supplies and equipment," Hopkins said.

"Our goods are big business in China," Stillwell confirmed.

"It's a small price for us to pay to keep China in the war and attacking Japan's flank," FDR said. He then looked over at Hopkins and said, "Harry, we need a declaration for the press conference tomorrow."

"How's this," Harry replied quickly. "The United States, Great Britain, and the Republic of China, Allies, pledge to continue the war against Japan and to eject the Japanese forces from all territories they have conquered, including the Chinese territories, Korea, and the Pacific Islands."

"Perfect," Churchill commented, and though his response suggested otherwise, he sounded thoroughly despondent. He rose from the table and began collecting his papers.

It was already clear to everyone at the table that China was going to be a significant problem when all of this was over. With Mao Zedong and his communists making the Japanese pay dearly for their infractions in the north, and Chiang's staggering ineffectiveness and blatant corruption in the South, new lines were already being drawn for a turbulent and very challenging post-war China.

As the meeting broke up, Mike Reilly, the President's lead Secret Service agent, entered the conference room and approached FDR. "Sir? Can I have a word?" asked the thirty-three-year-old man from Montana who had broad shoulders and was thick like a prize fighter.

Hopkins immediately thought it had something to do with Chiang, but he was mistaken.

"We've received word from Russian security that the Germans are planning to assassinate you at the conference in Tehran," Reilly said.

"They aren't able to get into our embassy, are they?" FDR asked.

"No, sir," Mike answered. "They would, however, be able to attack us as we traveled back and forth from our embassy to the conference at the Russian Embassy."

"Is this credible?" asked Hopkins.

"The Russians say the Germans are parachuting men into Iran specifically for this mission."

"What do you suggest?" Hopkins asked Reilly.

"Marshal Stalin has invited you both to stay in a villa inside the Soviet Embassy compound," Reilly informed them.

"What about Churchill?" Harry asked.

"As far as I know, they have only invited you and Mr. Hopkins," Reilly replied.

"Our friend will not like that at all," FDR worried.

"It would be safer if you stayed inside the gates of the Russian Embassy," Reilly said in a way that made it clear that was his recommendation for FDR and Hopkins.

"Thanks, Mike," FDR said and then added, "I will let you know."

"Yes, sir." Reilly nodded and left the room.

"Made up?" FDR asked Hopkins.

"Probably," replied Harry. "Could be helpful though."

"How's that?"

"Gives you a perfect excuse for alone time with Stalin," Hopkins said.

"It would indeed," FDR replied with a wry smile.

#

Harry Hopkins occupied a spacious suite at the Mena Hotel, second in size and splendor only to the one being used by the President. Harry's digs included a dining room, a butler's pantry, a living room, and two bedrooms, and from a large window in the dining room, he had a stunning view of the pyramids. He was gazing at them while finishing his breakfast the next morning when Averell Harriman walked in with a younger man.

"Great to see you, Ave. How's Moscow treating you?" Harry asked, shaking Harriman's hand.

"I liked it a lot better when I was just handling Lend-Lease stuff. Now that I'm an ambassador, they seem to be less interested in what I have to say. Amazing how that works." He smiled, and then added,

"Harry, this is Charles 'Chip' Bohlen. If there's anyone who can interpret Stalin's words, as well as his intentions, it's Chip."

"High praise coming from Ave," Hopkins replied, shaking hands with Bohlen. "Foreign Service?" Hopkins asked.

"Yes, sir," replied Bohlen. "Averell and I work together at the Moscow Embassy."

Bohlen had an easy-going and boyish manner and had been an original part of the American presence in Moscow since FDR normalized relations with Russia in 1934. No other diplomat, other than perhaps Joe Davies, knew the Russians better. Bohlen was fluent in their language, well-versed in Russian literature, and an expert on the tenets of Bolshevism. Chip's real knack, though, was his innate understanding of what made Stalin and all of the country's diehard communists tick. Harriman, like Davies and others in Moscow, leaned on him.

"Chip, I have met a lot of foreign service guys in my travels, and—" Hopkins started, and Bohlen jumped in.

"…and they didn't impress you?" Bohlen questioned, smiling at Hopkins.

"With all due respect, most struck me as a bunch of cookie pushers and pansies—and they were usually isolationists to boot. I've never been able to reconcile that one, a State Department that didn't want to get involved with foreign countries."

"I understand, Mr. Hopkins, but…" replied Bohlen

"Harry," Hopkins interrupted.

"Harry," Bohlen repeated. "Right now, we are using our hard power—our military—against our enemies. When this war is over, it will be the State Department's cookie pushers and pansies around the world who will be on the front lines—using our influence to persuade our friends and enemies alike they should follow us.

"And how will the Soviet Union respond when we try to persuade and influence them to follow us?" Hopkins asked Bohlen.

"I think you know," Bohlen replied. "The Russians only understand hard power."

"So, we will have to go to war with them?" asked Hopkins, trying to vet the young specialist.

"No, no," Bohlen said quickly. "Stalin cannot continue to make war without our support. For the moment, Stalin will use his alliance with us to push the Germans back and expand as far west as he can."

"Will he take Poland?" asked Hopkins.

"Five will get you ten he will try," Bohlen assured Hopkins. "And he will try for Hungary, Czechoslovakia, the Balkans, and as much of Germany as he can grab. My bet is Stalin sees a post-war world divvied up between the Soviet Union on one side and the United States on the other."

"What are the odds?" Hopkins asked.

"Better than even," Bohlen replied.

"What does he think about Great Britain?" asked Hopkins.

"I don't think Stalin believes Great Britain is worth the candle. If I'm right about that, you will see it in his behavior at the Tehran Conference," Bohlen said easily.

"Stalin is not shy," Harriman confirmed.

"The Russians invited the President to stay inside the Soviet Embassy compound in Tehran," Hopkins informed Bohlen.

"They probably said they want to protect the President," Bohlen commented, and Hopkins nodded. "The real reason is they want to listen in on you and the President."

"No kidding?"

"Every room." Bohlen nodded. "By the way, every person you see in their Embassy in Tehran—even the maids—all work for the NKVD—the Soviet Secret Police."

"Sounds like this is going to be a very relaxing trip," Harriman cracked.

"It won't be that bad." Bohlen smiled. "You just have to remember not to say or do anything in the privacy of your room that you wouldn't say or do in front of Stalin. Other than that, you should feel free to express yourself," Bohlen cracked.

Hopkins understood why Harriman liked this guy.

#

The Russian Embassy in Tehran was located at Atabak Garden. It looked more like a Tsarist palace than a diplomatic outpost and featured a main building with a long flight of stairs leading to a colonnaded portico over its front door. It was surrounded by several smaller structures, including the villas where Roosevelt, Hopkins, and other Americans would stay during the conference.

The compound was swarming inside and out with Russian soldiers and dozens of NKVD agents who circulated dressed in white waiters' jackets and housekeepers' frocks. All of the agents carried guns, evidenced by a visible bulge under their clothing.

Hopkins arranged for Chip Bohlen to brief FDR on the likely strategy and tactics the Soviets would use at the upcoming meeting, and Bohlen gave them, as much as anyone possibly could, an insider's view of Stalin's motives and modus operandi. It was good for both FDR and Hopkins to confirm their own thinking on the Soviet leader and learn what they were missing from the insights offered by Bohlen. He did a great job bringing them up to speed, and Hopkins could not have been more pleased that Averell brought Chip to his attention.

After Bohlen's briefing, Hopkins went to his room to rest, and there was a knock at the door to FDR's villa. When a military aide opened the door, he found two men in the doorway—Marshall Josef Stalin and his interpreter, Vladimir Pavlov.

Bohlen instantly greeted the Soviet leader in Russian. "Welcome, Marshal Stalin. Please, come in."

Pavlov responded, "Spasibo."

FDR was seated at a table, and Stalin went directly to him with an extended hand. The two men shook hands. Stalin sat next to FDR at the table, and they exchanged cigarettes. They each toasted each other with drinks.

"How are things at your front?" Roosevelt asked.

"Difficult," Stalin replied.

"We hear the Germans are trying to regroup and are moving east."

"Yes. They continue to probe and counterattack across our front," said Stalin.

"Well, during our time here in Tehran, we'll discuss measures that will require the Germans to move thirty or forty divisions away from your front," FDR assured him.

"That will be very helpful," answered Stalin, and then suddenly changing the subject, "I hope you are comfortable here."

"I could not think of better or more convenient accommodations," replied FDR with a broad smile. "Thank you!"

"You will be safe here."

"I have no doubt." FDR smiled.

It seemed that Chip Bohlen knew Stalin very well. FDR wondered why Stalin chose to suddenly remind him of the supposed assassination plot with, "You will be safe here," and remembered one of Bohlen's insights, "Stalin always looks for leverage he can use to his advantage over friends and enemies alike."

It was Stalin's way of telling FDR he had done a favor for him, and of course, remind him of his obligation to reciprocate.

The conference negotiations had begun.

CHAPTER TWENTY-EIGHT

"Not one American soldier will die on that goddamned beach!"

The "Big Three" began their meetings the next day in earnest, in the Soviet Embassy's Conference Room. Waiting for the meeting to begin, Hopkins stood at his place with Harriman, Admiral King, Admiral Leahy, Anthony Eden, Pug Ismay, General Brooke, John Dill, Portal, Molotov, and Soviet General Voroshilov.

Stalin was the first of the leaders to enter the room, and when he saw Hopkins, he walked directly to him with a big smile on his face and warmly shook his hand. Pavlov, Stalin's interpreter, was not expecting Stalin to go to Hopkins and had to catch up to him.

"It is good to see you again," Stalin said to Hopkins, shaking his hand, while his left hand held Hopkins's arm.

Averell Harriman was astonished. He had never seen Stalin greet anyone that warmly.

"It is good to see you looking well, Marshal," replied Hopkins.

"I am aging too quickly," the Soviet leader answered with a crooked smile.

"You have good company," Hopkins replied.

"Not true. You look younger than the last time I saw you."

"I appreciate your kind words."

Stalin turned to see Elliott Roosevelt pushing his father into position at the table and Churchill following closely behind. Stalin walked to grcct the two men, and they all sat.

Churchill began. "Marshal Stalin, we appreciate you graciously hosting our first conference together. With your agreement, I suggest that President Roosevelt serve as our Chair."

Through Pavlov, Stalin replied, "I agree."

FDR took the helm. "Thank you both. I am very pleased to welcome Marshal Stalin and the Russians as new members of the family circle, and to assure them that these conferences are always conducted as gatherings of friends with complete frankness on all sides."

Churchill said, "Seated here is the greatest concentration of power the world has ever seen in the hands of those present. Here is the future of mankind. I pray we are worthy of this God-given opportunity."

Stalin added, "This fraternal meeting is indeed a great opportunity, and it is up to those here to wisely use the power given to them by their respective peoples."

"I will begin our conference," FDR announced, "by providing a summary of America's progress in the war. The United States is most directly affected by the war in the Pacific. US forces are bearing the brunt of the fighting there with help from British and Australian troops. We still maintain that the European theater is the most important, and throughout all my conferences with the Prime Minister, our military plans have revolved around relieving pressure on the Soviet front. We have set the date for what we believe will be the decisive battle in Western Europe. In May of 1944, we plan to cross the English Channel and invade France. We are calling it 'Overlord.'"

As Stalin doodled on a notepad in front of him, he spoke quietly and deliberately. "The Soviet Union welcomes America's successes against the Japanese. When Germany is defeated, we will be able to send Russian troops to Eastern Siberia, and we shall be able by our common front to defeat Japan. The front today against the Germans inside of Russia remains a challenge. While we have had some successes, as we advance over captured territory, we find the Germans have systematically destroyed all things needed for communication and supply. We are pleased a date has been set to invade France, which is the only direct way to strike at the heart of Germany. I do not mean to belittle the significance of the North African Italian campaigns, because they both had real value. But continuing in Italy, or through the Balkans, is secondary to the main thrust of Overlord."

Churchill said, "Both the President and I have long agreed on the necessity of cross-Channel operation. Overlord will put more than one million men on the Continent of Europe in May, June, and July next year. We should be mindful, however, that there may be delays due to a shortage of landing craft. The Allies should not remain idle. If we can enlist Turkey in the war..."

FDR cut Churchill off. "Turkey would certainly demand a heavy price in airplanes, tanks, and equipment to enter the war on our side. That would result in an indefinite postponement of Overlord. Perhaps we should consider an operation across the Adriatic assisted by Tito's partisans in Yugoslavia."

Stalin shook his head and countered, "I don't think it is wise to scatter forces all over the Mediterranean. Overlord should be the basis of all operations in 1944. After Rome is captured, the forces there should be sent to Southern France as a diversion to Overlord. We have had success here when the Red Army has launched an offensive from two converging directions."

Shortly after the meeting broke up, Hopkins, King, and Harriman walked out of the Russian Embassy and down the steps. General Marshall was there waiting for them. "There you are," King said, wondering where the general had been.

"I was stuck in the city," Marshall said. "How did the meeting go?"

"Churchill immediately started in on Turkey," King informed Marshall. Churchill's imaginings were a pet peeve for the caustic admiral.

"Who the hell put that Adriatic idea in the President's head?" Hopkins asked, wondering if Churchill was behind FDR's suggestion.

"I think that was his own brainchild," King said.

"How was Stalin?" asked Marshall.

"Focused on the second front. A lot grayer than he was the last time I saw him," Hopkins reported.

"I've never seen him more cordial or open with anyone than he was when he saw you today, Harry," Harriman said.

Marshall nodded. "Stalin will never forget that Harry came to him at their worst time and promised to help him and his people when they needed it most. And he delivered."

#

After his foray into the subject of Turkey was summarily dismissed at the afternoon session, Churchill was feeling like he and the United Kingdom were being ignored by the elephant and the bear. Determined to be heard, he called a meeting at the British Embassy, some fifteen miles away, for later that night with Marshall, Brooke, King, Leahy, Portal, and several aides.

Churchill began with, "I appreciate you all coming here this evening to discuss and align our future strategy."

"I thought our future strategy had already been set and aligned," replied Admiral King. "Operation Overlord first in six months and then Operation Anvil."

"That is our challenge," Churchill responded. "Six months. We should not allow our forces to remain idle while the Russian Army continues its fight against the Nazis. We should exert and maintain pressure on our common enemy, and we should consider using our gains in Italy to deploy troops into Greece via Rhodes."

"Rhodes?" Marshall repeated in disbelief.

"Yes, Rhodes," Churchill insisted. "Landing on the beach in Rhodes will—" The Prime Minister didn't get to finish that sentence.

"Not one American soldier will die on that goddamned beach!" Marshall declared, leaving no room for discussion.

After a few awkward moments of silence, Churchill tried to speak, "I want to remind—" but he was cut off again.

"Not one!" Marshall repeated.

On the way back to the Russian Embassy in their car, King could not resist venting, partly because he knew Marshall had enough of Churchill's flights of fancy, and partly because he wanted a drink. "How much more time do we need to waste listening to him?" King asked Marshall.

"No more," Marshall said with such coldness that King knew not to press Marshall further. "American soldiers will not pay the price for a mission that has nothing to do with defeating our enemy. Not while I'm Chief of Staff."

#

The following morning, FDR sat in his villa going through a pile of papers while Hopkins wrote at a desk. Knowing that all of the white-coated servants worked for the NKVD, when they were present, small talk abounded, and handwritten messages were used to share and trade information.

"Busy bees," FDR said out loud, referring to the stack of papers.

"Who?" asked Hopkins.

"Congress," FDR said.

"Always," Hopkins said, rising from the desk and handing FDR a note.

FDR opened the note, and it read: "*EVERYONE must stay focused on Overlord today and not spend time on any new strategies or adventures.*"

"You read my mind," said FDR.

That afternoon, as the second plenary meeting in the embassy's conference room drew toward a close, Churchill added a touch of ceremony. A British officer carrying a beautiful sword entered the large room. The special sword had been crafted by the Wilkinson Sword Company and designed by an Oxford professor who specialized in Russian history. It was four feet long, and its grip was bound in gold wire. Each end of the silver cross guard was shaped like a leopard's head. The crimson sheath was made from Persian lambskin and bore the coat of arms and royal cipher of the British Sovereign.

Churchill stood in front of Stalin with the sword in his hands. "Marshal Stalin, on behalf of King George VI, I would like to present you with the Sword of Stalingrad to commemorate your victory and the victory of your people over the German Army at Stalingrad."

Stalin was deeply moved. He raised it from Churchill and kissed the blade. Then he said, "Spasibo. This sword is for all of our soldiers and people who gave their lives in defense of our great country!" Stalin handed the sword to an aide, and Churchill and Stalin hugged with kisses on each other's cheeks. It was a moving moment that in an instant seemed to confirm the goodwill between the Allies.

The sword was taken from the room, and when everyone was back in place at the table, FDR moved to bring the day's session to a conclusion. "We will end today with a report from this morning's meeting of our military leaders. General Marshall?"

"At this morning's meeting," Marshall immediately began, "we all agreed the US and British should execute a cross-Channel invasion of France, Operation Overlord, that will be targeted for May 1944, subject to change, with a concurrent invasion of Southern France called Operation Dragoon. Overlord will be the main focus of our joint efforts. We also agreed that when Overlord commences on D-Day, the Soviet Army will launch an offensive called Operation Bagration to prevent the Germans from transferring troops from the Eastern to the Western Front. We further acknowledged that the Overlord invasion can only be as large as the number of our landing craft will allow. There was a broad agreement to support the Yugoslav partisans with supplies and equipment..."

As Stalin listened, he became agitated and finally interrupted Marshall. "Excuse me," the Soviet leader said. "You did not say that Overlord was definite, and who will command Overlord?"

FDR chose to answer for Marshall. "We haven't decided yet," the President said.

Stalin looked at Marshall. "You said the date was subject to change," and then he turned to FDR, "Without a commander, Overlord will not happen."

"The decisions we take here in Tehran will influence our choice for the command of Overlord, Marshal Stalin," FDR explained.

And then seeing an opportunity to promote his agenda, Churchill jumped in. "Before finalizing our plans for Overlord, we must also survey the entire landscape of military matters from the south up through the north. The Mediterranean, Italy, Yugoslavia, Turkey."

Stalin held up his hands toward Churchill and then, turning to FDR, said emphatically, "If we three are here to discuss military matters, then the Soviet Union considers Overlord to be the most important and decisive operation in Europe, and the commander of Overlord must be appointed."

"But, Marshal Stalin, we should not dismiss the strategic importance of Turkey in our decision-making," Churchill declared.

Stalin looked directly at the Prime Minister, his eyes squinting, and said, "I would like to ask you an indiscreet question. Do the British really believe in Overlord, or are you expressing approval of it merely as a means of reassuring the Russians?"

"Britain will hurl every ounce of her strength across the Channel against the Germans if that is what we decide here," Churchill replied passionately.

The goodwill of Britain's sword presentation just minutes before was replaced with suspicion and doubt, and the possibility that guns and daggers were about to be placed on the conference table.

Hopkins knew it was not a good sign to have the Soviet leader on the prowl for leverage he could use, and he decided to step into the breech. "Surely, Mr. President," Hopkins addressed FDR directly, "Overlord must be decided once and for all. Here and now, before we leave Tehran. Perhaps the Combined Chiefs can convene again and come to a final decision on this issue?"

FDR was glad to have Hopkins in the water. He smiled and said, "Thank you, Harry. I agree. And since it is getting late and Marshal Stalin is hosting dinner this evening, the military chiefs should meet again in the morning to wrap up everything about Overlord." Then he closed his folder, smiled broadly, and added, "I shall see you all in about an hour!"

Most of those at the table were stunned that the meeting had come to such an abrupt and unexpected conclusion. FDR left the room, followed by Churchill. Hopkins remained gathering his papers and stealing looks at Stalin, who remained seated, doodling on a pad of paper. Hopkins suspected the Russian leader stayed at his seat to see if he was approached with a sidebar conversation by one of his Allies. There were no separate conversations that evening, and the Russian leader was the last to leave the room.

Hopkins caught up with FDR and Elliott as they walked back to the villa from the embassy with four Secret Service agents around the President. Speaking outdoors during the walks back from the embassy to the villas was the safest and most secure way to communicate.

"Glad you jumped in when you did," FDR said to Hopkins as they walked.

"We were losing Uncle Joe with all of the back and forth with our friend," replied Hopkins.

"I like him. He doesn't mince words," FDR said. "He and I can work together. I think he's gettable."

"He's annoyed right now."

"With us?"

"No. I think he feels indebted to us."

"Our friend?"

"Maybe, but I don't think so," Hopkins ventured. "Stalin always has the final word. In fact, his is the only word. My guess is he doesn't understand why we would ask the military to decide the Overlord issue... or anything for that matter. He probably expects you three to make the decision alone, right at that table."

"Wouldn't that be nice for a change." FDR cackled. "I think I might like that experience."

#

Later, after they finished Stalin's sumptuous Russian dinner that included champagne, vodka, wine, caviar, eggs, oysters, shrimp, crab, pheasant, rabbit, and lamb, the white-coated NKVD agents cleared the dishes, and Churchill tapped his glass with a spoon to get everyone's attention.

"I would like to propose a toast to President Roosevelt and Marshal Stalin," he declared, and everyone quieted. "President Roosevelt has devoted his life to the cause of the weak and helpless. Indeed, it was his courage and foresight in 1933 that prevented a revolution in America and has guided his country along the tumultuous stream of party friction and internal politics amid the violent freedoms of democracy," he said, with typical eloquent flair.

Glasses were raised, and a chorus of "To President Roosevelt" and "Na Zdorowie" resonated around the room.

Churchill continued, "And to Marshal Stalin. You, sir, are worthy to stand with the mightiest figures in Russian history. You merit the title, 'Stalin the Great!'"

After the chorus of agreement calmed, Stalin said, "Thank you. But the honors you pay me really belong to the Russian people. It is easy to be a hero or a great leader with the Russian people. It is true that the Russian Army fought heroically, but the Russian people would not tolerate any other quality from their armed forces. Even persons of medium courage and even cowards became heroes in Russia."

Stalin then turned toward Roosevelt and Hopkins and, with his glass raised, continued, "And we all recognize that without American production, the United Nations would not win this war. Na Zdorowie!"

There were shouts of "To America," "Hear, hear," "Na Zdorowie," as everyone raised their glasses to FDR.

FDR raised his glass and began, "By our decisions here at this Tehran Conference, we have already increased the hopes for a better world. And by a better world, I mean a world in which each ordinary citizen can be assured the opportunity for peaceful toil and the just enjoyment of the fruits of his labors."

"Great Britain shares your vision, Mr. President," Churchill exclaimed.

A smile came across Stalin's face as the words of the President and Prime Minister were translated to him. He then looked at

Churchill and teased, "I am pleased to hear that Great Britain believes in its ordinary citizens and workers."

"I have made a long and thorough study of the British Constitution, which is unwritten, as is that of the War Cabinet, whose authority and composition are not specifically defined," Hopkins said, and all eyes shifted his way.

The room went quiet as each person around the table watched Hopkins, not sure where he was going.

"As a result of my study," Hopkins continued, "I have learned that the provisions of the British Constitution and the powers of the War Cabinet are just whatever Winston wants them to be at any given moment."

The entire table, including Churchill, started laughing.

Stalin again raised his glass, "To Overlord!"

"To Overlord," FDR replied, cackling.

Churchill, who seemed lost in thought for a moment, did not respond, prompting Stalin to ask, "No, Prime Minister?"

"I was just thinking that to secure the peace, Turkey must enter the war on the side of the Allies," Churchill said, intent on making his point about Turkey.

Hopkins thought to himself, *Bad timing, Winston.*

"I don't understand," Stalin said, baiting Churchill. "In 1919, all you wanted to do was fight. What happened? Is it advancing age?"

"I love to fight." Churchill scowled. "In addition to agreeing to Overlord, I proposed taking Rhodes in the near term."

"Rhodes?" Stalin replied with shock on his face.

FDR stepped in and joined the teasing, "Winston is an old imperialist. He's always on the prowl to expand the British Empire."

"Are you pro-German?" Stalin laughed.

Clearly, Churchill was not amused. "As a matter of fact, I am all for the German people." He paused for effect. "Not the Nazis, of course, but all of the German people who have been duped by Hitler into this catastrophic war. As I am also for the French, the Danes, the Poles, the—"

But before he could finish his thought, Stalin interrupted. "The French? They are rotten to the core and should be punished for their weakness. De Gaulle is a buffoon."

"Europe will require a strong France. And a strong Germany after the war," Churchill rebutted.

"After this war is over, we must not have any more German wars," Stalin said, lighting his pipe and looking toward FDR. "I propose that we liquidate the German General Staff. Hitler's mighty armies depend upon about 50,000 officers and technicians. If they were rounded up and shot at the end of the war, Germany's military strength would be destroyed."

"Uncle Joe, I would like to mediate that effort," FDR chimed in. "Maybe just 49,000 would do the trick," he said with a smile.

Though there were a few snickers heard around the table, Churchill was livid. "I am not sure what to make of this," he said. "Candidly, I am outraged at such a proposal and discussion. Great Britain will not participate in any action involving the cold-blooded execution of soldiers who fought for their country. I'd rather be taken out into the courtyard and shot!" he finished with his voice rising. Churchill then stood and walked briskly out of the room and down a corridor as everyone at the table watched in stunned silence.

Stalin looked at FDR, realizing too late that he pushed Churchill too far. Hopkins's impulse was to retrieve his petulant friend, but he stayed in his seat when he saw Stalin rise and hurry after the Prime Minister. Though Churchill heard the sound of following footsteps on the stone floor, he continued walking and refused to stop.

"Prime Minister," Stalin called out. "I made a poor attempt at a joke. I was only teasing," Stalin called after Churchill, who finally stopped to face the Soviet leader.

"I will not be part of any discussion regarding wholesale murder," Churchill told Stalin emphatically.

"I was teasing," Stalin said. "Please forgive my bad manners. Foolish play. Come back to the table. I apologize."

Churchill stood silent for a moment, then the two men made their way back to the dining room. Once they were again seated, Stalin rose with his glass raised. "Like all friends," he began, "we may tease each other too much occasionally. But every single person in Russia and the world knows that when every European country was defeated by the German Army, it was you and your British Royal Air Force who stood firm against the Nazi onslaught and defeated them!"

Churchill raised his glass.

Then FDR said, "We came here with hope and determination and we leave here friends in fact, in spirit, and in purpose."

After dinner, as Churchill and his entourage made their way down the steps in front of the embassy, Hopkins caught up to him. "Winston. Are you all right?"

"My dear Harry, if you are going through hell, keep going," Churchill responded, his "Black Dog" rearing its head.

"They were a bit overdone tonight," Hopkins commiserated with him.

"I have been successfully reminded of just how insignificant England is becoming."

"Not so," Hopkins replied instantly. "The tension you feel is because of your importance and the importance of your ideas. That said, it is time for you to gracefully accept Overlord. Let it go, Winston."

Churchill thought for a moment and then said, "I am always ready to learn, though I do not always like being taught. Good night, Harry."

Hopkins watched Churchill get into his car and head back to the British Embassy.

#

The next afternoon, the tension of the previous day's meeting was gone, and there seemed to be light conversation and laughter around the conference table while they waited for Stalin to join them.

FDR began the meeting promptly when everyone took their seats. "I am pleased to inform everyone," the President said, "that General Marshall reports that the Combined Chiefs of Staff met this morning and unanimously agreed to launch Operation Overlord in May with a supporting operation in the South of France on the largest scale permitted by the landing craft available at that time."

Stalin said, "This is a welcome decision, Mr. President. When will the commander be named?"

"I will need several days to discuss it with my staff," FDR said.

"Victory is now assured!" Stalin exclaimed.

#

On the last day of the conference, as Hopkins walked to his car, shaking hands with all of the conference attendees, Vyacheslav Molotov, the man who Lenin called "Iron Ass" for his stone-cold demeanor, approached with his hand extended.

"I greatly enjoyed the conference," Hopkins told the dry foreign minister. "The meetings between the President and Marshal Stalin have done an infinite amount of good in bringing our two countries closer together to wage the war and the peace."

"I agree," Molotov replied. "I cannot but express my satisfaction with our work together at the conference. The meeting between our two leaders will help to speed our victory and post-war collaboration."

Hopkins smiled, knowing that if Molotov looked happy, there was hope and the promise of victory in the air.

#

On their way back to Cairo and the Mena Hotel after the Tehran Conference, Hopkins raised the decision to make George Marshall the Supreme Allied Commander. Knowing the persuasive skills of his good friend, Harry worried that Churchill had convinced FDR to give the job to one of his British generals, and that was why FDR did not mention him to Stalin or Churchill at the conference.

As they sat alone in the rear of The Sacred Cow, the President expressed concern over Marshall's appointment to the top job, and Hopkins thought his worst fears might be true. Harry thought about challenging FDR, but instead decided to let the President grapple with his decision. He did remind FDR, however, that Marshall was his top pick, and if not him, then in light of America's contribution to the war effort, it was critical that an American general hold the top post. FDR easily agreed with Hopkins's assessment.

After landing in Cairo late that afternoon, Marshall and Hopkins shared a car driven by a US officer back to the Mena Hotel. As they pulled up to the front of the hotel, they planned to debrief with each other over dinner.

"What time for dinner?" Hopkins asked.

"Give me an hour," replied Marshall.

"I want to give you a heads up," Hopkins said to Marshall, and he had the impression the general already knew what he was about to say. "The President has some concerns about your appointment as Supreme Commander."

"I thought that might be the case," Marshall said evenly. "Don't worry. I will do whatever the President decides," Marshall told Hopkins. "See you in an hour."

Once in his suite, Harry collapsed into a chair, beyond exhausted. After a few minutes, he got up, threw his small suitcase onto the bed, opened it, and removed a small bag. He fumbled with it, but when he finally got it open, he took out a vial and a syringe.

Dropping his trousers to the floor, Harry sat on the bed, inserted the syringe into the vial to withdraw its contents, and then gave himself a shot in his right thigh.

Without picking up his trousers, he reached for the phone and asked the hotel receptionist to call him in forty-five minutes. He lifted his pants and lay back on the bed. He was done—at least for the next forty-five minutes.

When Marshall arrived in his suite, there was a message waiting for him from FDR asking the general to come to his room. Marshall immediately turned and headed to the President's suite.

"Good afternoon, Mr. President," Marshall said, entering the suite and finding FDR alone, smoking a cigarette with a martini in his hand.

"Thank you for coming by, General. Can I get you something?" FDR asked.

"No, thank you, sir."

"I asked you to come by because I want to discuss the Supreme Allied Commander role with you, and I thought between the two of us, we could figure it out."

"Yes, sir."

"Now, I know I said I wanted you to have the Supreme Commander job, but frankly, General, you are too good at your job as the head of Joint Chiefs."

"Thank you, sir."

"What do you think about it?"

"Sir, I shouldn't attempt to judge my own capabilities," Marshall said without any trace of emotion. "You have to do it."

"No feelings one way or the other?" asked FDR.

"The issue is too important for personal feelings to be considered," Marshall stated. "I will wholeheartedly support whatever you decide."

"The damn problem is you are too good at your job," replied FDR. "I wouldn't be able to sleep at night if you were out of the country. If you agree, I think we should appoint Eisenhower as Supreme Allied Commander," FDR said, cutting to the decision.

"Yes, sir."

"It is an honor to be in this fight with you," FDR said.

Judging by his appearance, anyone who saw Marshall when he left the President's suite would never have known his profound disappointment in not being given the role of Supreme Allied Commander. Some would have pointed out that the job was actually a demotion for Marshall, but the truth was that it didn't matter. The best position for an old warrior in the greatest conflict the world had ever known was as the most senior commander on the battlefield, responsible for all of the soldiers fighting in the war. And Marshall just gave it up. He could have insisted, but instead he recognized the decision was not his but belonged to his Commander-in-Chief, and his duty was to his commander and his country.

Minutes after Marshall left the President, Elliott, FDR's son, returned and found FDR in his chair with his head thrown back and his eyes closed.

"Are you all right?" Elliott asked, and FDR stirred.

"Help me get inside. I need to hit the sack," FDR said.

"Let me call Dr. McIntire," insisted Elliott.

"No," FDR replied firmly. "It's just a headache. Just help me into bed and get a couple of aspirin for me."

Elliott went behind the President's chair and pushed him toward the bedroom.

#

On December 7, two years to the day after the attack on Pearl Harbor and America's entrance into the Second World War, Hopkins boarded The Sacred Cow and flew with the President to Tunis, where General Dwight David "Ike" Eisenhower was waiting for them. As soon as Ike climbed into the President's car, Roosevelt said, "Well, Ike, you are going to command Overlord."

After months of debate and disagreement among the Allies, the cross-Channel invasion—the operation that Marshall had wanted since his first meeting with the British back in December 1941—finally had a commander, and it was going to happen.

And George Marshall would not be there. He would be in Washington, DC.

CHAPTER TWENTY-NINE

"Your son, my lord, has paid a soldier's debt!"

As 1943 drew to a close, Harry was filled with hope—hope for victory and for peace. The conference at Tehran had accomplished many things, but even more than the military strategies and supply issues discussed was the overall change in the mood of the Allies. There was a clear and marked shift in the Soviet Union's attitude toward Great Britain and the United States. The Russian people seemed to have moved, certainly following the cues of their leader, toward what was being described as widespread enthusiasm. Reluctance and suspicion had been replaced with a warm international embrace.

It seemed like a Christmas miracle.

When he returned, Harry took a little time to focus on domestic matters—not domestic politics, but his own living arrangements. After three-and-a-half years of living in the White House, it was time for him and Louise to move to their rented house at 3340 N Street in Georgetown and settle down in a home of their own. That Christmas would be the first not spent with the Roosevelts in years.

Hopkins wanted to make new memories with Louise and Diana, and like many across America, he and Louise held places around the Hopkins holiday tree and their table for his boys, who were serving. David, his oldest, was in the Navy on an aircraft carrier somewhere, Robert was with the Army in Algeria, and Steven was in the South Pacific with the Marines.

While they sat in their living room on Christmas Eve, a group of carolers came to their front door singing *O Come All Ye Faithful.* When Harry, Louise, and Diana opened their door, they found a group of eight red-faced men and women, dressed in red and singing at the top of their lungs. The carolers' song had cars slowing on the street and neighbors stepping outside of their homes to listen. Everyone was war weary and was grateful for the song and the chance to feel joyful, however brief it may be. Harry stepped away while the group sang, and he returned with a bottle of Scotch for them and handed it to the carolers' leader.

"Thank you!" the leader said loudly, sounding like he was already more than halfway to being fully inebriated. Louise smiled and thought it was amazing he could sing as well as he did in his condition.

When the Carolers moved off to their neighbors, Louise and Harry tucked Diana in bed and returned to sit in their darkened living room in front of their first Christmas tree and fireplace with drinks. Hopkins sat quietly next to Louise, watching the fire and sipping his drink.

"Are you okay?" Louise asked, looking into Hopkins's eyes.

"I'm fine," he replied. "Just missing the boys."

"They'll be home before you know it," Louise assured him.

"I know. I'm turning into an old softy. You have made this the best Christmas I have ever had," he said and kissed her.

"For me too. I love you," she said and kissed him again.

#

The dining room in Springwood, FDR's home in Hyde Park, was perfectly decorated for Christmas dinner with a hand-painted Christmas ornament resting at every person's plate, and a handcrafted wooden sleigh holding everyone's napkin. With more than a dozen people at the table, Eleanor made sure the staff ordered a sizable turkey with more than enough trimmings. She was especially happy to know that Anna Boettiger, her pretty thirty-seven-year-old daughter, and her five-year-old grandson, John, were there to spend the holidays with them.

The servants brought out a huge golden turkey sitting on a silver tray with all of the implements that FDR would need to carve it for his guests. They placed the tray in front of FDR at the head of the long table that glistened with its polished silver and glassware.

FDR looked at his guests seated at the table. "I think a prayer is appropriate," he said, and everyone grew quiet and bowed their heads.

"Dear God," FDR began, "as we welcome your son into our homes and hearts this Christmas, we thank you for the food we are about to eat and for all the blessings you have given us this past year. Please protect and watch over America and all of her sons and daughters who are in harm's way, and provide each of them with the strength of your courage and grace. Amen."

"Amen," everyone responded, and all exchanged looks and smiles as many conversations started up again around the table.

FDR looked at Eleanor. "Merry Christmas. I wish Harry were here," FDR said to her quietly.

"And Diana," Eleanor replied.

FDR looked down the table and found his daughter, Anna. "Anna," he called to her, "Would you come here, sweetheart, and help me serve our guests?"

"I would love to," replied Anna, rising from her seat to go to her father. She loved being included in his life.

"Merry Christmas, everyone!" exclaimed FDR, and he picked up the large knife and fork to start carving the turkey.

#

On New Year's Eve, Harry and Louise hosted a small dinner party for their close friends in their new home. Joining them were Henry and Mabel Stimson, Pa and Frances Watson, Sam and Dorothy Rosenman, and Bob and Madeline Sherwood. Dinner was great, and the mood was celebratory—a kind of feeling those in the group hadn't felt in a long while.

They listened to music over Hopkins's radio all night long, and at midnight, they all lifted their glasses of Pol Roger champagne in honor of Winston as the announcer on the radio counted down the remaining seconds of 1943. When Guy Lombardo's Royal Canadians played Auld Lang Syne from the Roosevelt Grill in New York's Roosevelt Hotel, Bob Sherwood raised his glass and shouted, "Here's to a splendid 1944!"

"Let's hope so," Henry Stimson said with his glass raised. "Happy New Year!"

Hopkins took a sip of champagne and kissed Diana and Louise. That was when Louise noticed the odd look on his face.

She watched Harry go back to his seat at the dining room table and saw his eyes glaze over. A moment later, his head sagged, and he seemed to drift to his side and fall from his chair. Bob Sherwood was watching too and ran over to catch him before he fell. "Harry?" he called out.

Hopkins responded weakly, "I'm... I'm... okay."

Louise was quickly at his side and urging him to stand. "We need to get you to bed, Harry." Louise then turned to Pa Watson. "Pa, please call Dr. McIntire," she said as she and Sherwood lifted Hopkins to his feet.

In the commotion, everyone forgot Diana was awake and scared. She had tears in her eyes as she watched the whole scene.

After they checked Hopkins into Bethesda Naval Hospital, the doctors thought at first it was the flu. But it didn't take long for them to realize his old malady had returned with a vengeance. He was unable to absorb nutrients, and he was losing weight fast. Though Hopkins promised himself he would avoid the hospital treatments at all costs, he knew this was all there was for him if he wanted to see the war's end and watch Diana grow up.

When Marshall told John Dill about Harry's condition, Dill immediately informed Churchill of Harry's sudden hospitalization, and Winston immediately contacted FDR for a prognosis.

The President assured Churchill that it was just a touch of the flu.

#

A month later, when Hopkins was on the Silver Meteor train on his way to John Hertz's palatial Miami estate for rest and recovery, Steve Early entered the President's office looking somber and handed him a note. One look at Early, and FDR knew it was not good news. He read the note and then turned it over on his desk, almost as if he believed that if he did not look at it, the news would go away.

"Where's Harry now?" FDR asked his press secretary as he removed his glasses.

"We think he's on a train heading down to John Hertz's place in Miami," replied Early.

FDR put on his glasses and, on a piece of White House stationery, wrote a note to Hopkins and handed it to Early. "Get this to him without delay," he ordered.

Harry's train had just entered Florida and was a bit south of Jacksonville. He was traveling with Adda Johnson, a nurse whom Dr. McIntire insisted he take with him while he recovered. They sat in the Club Car, she reading a magazine and Hopkins looking out the window, watching north Florida race by. The cadence of the train and the streaming landscape outside his window were having their desired effect, relaxing Hopkins and pulling him ever closer to an afternoon nap.

In the back of his brain, Hopkins thought he heard a man's voice nearby speaking to Nurse Johnson, but he decided he was too tired to be curious. That was until he heard the man say, "The President."

Hopkins was instantly awake and alert and turned toward Nurse Johnson. He saw she held a note in her hand.

"Is that for me?" Hopkins asked.

"Yes, sir," Johnson replied and handed the note to Hopkins. "It is an urgent message from the President, Mr. Hopkins."

Hopkins opened the note.

"I am terribly distressed to have to tell you," FDR wrote, *"that Stephen was killed in action at Kwajalein. I am confident that when we get details, we will all be even prouder of him than ever. I am thinking of you much, FDR."*

Nurse Johnson watched for a moment and couldn't resist asking, "Is everything all right, Mr. Hopkins?"

Hopkins, with his voice quivering and tears welling in his eyes, said, "My son Stephen was killed in the South Pacific."

He turned back to look out of the window while he held the note in his hand. Nurse Johnson watched him for a long while and finally went back to her seat. Hopkins never moved and kept looking out of the window.

Marine Corps Private First Class Stephen "Hoppy" Hopkins was buried at sea. In the days following Harry's arrival at Hertz's home on Miami Beach, hundreds of condolences made their way to him.

In addition to her nursing duties, Nurse Adda Johnson found herself doubling as Hopkins's secretary. There were messages from Chiang Kai-shek, T.V. Soong, General Marshall, General Eisenhower, Lord Mountbatten, Halifax, Dill, King, Leahy, Stimson, Sherwood—the list went on and on and on. And then there was the note from Churchill, who sent the most eloquent message to his friend on a parchment scroll written in elegant calligraphy. It read:

"Your son, my lord, has paid a soldier's debt;

He only liv'd but till he was a man;

The which no sooner had his prowess confirm'd

In the shrinking station where he fought

But like a man he died." — Shakespeare

Stephen Peter Hopkins, aged eighteen

13 February, 1944

When he read it, Hopkins began to weep and could not stop. He cried for his son and for all the sons who were killed in this horrendous conflagration. Unsurprisingly, his overwhelming grief did not help him recuperate, and Harry's body refused to rally. After a few weeks, it was clear to his medical team that another surgery would be required.

On March 29, Hopkins returned to the Mayo Clinic, where the surgery was performed. Shortly after, Churchill wrote to FDR. *"Though his is an indomitable spirit,"* Churchill wrote, *"I cannot help feeling anxious about his frail body and another operation. I shall always be glad for news about him."*

After he returned to Washington, on May 7, General Marshall dispatched an Army airplane to fly Harry to the Greenbrier in White

Sulfur Springs, West Virginia. The posh antebellum resort had been requisitioned by the military and converted into a convalescent center and renamed as "Ashford General Hospital."

#

"What news of Harry?" Churchill asked the President. It was late in London, and Churchill took advantage of a short break before his meeting with Eisenhower to call FDR and find out about Hopkins.

"They are trying to fatten him up now at Ashford Army Hospital in West Virginia. He will be back in action soon," FDR assured Churchill.

"General Eisenhower has just arrived," Churchill informed FDR.

"Please tell Ike I said hello. You should listen to what he has to say, Winston," FDR remarked.

"Courage is what it takes to sit down and listen, Mr. President."

"Well, then, all is well because you have courage by the bushelful. Goodbye, Winston."

Churchill hung up the phone, lit his cigar, and looked across the desk at Eisenhower, who sat in a chair in front of the Prime Minister's desk. "The President said I should give you my undivided attention, General."

"I won't take up too much of your time," Eisenhower said, jumping right in. "The long and short of it is that we will not be able to execute Overlord and Anvil if we continue to try to execute other initiatives in Italy and the Mediterranean."

"General, our commitment to Overlord does not mean we should stop trying to apply ourselves elsewhere in Europe," Churchill replied.

"Mr. Churchill, we cannot," answered Eisenhower, and he sounded immovable.

"What do you mean?"

"We have reached the practical limits of our resources."

"Explain," prodded Churchill.

"For example, landing craft. Right now, we don't have enough landing craft here in England to execute Overlord."

"Why not use some of the landing craft we have in Italy?"

"Actually, that is the point. We need the landing craft from Italy, and when we move it, it will limit what we can do there and elsewhere in the Mediterranean."

"But surely we can find additional landing craft in other theaters," Churchill scoffed. "What about the Pacific?"

"They don't have enough for their own plans," the general countered.

"Can't we make more?"

"Certainly, sir. But not in time for D-Day. For Overlord to succeed, we need every single landing craft we own just to land enough men and material in France and to keep the Germans from pushing us back into the Channel."

"How about Anvil and invading Southern France?" Churchill asked. "How will we be able to do that?"

"We will need to reuse any Overlord landing craft that is not damaged in the landing," Eisenhower said in a way that told Churchill there was no way around the problem.

It was the first time since their relationship began that Churchill realized the Allies were resource-constrained. For years, Churchill had come to rely on the seemingly bottomless pit of US equipment, supplies, and manpower for any initiative the Allies wanted to tackle. This landing craft issue made him think about Hopkins and how easy he always made it seem to provide Great Britain with exactly the right equipment or machinery, or supplies whenever they were needed.

Churchill puffed on his cigar and, through the haze of smoke, looked across his desk at Eisenhower.

"Where is Harry when we need him?" he asked Ike.

#

Shortly after the attack on Pearl Harbor, the US Army had purchased the Greenbrier Hotel, a luxurious resort in White Sulphur Springs in the Allegheny Mountains, for $3.3 million. Their plan was to use it as a hospital, and after more than $2 million spent on renovations, it reopened for that new purpose. Over the course of the war, nearly 25,000 soldiers were treated at the new Ashford Army Hospital.

Marshall was glad to have the chance to inspect the new facility with his friend and colleague Sir John Dill, and he used his inspection tour to check in on Hopkins. They surprised Hopkins when they walked into his room.

"What are you guys doing here?" Hopkins was truly pleased to see Marshall and Dill, and immediately felt better upon seeing them.

"The Prime Minister ordered me to have my eyes on you," Dill said. "He wants to see you back in full operation."

"Even the Russians are missing you, Harry," Marshall added.

"Stop." Hopkins smiled.

"I can tell you we British feel pretty lost with you out of harness," Dill confided.

"Everyone misses your knack of getting to the point," Marshall said.

"My friends in the press think otherwise," replied Hopkins.

"The press?" Dill said with scorn in his voice.

Marshall jumped in. "You'll be happy to know that when the press asked Secretary Stimson why you were entitled to be treated in an Army hospital, he told them, as 'Chairman of the Munitions Board, Mr. Hopkins is entitled to the finest care our military has to offer.'" Marshall smiled.

"Harry, do not allow the press to get under your skin," Dill chimed in. "I know of no one who has done more by wise and courageous advice to advance our common cause than you. I'm sure that someday that truth will be known."

"When are you getting out of here?" asked Marshall.

"I hope in a couple of weeks," Harry replied.

"I could put in a word for you, Harry," Marshall said, half in jest. "I think I may have a little pull here."

"Doc McIntire would have your neck." Hopkins laughed.

"I'm pretty sure I can still take that old sawbones." Marshall smiled.

Harry lingered at Ashford for the rest of the month, and during the first days of June waited and wondered in his hospital bed about the most important Allied operation of the war.

CHAPTER THIRTY

They had been waiting for a long time on the field at Greenham Common Airfield in Berkshire, England, but they sensed their wait was coming to an end. They were members of the 101st and 82nd Airborne, men who would soon be jumping over France from the dozens of C-47 transport planes parked on the tarmac. Tonight, they were tasked with parachuting into Normandy, France, behind beaches that the Allies had code-named: *Omaha* and *Utah*.

The men were dressed in their jump uniforms and boots, with their faces painted black and camouflage netting atop their helmets. Some were lying on the grass, some playing cards, some were cleaning their weapons, while others sharpened their bayonets, wondering if they'd be using them in the way they had been trained to do. Almost all were smoking cigarettes, and almost all were too tense with anticipation to be bored.

A green Packard with five stars on a green frame attached to its front bumper pulled through the airfield's security gates and came to a stop near the hundreds of paratroopers in the field. The driver's door opened, and Kay Summersby, Eisenhower's driver, exited as General Dwight Eisenhower emerged from the rear seat.

"Holy shit!" a voice rang out. That's Ike!"

Men with blackened faces and wearing heavy combat kits scrambled to their feet and rushed toward Eisenhower as he approached in his trademark half-jacket. "There's Ike!" could be heard over and over again from different voices throughout the crowd of young soldiers. As Ike approached closer, a voice rang out, "Ten-hut!" and the paratroopers snapped to attention.

"At ease," Ike said as he pulled out a pack of Camel cigarettes and quickly lit one. "Smoke 'em, if you got 'em," he said to the troops and held out his pack to a couple of soldiers. They couldn't believe they were being asked to share a smoke with their Supreme Commander. *This is like having a cigarette with Jesus,* one of them thought.

"Gather 'round, fellas," Ike encouraged, and the soldiers pressed toward him. "We go tomorrow. You all set?" asked Ike.

"Can't wait!" a number of troopers responded.

"Know your assignments?"

"Yes, sir!"

"You guys are the best of us!" Ike shouted to the men. "The best-trained, the best-equipped—the toughest damned Army the world has ever seen."

All of the men around him let out with a rousing cheer. One lieutenant close to him said, "Sir, we are going to kick the shit out of the Germans!"

"Just don't hurt the French." Eisenhower laughed.

"No sir!" a few of the soldiers replied, and they were joined by many voices in the crowd that called out, "You leave it to us, sir," "We love French girls," "Those bastards will be running back to their Momma's in Berlin," "They won't be running, they'll be in a box."

Eisenhower walked into the crowd, and a circle of men immediately formed around him. He shook their hands and looked each man in the eye.

"Look out for each other over there," Eisenhower said quietly to one of the men, and the soldier responded, "We won't let you down, sir."

"Proud of you," he said to another, and to another, "Good luck."

"You too, sir," the trooper replied.

"Don't you worry, General," said a trooper who had shaved his head. "The 101st Airborne will take care of it!" and all of the men cheered again, louder than the last time.

When the cheering died down, Eisenhower looked around at the faces and with a big, broad smile. "Which one of you guys is from Kansas?"

He loved being with those men. He knew that in a few hours, Overlord, the cross-Channel invasion of France, would all come down to these brave men and the millions of other troops who were prepared to defeat the monstrous regime in Germany. They would walk onto French soil through unrelenting, deadly swarms of machine gun bullets and heavy artillery, and in planes, tanks, jeeps, and landing craft, to begin the long and difficult fight to Berlin.

There was nothing more for him to do. The die was cast.

D-Day was now in the hands of men mostly under the age of twenty, who came from their homes in America to fight against the idea that some people are better than everyone else, and for the idea that every person, everywhere in the world, should be able to express themselves freely, worship who they pleased, and live their lives free from fear and want.

It was what Eisenhower called "the Great Crusade."

#

After their early successes on D-Day, June 6, the American, British, and Canadian Forces were stopped by the German Army, who cleverly used the hundreds of thick hedgerows in upper Normandy, France, to pin down the Allied forces. With each passing day, Eisenhower worried that a coordinated German counterattack would push the Allied soldiers back into the English Channel.

Finally, back in DC, on the evening of July 20, Hopkins went to the White House for cocktails with FDR and Pa Watson. On the same day, Eisenhower was putting the final touches on Operation Cobra—a plan to carpet bomb the town of St. Lo starting on July 25 and create a path for the Americans out of the Normandy hedgerows onto the wide-open plains in central France.

When Hopkins entered FDR's study, Pa Watson caught Hopkins's eye and held his thumb and forefinger in the air about two inches apart to ask Hopkins if he would like a drink.

"Just a short Scotch, please, Pa," Hopkins said, and Pa went to the liquor cart to pour it.

"It's good to have you back, Harry," FDR said, raising his glass to Hopkins.   "Today was a very good day, indeed."

"Congratulations on your nomination. Here's to your fourth term," Hopkins replied, taking his Scotch from Pa and raising his glass to FDR.

"And they tried to kill Hitler today, Tojo resigned, and Marshall tells me Ike has a plan that will break us out of Normandy in a few days. Today was a very good day."

"Cheers," Hopkins responded again, raising his glass and taking a sip of his drink.

"Have you spoken to Winston recently?" FDR asked.

Hopkins nodded. "Still pushing his agenda," he informed FDR. "He wants to delay invading Southern France."

"And do what?" FDR asked, worried that Churchill's ideas might only cause more confusion.

"Probably his underbelly strategy again," Hopkins said, sounding dismissive of Churchill's "fight north through Italy into the Balkans and then on to Germany" strategy.

"That's because the British under General Montgomery have been stuck outside of Caen for more than six weeks," FDR said.

"I heard Eisenhower asked Churchill to visit Montgomery in person and persuade him to get on his bicycle and start moving." Pa Watson laughed.

"Winston and I should meet again," FDR suggested, and immediately Hopkins's antennae went up.

"If there are matters you need to take up with Churchill, I recommend you make sure that he comes to you," Hopkins said. "You should avoid going anywhere to meet with Churchill alone."

"I agree," FDR replied.

"I hope you will kill the idea that the war is over," Hopkins suggested. "I think our Allies and the American people have no idea of the severe tests we have ahead of us, particularly in the complete defeat of Japan."

"You're right, Harry."

"And the next time you do speak with Winston, please tell him how strongly you feel about knocking down some of their trade barriers," advised Hopkins. "Lately, he's been maneuvering for me to support their Imperial Preference. Winston needs to know that you want global free trade at the end of this thing," counseled Hopkins.

"Like I said, it's good to have you back."

#

No sooner did Harry come up for air than some in Congress and the press were all over him. Again.

The latest stories, created with the help of FDR's political adversaries and the creative writing of ambitious reporters,

521

suggested that Harry was going to use Lend-Lease to rebuild England after the war, and lambasted him for being under foreign control. Accusations appeared in print that he was under British or Russian influence, and even under the spell of Madame Chiang and the Chinese.

When Steve Early came to FDR's office to tell the President as gently as possible that he thought Harry was a political liability for his upcoming campaign, FDR already knew Early was right. One of Louis Howe's great legacies was his advice to look in and under newspaper stories, and FDR knew you didn't have to dig very deep to know Hopkins would be used to discredit him.

As much as FDR wanted to challenge the press's focus on Hopkins, he knew it would be a futile exercise, and he would lose that battle. The political wizard he was, FDR realized that if he helped his enemies make Harry Hopkins the story in the upcoming election, FDR would lose the next election, the chance to win the war, and the right to finish the job at hand.

Early did not have to do much convincing. Practical as always, FDR and Hopkins met and decided that Harry would have to help the wizard by staying out of the light behind the wizard's curtain until after the election.

#

Operation Cobra allowed British general Bernard Law Montgomery to finally break out from Caen in the north and General Patton to chase the Germans east across France. The British and

American armies caught the escaping German troops between them in Falaise, and hundreds of thousands of German soldiers were captured in what became known as the "Falaise Pocket." Allied troops went from being stuck behind the hedgerows to winning victory after victory, and on August 25, Paris was liberated after four years of Nazi occupation. The world was jubilant.

In September 1944, a little more than a year after their first meeting at the Frontenac Hotel in Quebec, FDR, Churchill, and the Combined Chiefs met again at the famed historic hotel. Despite the entreaties of Churchill and FDR, and Hopkins's own preference, at the insistence of Louise and the doctors at the Naval Hospital, Hopkins remained at his Georgetown home recuperating from his last episode.

The second Quebec Conference was code-named *Octagon,* and the discussions there were quite different and far more positive than almost all prior Allied conferences. Churchill and FDR now fully expected to defeat Germany and in preparing for their victory held wide-ranging and important discussions over the four days covering occupation zones in Germany, continued Lend-Lease aid to Great Britain, the Royal Navy's participation in the continued fight against the Japanese, the plan to drop an atomic bomb on Japan, and Henry Morgenthau's plan to demilitarize Germany.

Morgenthau's original memorandum for the plan was written between January and early September 1944 and called for the complete demilitarization of Germany, including the removal or destruction of all of Germany's war material, the German armament industry, and the removal or destruction of other key industries. In addition to recommending the partitioning of Germany into various smaller states, Morgenthau believed that the Ruhr, the heart of Germany's industrial might, should never be used for industry again.

Morgenthau briefed the Conference attendees on his plan, and while FDR initially endorsed the plan, Churchill did not. After some not-so-subtle persuasion by Morgenthau and others regarding Britain's financial condition, Churchill was finally convinced to agree to Morgenthau's plan to turn Germany back into an agrarian society.

When FDR returned in mid-September, it was plain to everyone that the cumulative stress of the last eleven years was exacting a toll on his health. As summer gave way to autumn, the great campaigner who in the past always rallied voters was barely engaged. New York's Republican Governor, Thomas Dewey, appeared to be winning, and FDR was doing very little to get himself elected.

Pa Watson and Grace Tully, who spent the most time with FDR every day, were downright worried. Not only because FDR was not fighting back against the assaults thrown at him by Dewey in his bid for the President's chair, but also because the President looked very ill and very tired. Watching him throughout the day, they both were becoming convinced he didn't want any of it anymore. And to make matters worse, they believed the awful news about Missy would slow him down even more.

"He just doesn't seem to give a damn," Pa said, very concerned.

"I don't think he's feeling well," Tully excused her boss. "I know Eleanor and Anna are not happy and want him to change doctors," Tully whispered.

Hopkins turned the corner into FDR's outer office, and he could see he had interrupted a private conversation.

"Hi, Harry," Tully said quickly. "He's expecting you."

When Hopkins entered FDR's office, both Pa and Tully had the same idea at the same time. "I swear," Tully whispered to Pa after Hopkins entered FDR's office. "The two of them look like they are going to keel over."

Hopkins found FDR sitting at his desk in shirtsleeves with his head in his hands, massaging his temples. Though it was closed, his shirt collar appeared to be too big for his neck, his face was drawn, and he had dark, puffy circles under his eyes. He looked the way Hopkins felt.

"Bob Sherwood is on his way," Hopkins informed the President as he entered the room.

"Missy died today, Harry," FDR said, his head in his hands.

"Damn." Hopkins exhaled. Perhaps this news explained why the President looked so bad. FDR loved Missy as much as he had ever loved anyone.

"McIntire said it was a cerebral hemorrhage," FDR said quietly, lifting his head to look up at Hopkins. "I always believed Missy would get better," he said to Hopkins with more feeling than Harry expected. FDR was not apologizing, but his voice sounded filled with regret.

"Have you seen the new doctor?" Hopkins asked, very concerned about how poorly FDR looked.

FDR waved his hand at Hopkins, encouraging him to change the subject. "He said I have to cut down on my cigarettes and martinis."

"Make sure you listen to him," replied Hopkins. "How was Quebec?"

"You were missed," FDR replied instantly. "We agreed to Morgenthau's plan for post-war Germany, and also agreed to put Lend-Lease under a new committee going forward. I hope you don't mind," FDR added, checking Hopkins's reaction to the news of his demotion.

"The new committee is a smart decision, especially with all of the noise about me being in Churchill's pocket," Hopkins said evenly.

The door to the office opened, and Grace Tully entered with Bob Sherwood. "Mr. Sherwood, Mr. President," Tully announced.

"It's good to see you, Bob," FDR greeted Sherwood warmly. "How was Paris?"

"Coming back to life. Hi, Harry," Sherwood said.

"Sorry to cut your trip short," Hopkins apologized, "but we need a little of your magic for the campaign."

"Have you heard any of the speeches Dewey has been giving about me?" FDR asked Sherwood.

"A couple. He is not very imaginative," Sherwood said easily.

"I have to give a speech next Saturday night for Dan Tobin's boys and the Teamsters, and I want to have some fun with it. And I would like you and Sam to write a speech for me along these lines," FDR said, picking up a sheet of paper with handwritten notes on his desk.

FDR read his notes out loud for Sherwood and Hopkins. "The Republican fiction writers have concocted a story that I left my dog, Fala, behind in the Aleutian Islands, and I sent a destroyer back to find —at a cost of two or three million dollars to the taxpayers. Well, when Fala found out his Scotch soul was furious. He has not been the same dog since. I am accustomed to hearing falsehoods about myself, but I think I have a right to object to libelous statements about my dog."

Sherwood and Hopkins laughed out loud. "I know exactly the kind of speech you want," Sherwood said.

"A little playful and a lot of sarcasm," replied FDR.

"Don't worry, sir," Sherwood assured the President. "After you give your speech, everyone will think Dewey is running against Fala.

"That's the ticket." FDR cackled.

Hopkins watched FDR laughing and realized that it took just a few minutes for him to look better following the awful and disturbing news about Missy. Hopkins wasn't sure whether it was Dewey's challenge or just FDR's uncanny ability to compartmentalize information that energized him. Whatever the reason, Hopkins was glad to see FDR moving forward again.

#

As they had done for all four elections, FDR and Eleanor spent election eve at Springwood, in Hyde Park, New York, listening to the election night reports on the radio and monitoring the returns. Hopkins again joined them, as he had for the last three elections.

"It's in the bag," Hopkins said, reviewing reports on the conference table.

"You are not the best political prognosticator," FDR teased.

"You will certainly win, Franklin," Eleanor agreed with Hopkins. "And as we get closer to the war's end, you must keep in the forefront of your mind the domestic situation here at home," she preached, making sure she made her opinion known even before the results were official.

"Always," FDR said, hoping his one-word answer would end the conversation.

But Eleanor would not be silenced and was determined to make sure her points were made. "Americans are in no mood for you to spend your time and attention in Great Britain or France when there is still so much work to be done here at home," she insisted.

"Except for another meeting with Churchill and Stalin, I will be here," assured FDR.

"And this goes for you as well," Eleanor said, turning to Hopkins. "There is still a lot of work to be done."

"Yes, Eleanor," Hopkins replied, and FDR rolled his eyes.

"You have a moral obligation to see your domestic reforms through," she instructed Hopkins. "Particularly ensuring that everyone at home has a job. Especially after the war."

"Eleanor," FDR said, "I haven't been officially elected yet, and you are already putting us back to work."

"You will win tonight," she said, "and you both have an overwhelming task ahead of you here in America that won't be settled by making speeches. We have work to do."

"We could not have done any of this without you," FDR said, and though he smiled at Eleanor, there was no hiding the fact he was very weary—of the work, the war, and his wife's moral intensity.

"Now you must finish what we started," she said.

Eleanor never gave up.

#

The following morning, November 7, 1944, the American voters elected FDR for the fourth time, though his bout with Dewey was the closest of all his elections.

CHAPTER THIRTY-ONE

"I have miles to go before I sleep."

A week after FDR's election to an unprecedented fourth term as President, Henry Stimson was worried about the unintended consequences of Morgenthau's memorandum. Of course, the Nazis were aware of the plan and used it to strengthen resistance among their troops and the German people, making life more difficult for Allied troops marching toward Germany. Even Eisenhower reported that resistance had stiffened along the front lines since the content of the plan became public.

Stimson called Hopkins and asked to meet him and Cordell Hull at his office in the new Pentagon, and Harry was surprised by Stimson's passion and agitation. "Morgenthau went too far," Stimson told Hopkins emphatically. "He is proposing to send Germany back to the Dark Ages."

When they met the next day, Hopkins held Morgenthau's memorandum in his hand while he, Stimson, and Hull sat at Stimson's conference table.

"These are the President's and Churchill's initials," Hopkins said, pointing to the document, confirming what he already knew to be true.

"They are," Stimson replied.

"Germany will not survive without an industrial economy," Hull said matter-of-factly.

Hopkins knew Hull and Stimson were right and Morgenthau had gone too far in his desire to ensure that belligerent Germany never breathed another militant breath again. The challenge, and it was a real challenge, was to get FDR and Churchill, the two prima donnas, to backtrack from their decision to support Morgenthau's proposal.

Hopkins felt the burst of energy that always seemed to grip him when there was something important to be done. It occurred to him that he and Churchill were very similar in that respect. They were both energized by important work.

"Leave it with me," Hopkins told Stimson and Hull.

#

Hopkins did do the important work and immediately informed FDR of their faux pas. As it turned out, FDR and Churchill were easy to convince and immediately grasped the disastrous implications of a crippled Germany in a post-war world sandwiched between two vindictive enemies—Russia on one side and France on the other. After Hopkins informed Morgenthau that his plan would not be accepted, he reported back to FDR several days later while the President was shaving.

"I spoke with Morgenthau," Hopkins said. "He understands, but he is not happy."

"I wish you were with me in Quebec," FDR said, wiping his face with a towel and turning in his wheelchair to face Hopkins.

"I'm sorry I wasn't there," replied Hopkins, holding a cable in his hand.

"What have you got there?" asked FDR, looking at the paper in Hopkins's hand.

"Your cable to Stalin about Churchill's meeting with him. It will be misinterpreted."

"How so?" asked FDR.

"You are giving Stalin the impression that when he and Churchill meet, Churchill will speak for the United States," Hopkins said.

"That isn't true," FDR said, concerned.

"You cannot stop Churchill from speaking with Stalin about anything they want," instructed Hopkins, "but it's of the utmost importance you let both of them know that any decisions they may reach on whatever topics they may discuss will not be considered valid until they are discussed with the United States."

FDR was stunned. It had been terribly careless of him to allow Churchill to speak for Britain and America in front of Stalin. He looked at Hopkins, and a chill ran through him as he realized that unless he explicitly said otherwise, the United States would be held accountable for commitments made by Churchill during his meeting with Stalin.

"We must stop my cable, Harry," FDR said, sounding alarmed.

"I already did," Hopkins replied calmly. "Chip Bohlen is on his way here now to draft a cable for you to send to Stalin."

"Good," FDR replied.

Hopkins continued. "We should ask Stalin if Averell Harriman can accompany Churchill to the meeting as an observer."

"Let's get a message to Averell," FDR agreed.

"I will," Hopkins replied and turned to exit.

"Harry," FDR called out, and Hopkins stopped and looked back. "Thank you."

Hopkins sent the cable to Stalin requesting permission for Harriman to attend his meeting with Churchill, and to clarify Churchill's position relative to the United States. The following day, Hopkins received a cable from Stalin, in which the dictator approved of Harriman observing the meeting and thanking FDR for clarifying Churchill's role. In his response, Stalin told FDR that before he received FDR's cable, he was under the impression that Churchill was authorized to speak for himself and for FDR as well.

"Thank goodness," FDR quietly told Hopkins.

#

There was a noticeable change in the White House and throughout all of FDR's administration as 1944 came to a close. Churchill used to say that the human mind was like a culvert capable of handling a limited amount of inbound information before the rest just spilled over. It was clear that everyone's culverts in FDR's administration were overflowing.

Despite their exhilaration in winning a fourth term, the seismic changes and enormous challenges faced by FDR and Hopkins since they began twelve years earlier left both men perpetually and chronically worn out. And they were not alone. Many in FDR's administration and Cabinet who had made the long, hard slog through the years of the Great Depression into World War II seemed to be slowing down, with little energy left to respond quickly to the problems at hand. It was almost as if they were suffering in varying degrees from what people used to call "shell shock" in World War I—a deep, debilitating, stupor and numbness.

It was just after Thanksgiving, when the first of FDR's administration gave out. Cordell Hull, FDR's longtime Secretary of State, visited with FDR in his office, looking tired and very ill.

"I am sorry, Mr. President," Hull said, his normally robust voice sounding thin and his usual crisp pronunciation sounding garbled. "I must resign. The doctors say I must give up all of my responsibilities immediately. I don't even have the energy to sit at my desk any longer. I am sorry." He handed FDR an envelope containing his resignation.

"So am I, Cordell," FDR responded. "I don't want to accept it, but I understand. Our country owes you enormous gratitude for your impeccable service during these historic times."

"Thank you, sir," replied Hull. It was my privilege and honor to serve you and to serve our country."

FDR asked Hull who he thought should replace him. Hull immediately responded that he thought former Supreme Court Justice James Byrnes should be the next Secretary of State. After he left the Supreme Court, Byrnes ran the Office of War Mobilization. Though Byrnes was a candidate to replace Henry A. Wallace as Roosevelt's running mate in the 1944 election, it was Harry Truman who was ultimately selected as Vice President.

After Hull left FDR's office, FDR met with Hopkins to discuss Cordell's resignation and get his opinion on the next Secretary of State.

"Ed Stettinus," Hopkins replied easily.

"Not Jimmy Byrnes?" FDR asked.

"No," replied Hopkins. "Ed has Lend-Lease, State Department experience since '43, and he just chaired the Dumbarton Oaks Conference." Both FDR and Hopkins knew how important Dumbarton Oaks was as a precursor to the formation of the institution that would become known as the United Nations.

"Ed Stettinus it is," replied FDR.

#

The smoke-filled Old Ebbitt Grill was jumping with dozens of people layered up against its bar shouting drink orders and debating the Allies' latest maneuvers to win the war. Always a loud and vocal bunch, this night the reporters, misfits, raconteurs, salesmen, soldiers, ne'er-do-wells, and politicians at the bar were particularly boisterous and happy, inspired by their drinks, the incoming holiday season, and the fact that it looked like the end of the war in Europe was in sight. With the Soviets on the move heading west, and Patton's run across Southern France to pincer the escaping Germans at Falaise, most at the bar believed it would be a very, very Merry Christmas in 1944.

Thanks to Phil LoScalco's size and girth, he was able to occupy and cordon off a significant piece of the bar for himself and his fellow reporters Mike Brannigan, Mickey Porter, and Charlie McAllister. They always made it a point to meet up at the end of the year to wish each other a Merry Christmas, compare notes from the prior year, and make bets on the next. A little money at stake throughout the year kept the day-to-day sameness and drudgery of reporting the news a little more bearable and, at times, exciting.

LoScalco saw several politicians circling a group of pretty-looking WACs at the bar, and his antennae were up. "Look at that," LoScalco said to his buddies. "Five years ago, a woman wouldn't be caught dead at this bar, and now they're here in uniform."

"Hickok always came here," Porter replied.

"Like I said, a woman wouldn't be caught dead in this place," LoScalco cracked. Every reporter in DC knew Lorena "Hick" Hickok, and anyone who hung out at the Old Ebbitt did, as well.

"Hey, stop changing the subject," Charlie McAllister said to LoScalco. "It's time to settle up. Five bucks, fat boy. Get it up."

"What's right is right," Brannigan chimed in.

"You did say Hopkins was too sick and would be out to pasture," Porter confirmed with LoScalco.

"Didn't I tell him?" McAllister asked the others, encouraging them to continue their support. "I told you," McAllister told LoScalco. "Don't count out Hopkins. Five bucks. Cough it up."

"How do you know he's still pullin' da strings?" LoScalco asked.

"C'mon, Phil. You think Stettinus was named the new Secretary of State on his own?" Brannigan asked, knowing Hopkins was behind it.

"Who do you think knocked off Byrnes?" Porter jumped in.

"Everyone knew the Secretary of State job was going to Byrnes. Even Hull thought so," McAllister added, taking a long swig of his bourbon.

"There's lots of bad blood between Harry and Byrnsie," Brannigan said, tapping his glass to ask the bartender for a refill.

"Hopkins definitely put the kibosh on Byrnes," Porter said, certain that Hopkins was the one who backed Stettinus.

"Ante up, big guy," McAllister said to LoScalco with the palm of his hand extended and turned up. "Gimme."

LoScalco reached into his front pocket and removed bills that were folded in half and held together by a rubber band. He removed the band and a five-dollar bill from the fold and tossed the bill onto the bar in front of McAllister.

"Thank you," McAllister said cheerfully as he snatched the bill off the bar. "Hey, Phil," McAllister said, putting the bill in his wallet. "Five'll get you ten that Hopkins goes to the next meeting with Stalin and Churchill."

"I'm done bettin' on Hopkins," LoScalco sulked.

"I have a better idea," Brannigan jumped in. "Let's start a pool in '45. A buck each. Who will be the first member of the Cabinet to resign? I'll take Stimson," Brannigan finished and put a dollar bill on the bar.

"No way," LoScalco announced. "He'll stay until da war's over."

"Perkins. Maybe Ickes," Porter said out loud.

"Ickes will never leave," McAllister said.

"How 'bout Truman?" LoScalco asked.

"He's the Vice President, not a Cabinet member," Brannigan said. "Besides, he's not going anywhere. That guy's just glad he's got a job."

"I'll go with Frank Walker," Porter said, putting a dollar onto the bar. "He's been around a long time."

"Definitely Stettinus," McAllister said, throwing a dollar on the bar and sounding very sure of his pick, turned to LoScalco. "Another buck coming my way, big guy."

LoScalco glared at McAllister as he put a dollar on the bar. "I'll go with Perkins," he told the group, convinced he had made a smart choice.

Big Phil LoScalco would lose another buck to Charlie McAllister in 1945.

#

Construction of the new Pentagon had begun three months before the Japanese attacked Pearl Harbor, and it was an enormous undertaking. Sitting across the Potomac River in Arlington, the building was designed as a five-sided building of more than six million square feet to house the War Department and everyone who supported the US military. When it was completed, it was the largest office building in the world.

No one expected Hull's resignation to reverberate around Washington, DC, but before long, the law of unintended consequences and DC rumors had Hull's resignation taking on a life of its own. "They," whoever "They" were, wondered whether FDR actually fired Hull or if Stettinus engineered a coup, or if Harry Hopkins got rid of Hull so that he could put Stettinus in as Secretary of State.

After Hull's resignation and Stettinus's appointment, "they" concluded that Hopkins engineered both. "They" naturally picked up on the Hull and Stettinus intrigue to start the Jimmy Byrnes saga. "They said" it was widely known that Hopkins did not like Jimmy Byrnes, and so he squashed Byrnes as FDR's running mate for Vice President in '44, and Hull's replacement. "So, they said."

When Hopkins and Henry Stimson finished their lunch of meatloaf and potatoes in Stimson's office at the Pentagon, the two men actually had the same thought about each other: "He looks tired and worn."

Secretary of War Stimson, who was seventy-seven years old, was appointed by FDR in July 1940 and, working with George Marshall and with support from Hopkins, built the US Army and Air Corps from a force of less than 200,000 men to a sophisticated, technologically modern Army of sixteen million people in a matter of five years.

"Harry, does the President want me to resign?" Stimson asked, stirring sugar into his coffee.

"What?" a startled Hopkins replied.

"I've gotten a little long in the tooth, Harry.   You know I'm not as strong as I used to be," Stimson said.

"Henry, we're all tired," Hopkins replied.

"There are a lot of people in the press bringing up my age lately," Stimson said.

"If those guys knew what they were talking about, they would be dangerous."

"It might be wise for the President to have me resign now.   Get someone younger in here."

"Henry. You are the most respected member of the Cabinet. You have the respect of the American people, the rank and file in the Army, and George Marshall himself," assured Hopkins.

"Thanks for saying that, but..." Stimson started, but Hopkins cut him off. He did not want to hear any more of Stimson's musings about resignation.

"Most importantly, Henry," Hopkins said over Stimson, "you have the complete confidence of the President. So, no, I don't think you should resign. The President doesn't want you to resign. And neither do I nor anyone else."

#

After losing more than 800,000 soldiers at Stalingrad, in January 1943, German General Friedrich von Paulus surrendered his Sixth

Army to the Russians. For the first time since the war began, the German government informed its citizens of a German loss, and Joseph Goebbels, Hitler's Minister of Propaganda, began telling German citizens to be prepared for total war. And that was when Adolf Hitler began talking about Germany's new "Wunderwaffen"—wonder weapons—that were being developed, which would vanquish their enemies.

As the German Army continued to suffer defeats and death at the hands of the Allies, the idea of Hitler pulling a rabbit out of his hat to save the German people helped to keep hope alive among Germans and their military. By the Fall of 1944, one of Hitler's promised wonder weapons, the V2 rocket, made its appearance, and as 1944 came to a close, it wreaked havoc with more than 1,000 rockets descending on London. After years of bombings and finally peace in the skies over their heads, suddenly Londoners were once again the recipients of the terror and whims of falling Nazi bombs. The V2 in particular was terrifying in its indiscriminate and uncontrolled attacks on London.

Unlike the V1 rocket, which Londoners called the "Buzz Bomb," Londoners couldn't hear the new V2 rocket as it approached the city. The old V1 rocket would loudly fly at very high speed above London, the sound of its engines drawing everyone's attention, until the engine stopped and it descended to detonate and destroy whatever it came in contact with.

The much bigger, new V2 rockets, however, were fired from launch sites in Germany and France and flew at supersonic speeds day or night to some fifty miles above the earth. When a V2 rocket's engines shut down, it would silently free-fall to Earth and detonate wherever it landed. And no one, not even the Germans who launched it, knew exactly where it would land. It was all indiscriminate, and if you happened to be in its flight path, it was just bad luck. More than 10,000 Londoners had their luck run out in the path of a V2 rocket.

Churchill sat in his office on his phone, and though he didn't hear the V2, he could hear the cries of British civilians on the streets below shouting about a rocket in the sky. He stood with the phone to his ear, looking outside his window and searching the sky to see if he could spot the V2 on its way to its destination. He could not.

"Harry? Harry? Are you there?" he shouted into the static-filled connection between him and Hopkins.

"Winston?" Hopkins responded.

"What is Stettinus talking about?" Churchill was upset, but the static on the line masked his emotion.

"Stettinus?" asked Hopkins, trying to be sure he heard Churchill correctly.

"Yes!" an exasperated Churchill shouted. "What does he mean the British and Italian governments have been notified that Italy must work out its problems along Democratic lines? Does that apply to Greece?"

"Winston, I'm sorry," Hopkins's voice came through sounding frustrated. "What about Greece?"

"How dare Admiral King say he will not allow American landing craft—your LSTs—to be used to deliver supplies to Greece."

"Admiral King?" Hopkins shouted, trying to make sense of the conversation through the static and missed words.

A very frustrated Churchill shouted into the phone, "Harry, I will ask Lord Halifax to contact you!" Churchill slammed down the phone. "Blasted device."

After Churchill hung up, Hopkins reached Admiral Leahy, the Chief of Staff for the US Armed Forces, and asked to meet in the Map Room in the White House. The White House was already looking festive with Christmas decorations, and in the Map Room, there stood a small Christmas tree, put there by the duty officers.

"Yes, that's true, Harry. Admiral King did tell Admiral Hewitt not to use our LSTs to ferry supplies to Greece," Admiral Leahy said as they stood in front of a map of Greece and its surrounding islands.

"Admiral King has now got himself into a political area he wants no part of," Hopkins informed Leahy. "We told the British they could use our planes to move troops into Greece, and pulling the LSTs from them certainly doesn't reconcile with that."

"I'll call King and tell him to countermand the order," Leahy promised.

A short while later, Hopkins and Lord Halifax had lunch in the White House dining room, and Halifax told Hopkins, "I wish I did not have to be the one to communicate this to you, Harry, but the Prime Minister intends to send a very strong protest to the President about this Greece business."

"Not necessary," replied Hopkins. "Admiral King has already told Admiral Hewitt to disregard his original order."

"That may very well be the case," Halifax responded, "but I rather understand why the Prime Minister would want this episode escalated to the President."

"I recommend you cable the Prime Minister and tell him that I said any cable from him would serve no purpose at this point since the matter is settled," instructed Hopkins.

"You should know, Harry, that I am in favor of sending a protest to the President."

"Lord Halifax," Hopkins responded, sounding formal and firm. "A protest would be a waste of time, and it would put unneeded pressure on the relationships between the United States and Britain. US public opinion already believes that Great Britain has messed up the situation in Greece," Hopkins informed Halifax.

"I must say that is rather direct," Halifax replied.

"If the PM lodges a protest over this, it will not serve either America or Great Britain," Hopkins assured the imperious Halifax.

The following morning, Hopkins was in the Map Room, going over the latest convoy reports with the military officers on duty, when the communications officer handed Hopkins a communication. "This just came in for you," the officer told Hopkins.

From: W. Churchill

To: H. Hopkins

Many thanks for your timely advice to Lord Halifax. I greatly appreciate your actions on this matter. I have canceled my dispatch to the President.

"Can you fit me in?" Hopkins asked the communications officer after reading Churchill's cable.

"Sure, Mr. Hopkins," answered the officer and walked to his station with Hopkins following.

"Okay if I dictate?"

"Sure."

"It's to Churchill," Hopkins said, and the communications officer began to type.

"No one knows better than I what a gallant role you are playing in the greatest drama in the history of the world," Hopkins dictated, and the officer typed. *"On this fateful Christmas, I want you to know that I am well aware of the heavy burdens that you carry. I am proud to be known and even to be attacked by some of my countrymen as your good friend. Merry Christmas!"*

#

It didn't take long before the exhilaration of winning a fourth term, the Allies' successes on the battlefield, and a Christmas season brimming with hope and goodwill were undermined by news from the front that the Germans were on the move.

On December 16, a little more than a month after FDR won the election, the Germans drove their tanks through the Ardennes Forest and slammed into America's lines in Belgium and Luxembourg in their mission to reach Antwerp. Their goal was to cut the British and American forces in two, and for their effort, they created a bulge in the American lines as American forces retreated west under the weight of their assault.

The Battle of the Bulge, as it became known, was now focused on the soldiers in America's new 101st Airborne Division who were surrounded by the Germans in the Belgian town of Bastogne.

In the midst of this threat, the Allied leaders agreed on another conference, and this time, Stalin would be able to attend. Their meeting was set for early February in the city of Yalta in the Crimea.

Hopkins sat in the residence, sipping his Scotch, smoking his cigarette, and watching FDR and Eleanor spar with each other. Even though they each gave it their best, neither Eleanor nor FDR had the energy to go a full round with each other, punch for punch. Lately, Eleanor found that the President gave in to her far more easily than he ever had in the past.

"Why are you traveling all over the world, Franklin?" Eleanor asked, seemingly very upset with her husband. "Stalin and Churchill should come to you for a meeting."

"There is still heavy fighting in Russia, and Stalin cannot leave, plus Europe is not yet secure." Though FDR answered her, he sounded like he had no interest in doing so.

"You must take care of yourself," Eleanor said, and though it could've been interpreted as a loving comment from someone who loved him, Eleanor's tone reeked of criticism.

"And you, too," Eleanor said, turning to Hopkins. "Churchill has you two running ragged," she said and left the room in a huff.

"She cares about you," Hopkins said evenly to FDR in the silence left by Eleanor's departure.

"Don't I know it. Missy used to do a great job screening me from all that love." FDR cackled.

"I miss her," Hopkins said, surprised at the intensity of the feeling that welled up in him at the mention of Missy's name.

"So do I," FDR replied, and then, as if he was shaking himself free of something holding him, changed the tone and volume of his voice and the direction of their conversation. "I want you to go to Europe, Harry, before Yalta," ordered FDR. "Churchill has been very chilly lately."

"I'll meet with him."

"And while you're over in Europe, you should also spend time with De Gaulle."

"I've never met anyone more determined to be disliked than De Gaulle."

"Nor anyone as good at it as he is. That fellow makes me itchy, but we do need a strong France with a strong England and Italy to help stabilize Europe after the war is over," FDR replied.

"I'll put him on the schedule," Hopkins agreed. "In your upcoming State of the Union, you should mention our historic friendship with France and the heroism and courage of the French Resistance," suggested Hopkins.

"Good idea."

"And the success of Allied unity, especially when it comes to challenges like Poland and Greece," added Hopkins.

"You mean how we continually have to ask Winston to stop trying to screw up Europe when the war is over?" FDR snickered and Hopkins laughed.

"Actually, Winston probably would prefer to give your State of the Union address himself."

"He probably would." FDR laughed.

"No, on second thought, he definitely would." Hopkins laughed.

#

FDR suggested that Hopkins fly to Europe using the President's "Flying White House," a Douglas VC-54C Skymaster. The airplane, which was nicknamed "The Sacred Cow" for all of its elaborate security, was the first plane ever built to specifically fly a US President. Though the cabin was unpressurized, requiring the aircraft to fly below an altitude of 12,000 feet, it included a conference room, desk, private lavatory, bed, refrigerator, and bulletproof windows. There was even an elevator in the rear of the aircraft to allow FDR to easily board the plane.

On January 6, FDR delivered his State of the Union address and provided Americans with a comprehensive look at the state of the war, the country, and its military. He concluded his address with, *"This new year of 1945 can be the greatest year of achievement in human history. 1945 can see the final ending of the Nazi-Fascist reign of terror in Europe. 1945 can see the closing in of the forces of retribution about the center of the malignant power of imperialistic Japan. Most important of all, 1945 can and must see the substantial beginning of the organization of world peace. This organization must be the fulfillment of the promise for which men have fought and died in this war. It must be the justification of all the sacrifices that have been made, of all the dreadful misery that this world has endured. We Americans of today, together with our Allies, are making history—and I hope it will be better history than ever has been made before. We pray that we may be worthy of the unlimited opportunities that God has given us."*

Hopkins brought Chip Bohlen with him on his European trip, and though he anticipated turbulence in his upcoming meetings with Churchill, De Gaulle, and the pope, he was energized by the prospect of victory in Europe and Japan, and the possibilities for a world at peace. This was in spite of the fact that the ties that bound the Allied relationships were becoming stretched at best or unraveled at worst. Hopkins realized that much of the difficulties circulating inside the day-to-day dealings between the Allies emanated from Great Britain and Churchill's recognition that their role and influence in the world were diminishing daily.

"Lunch tomorrow with Churchill," Hopkins said as he and Bohlen sat on The Sacred Cow reading.

"How can I help with him?" Bohlen asked.

"Give him lots of room to get everything off his chest. And trust me, he will."

"You know him well."

"He is a good friend," Hopkins said, and then, smiling, held out a document for Bohlen. "The President designated Robert, my son, the official photographer for the Yalta Conference."

"I hope Robert knows you are to be in every photo?"

"Not yet." Hopkins laughed and added, "Though I should probably tell Robert to make sure Winston is."

An Army Air Force captain entered the main cabin from the plane's cockpit, walking up the narrow aisle to Hopkins and Bohlen.

"What's going on?" asked Hopkins.

"Fortunately, not much," the captain answered. "I came back to tell you we are about an hour out from Heston Airport and the skies over London are clear of everything, including V2s and the Luftwaffe," he said to Hopkins and then looked out the side windows.

"Thanks, Captain."

"Here's our escorts now," the captain added, pointing outside the aircraft.

Hopkins and Bohlen looked out the windows, and there was a British Spitfire flying on either side of the aircraft.

#

London's weather in January was predictably overcast, gray, and cold, and there was a fire blazing in Churchill's office at 10 Downing Street. While Churchill paced the room with something weighing on him, Hopkins sat closest to the fire in an easy chair, and his Fleet Street long underwear, while Bohlen stationed himself at Churchill's conference table.

"There is the persistent perception here in England that the relationship between the United States and England is evaporating before our eyes and we are increasingly under the thumb, or should I say the boot heel, of Stalin," Churchill said while pacing, smoking, and not looking at either man.

"Winston. You know that is not true," answered Hopkins matter-of-factly.

"It isn't?" Churchill asked rhetorically as he puffed his cigar and stopped pacing. "Yalta?" he exclaimed disbelievingly. "We could not have found a worse place for a meeting if we had spent ten years on research. Why would Franklin agree to go to Yalta of all places?"

"Are you asking me?" Hopkins was losing patience.

"I am."

"Because the President believes a meeting between the three of you is most important, and where that meeting takes place is not," answered Hopkins.

"It seems to me, my dear Harry, that England is being squeezed between two behemoths who are determined to suit themselves without any regard for little old England."

Churchill began pacing again.

"Winston, who have you been talking to?" Hopkins asked, recognizing his friend was spiraling into his "Black Dog."

"Myself."

"Okay, then answer these questions for yourself," Hopkins replied. "Why would America abandon Great Britain and all that we have already accomplished together?"

Churchill grunted and stopped to look at Hopkins through the smoke swirling around him.

"Why would America discard the goodwill developed between our two countries," Hopkins continued, "after fighting side by side during the darkest days either country has ever known?"

Churchill started with "I don't..." but Hopkins continued over him.

"And good will aside... selfishly speaking, now—why would America turn its back on the significant investment it has made in Great Britain in blood and treasure over the last five years?"

"You wouldn't," Churchill said simply.

"Of course not."

Churchill turned to look at Chip Bohlen. "Lord Root of the Matter," he said, pointing to Hopkins.

"It's just easier to see from a distance. Especially when you are not the one putting the bricks on the wall as fast as you can and covered from head to toe in cement," Hopkins replied.

"And not even sure if the wall you are building is going up straight," Churchill confirmed.

"Winston, you have done more during this war in furtherance of the Allies' cause and victory than anyone ever believed was humanly possible," Hopkins said and meant it.

"I have miles to go before I sleep." Churchill smiled.

"One step and one brick at a time, Winston."

"Are you going directly to Yalta?"

"Seeing De Gaulle in Paris next."

"He who represents all Frenchmen has deigned to meet with you? Have I told you he is unbearable?" Churchill asked, and turned dark again. "Harry, I want to be clear. De Gaulle is not welcome at the conference table in Yalta."

"Leave it with me."

After Harry and Bohlen landed in Paris and were driving down the Champs-Élysées, the sight of hundreds of Frenchmen and Allied Soldiers sitting unafraid in cafés and walking along the famous boulevard made Hopkins wish Louise were with him. Paris was free again. Despite the heavy, dark clouds above the Eiffel Tower and the city's temperature hovering near freezing, there was no mistaking the feeling of liberty and lightness that seemed to envelope the historic city and everyone in it. Though wrapped in their heaviest wool and fur coats, hats, and gloves, the people of Paris and their city were once again truly alive.

General Charles De Gaulle had arrived in Paris five months earlier on August 25 and walked at the head of the French Resistance fighters and Allied armies as they marched down the famous boulevard to liberate the City of Light. Since that time, from his offices near the Arc de Triomphe, De Gaulle worked to form coalitions of the many fractured political parties remaining in France. He wanted a unified French government with him at its head, and his goal for France was to reclaim its leadership position in the world, secure a zone of occupation within defeated Germany, and have a seat on the newly formed United Nations' Security Council.

De Gaulle's office, a nicely appointed Art Nouveau office looking out over the Champs-Élysées, was seized from a Vichy functionary who was then handed over to the French Resistance for summary execution. Since France's liberation, any and all Nazi collaborators were hunted, and even if they were given a trial, more often than not, they were executed.

De Gaulle sat with Hopkins and Bohlen, his imperious and aloof manner unchanged from the last time Hopkins saw him in Casablanca.

"I believe that relations between the United States and France can be improved," said Hopkins, trying to paint an optimistic picture for the relationship between the two countries.

"If relations between the United States and France are not all they should be currently, why don't you do something about it?" asked De Gaulle, thinking he was being clever, turning the tables on Hopkins.

When Hopkins heard De Gaulle's dripping arrogance, he quickly decided he didn't have the stomach or the patience to dance with this delusional Frenchman.   Bohlen, who had spent enough time with Hopkins, immediately knew this was not going to be a pleasant meeting.

"The United States has already done an enormous amount," Hopkins said evenly.

"Why was I not invited to the Yalta Conference?" asked De Gaulle, and Hopkins decided to lower the boom.

"The cause is above all the stupefying disappointment we suffered when we saw France collapse and surrender in the disaster of 1940," Hopkins replied, and when De Gaulle tried to interject, he continued over him. "And add to that the fact that those French military or political leaders in whom we successively placed our trust did not show themselves worthy of our hopes. That's why," Hopkins finished and stared unemotionally directly at De Gaulle.

Bohlen smiled to himself, knowing he had predicted Hopkins's reaction.

Despite his best efforts to appear otherwise, it was evident De Gaulle was unsettled by Hopkins's candor and tried to push back. "During those years, the United States did not help or encourage France to keep fighting," he replied, suggesting that France's predicament was America's fault.

"Yeah, well, it was American material and soldiers who liberated Paris and France," Hopkins said, never taking his eyes off the man in front of him.

"That is true, but you always seem to assist us grudgingly and under pressure," cried De Gaulle.

Sitting there and taking the measure of the man, Hopkins realized that De Gaulle was like a petulant, spoiled teenager blaming everyone but himself for his own shortcomings. He had had enough of this guy.

"When everyone turned their backs on France, it was the United States who insisted on your liberation," replied Hopkins off-handedly, knowing full well the scale and reality of America's help would have no impact at all on the haughty Frenchman's perspective.

"The future of Europe will be decided at the Yalta Conference," De Gaulle said, telling Hopkins that his attendance at the conference was most important for him. "I cannot accept that France will have no say in those matters."

"You will not participate in the Yalta Conference," Hopkins said definitively, leaving no room for doubt.

"But France deserves..." protested De Gaulle, and Hopkins waved his hand, cutting him off.

"I will try to persuade the Allies to offer France a zone of occupation in Germany after the end of the war and a role on the Control Commission," Hopkins said this like it was the best he could possibly do for De Gaulle.

"What type of zone?"

"To be determined," Hopkins said, and fell silent. Chip Bohlen thought to himself that there was nothing diplomatic about Hopkins's demeanor with the general, and the word "hardball" popped into his brain as Hopkins sat there looking unperturbed, silently observing an angry De Gaulle.

"Maybe I can arrange for you and the President to meet after the Yalta Conference. Perhaps in Algiers," offered Hopkins, like it was an afterthought, and he was only trying to be polite.

"We should," an infuriated De Gaulle replied.

"Very well," Hopkins said, rising from his chair. While he and Bohlen put on their coats and hats, De Gaulle sat stewing in his chair, and no one spoke.

"General," Hopkins said in lieu of goodbye.

"Good day, Mr. Hopkins," De Gaulle replied, his nose held firmly in the air.

#

Perhaps the most surprising stop on Hopkins's pre-Yalta European trek was his visit with Pope Pius XII in Rome. After walking past hundreds of people in Piazza San Pietro outside of Saint Peter's Basilica in the Vatican, Hopkins and Bohlen were escorted by the Vatican's Swiss Guards to the pope's Private Library in the Apostolic Palace. Inside the ancient palace, Hopkins and Bohlen were overwhelmed by the incredible wealth displayed in furnishings, art, and books as they made their way to and into the library.

Pope Pius was already sitting comfortably in an ornate red and gold chair with his feet settled on an upholstered footstool when they entered. Hopkins and Bohlen sat in front of him on functional wooden chairs, their seats below the pope.

The sixty-nine-year-old Pope Pius was elected six months before the start of World War II, and since that time, he tried to navigate the Catholic Church as a neutral entity while Europe burned around the Vatican. Despite his intentions, there were a number of allegations regarding the Church's inaction in the face of the Nazis' mass murder of Jews and others throughout Europe.

While there were some Americans, British, and Europeans who blamed the pope for his inaction in the face of the Nazis' genocide, Stalin blamed Pius for publishing a Decree against Communism. The Decree informed Catholics who followed the tenets of atheistic Communism that they would be excommunicated from the Catholic Church.

Stalin did not appreciate the pope's views and sentiment regarding Communism, to say the least, and subsequently, there were mass deportations of Catholic clergy from the Eastern Bloc. There were some who thought the deportations showed Stalin was getting soft in his old age. Ten years earlier, all of the clergy would have been killed and their dead bodies left behind to burn with their churches.

Sitting with Pius and Bohlen, Hopkins was certain that no one in the pope's library that day was pure, innocent, and without sin—and that included the two priests flanking Pius's chair.

"When the war is over," Hopkins told the pope, "we believe Russia, England, and the United States will occupy Germany, and Poland will form its own government."

"Thank you for sharing the goals of the Allies with me," Pius replied.

"Your Holiness. The President has a very high regard for you and for the Church's unfailingly sympathetic attitude toward America during these difficult years," Hopkins informed the pope.

"America is a beacon of hope not only for the many people in Europe who have suffered through this ordeal, but for every person in the world," replied Pius.

"That is very kind. We hope to be worthy of that responsibility," answered Hopkins.

"As you know, Mr. Hopkins, God shed his light on thee." The pope smiled.

"As we sing in our national anthem," Hopkins returned his smile. "We also hope to be worthy of His light."

"I trust you will," Pius replied and raised his hand in the air, extending it toward Hopkins and Bohlen, who in turn bowed their heads.

"May God bless you and America in your momentous endeavors in the coming months, and keep you from harm, and may he bless you and America with the abundance you will need to help heal the world. I ask this in Jesus's name. In the name of the Father, and of the Son, and of the Holy Spirit. Amen," the pope concluded.

They both uttered "Amen," softly, and when they lifted their bowed heads, Bohlen could see that Harry was misty-eyed.

CHAPTER THIRTY-TWO

"He speaks according to his soul."

It was just before the Yalta Conference when it became clear to FDR, Hopkins, and Churchill that Stalin was seeking much more than a pound of flesh for his country's blood and sacrifice. Though the Russian Army was rightfully on the march to expel the Germans from their borders, it seemed that there was an even greater intensity and new urgency to their fighting. It was not only retribution that motivated Stalin and the Russian Army, but also their desire to acquire as much land as possible in their drive to push the Germans back to Berlin.

Word began to bubble up within diplomatic circles that Stalin was after an iron-clad security guarantee for his borders and his government. There were reports that he wanted to move the Polish border further west and increase the buffer between Berlin and Moscow, and wanted to be sure the Free Polish government in exile in London would have no say in Poland after the war. Ever paranoid about his Western Allies' intentions, Stalin wanted a government in Poland that he could control.

While the friction among the Allies increased in their quest to ensure a safe and sound Europe at the war's end, there were still two dangerous and ruthless enemies who were determined to leave their indelible black marks on the world. While the Germans committed wholesale murder and destruction across Eastern Europe, the Japanese sent Kamikaze into US warships and fought until the last of their soldiers at each of their Pacific-island installations gave their lives to the Japanese emperor, sometimes by their own hand. Humankind had never experienced a war as brutal, terrifying, or unforgiving.

When the British delegation arrived, Hopkins and Bohlen stood on the tarmac with Soviet Foreign Minister Molotov at Saki Airport in the Crimea, surrounded by hundreds of Soviet soldiers. Churchill and his daughter Sarah exited the aircraft first, and after Hopkins greeted them, Lord Moran, Churchill's personal physician, shook hands with Hopkins and confided that the Prime Minister had a very high fever. Bad timing, especially since the negotiations over the next several days would require all of the energy and clarity the Prime Minister could muster.

A short while later, Pa Watson, Ed Stettinus, George Marshall, and Admiral King arrived with the President and walked across the tarmac. The President, who was traveling with his daughter, Anna Boettiger, was settled in the front passenger seat of a jeep and was slowly driven across to meet the others. Along with the hundreds of

Soviet soldiers, there were dozens of military and foreign service officers in the delegations from all three countries on the tarmac.

Marshall and King were the first to reach Hopkins and shook hands with him.

"I heard you threatened to resign," Hopkins quietly greeted Marshall and shook his hand.

"You should have seen it," Admiral King answered for Marshall. "The British kept bitching and moaning about Eisenhower's plan. Blah blah blah..."

"I could not put up with their bickering, so I finally said if they adopted the British plan and it was approved by the Prime Minister and the President, I had no choice but to resign," explained Marshall.

"That got their attention." Hopkins smiled.

"Harry, before we get to Yalta, you should know the Chiefs decided to transfer any available American shipping to the Pacific after we win in Europe," King relayed one of the decisions reached at their recent meeting.

"We shouldn't do that," Hopkins said simply.

"Why not?" asked Marshall, surprised that Hopkins disagreed.

"We need that shipping to help rehabilitate the civilian population throughout Europe," Hopkins explained. "There will be no recovery, no peace, and no democracy if the people in England and Europe don't have enough to eat or the tools to get back to work."

"What do you suggest?" asked King.

"Leave the shipping allocations with me," Hopkins said.

"Okay by me," King said.

"I will inform the Chiefs," confirmed Marshall.

FDR's jeep approached at the pace of a slow walk, and Harry approached to greet FDR. As he got closer to the jeep, Harry was startled by how pale, worn, and sickly the President appeared. He seemed to have lost weight since Hopkins left for his European trip, and looked exhausted and ill. Hopkins couldn't help but think that the British and American contingents might have their hands full during the conference with everyone so severely under the weather.

"Harry, did you take care of my Sacred Cow?" FDR asked.

"It's in great shape," replied Hopkins.

Admiral King, who was standing off to the side with Marshall watching FDR and Hopkins, was struck by how worn out they both looked. "Is it my imagination, or do those two look like they're about to croak?" King whispered to Marshall, who did not react.

FDR's jeep slowly drove away with Churchill walking beside the jeep toward the cars that would take them on the 150 km, five-hour drive from Saki airport to Yalta. Lord Moran was not happy about his Prime Minister walking next to FDR in his car, who, according to Moran, looked like "an Indian attendant accompanying Queen Victoria."

Harry's son, Robert, the official American photographer for the conference, was standing on the perimeter and approached his father when he saw the chance.

"It's great to see you, Dad," Robert said, hugging Hopkins.

"You look good for a married man," Hopkins said.

Robert had recently gotten married in London. "I can't wait for you to meet Brenda."

"Neither can I." Hopkins smiled and walked with Robert to their cars.

Again, Stalin started his negotiations early, pressing for an advantage from the moment his "Allies" planes touched down in Saki. He decided he would not greet his Allies at the airport, and he made sure on their five-hour drive to Yalta, they would see and feel the devastation, carnage, and death Russia had experienced in its fight with the Germans.

Almost everywhere they looked during their drive, the British and the Americans saw destroyed buildings, corpses, and dead animals littering fields. The sights were intentionally haunting and designed to show how much Russia had suffered and how much Stalin's "Allies" hadn't.

Yalta, which was located on the southeastern coast of the Crimea, offered the Czar and Russian aristocrats at the end of the nineteenth century a beautiful summer resort area on the Black Sea. Populated by old, worn-down palaces and dilapidated, but once opulent homes that still spoke of the bygone era of the monarchy, Stalin decided to restore and refurbish the old buildings for the conference and ordered new furniture brought by convoy from Moscow. Stalin, who controlled every bit of the conference agenda, dictated that FDR, Hopkins, and the American contingent would stay in the Livadia Palace where the conference would be held, while Churchill and the British entourage would stay at Vorontsov Palace, some 15 km away. Churchill noticed.

By the time they arrived in Yalta on a clear and very cold star-filled night, Churchill was burning up with fever, and both FDR and

Hopkins were completely exhausted. FDR's 8,500 km trip, which began on the USS Quincy twelve days before and ended on a plane from Malta to Saki, was an arduous journey even for someone who was in the best of shape. Though FDR relished sea journeys and always found them restorative, in his current condition, he felt like he had pushed his wheelchair across the entire Atlantic. Like Hopkins, FDR's health was failing him.

The following morning, Dr. McIntire examined FDR while he sat in the living room of his suite at Livadia Palace. Everyone in the entourage was briefed that they should assume that everything they did or said would be seen or overheard by the maids and butlers and reported directly to Stalin. In short, they would be spied on. With that in mind, Dr. McIntire finished his examination of FDR and cheerfully returned his stethoscope to his bag.

"I'm fine," FDR said out loud, but knew he was not well. He was very, very tired.

McIntire did not respond to FDR's comment. He was worried and did not like the way the President looked or how his heart sounded. Knowing they were being watched, he decided some benign instructions might help. "You should try to limit your cigarettes to eight or ten per day for the conference and try not to drink," he told FDR.

"Right." FDR smiled. "Eight or ten per day and no more drinking!"

"Rest whenever you can."

"I will," FDR said and asked, "How is Harry?"

McIntire moved his hand back and forth, telling the President, "So, so."

"He'll be fine," FDR said cheerfully.

No sooner than Dr. McIntire finished his examination than a Secret Service agent entered with Stalin and Molotov. Stalin decided to visit FDR to greet and spend time with him before the official start of the conference and the plenary sessions, which would take place later in the afternoon. He had already done the same with Churchill.

"Premier Stalin would like to say hello, Mr. President," Molotov said.

"What a wonderful surprise!" replied FDR in his best campaign voice. "Please come in."

Stalin acknowledged McIntire and walked directly to FDR with his hand extended. "It is good to see you again."

"I am so glad you stopped by," FDR said with a broad smile.

"I hope I haven't interrupted," Stalin said, looking at McIntire.

"Not at all. This is Dr. McIntire," FDR said, and Stalin nodded to McIntire. "He takes care of my sinuses. I was just about to make myself a martini. Would you like a drink?" asked FDR as he lit a cigarette and wheeled himself over to the liquor cart to begin mixing his famous martini.

McIntire could not believe his eyes. So much for doctor's orders.

"Yes, thank you." Stalin smiled.

"Foreign Minister?" FDR asked Molotov.

"No, thank you," replied Molotov.

"Admiral," FDR said to McIntire. "Would you ask Robert Hopkins to come in? We should have some photos," instructed FDR.

"Yes, sir," McIntire answered and exited the room, shaking his head.

"You are feeling well?" asked Stalin.

"Yes. And you?" asked FDR

"Well."

FDR completed his mixing and poured Stalin a martini. Reilly, FDR's lead Secret Service agent, brought the glass to Stalin and handed FDR his.

"Cheers!" FDR said, holding up his glass.

"To your health," Stalin replied.

"I need to ask you, Marshal Stalin," FDR said. "What are your thoughts on De Gaulle?"

"He seems very impressed with himself and not realistic about France's contribution to the war effort," Stalin replied instantly.

"There are some disagreements between Great Britain and me about the policy toward France and also the zones of occupation in Germany," FDR shared.

"Do you believe France should occupy Germany?" Stalin asked in a way that did not indicate what he thought about the subject.

"It is a complicated topic," FDR said.

"I cannot see why they should," Stalin admitted.

"We have much to discuss while we are here," FDR replied.

Robert Hopkins entered the room with several cameras around his neck.

"Ah, there he is," FDR exclaimed. "This is Robert Hopkins. Harry's son," he informed Stalin.

"It is an honor to meet you, sir," Robert said, shaking hands with Stalin, who nodded.

"Where is your father?" Stalin asked.

"In his room, I believe," Robert replied.

"Robert. Would you take some photographs of Premier Stalin and me?" instructed FDR.

"Of course, sir."

#

Inside Hopkins's suite, Dr. McIntire was examining Hopkins, who was lying in his bed. Hopkins was pale and weak, and though McIntire had injected him with one of his magic elixirs, it did not seem to have any beneficial effect on Harry.

"You cannot go," McIntire ordered. "The first conference meeting is in twenty minutes, and you should not—I repeat, not—leave this bed. That's an order."

"I'm a civilian," Hopkins replied.

"I don't care. You are confined to your bed. In fact, in your condition, I really should move you out of here."

"Where would you move me to?"

"The USS Catoctin. It is docked in Sevastopol, and I can take better care of you there."

"I am not leaving here."

"Well then, skip today's session at least."

"You tell Harriman, Bohlen, and Stettinus to come here after the meeting and brief me," instructed Hopkins.

"Okay, it's a deal," McIntire answered. "But you must promise me you will stay in bed."

"Yes, sir," Hopkins agreed.

McIntire did relay Hopkins's instructions and, as directed, later that night, Secretary of State Ed Stettinus, Chip Bohlen, and Averell Harriman visited Hopkins in his room, briefing him on the day's meeting. Hopkins sat at the end of his bed.

"The President chaired the meeting as he did in Tehran," Harriman reported.

"How's the room, Harry?" Stettinus asked, wondering if there were listening devices.

"Good," answered Hopkins. "Our guys checked it."

"In a nutshell, here it is," Harriman continued. "When the war is over, Stalin wants Germany weak and divided and wants them to pay reparations. He wants to control Eastern Europe—his sphere of influence—especially Poland.

"How far is the Red Army from Berlin?" asked Hopkins.

"About sixty miles," Stettinus answered, sounding discouraged.

"He's in the driver's seat," Hopkins confirmed Stettinus's view.

Harriman continued. "For his part, the President made it clear he wants the "Allies" to remain allies after the war, and he pushed for establishing the United Nations as a peacekeeping institution with a Security Council made up of the Allied powers. There are lots of questions and unsettled issues about voting in the UN Security Council."

"And the President pushed for some assurance from Stalin about Russia joining the fight against Japan," Bohlen added.

"Good. Churchill?" asked Hopkins.

Harriman answered. "Churchill seemed focused on how Germany is to be divided after the war and the idea that France should be given a zone of occupation there. He also seemed very concerned about Poland."

"It's clear Stalin wants to control the government in Poland," Bohlen added. "He wants a buffer between him and Western Europe.

"Harry, you should know the President supported Churchill and asked that the London Poles be included in any new elected government in Warsaw," Harriman said and then turned to Bohlen and Stettinus. "Did I leave anything out?"

"That was the gist of the meeting," Ed Stettinus confirmed and then turned to Hopkins. "Harry, Stalin seemed undecided and even evasive on the fate of Poland and on the voting issues in the United Nations. But he did agree to assist us in the fight in the Pacific when the war in Europe is over."

"Give me Poland and I will fight with you in Japan?" Hopkins asked.

"I think that is where we are heading," Stettinus agreed. "If they join us against Japan, it will save hundreds of thousands of American lives."

"For whatever it's worth, Harry," Bohlen weighed in. "I don't think the President fully understands the profound differences that exist between Russia and the United States and between him and Stalin."

"The President thinks he can persuade Stalin to alter his point of view on matters that Stalin will never agree to," Harriman commented. "The Russians will settle matters in their own manner, on their own terms, and in their own time."

"I will be at tomorrow's meeting," Hopkins said, determined that if he was able to fog a mirror in the morning, he would attend the meeting.

"You should rest," advised Harriman.

Hopkins simply shook his head and said, "I will be there."

#

The plenary sessions of the conference were held in the Livadia Palace's Grand Ballroom with its large floor-to-ceiling stone fireplace at one end of the room, and a large round table capable of seating all of the leaders and their advisers in the middle. FDR, Hopkins, and Ed Stettinus sat at the table the next day.

The big issues were a free Poland, a new global peacekeeping institution that would be called the United Nations, managing a defeated Germany, and the war with Japan. Each of the Allies had their own views on each topic and were determined to leave the conference with a favorable agreement. While the discussions were generally collegial, there were times during the conference when Stalin, whose spying gave him invaluable insights into British and American intentions, created significant tension between the "Big Three" in their search for an endurable peace.

"We should agree right now that the Soviet Union can have two or three additional votes in the United Nations," demanded Stalin.

"What is the purpose of these additional votes?" Churchill asked, and Hopkins could tell Churchill was gearing up for a street fight debate with the Soviet leader.

"I would like to invite Ukraine and Byelorussia to sign the UN Declaration and join us at the first meeting in San Francisco," explained Stalin.

"These additional votes," FDR said, "Do you believe they should also be used in the Security Council?"

"No," answered Stalin. "Only the General Assembly."

"If we abide by this logic," Churchill jumped in, "then Great Britain should..."

As Churchill rambled, Hopkins leaned into FDR. "You should try to get this referred to the foreign ministers before this issue turns into trouble," Hopkins whispered.

"On that basis," Churchill continued, "we all should have additional votes, and the United States might even ask for forty-eight additional votes for its states."

"Perhaps we should ask our foreign ministers to fully discuss this issue and present us with a credible solution," FDR suggested.

"I agree," Stalin said.

"Very well," conceded Churchill.

FDR continued his chairmanship of the session and referred to his notes for the next discussion topic. "On the subject of France being assigned a zone of occupation in Germany and a member of the Control Commission," FDR introduced the topic. "I believe we should grant both to the French."

Stalin was taken aback, having heard the opposite from the President just the day before. "What changed your mind?" Stalin asked, though he already knew that FDR was inclined to favor France.

"I considered this issue carefully and concluded it will be easier for us to deal with France if they are part of the Commission than if they are not," FDR said simply.

"Agree," Stalin said, knowing that while the others perceived this as him conceding to the British and Americans, it really wasn't a material issue for his goals. From Stalin's perspective, the French could not get out of their own way, let alone threaten the Soviet Union. He was happy to let the Americans and British deal with them.

"As do I." Churchill was pleased that France would participate in the post-war Germany.

Immediately after his "concession," Stalin said to FDR, "I would like us to discuss the issue of German reparations. There was a proposal made by the Soviet Union of a payment of twenty billion dollars, half of which—ten billion dollars—would be paid to the Soviet Union by Germany."

Before FDR could respond to Stalin, Churchill opened the discussion. "Considering the outcome of the Great War's reparations burden on Germany by way of the Treaty of Versailles, I am confident British public opinion will not tolerate reparations of twenty billion or even ten billion dollars payable by Germany."

"I also believe American public opinion would be against such an arrangement," FDR agreed.

"To overcome the objections of your people, you must subject them to a propaganda campaign," advised Stalin.

"Perhaps the American and British people should learn to obey their leaders," Molotov suggested sarcastically.

"One of the greatest rights of our people is their right to dissent and disapprove of their leaders, providing they…" Churchill was off and running in a mini-lecture about the value of free speech and democracy.

Seeing his opportunity, Hopkins leaned into FDR. "Let the British disagree if they want to," he told FDR. "Simply say it will all be referred to the Reparations Commission and note that the British disagree with the proposed amounts."

Though FDR heard Hopkins again, he did not acknowledge him as they both focused on Churchill concluding his talk.

"That said, we treasure our free press, which we recognize as the sleeping guardian of the rights that all in Great Britain prize," Churchill concluded.

"I propose we place this matter in front of the Reparations Commission," FDR said to the table, "to determine what, if any, reparations might be due from Germany to Russia and the Allies."

"That is satisfactory," Churchill said.

"Where will the Commission meet?" asked Stalin.

"I have no objection to the Commission meeting in Moscow," conceded FDR. "Do you, Winston?"

"That would be fine," Churchill answered.

"Agree," Stalin confirmed.

#

It was a gray, overcast, and cold day in Yalta when, just two days before the end of the conference, reporters gathered in front of FDR, Churchill, and Stalin in the courtyard outside the palace. Robert Hopkins positioned himself, preparing his camera in front of the leaders as they chatted with each other before sitting to face the press. Churchill sat to FDR's right and Stalin to his left. Though the air around them seemed to be less tense, all three men showed the emotional wear and tear of the intense and detailed discussions of the past five days. Stalin appeared to be the most at ease of the three.

Robert Hopkins started taking pictures of the leaders and the many attendees at the conference. Alan Brooke, George Marshall, Admiral King, Admiral Leahy, Ed Stettinus, Gil Winant, Averell Harriman, Chip Bohlen, Anthony Eden, Molotov, Maisky, and many, many others who stood behind the leaders, talking and milling about, waiting for the press conference to begin. Though not evident in his photographs, all who were there that day were acutely aware that the conference was historic and believed the decisions they reached would positively impact the lives of millions for generations to come. Despite the friction between the Allies, every single person standing there envisioned a better future.

"We have done much here to ensure peace in our time," Churchill said to Stalin as the reporters settled in behind the cordon. The

Prime Minister was seated to FDR's right and was dressed in a heavy coat and holding his hat in his hand.

"It was a good meeting," Stalin said, seated on FDR's left, his hands clasped together in front of him and dressed in a military overcoat and hat.

"Somehow, I suspect the press will have a different opinion," FDR snickered.

"I do not have that problem," said Stalin, looking straight ahead, and though he seemed to smile at his own joke, his eyes told a different story.

FDR, who had a cigarette in his left hand, turned forward toward Robert Hopkins and then smiled at his friend's son.

As Robert snapped the photo of the "Big Three" that day, he thought that FDR, sitting with his cigarette in hand and Churchill with his hat in hand, looked like two old athletes after they played an overtime game. The skill and poise of days past were there, but the stamina was gone.

Stalin, on the other hand, looked ready for more.

#

By the time the Yalta Conference wound down to its final days, the British, American, and French armies had liberated all of France and Belgium, and they were pushing against the Western border of Germany. In the east, Soviet forces pushed the Germans out of Russia, Poland, and Bulgaria and now stood some forty miles from Berlin.

The die was cast.

On the eve of the final day, Hopkins sat with FDR, Marshall, Harriman, Stettinus, Admiral Leahy, King, and Chip Bohlen in FDR's living room to discuss the summary of agreements reached over the past ten days. Each was historic in its own right and had profound implications for the future of Europe and the world. Ed Stettinus briefed the group.

"First and foremost," Ed said, reviewing his briefing document, "the Allies agree on the unconditional surrender of Germany. The second critical agreement was on the formation of the United Nations as an institution and the veto power of the permanent members of its Security Council. Next is the unanimous support of the Declaration of Liberated Europe, which follows the Atlantic Charter's principle of self-determination for every country, and the European Advisory Commission, which will set the boundaries of post-war occupation zones for Germany for each of the three principal Allies. The US and Britain agreed to give France a zone inside Germany created from their two zones. The French will also have a position on the Allied Control Council for Germany," Stettinus said.

"De Gaulle should send a thank-you note to Churchill for that," Hopkins said.

"I felt I had to back Winston after his many long years of putting up with that man," FDR explained.

"Stalin still will not allow De Gaulle a seat on the Allied Reparations Commission," Stettinus said, and then continued. "Germany is to be subject to demilitarization and denazification, and its war criminals are to be brought to trial. The issue of war reparations would be decided by the Allied War Reparations Commission, which will meet in Moscow, and payment would be made in the form of money, assets, and forced German labor to repair the damage done to other countries." Stettinus stopped and took a drink.

"Last but certainly not least as far as Europe is concerned," Stettinus continued, "we agreed to move Poland's eastern border with the Soviet Union west to the Curzon Line, and as compensation for Poland, give them more territory from Germany. Though there was agreement that the provisional government of Poland should, quote, 'be pledged to the holding of free and unfettered elections as soon as possible,' end quote, Stalin insisted that the Polish Government in Lublin should be the basis for the new Polish government. There was an agreement that members of the Free Polish Government in Exile in London would be included in the new Polish government," Stettinus finished.

"We cannot evade the fact that we have placed more emphasis on the Lublin Poles," FDR told the group. "If we do, it will look like we are going back on our agreements." FDR wanted to be sure there were no misunderstandings when the American contingent returned home.

Admiral Leahy spoke up. "Respectfully, sir, the language regarding Poland is so vague we can stretch it all the way from here to DC and never break it."

"I'd rather not give our ambitious press any ammunition," replied FDR, and turned to Stettinus. "Please continue, Ed."

"And that brings us to Japan," Stettinus said. "The Soviets agreed to join us in the fight against Japan shortly after Germany has surrendered. In return, we agreed that the Soviets would take possession of Southern Sakhalin and the Kuril Islands, the port of Dalian, and Port Arthur," Stettinus concluded. "Those were the major agreements."

"This has been an important meeting," FDR mused. "Not only to map out the future of Europe after Germany surrenders, but to prove that we can work together with Stalin and the Soviets for a better world."

"There's hope," Hopkins said.

"Indeed," replied FDR.

#

That evening, Stalin visited FDR and Hopkins in the President's suite inside the palace.

"I wanted to see you before you left tomorrow to thank you for making this long journey for all of your help making our important meeting a great success," he said, shaking FDR's hand.

"We have accomplished a great deal together these last days," replied FDR.

"It is a privilege to be associated with you in this great fight. Please take good care of yourself."

"The privilege is mine."

Stalin then turned to Hopkins and shook his hand. "It is always good to see you," he told Hopkins, his focused, steely gaze belying the crooked smile on his face.

"I hope the next time we see each other, the guns will be silent," replied Hopkins, "replaced by the sound of children laughing."

"I as well," Stalin said, still holding onto Hopkins's hand. He turned to look at FDR and then pointed his finger at Hopkins.

"He speaks according to his soul."

#

FDR, Hopkins, and the US entourage returned to the USS Quincy. The plan was to sail first to Alexandria, Egypt, then to Algiers for a meeting with De Gaulle, and then through the Straits of Gibraltar and across the Atlantic to the United States.

The USS Quincy was at anchor in Alexandria's harbor on a bright sunny day, sitting in flat seas and surrounded by heavy cruisers, battleships, destroyers, and a submarine, defending the ship from potential attacks from below the surface. Despite it being February, the remarkably warm and beautiful day on the calm Mediterranean Sea seemed to reinforce the goodwill and good feeling everyone carried from the conference. It certainly felt like there was a bright future ahead.

FDR, Hopkins, Pa Watson, and Churchill finished their lunch inside the officers' dining room on the Quincy, and each man showed the classic signs of exhaustion—pale skin, hollow eyes, and slackened jaws. Even Churchill seemed subdued.

Pa rose from the table. "Forgive me for abandoning my post, but I have a little indigestion," Pa said.

"Ask Dr. McIntire for something to help," FDR suggested.

Almost immediately after Pa left for his stateroom, an officer entered carrying a cable for Hopkins. It was from De Gaulle.

No rest for the weary.

"De Gaulle changed his mind about meeting me?" FDR shouted. "Well, he is about to find out that I have changed my mind! About him!" Hopkins was not surprised that the fickle Frenchman's latest gambit pushed FDR over the edge.

Concerned that De Gaulle could upset all that was accomplished at Yalta, Churchill tried to calm FDR. "I know how frustrating he can be, but we made progress for France these past days," he said, trying to persuade him to tread easily.

"Let me get Chip Bohlen to draft a cable to De Gaulle," suggested Hopkins.

"No, no. I am going to write it," FDR responded firmly.

Normally, Hopkins would have persuaded FDR against listening to his darker angels, but the truth was he just didn't have the horsepower to push back.

"I need to rest," Hopkins said as he rose from the table without another word about De Gaulle.

Churchill stood up as well. "I will not see you again before I leave. You must take the best care of yourself."

"I will," assured Hopkins. "You as well. Please give Clemmie a hug for me."

Churchill turned to FDR and clasped FDR's extended hand in both of his.

"I want to tell you both that your leadership has brought the world," Churchill paused when Hopkins held up his hand, but then continued in earnest, "yes, the entire world, back from a dark abyss. You have guided us all to the sunlit uplands that will be enjoyed for generations to come. I am truly honored to be your Ally and your friend."

#

Later that afternoon, Chip Bohlen and Steve Early brought Hopkins, FDR's drafted response to De Gaulle. Both men were worried and didn't believe the President should send his cable. They hoped that Hopkins, who sat on his bed reading the draft, would agree and get FDR to come to his senses.

"He has his Dutch up," Early said as Hopkins read the draft. "He can't send that to De Gaulle."

Hopkins handed the draft back to Early and took a pen and pad from his desk. "Chip," Hopkins said, "give this note to the President. Hopefully, he will calm down."

"Why don't I ask the President to visit with you here?" Early suggested, believing a face-to-face with Hopkins would soothe the boss.

"Unfortunately, there is no way for him to get here in his wheelchair. The passage is not big enough," explained Hopkins. "Let Chip see what he can do with him."

"What if I can't persuade him?" Bohlen asked.

"If he burps, let me know and we'll try a different tactic," Hopkins assured Bohlen. "It'll be fine. There's no sense destroying two centuries of friendly relations between France and the United States all because of one pompous ass."

"Thanks, Harry," Early responded.

"I was referring to De Gaulle, of course," Hopkins added, and both Early and Bohlen laughed.

"The President also wants you to help him work on the draft of his speech to Congress," Early informed Hopkins.

Hopkins picked up the pen and pad again and started writing another note.

"I have to leave the ship when we get to Algiers. I need to rest on land in a real bed. I'll stay in Algiers for a few days to recharge and then fly back to DC."

When Bohlen and Early left Hopkins's cabin on their way to see FDR, Early turned to Bohlen. "I actually can't tell who is in worse shape, Harry or the boss. It's like they're in a race trying to see who will be the first to crash."

Minutes later, Bohlen and Early stood in FDR's cabin watching FDR read Hopkins's note. He tossed the note on his desk.

"The United States has been insulted, and it requires an appropriate answer," FDR said.

"Sir," Chip Bohlen spoke up. "We can all admit that De Gaulle is one of the biggest sons of bitches who ever straddled a pot. But we shouldn't..."

And just like that, FDR cut him off. "Oh, go ahead," FDR said, waving his hand. "You and Harry try your hand at the draft to De Gaulle."

There was a knock on the door, and when Steve Early opened it, a grim-faced Dr. McIntire stood in the doorway. McIntire did not have to utter a word, and Steve Early knew something terrible had happened.

McIntire entered FDR's cabin, and when FDR saw him, he thought he had come to check on him. "I am fine, Doc. Go find someone else to bother. Go check on Harry," FDR said.

"Sir," McIntire started, "I'm sorry to tell you that Pa died about twenty minutes ago in his cabin."

"What?" FDR exclaimed, examining McIntire over his pince-nez glasses.

"It looks to me like he had a massive stroke," McIntire informed the President.

"Dear God," FDR whispered, removing his glasses.

After several moments, FDR looked at a stunned Steve Early. "Steve, please cable Frances and tell her what has happened," ordered FDR. "And please inform my missus and ask her to plan a memorial for Pa when we return."

"I will, Mr. President," Early replied, surprised at the emotions welling up inside him. "My condolences, Mr. President." Early knew how much Pa meant to FDR.

"To all of us," FDR responded. "Pa was a good man. A good friend," he said, and turned away from the men with his papers in hand.

CHAPTER THIRTY-THREE

"... we have lost one of our greatest friends and the world its most outstanding champion of freedom and justice."

Much to FDR's dismay, Hopkins did get off the ship in Algiers for rest and relaxation before flying home. FDR was not happy to lose Hopkins on the journey home, but Harry was beyond caring as he felt himself walking on the razor's edge between the here and now and no more tomorrows. The weight, strain, and duress of the last twelve years seemed to have accumulated in his body and finally put him down.

FDR was not only very upset with Hopkins for leaving him on the Quincy, but as the weeks passed with Harry unable to work, FDR became frustrated with Hopkins's absence in the White House. Of course, FDR understood the strain of Harry's tenuous health, but nonetheless, he felt like he had been abandoned by his most trusted adviser. The idea of Hopkins not being around, available, and seated at the table grated on FDR.

After returning from Algiers, Louise insisted he immediately confine himself to quarters in his Georgetown home. Though he ordinarily would have rebelled, he surprised himself and Louise by waking up late each morning and taking those afternoon naps in bed as Churchill had once suggested. Even more surprising for Louise was his lack of desire to return to the White House and the work ahead. It almost seemed like he was satisfied for Yalta to serve as the exclamation point on all the work he had done since he arrived in DC in March 1933. That concerned Louise the most because she knew that Harry was never satisfied.

Hopkins was sitting up in bed, smoking, when Louise entered carrying sandwiches for his lunch and a coffee pot.

"How are you feeling?" Louise smiled, putting the tray on their bed.

"Ah, Louie. Not so good today," replied Hopkins, sounding like he wished it wasn't so. Another surprise Louise had noticed since he arrived home from Yalta was Hopkins's willingness to tell her how he was really feeling.

"Give yourself some time," she said with another smile. "That was a very long trip."

"I've seen this movie before. I think I should get to the Mayo."

"I'll call," Louise responded immediately, pleased that he would proactively look into his illness.

As she headed toward the door, Hopkins called out. "Louie, I'm sorry."

Louise stopped and returned to his side to kiss him. "We're going to get you fixed up," she said confidently, "so we can visit all your friends up at the Saratoga race track this summer." She smiled.

"I can't wait," he said, and kissed her again.

When Louise left the room, Hopkins moved the tray with his sandwiches and coffee and lay flat on the bed.

He stared up at the ceiling, too tired to be frustrated or hungry or angry.

It felt like his engine was running on fumes.

#

Though the President's daughter, Anna Boettiger, provided the kind of companionship and company FDR always craved, she could not replace the work that Hopkins performed. FDR missed Hopkins and, in fact, found himself downright angry with his best man for leaving him to fend for himself. The two had not seen each other since they said goodbye on the USS Quincy.

In April, FDR invited his friend Henry Morgenthau, his daughter Anna, and his former lover, Lucy Mercer, to The Little White House in Warm Springs, GA. Though Mercer married after her affair with FDR during World War I, her husband had died, and whenever possible, FDR would arrange for her to secretly visit him. Her name in the White House logbook was Mrs. Paul Johnson.

It was a pleasant, early spring evening in Warm Springs with Secret Service agents and Marines stationed around the perimeter of the President's "Little White House." FDR sat inside the small living room with Lucy Mercer, while Henry Morgenthau and Anna prepared FDR's favorite cookies in the kitchen.

"Does Eleanor know Lucy is here?" Morgenthau asked Anna.

"No," Anna replied, feeling guilty that her mother did not know she allowed her father's former lover to visit him.

"Anna, he needs a doctor," Morgenthau insisted.

"He won't listen," Anna replied. "I would appreciate it, Henry, if you could help me convince him," Anna said and took the plate of cookies into the living room with Morgenthau following behind. Anna was chilled, and Morgenthau was shocked when FDR turned to watch them enter the room, and they saw his hand shaking as he put down his coffee cup.

Had anyone who was with FDR just weeks ago at Yalta or on the Quincy seen him that day, they would have immediately rung the alarm. Though it was obvious he was not well when he was in Yalta, the difference and deterioration in his appearance between then and now were startling.

"There they are. My favorites," FDR said.

"People? Or the cookies?" Anna cracked.

"All of the above. My daughter, my Secretary of the Treasury, and my favorite Georgia Chocolate Chip Cookies," FDR said, removing his glasses and rubbing his eyes and temples. "This Georgia pollen has my sinuses acting up."

"You need to be in fine form for your portrait," Anna reminded FDR. "Elizabeth Shoumatoff will be here shortly to finish painting you."

"We would all be better off if she just painted the outside of the cottage instead," FDR complained.

"Oh, Father," admonished Anna, passing the plate of cookies to FDR.

"I wish we could get these cookies in Washington," FDR said, taking a bite of the warm chocolate chips.

"I can arrange that for you, Franklin," Lucy said, pleased to see him a little more cheerful.

"Whatever you do, please do not use the US Treasury, or it will be in all the newspapers." Morgenthau smiled at FDR. "The President spends taxpayer money to bring chocolate chip cookies from Georgia to Washington, DC." Morgenthau laughed, as did the others.

FDR rubbed his temples again and the back of his head.

"Damn sinuses," he said.

#

Hopkins and Louise opted to return to the Mayo Clinic in the hopes that in the years since his last visit, the country's leading medical institution would have been able to fill in the gaps regarding Harry's condition. As usual, the care Hopkins received at the Clinic was superb, and the doctors were extraordinary. After a couple of weeks, he felt like he was turning the corner and began to feel like his engine was running again.

It was late afternoon on Thursday, April 12, when the phone in Hopkins's Mayo Clinic room rang, and Hopkins answered it, hoping it was Louise and Diana. He missed them.

It was Chip Bohlen calling, and all that Hopkins remembered from the call was Chip saying: "The President died…" "Warm Springs…" and "they're bringing him back here," and his own voice telling Bohlen: "I better be going to Washington. I'll reach out to Churchill."

After he hung up, Hopkins rang for his nurse to begin the process of getting discharged from the Clinic. Struggling to fight back tears, he swung his legs off the bed and picked up the phone again.

"Connect me with the White House," Hopkins said into the phone, and after several moments, "This is Harry Hopkins. Please put me through to the Map Room."

As Hopkins waited for his connection to the Map Room, he drafted and re-drafted the message he wanted to send to Churchill in his head. He always preferred to go to the heart of a matter, but today he could not find the right words. A lieutenant in the Map Room answered, and Hopkins decided to just plow forward with the best he could muster in the moment.

"Lieutenant, this is Harry Hopkins. I have a cable for Winston Churchill."

"Whenever you are ready, Mr. Hopkins," the lieutenant replied.

"I cannot tell you what goes through my mind and heart," Hopkins dictated slowly with none of his characteristic confidence. "All I know is that we have lost one of our greatest friends, and the world its most outstanding champion of freedom and justice. I will leave the hospital tonight and be back in Washington tomorrow. Will cable you all the details tomorrow."

#

Until then, Louise had never done any work for her husband, secretarial or otherwise. So, when she started answering his phone calls in their Georgetown home, taking and relaying his messages, greeting his guests, and seeing to his well-being, she was surprised how her feelings for Harry seemed to deepen. She knew what she was doing for him was not going to alter the course of history, but as the day continued, she felt herself a part of his life in a way she never had before.

The phone in their home had not stopped ringing since Harry arrived home from Rochester the afternoon before. Louise and Harry were woken at 7 a.m. by T.V. Soong calling Harry to offer his condolences, and shortly after that, the calls started coming in at a rate of almost one every five minutes. When Harry refused every call, Louise shifted gears. She stopped telling Harry who was calling and began the process of taking names, numbers, and messages. He would call back those he wanted to.

When Bob Sherwood came by late in the morning to visit Hopkins, Louise was so happy to see Sherwood that she immediately tried to enlist him to take over her phone duties in the afternoon when Admiral Leahy, General Marshall, Sam Rosenman, and others were scheduled to visit. By this time, Louise told Sherwood, she had her patter down regardless of who called for

Hopkins. "It goes like this, Bob," Louise instructed Sherwood, "I'm sorry, whoever you are—Prime Minister, Ambassador, Foreign Secretary, General, Admiral, insert the title—Mr. Hopkins is not available. May I take a message? That's all there is to it, Bob," Louise told Sherwood, relieved she would have some help. "Harry's upstairs in our bedroom."

Sherwood found Hopkins sitting on the edge of his bed with his elbows on his knees, scanning the dozens of condolence messages and cables from the world's leaders. He sat next to Hopkins as Louise continued her receptionist duties on the downstairs phone.

"How are you holding up?"

"You know, Bob," Hopkins answered, reading the names of the callers on the papers in front of him. You and I have got something great we can take with us for the rest of our lives. Because we know it's true what so many people believed about him, and what made them love him. The President never let them down. That's what you and I can remember. Oh, we all know he could be exasperating in the little things. But in the big things—all of the things that were of real, permanent importance—he never let the people down."

They heard the phone ring again and Louise say loud and clear, "Yes, sir. One moment, please." She ran up the stairs to their bedroom.

"It's Harry Truman," Louise said out of breath.

Hopkins walked to the phone on his night table and picked it up. "Mr. President," he said into the phone and listened while both Sherwood and Louise examined Hopkins's face for any information it might give them.

"What time would you like me there?" Hopkins asked, and after a moment he answered, "Yes, sir," and hung up the phone.

"Truman wants to meet me before the funeral on Saturday," Hopkins told Louise and Sherwood.

#

April 14 was the day of FDR's private funeral service in the East Room of the White House. For five hours leading up to that event, thousands of mourners filed by his casket in the center of the room with handkerchiefs clutched in their hands to say goodbye to their beloved leader. For some on the line, he was their savior. For others, their hero. And for still others, the father they always wished they had.

While almost all of the mourners in the line were adoring fans of Roosevelt, there were many in the country that day who viewed their former president as a cold-hearted enigma, a traitor to his class, a socialist, or a leading threat to their ideas of what America should be. A man who, according to some, saved America twice, and who, to others, gave America away to its foreign and domestic enemies and to the devil's forces alight in the world. The same man.

When Hopkins was driven past Lafayette Park that Saturday for his meeting with the newly sworn-in President Truman, there were thousands of mourners standing in the park gazing at the White House. The scene reminded Hopkins of his first visit there in '33 when all of the supplicants stood looking up at the portico waiting for FDR to appear. Hopkins noticed that the crowd that day in

Lafayette Park had the same look in their eyes. They too longed to see and hear their President one more time.

It felt downright weird for Hopkins to be standing in the Oval Office, the same office Hopkins had spent countless hours in. Not only was FDR not there, but the office was barren as FDR's furniture and items were being removed and replaced by new furnishings chosen by Harry Truman's wife, Bess. Truman ordered sandwiches from the White House Kitchen for the two of them, and after their meeting, they would both attend FDR's funeral service.

"Harry, it's most important for our country that I get up to speed on our foreign affairs," Truman said to Hopkins, taking a bite of his turkey sandwich. "I must understand the whole situation with Russia, Poland, and the United Nations, and I need firsthand information about the various heads of state and, in particular, about Stalin."

"I can help," replied Hopkins, and began taking President Harry Truman through all of the major events and conferences since the beginning of the war in 1939. The briefing was long, and Truman listened intently. Hopkins even included information on the shift from the New Deal to Total Defense, Lend-Lease, his missions to Churchill and Stalin, the Atlantic Charter, the Arcadia Conference, the Pacific Council, Britain's intransigence concerning the cross-Channel invasion, the Casablanca Conference, Quebec, Tehran, Yalta, and more. Most importantly, Hopkins gave the new President insight into the character of most of the world's leaders with a particular focus on Churchill and Stalin.

When Truman asked him for his summary of Stalin, Hopkins replied, "Stalin is a candid, rough, tough Russian. A Russian partisan through and through. Always thinking first about Russia. He can be talked to frankly," advised Hopkins.

"Harry, I can't tell you how helpful this has been," Truman said.

"Will you continue FDR's policies?" Hopkins asked.

"That's my plan."

"I will do my best to give you all of the assistance I can."

"How 'bout you?" Truman asked. "What are your plans?"

"I planned to retire from the government next month."

"Your health permitting, Harry," Truman said, "I would like you to consider continuing with me in the same role as you did with President Roosevelt."

"I promise I will seriously think about it," Hopkins replied.

When Truman and Hopkins entered the East Room for FDR's service, everyone was already in their seats. The two men walked to the front row with Truman sitting next to FDR's children, and his wife, Bess. Hopkins sat next to Louise and Bob Sherwood. Eleanor entered the room and as she walked to her seat in the front, an organist began to play "Eternal Father, Strong to Save," one of FDR's favorite hymns.

As the people sang the hymn, Hopkins stood and began to sob quietly. He couldn't help it. The emotion came in waves, accompanied by so many memories, he was unable to push back the grief that gripped him. After losing Barbara and Stephen, Hopkins knew this is exactly what real loss felt like, and it would take a long while for him to get over it—if he ever did.

Louise wrapped her arm around Hopkins, and as she held him tight with her head on his shoulder.   Eleanor turned to look at Hopkins, and when she saw him sobbing, a deep sadness fell over her. Not only for the loss of Franklin, but also for the loss of all that she and Franklin and Hopkins had been through together, and the knowledge that those things would never take place again.

CHAPTER THIRTY-FOUR

"You can't beat destiny."

Though Hopkins had left the Mayo Clinic weeks before, he was still under the weather and needed regular visits to the Naval Hospital for his doses of their magic elixirs—courtesy of Henry Stimson and Dr. McIntire. When Harriman and Joe Davies visited him in Georgetown, unexpectedly, Harry was at the peak of his revolving health cycle and looking fairly well. Joe Davies, on the other hand, looked like Hopkins usually did.

"The word is you are retiring," Davies said, his voice sounding weak.

"It's time, Joe."

Harriman had debated with himself before his visit whether or not he would bring up helping Truman. But when he saw how good Hopkins looked and heard Hopkins tell Davies it was time for him to retire, he decided to make his pitch.

"Truman needs your help," Harriman said.

"I heard," replied Hopkins. Stimson and Stettinus had informed Hopkins that Truman was treading water with the Russians.

"Molotov told Truman last week the Russians have the right to veto discussions in the UN Security Council," Davies told Hopkins.

"Stalin is testing him," Hopkins said quickly. "That's not what we agreed to at Yalta. What did Truman say?"

"He told Molotov the United States expects Stalin to stick to his word on all of the agreements reached in Yalta and especially agreements on Poland," reported Davies.

"And then Molotov told Truman he's never been talked to like that in his entire life, and Truman said, 'Keep your agreements and you won't be talked to like that.'"

"Subtle," Hopkins said sarcastically.

"A kick in the balls," Harriman agreed. "Truman wants the Polish issue settled before the opening meeting of the United Nations."

"We had it easy all this time because we knew FDR was there," Hopkins said. "Well, he isn't there now. Roosevelt knew after Yalta that Stalin was going to be a problem."

"I saw FDR about three weeks before he died," Davies said, "and he told me Stalin broke every one of the promises he made at Yalta."

"You know Joe," Hopkins began, "in our hearts, we really believed a new day had dawned at Yalta. We were all convinced we had won the first great victory for peace, and when I say we, I mean all of us, all civilized mankind. The Russians had proved that they could be reasonable and far-sighted, and at that moment neither the

President nor any of us had the slightest doubt that we could live with them and get on peaceably with them far into the future."

Davies shook his head slowly. "There is no such thing as civilized mankind for Stalin. Too many Russians dead and too much lost."

"Harry, Stalin respects you like no one else," Harriman said, still pressing forward. "If you agree, Joe and I would like to ask Truman to send you to speak directly to Stalin."

"Are you up for that?" Davies asked.

"You know I'll do what I can," answered Hopkins.

#

It had become clear to everyone around him in the bunker that the Russians were closing in on their position in Berlin while the rest of Germany west of the city was lost to the Americans, British, and French. And with each passing day, it was also clear to those around him that their Führer, Adolf Hitler, was becoming more and more delusional. Though he believed there were German armies available to him to defend the city and counterattack, the reality was that Berlin's defense was in the hands of children and old pensioners. On April 30, Hitler and his wife Ava Braun succumbed to the reality above their heads and, rather than allow themselves to be captured, they committed suicide in the bunker. As Hitler ordered before he died, their bodies were removed by aides and burned in shallow graves outside the bunker.

Just days later, in the early morning of Monday, May 7, General Alfred Jodl, the Chief of Staff of the German Army, sat in the

Supreme Headquarters of the Allied Expeditionary Force in Reims, France, and signed Germany's unconditional surrender to the United States, Great Britain, the Soviet Union, and France. General Bedell Smith, who was General Eisenhower's Chief of Staff, accepted the surrender, and only after the surrender was signed did Eisenhower agree to meet Jodl. When he came to the room from his second-floor office, he told Jodl that he would be held personally responsible for any failure to keep the terms of the surrender and then dismissed him. With that, World War II in Europe came to an end.

The next day was V-E Day, Victory in Europe Day, and celebrations were held in London, New York, Moscow, Paris, Rome, and countless other European and American cities. After six years of fighting and more than fifty million people dead, millions of the living took to the streets relieved they were finally free of the chronic terror that had gripped them for the last six years, while millions of others took the time to give thanks in their places of worship. For Americans, hope, that elusive feeling since the days of the Great Depression, was again alive in the air they breathed, and palpable in their hearts.

In his radio address to America on that day, President Truman told the American people, "This is a solemn but glorious hour. I only wish Franklin Roosevelt had lived to see this day."

#

Hopkins looked forward to spending time with Marshall and vice versa. The two had worked together for years to build America's armed forces first to defend the nation, and then to achieve victory over the darkest governments and forces the world had ever known. For Hopkins, George Marshall was one of the greatest Americans he had ever known.

Marshall's orderly put down plates of sandwiches on Marshall's conference table in his office at the Pentagon. Marshall rarely, if ever, had someone in his office for lunch and usually spent his lunch with his wife, Katherine, at their home in Fort Myers. Today, however, he wanted to spend as much time as possible with Hopkins and ensure they both had privacy away from aggressive reporters looking for a story, or an ambitious Senator or Congressman trying to make a name for himself.

One of the traits that Hopkins and Marshall shared, and one of the things they liked most about each other, was their preference to cut to the chase and not beat around the bush. Both usually went to the heart of things, and today was no exception.

"Now that it's over and before you leave the government, I wanted to tell you something," Marshall said directly.

"Sure," Hopkins answered, though he was unsure where the general was headed.

"You have literally given your physical strength during the past three years to a degree that has been, in my opinion, heroic and will never be appreciated except by your intimates," Marshall told Hopkins, surprising him.

"That means a great deal to me coming from you," responded Hopkins, "Thank you."

"I wanted you to know that you personally have been of invaluable service to me in the discharge of my duties in this war."

"You and I did what we had to do."

"No," Marshall disagreed, "much more than that. Time after time, you did for me things that I found exceedingly difficult to do for myself, and always, it seemed, in matters of the gravest import. You have been utterly selfless as well as courageous and purely objective in your contribution to the war effort," Marshall said, holding Hopkins's eyes in his own. "You have rendered a service to this country which will never even be vaguely appreciated," insisted Marshall.

"Thank you for that," replied Hopkins, truly touched by Marshall's compliments. "But I am certain about one thing. Certain. Without you and the work you did building up our military and production capabilities," replied Hopkins, "and the work you did with the military leaders of our Allies, the Soviet Union would never have prevailed against the Nazis, England would never have survived Germany's onslaught, and America would most certainly not be the leader in the world we are today."

"That means a great deal to me coming from you," Marshall repeated, "Thank you."

When Hopkins returned home, he released his driver, knowing that he was done for the day. He immediately went to his bedroom and lay on top of his bed. It felt good to rest. Louise came into the room with envelopes in her hand and was startled to see him.

"I didn't hear you come in," she said. "Are you all right?" she asked, kissing him.

"Fine. Just wanted to take advantage of a free afternoon," replied Hopkins.

"I am glad to hear you are going to rest," she said. "A couple of things: these came for you," Louise held out the envelopes in her hand. "I think they are cables," she added. "And Bernard Baruch and Admirals Leahy and King would like to stop by tomorrow afternoon to see you."

"Yes, to Bernard and the admirals, and please read the cables for me," Hopkins replied with his head on the pillow and his eyes closed.

Louise sat down next to him on the bed, and Hopkins took advantage of her proximity to put his arm around her and caress her thigh while she opened the first envelope.

"It's from Ed Stettinus, Anthony Eden, and Molotov at the opening of the United Nations in San Francisco," Louise announced, removing and opening the cable. "It says... '*At a dinner last night, we three drank a special toast to you in sincere recognition of the outstanding part you personally have played in bringing our three countries together in the common cause. We regret you are not with us at this moment of victory. With our affectionate personal regards.*'"

Hopkins opened his eyes and smiled at the thought of Ed Stettinus tangling with Molotov and Eden over the wording of their communication to him. Hopkins knew those two never approved anything without their boss's approval.

"This one is from Pug Ismay. He says, *'I shall always regard you as one of the few outstanding figures of these war years, and I shall remember your courage, your helpful kindness, and warm friendship as long as I live.'*" Hopkins smiled.

"And this one is from Beaverbrook," Louise said, "and no, he is not giving me an emerald necklace." They both laughed, and Louise continued, "He writes, *'I must say that you have made the largest contribution outside that of your dead friend and I ever remain your admiring, devoted, and affectionate friend.'*"

"Oxford University," Louise continued with the next cable, "is giving you an honorary degree of Doctor of Civil Laws in recognition of your eminent services to the Allied cause, and Winston sent this one."

Hopkins opened his eyes and turned to look at her as she opened Churchill's cable.

"Winston says, *'Among all those in the grand alliance, warriors or statesmen who struck deadly blows at the enemy and brought peace nearer, you will ever hold an honored place.'* That's the last one today," Louise said, stacking the cables on Hopkins's night table.

"I am very proud of you," she said, and leaned over to kiss him.

#

It was just weeks later, but miraculously, Hopkins looked more like himself again. Louise could see it, and Hopkins could feel it.

Energized, focused, and determined. There was a mission to be done, and he would do it.

The new Truman administration kept bumping up against Stalin and the Soviets, and Truman needed answers to proceed with the inauguration of the new United Nations and to maintain the peace in Europe. It was only a month after the war had ended in Europe when Truman asked Hopkins to go to Moscow and speak to Stalin to try to convince the Soviet leader to agree to several critical issues.

"Here is what we need," Truman told Hopkins. "One, an agreement on a new Polish government; two, the Soviets must name someone to the German Control Commission; three, they must participate in the UN Meeting in San Francisco; and four, we need to arrange a new Big Three meeting. I also want Stalin to know that Americans do not make commitments we do not expect to carry out to the letter, and we expect him to carry out his agreements. Feel free to use diplomatic language or a baseball bat if you think that would be more effective."

"Leave it with me," Hopkins told the new President.

#

When Hopkins and Louise boarded the plane that would take him to Moscow, he smiled as he thought what a far cry it was from the PBY that flew him to Russia the first time. Louise was awestruck by the interior of the aircraft, which had rich leather easy chairs, a dining table, a galley, and a bedroom with its own bath.

"This is swanky," Louise said, looking at the plane's luxurious interior.

"Only the best for my sweetheart," answered Hopkins.

Hopkins watched Louise explore the plane, and when she opened the bedroom door, she turned and said, "It's a flying boudoir."

Hopkins and the lieutenant who was assigned to them laughed.

"Yes, ma'am. It's a long flight to Moscow," the lieutenant commented.

"I want you to get settled back there," Louise told Hopkins. "It would be good for you to rest."

"I will after we take off," Hopkins replied.

"Can we get Mr. Hopkins settled into the bedroom?" Louise asked the lieutenant.

"Of course. Right this way, Mr. Hopkins," the lieutenant responded, guiding Hopkins to the bedroom in the rear of the plane.

"I'll get your medicine," Louise said.

#

June was one of the best months when it came to Moscow's weather, and the day Hopkins and Louis arrived was one of the best days of the year so far for Muscovites.

Hopkins and Louise were greeted by Harriman, Bohlen, Molotov, and Maisky at the airport, and later that evening, they were the guests of honor at a dinner hosted by Stalin. As usual, Stalin spared no expense serving the best food available in the Soviet Union and gallons of the best vodka and wine. The lavish affair was attended by everyone and anyone of importance in Moscow.

The next day, as Hopkins, Averell Harriman, and Chip Bohlen approached the gate in their car for their meeting with Stalin, Hopkins was proud of himself for artfully staying clear of the usual successive vodka toasts the night before with his Russian hosts. He was focused, clear-headed, and glad to have all of his wits about him for his meeting with Stalin.

When Hopkins entered Stalin's office, the Soviet leader smiled broadly. "It is good to see you again. You are looking fit," Stalin said.

"My wife takes good care of me," replied Hopkins.

As they spoke, Hopkins heard Molotov, Pavlov, Harriman, and Chip Bohlen file into the room behind him.

"And she is also very pretty, smart, and charming," Stalin said appreciatively as they all took seats. "I look forward to seeing her again at this evening's dinner," Stalin added and pointed to a chair, inviting Hopkins to sit. "I am pleased President Truman sent you to visit with me here in Moscow."

"I would not have come here if I didn't believe the future well-being of hundreds of millions of people depended on the relationship between the United States and the Soviet Union," Hopkins replied, and then, as usual, went right to the heart of the matter. "If the Marshal would not mind, please tell me your concerns."

"There is a perception here in the Soviet Union," Stalin told Hopkins immediately, "that once Germany was defeated, America behaved like Russia was no longer needed."

"President Truman expressed to me his great concern over the coolness that has developed between the Soviet Union and the United States and wants you to know his desire to continue President Roosevelt's policy of working with the Soviet Union," replied Hopkins evenly.

"There are five questions I have," responded Stalin. "The first is, why was Argentina invited to join the United Nations? The second is why France—a country that surrendered to Hitler—was given a seat on the Reparations Commission. It is an insult to the Soviet Union, and…"

#

After several days of meetings and discussions, Hopkins had introduced all of Truman's critical issues and moved the Soviet leader forward toward agreement. Harriman, who was the current US Ambassador to the Soviet Union, marveled at Hopkins's ability to get the Soviet leader to engage.

The night before he and Louise were to leave, Stalin gave another lavish dinner in their honor. While Hopkins and Stalin spoke off to the side with drinks in hand, Louise was surrounded by a number of Russian military officers and diplomats. It appeared her audience was hanging on her every word and laughing at most of them. From a distance, it looked to Hopkins like she was holding court.

"My people are in love with your wife," Stalin said, seeing Hopkins watching Louise.

"They have good taste," replied Hopkins, and Stalin laughed.

"You know. Just by herself, she says a great deal about the man who was able to marry her." Stalin smiled.

Hopkins turned to look directly at Stalin. "I greatly appreciate the many kindnesses and courtesies you have shown Louise and me during our stay here in Moscow," said Hopkins. "Our meetings these last days have reassured me that the Soviet Union and the United States can find ways to work through our issues.

"I completely agree with your view," Stalin said. "Where will you go when you leave us tomorrow?" he asked.

"Berlin and Frankfurt before returning to Washington," replied Hopkins.

"It will be good for you to see the current state of Berlin."

"Who knows, I may even be able to find Hitler's body," Hopkins teased, but seeing the look in Stalin's eye, he was concerned his intended joke was lost in translation.

Stalin leaned toward Hopkins and said quietly, "I am sure Hitler is still alive," and then turned away from Hopkins to look across the dining room.

Harry wasn't sure if the Soviet dictator was serious or if they were just pulling each other's legs.

#

Moonscape was the only way to describe Berlin.

Berlin's unimaginable destruction throughout the city left him and Louise speechless. Children ran through the city in packs looking for food, while former German soldiers and women walked in pairs with their heads down, trying to avoid eye contact with marauding Russian soldiers. Rape was commonplace. Looting was rampant. Life was cheap. Everyone who was still alive in Berlin now intimately understood what it felt like to be a Jew under the Nazis. There was nowhere to hide, and there was no chance of help from anyone. These were desperate and dismal days for the Germans.

Seeing the trauma and destruction in Berlin made Hopkins think that those who were alive were walking dead, and those who were dead were fortunate. And despite the fact that bombs were no longer falling on the city, the war continued to leave its mark. Unexploded ordnance continued to take the lives of Germans and others throughout Europe.

While Hopkins and Louise were in Berlin, an unfortunate German fisherman tied up his boat to a ring along the wall on the Spree River, and he and his boat were blown to bits by an unexploded leftover bomb from an American B-29 that sat under the water. The bomb took the man, his boat, and three children who happened to be watching the fisherman from above. You didn't need to be a social scientist to know it would take many generations and huge amounts of money to repair the physical and psychological damage suffered by the Germans, and by all other Europeans because of them.

Hopkins and Louise proceeded from Berlin to General Eisenhower's beautiful country home outside of Frankfurt. Ike's home, which was surrounded by dense, beautiful trees and bright flower beds, was requisitioned by the US Army when he set up his headquarters in the city. He arranged to have lunch with Hopkins while his driver took Louise into Frankfurt for a tour of the city.

"What the hell took you so long?" Eisenhower laughed as he sipped his beer. "We have been trying to get the Soviets to name someone to the Allied Control Commission for months, and you get Stalin to agree to it in a couple of days. And with Zhukov, no less."

"I'm pretty sure Stalin will keep a tight rein on Zhukov." Hopkins smiled.

"No doubt."

"Stalin also agreed to our position on the voting procedure in the Security Council," Hopkins informed Ike.

"And Poland?" Ike asked.

"He agreed again to include some members of the Polish Government in exile in London with the Lublin Poles in the new Polish government."

"Well done, Harry," replied Ike.

"I'm pretty sure Poland will remain an issue," Hopkins confided.

"What does Churchill think?"

"We'll see. He wanted me to stop in London on the way home, but I told him I have to brief the President first."

"How did he react?"

"He called the President and asked him to send me. Truman told him no."

"Winston never gives in." Ike smiled.

"Never, never, never," agreed Hopkins with a grin.

#

Unlike when he left Washington, DC for his mission to Moscow, Hopkins's health was on the downswing when he returned home. The trip had taken all of the stuffing out of him. No sooner had he arrived on a sparkling June day than Truman asked him to come to the White House to share the facts and nuances of his three days of meetings with Stalin. Hopkins did as he was ordered and spent an hour briefing the President. He concluded with, "My final comment to you is really a recommendation. I encourage you to be very, very clear and candid when you meet with Marshal Stalin in Potsdam."

"I can do that," President Truman commented.

"Don't leave room for interpretation," Hopkins encouraged.

"I want you to join me in Potsdam," Truman said, his words sounding like he was giving Hopkins an order, but his tone suggesting it was a request.

"Respectfully, I don't think that's wise," responded Hopkins. "My presence at the conference will diminish Secretary of State Byrnes's position, especially since he is new to that role. Both Churchill and Stalin will look to me, and we need them to look to you and Byrnes for their answers and guidance."

"You did a great job in Moscow, Harry," the President said. "Thank you."

"I wish I were able to get a better, tighter deal for Poland, but—" Hopkins started to explain, but Truman cut him off.

"This was the best deal we could expect," Truman confirmed. "Listen, you saved the Potsdam Conference and the United Nations.

I want you to know that when I return from Potsdam, I plan to give you the Distinguished Service Medal for all you have done."

"I'm honored. Thank you."

#

In the late summer of 1945, just a few weeks after the United States dropped atomic bombs on Hiroshima and Nagasaki, and the Japanese unconditionally surrendered, Harry Truman did give Hopkins the Distinguished Service Medal. And just days after President Truman pinned the medal on him, Hopkins, Louise, and Diana left Washington, DC, and returned to New York City on the same train that had carried him to his destiny twelve years earlier.

His war was over.

When they entered Union Station's main hall that day, it was its usual lively blend of sound and activity. Over continuous announcements about lost items, and departing and arriving trains, there were hundreds of civilians and military moving about, waiting for arriving passengers, running to catch trains, in conversations, and being greeted by friends and family.

Over the loudspeaker, Louise, Diana, and Hopkins heard, "Train to Penn Station, New York City is now boarding on Track 22."

On board their train, they settled into their seats, and the train conductor shouted, "All aboard! Washington to New York train is now departing! All aboard."

Louise put her arm through his and squeezed him close as Diana looked out of the window.

After they returned from Russia, Louise observed a slow and steady decline in Harry's health and an inability to regenerate his batteries. He was having difficulty keeping food down, and the elixirs he used for recovery were no longer working—the peaks were getting shorter in duration and the troughs longer. Watching Harry's physical decline was difficult enough for Louise, but watching the light in his eyes slowly darken day by day broke her heart.

The International Ladies Garment Workers Union offered Harry a job at $25,000 per year, and though he accepted the job, he did little work. His new salary and wealthy friends like Bernard Baruch allowed him and Louise to live comfortably in one of New York's finer apartments.

They heard air escape from the train's brakes, and the train's wheels turned slowly at first but soon picked up their cadence as the train left the station. Hopkins looked out Diana's window and remembered seeing the four hobos who jumped onto a northbound train on the day he arrived in Washington twelve years earlier. Today, as he and Louise headed in the same direction, outside Diana's window, there were four railroad employees repairing a track.

#

January in New York City was always challenging, and 1946 was no different. The holiday high was gone, the frigid air had arrived, and everyone felt themselves settling back into that unique and frenetic New York grind. As usual, hundreds of pedestrians walked, and dozens of cars and taxi cabs inched their way along Park Avenue, beeping their horns and pushing clouds of smoke from their tailpipes into the cold air.

Fortunately for Hopkins and Louise, they were warm in Harry's hospital room inside Lennox Hill Hospital on 77th Street off Park Avenue, Harry in his bed and Louise sitting next to him, reading. She always spent afternoons with him. Since they returned in late August, Hopkins had been in and out of the hospital for brief stays until he came to Lennox Hill shortly after the new year.

He had not been home since.

Though it was extremely difficult and taxing for him, he sat up in his bed and decided to write a note to Churchill and Clemmie. He owed them one. Churchill and Clemmie came to New York Harbor before journeying to Florida and hoped Hopkins could meet them. He couldn't. Hopkins took out his pen and, with his notepad on his lap, began to write. He started to write the note in cursive but found it too difficult with his unsteady hand. He decided to print his note instead.

"Dear Winston," he wrote. *"Only being laid up in the hospital prevented me from meeting you at the boat the other day, and I do hope you'll find it possible to get to New York because it appears altogether unlikely that I could possibly be in Florida during the next month. All I can say about myself at the moment is that I am getting excellent care, while the doctors are struggling over a very bad case of cirrhosis of the liver—not due, I regret to say, from taking too much alcohol. The newspapers indicate you and Clemmie*

are having a quiet and delightful time, and I hope you won't let any Congressional Committee of ours bore you. Do give my love to Clemmie and Sarah. I hope to see you before you go back, and want to have a good talk with you over the state of world affairs, to say nothing of our private lives. Harry."

When Harry put down the pad and pen, he threw his head back against the bed, closed his eyes, and let out a long sigh. Just sitting up in bed and writing his note to Churchill was a bridge too far for him. Louise, who was sitting next to his bed, looked up and took his hand.

"What's on your mind, Mr. Hopkins?" she asked, smiling.

When Hopkins opened his eyes to look at her, Louise trembled, seeing how feeble he looked.

"You can't beat destiny," he said, smiling weakly at her, and Louise wondered what made him say that.

Louise put down her magazine and took his hand in both of hers. Hopkins closed his eyes, and his head sagged to the side.

He was gone.

#

The day after Harry Hopkins died, the *Los Angeles Times* ran an Op-Ed that read in part, *"...Americans need not concern themselves now whether Harry Hopkins was great or little or good or bad; their care should be that the phenomenon of Harry Hopkins in the White House does not recur."*

Hopkins was no longer needed.

EPILOGUE

April 1957

London

When Robert Hopkins finished writing to his wife, Brenda, telling her about his afternoon with Churchill, it felt as if his father, Harry Hopkins, was sitting with him in his hotel room. Robert was always grateful that he had the chance to spend time with his father while he was in the middle of some of the most poignant and important moments in America's history. But after today's meeting with Churchill, he realized that his father was much deeper than he realized and was guided by much more than his quick wit and emotional intelligence.

In his briefcase, Robert always carried copies of the speeches his father gave throughout his career. He would, from time to time, read them because he found he could hear his father's voice when he did.

It made Robert remember and feel close again to Harry. After his meeting with Churchill today, Robert was drawn to some of his father's words from a speech he gave when he returned to New York City in September 1945.

"America is now faced with two great tasks, both of which require immediate action. The one task relates to the transfer of a whole nation from a wartime economy to the attainment of economic prosperity in the pursuit of peace. The other encompasses the part the United States is to play in securing a lasting peace.

"If I speak of our domestic problems first, it is because every nation that would exercise its influence abroad must have within itself a moral vitality and economic strength that will give its citizens confidence in their own security and well-being. I believe most Americans interpret a good life in very simple terms. We desire an opportunity to earn a living, and we desire the establishment of conditions in which the basic rights can be fulfilled. There are some who recoil from this expression, feeling that in some mysterious way, the opportunity to earn a living would lead to the destruction of our lives by bureaucratic government, and worse, that it will destroy the incentive for hard work which has been so characteristic of our American tradition. I believe that neither of these fears have a solid base. I believe that full employment must and can be attained within the framework of our traditional Democratic processes. Having waged the total and successful war against the most powerful enemies on Earth, it is unthinkable that we cannot implement the energies of our private economic system to win peace at home.

The gateway to a secure and prosperous America is open. And I believe we shall, passing through that gate, find a way of life that will assure, for all time, the economic freedom of every American citizen.

"I have often been asked what interest we have in Poland, Greece, Iran, or Korea. Well, I think we have the most important business in the world—and indeed, the only business worthy of our traditions. And that is this—to do everything within our diplomatic power to foster and encourage Democratic government throughout the world. We should not be timid about blazoning to the world our desire for the right of all people to have genuine civil liberties and our belief that our dynamic democracy is the best in the world. Well, why not say so in a language the world will understand? But the forces of democracy are on the march in England, France, China, and a host of other nations. I believe that our country's interests throughout the world are jeopardized by the advent of any kind of totalitarian government, whatever its name or label. We rejoice in the promise of a world free and at peace.

We have an abiding faith in our way of life."

That was his father's voice, for sure, Robert thought.

His father, Harry Hopkins, did indeed have an abiding faith in America.

ABOUT THE AUTHOR

Steve Vesce is successful entrepreneur with a lifelong passion for Modern U.S. and European History. He has served as CEO of three pioneering companies, and has given more than a dozen seminars on the people, events, and issues that impacted America leading up to and including World War II. One Ordinary Man is his first novel.